Praise for *Or What Y*

"This gorgeous, deeply philosophical w—
—*Publishers Weekly* (starred review)

Praise for Jo Walton

"I love Walton's work for several reasons, not least of which is her ability to make a book feel like a conversation."
—Amal El-Mohtar, NPR, on *Lent*

"Fantasy doing with beautiful assurance what straight historical fiction can't, putting us right inside the gorgeous, idea-thrilled, demon-haunted imaginarium of the Renaissance—and making the best case for Savonarola in about five hundred years."
—Francis Spufford on *Lent*

"Rendered with Walton's usual power and beauty . . . It's this haunting character complexity that ultimately holds the reader captive to the tale."
—N. K. Jemisin, *The New York Times,* on *The Just City*

"Walton shines, as she always does, in the small and hurtful and glorious business of interpersonal relationships."
—Cory Doctorow on *The Just City*

"Has as much in common with an Alice Munro story as it does with, say, Philip K. Dick's *The Man in the High Castle.*"
—Lev Grossman on *My Real Children*

"A funny, thoughtful, acute, and absorbing story all the way through, but in the magic parts it is more than that . . . As in old ballads, the quiet, factual narration deepens the inexplicable experience, making strangeness real."
—Ursula K. Le Guin on *Among Others*

TOR BOOKS BY JO WALTON

OR WHAT
YOU
WILL

JO WALTON

TOR

A Tom Doherty Associates Book
New York

OR WHAT YOU WILL

A Tor Book
Published by Tom Doherty Associates
120 Broadway
New York, NY 10271

www.tor-forge.com

Tor® is a registered trademark of Macmillan Publishing Group, LLC.

The Library of Congress Cataloging-in-Publication Data is available upon request.

ISBN 978-1-250-30900-6 (trade paperback)
ISBN 978-1-250-30901-3 (ebook)

Our books may be purchased in bulk for promotional, educational, or business use. Please contact your local bookseller or the Macmillan Corporate and Premium Sales Department at 1-800-221-7945, extension 5442, or by email at MacmillanSpecialMarkets@macmillan.com.

First Edition: July 2020
First Trade Paperback Edition: July 2021

Printed in the United States of America

0 9 8 7 6 5 4 3 2 1

This is for everyone who ever had an
imaginary friend.

I know more than Apollo,
For oft when he lies sleeping
I see the stars at bloody wars
In the wounded welkin weeping.

—"TOM O'BEDLAM'S SONG"
ANONYMOUS, FIFTEENTH CENTURY

If this were played upon a stage now, I could condemn it as an improbable fiction.

—FABIAN, *Twelfth Night*
WILLIAM SHAKESPEARE

OR WHAT
YOU
WILL

1

THE BONE CAVE

She won't let me tell all the stories. She says it'll make them all sound the same. She's had too much of my tricks and artfulness, she says. I have been inspiration, but now she is done with me. So I am trapped inside this cave of bone, this hollow of skull, this narrow and limited point of view that is all I am allowed, like a single shaft from a dark lantern. She has all the power. But sometimes she needs me. Sometimes I get out.

"I have been" is a very Celtic way to begin a self introduction. (I have been a Celt.) It's as if the best way to present yourself is with an interlocking set of riddles, a negotiation of images and history and shared knowledge, creating a relationship between us where instead of information being imparted from me to you, you are instead asked to invoke your own wisdom and cunning and information stores to involve yourself in a guess. "I have been" in those long Celtic poems often gives way to "I am" more riddles, often boasting, phrased as sets of opposite qualities.

I have been too many things to count. I have been a dragon with a boy on his back. I have been a scholar, a warrior, a lover, and a thief. I have been dream and dreamer. I have been a god. I have stood by the wind-wracked orchard, near the storm coast.

I have been guardian of the good water. I am wise, but sometimes reckless. I am famed for my fast answers, but I would never proclaim that I am witty. You see, I am not modest. The sun my brother will never catch me napping, nor the lazy sunbeam warm my pillow. I am friend to monsters, companion to bees. I have been a stormbringer and a stormtamer. My silver tongue runs up and down, on and back, oh yes, I have been a poet. My prison now is the skull of a poet. I am deathless, but I have spent time on death's many paths. (Yes, time can be currency, especially now that I have so much of it that I can be profligate.) I have been a boy with a book, burning, burning. I have been a shepherd, and a fierce bearded goat looking down from a high path.

What am I? What am I? Figment, fakement, fragment, furious fancy-free form. I have been the spark that ignites in a cold winter. I have been the swell of a warm penis in the darkness. I have been laughter at daybreak, and tears before bedtime. I have been a quick backanswer. I have been too clever for my own good.

Especially that last.

I have been a character, and I have been a narrator, but now I don't know what I am.

She doesn't want to let me out again, that's the problem. I think she may be afraid, but she doesn't say that. She says she's used me too much and wants a change. When I say I can change, that I can be whatever she wants (I have been the roar of a lion. I have been a weaver, and torn cobweb blowing in the wind, and moonbeams enlightening a chink in a wall, and summer fields full of sprouting mustard seed . . .) then she says she needs to make up the world first. Imagine that power, to make worlds! I can make and shape and take no worlds. I slide myself into the worlds I am given and find myself, frame myself, tame myself into the space there where I can see to be me. I slither like quicksilver, fast flowing to fill up the form. But now she says she doesn't want me to. So I don't know what to do. I'm lonely. I miss you.

There are other people in here, so I am not quite solitary, but unless she will open for me the door into worlds, I am beating the bounds of a prison of bone, contemplating all I have been.

I have been a word on the tongue. I have been a word on the page. And I hope I will be again.

She says she is afraid she is going mad, talking to me. She says she used to do both sides of the conversation, but not anymore. She does, however, still talk to me. I take consolation in that. If she didn't, if she left me in the dark in the bone cage for long enough without light, then might I in time dissolve back into the grey mist? I have seen it happen to others.

That mist is one of the oldest things in her head, one of the oldest things she ever thought of, when she was a child. She walks into it when she wants a character, and it swirls around her. "Just make one up, just make me up!" the mist voices plead, and as she listens the tendrils thicken and solidify and take form and colour and follow her out into such solidity as she chooses to set them. I might have come from that mist, long ago, though that is not how either of us remember my origin. Still, I avoid the place where the mist pools, for fear of being lost and forgotten, for fear of drowning, or dissolving into the stuff of subcreation. There were others here with me before, almost as solid as I am, who are now only shadows and murmurs, ones who surged like the sea in spate who are only a whisper of waves on the distant shore. It would take a lot to invoke them now, a full-blooded sacrifice to call back no more than their hollow moth-voices. She has half-forgotten them, and I dare not summon them forth. I husband such power as I have. Though I know enough to be aware it is wrong to be selfish, still I have to protect myself. I must fasten my own oxygen mask before attempting to assist others.

I have been a runner quivering on the instant. I have been an imaginary friend. And a real friend, that too! I have been bound here, waiting, ready to do service.

She asks if that's really how I'm going to describe it, the deepest most numinous part of her head, the wellspring of everything? It isn't just *mist,* she says, grumpily. It's a place, a place swirling with potentiality. It's huge, and though you can't ever see far you feel that if the twining tendrils of mist thinned you might find unexpected vistas opening before you. It's the source, the foundation, the origin. It's the valley of the shadow, and the dreamcrossed twilight. It's Ginnungagap, where nothing is and all things start. (I have been a thief of words and so has she, though she might not as readily admit it.) The mist that is the essence of creation is of all colours and densities of grey and silver, from dark stormcloud to blown breath on a bright winter morning. It never stops moving, eddying, surging, and nobody can tell what is mist and what is shadow, not until shadow and mist transform and are shaped to become solid and walk beside you. She has been there many times but it has never become tame, there is always a risk, going in, of becoming lost, losing your way out, losing your very self into those drifts of being and becoming. There are cliffs, she says, huge cliffs, shaping the bounds of the space. When she goes into the mist she is always aware of walking between cliffs, and that is the way she comes out again, between the cliffs, but now in company. If you go too deep, she says, you might find yourself on the top of those cliffs, and drawing too close to the edge.

How would I know? I stay as far away from it as possible.

She says, besides, any normal person talking about the inside of her head would speak of her as "I" and of me as "he." But no, she's wrong there. A normal person would not speak of me at all, would grant me neither pronoun nor any least mote of reality. I have stood beside her in a circle of standing stones and at the top of the CN Tower, and yet to any eye she was alone. It is true I have seen with her eyes, but has she not seen with mine? I have been the flicker of fire that brings warmth. I have been a threshold.

I have been cocky. I have been assured. I have learned from Pythagoras himself, and from the masters of Bluestone Caves. I have knowledge and tools and a unique way of seeing. I have been a dragon in a university. I know more than Apollo. But I am afraid. I no longer want to escape to Constantinople, escape fate, escape her. I want her to make a world for me, for all that I am and could be, for me seen whole, not one where I have to pour as much of myself as will fit into an aspect she has shaped for me. "No," she says. "No. It would be too meta. Nobody would want that. The poor reader would recoil in horror. Anyway, all of what you are would not fit within the bounds of any page, the shape of any story. Besides," she says, when I don't answer, "what would it be about?"

"I could save you," I suggest, uncharacteristically tentative. Making up stories has always been her job, not mine. I simply tell them and act in them. She has always dealt with the question of what they are about.

"Save me? What from?"

"Some real world thing," I say, casually, but too fast, and she is wary.

"Oh, so it's the real world you want? You want to be real in the real world?"

"Like Pinocchio," I say. "Like the Velveteen Rabbit. Like the robot in *The Silver Metal Lover*." (Can you *believe* that there's a sequel?) But this is all the flick and flash and razzmatazz of distraction, and this time it doesn't work.

"That's not in my power," she says, and she is not laughing, not at all, she is dead serious.

For what, after all, could I save her from? Think about that, because we're going to have to face it now. She is the poet and I am trapped in her head. What I need to save her from has to be death. Because when she dies, where am I then? This bone cave is bounded in more than one way, for it is also bounded in time.

"Could I save you from mortality?" I offer, putting it out there plainly, still tentative, still careful, grateful she is speaking to me at all, that I am at least that far real, that she is giving me consideration. I don't want to frighten her away again.

She hesitates, there is a long pause, here in the darkness where we speak poised in space, two jewel-bright voices set in no setting, with nothing around us, not even the wisps of mist, neither heat nor cold nor scent nor touch nor taste, nothing but the expectation of electrical excitation, like the oldest poetry where simile stands in for senses. And she speaks, her words filling the silence, the blankness: "You don't understand. You're not real, you only think you are. And even if I acknowledge you are in any sense real, a real subcreation, you're still not a real god. Your powers are only in my worlds, in story, not in the real world, the outer world where I live and where I must . . . die."

"And if you die, must I die with you?" I ask.

"You'll live on in the stories," she says, but she doesn't sound certain.

"Then make me a new one, for all that I am," I ask, again.

"No. I have used you too much. I'm getting stale. Now I want to write this alternate Florence book, and it doesn't have you in it."

"But I love Florence!" I insist, which is the whole and holy truth. She doesn't answer. There's nothing I can do when she doesn't answer.

I am the egg of aspiration. I am the spaceship in the sunrise. I am hope, lurking amid the evils. At least, I hope I am. I'm getting desperate in here.

2

HER DEAD HORSE BOOK

Orsino, Duke of Illyria, is holding the head of a dying mare. They have both been up all night. The mare has given birth to a spindly chestnut foal, with white mane and tail, just like his mother. Orsino has already named the colt Leander. The foal is in the next stall drinking milk from the udders of the reliable Pyrrha, who has fed most of the foals in the Duke's stable, whether they were hers or not. Pyrrha, the colt, and the dying mare are the only horses in this particular stable, all the rest have been moved out for the birth, and now the death. The mother mare has twisted something inside, and is dying. Orsino has used all the healing magic he can, but it's not enough. He has been through this before. The pain of loving animals is even worse for the long lived. He is sitting in dirty straw, leaning against a manger, the mare's head heavy on his knees, one hand on her neck where the pulse beats. He is exhausted, dirty, cramped, and his back aches, but he stays where he is, occasionally huffing gently to the horses.

"Why did you call her Hero if you won't let her be one?" Olivia asks.

Orsino looks up blearily. Olivia has slept, and is washed,

bathed and fragrant in the blast of morning sunlight and cold autumnal air she has let into the stable. She is dressed in a gown of brown-and-gold brocade over creamy muslin, and her platinum hair is artfully arranged around a gold-and-bronze coronet. He can still remember when he loved Olivia, when he felt he would die if she didn't return his love. But time and change have happened, and though now the taste and smell of Olivia, and her somewhat demanding bed habits, are intimately familiar to Orsino, she never has come to love him. Usually they are comrades, but sometimes he almost hates her. He gentles the nose of the mare, Hero. "She is one," he says.

"Why don't you put her out of her misery?"

"I'm letting her die with dignity," he says. From experience he can tell when it gets too bad, the moment when a horse would choose death if she were human. Hero isn't far off, but she isn't there yet. She can see her foal and appreciate Orsino's touch, and she isn't (thanks to his magic) in pain now. "I'll be here a little while longer."

Olivia sighs, and takes a step into the stable. "Oh, the foal is lovely! Beautiful colouring. Can I have her?"

Orsino is tired, and beyond courtesy. "No, he's for Drusilla," he says.

"You spoil that child. Drusilla's too small for a proper horse," Olivia says.

"And he's too small to be ridden. Both these things will right themselves at the same time. You have plenty of horses of your own."

"I'm going back to the others." She turns, leaving the door open so that Orsino and Hero are left in a draft. He wouldn't mind for himself, but he wants the mare's last moments to be tranquil, so far as possible. "Are you ready, old girl?" he asks, when he's sure Olivia has gone. Hero shivers under his hand. He makes a gesture of drawing together with his other hand and the stable door bangs shut. It takes his eyes a little while to readjust to the semidarkness. The little curly white stable dog, named Horse by Drusilla when she was a puppy, comes up and settles herself down, warm against his leg. A bell rings in the high tower, and is answered by another, from a monastery across the city. Then the sounds die away, and Orsino can hear the breathing of the dog and the three horses. His own breathing is steady.

Half an hour or so later, Orsino's wife, Viola, comes into the stable. She is dressed as a young man, as always, except when she was too pregnant to fit into men's clothes. She is carrying a covered earthenware pot of warm gruel and a silver coffeepot. "It's all for her, but there's enough for you," she says. She sets the gruel down and pulls a delicate porcelain cup out of the pouch at her belt. "Here."

Orsino drinks the coffee gratefully. It has come all the way from distant Timbuktoo, by camelback across the deserts to Mizar, and by ship from there to Thalia. Every bean is worth its weight in gold, and at this moment Orsino thoroughly agrees with this valuation. As he sets the little cup down, Viola hands him the gruel and a horn spoon, also from her pouch. "You wouldn't have put cinnamon in it for her," he says, as he takes off the lid and the scent reaches him. "Cinnamon and honey," he adds, as he tastes it.

Viola grins at him, and moves on to see the new foal. "Isn't he lovely! And you're lovely too, Pyrrha, you're so good to feed him. Their legs look so long when they've just been born, all spindly, but you can see he's going to be a beauty."

"I'm calling him Leander," Orsino says through a mouthful of gruel, which tastes very good. "He's going to be for Drusilla."

Viola comes over and rests her hand on Orsino's shoulder. There is a lot to be said for having a wife who is a friend, Orsino thinks, as he leans his cheek against it. "Do you think Olivia and Sebastian would like to go off and rule a little outlying city on their own?" he asks, as he does sometimes ask.

"No, and however provoking Olivia was this morning, you don't really want them to."

"She's so spoilt!"

"Yes, but that's just how she is. And I'd be hopeless at being an ornamental kind of duchess, you know I would, and she and Sebastian are both very good at that end of things, and we're lucky to have them and much better off as things are." Viola kisses the top of Orsino's head.

Hero gives another shiver, and a kind of cough Orsino recognises. He draws his hand over her eyes, and twists with the other hand, almost the same gesture he made at the door. And with the same suddenness, the mare's heart stops beating, and she slumps, dead. The dog called Horse gets up and turns around where she had been lying, then barks once.

Orsino stands up, letting Hero's head slide to the ground. Pyrrha and the foal Leander don't react at all, but Horse runs to Viola, who pets her. Orsino sets his hands on the wall and bends, easing his cramped legs and stretching his back. "In an hour or so, after the stablemen have given Hero to the dogs, we can bring Drusilla down and show her Leander," Orsino says, his voice giving away nothing of what he feels.

"Are you sure?" Viola says, looking sadly at Hero's corpse, her fingers rubbing Horse's ears.

"Yes. There's nothing more sentimental than an animal graveyard. It would be sheer self-indulgence. And I don't want people thinking I've gone soft."

"Nobody would ever think that," Viola says loyally. She has loved, respected, and admired him for as long as she has known him, and shows no sign of stopping. It is a miracle, Orsino thinks.

"I have enemies," Orsino says. "They're always ready to leap on any sign of weakness. No, Hero's carcass goes to the dogs. It makes no difference to her now."

"Let's give what's left of the gruel to good old Pyrrha and go and find you something better," Viola says, as he straightens and stretches again, shaking away the aches of the night, "Your mother wants to see you."

"She's not here, is she?" he asks, alarmed, and suddenly tense.

"No. She sent a note. There was some kind of disturbance last night, an apprentice was killed. She said she'd be calling in to talk to you later this morning."

Orsino frowns, leading the way out of the stable into the yard. Horse follows them out, scuffling through the fallen leaves, wagging her tail. Doves scatter before her, white doves with plumed tails. Orsino stops at the fountain to wash. The water is very cold. The stablemen are already going into the birthing stable. Orsino looks up past them, to the palazzo with its many small windows, and up above it to the tower that from here seems so light and airy, but which weighs on him so heavily.

He puts his head under the cold water of the fountain to wake himself up, then abruptly pulls it out again, shaking drops everywhere like a dog. Horse jumps into the fountain to join in this new game. Viola grimaces as a shower of waterdrops hits her in the face.

"More breakfast, and more coffee, and clean clothes, and I'll be ready to play Duke and help sort out whatever it is," he says. "It must be something serious if it killed an apprentice and if Miranda wants to talk to me." Around their feet, doves coo and peck for grain as the little dog shakes herself dry.

3

DIRECT ADDRESS

That's her new book. What she calls the Florence book. It's a sequel to *Twelfth Night,* and also to three books she wrote long ago. And as you can see, I am not in it. Well, then. Let's try something else. Let's try to get at this tangentially.

Let me tell you what there is. Let me name and number the things so you can turn them over in your mind like people playing the old Kim game, where you are shown a tray and have to list the contents after it is covered up again. Let me tell you everything, so clear, so sharp that you can taste for yourself the tart purple berries exploding on your tongue, contrasting with the sweetness and the crispness of the folded pastry crust. Let me tell you—what, show you, you say? I can't *show* you anything. This isn't a picture book. It's all telling here. We only have words between us. But let me tell you, so you may, if you choose, weigh the qualities of different silences.

Now that I have addressed you directly, don't let it worry you that you are in this story. Nobody will make you do anything but what you are doing already, reading and making the story live in your mind. I'm not about to inform you that you are walking down a long hallway with fraying carpet, which brightens as you

pass a lace-curtained window, whose sill holds a single blossom of red geranium, drooping in a neglected flowerpot next to a dusty pile of books, their green and orange spines slowly fading to teal and lemon. I won't ask you to decide the colours of the carpet (vermilion and ash) or of the tired paint on the walls. Most especially I will not say you are putting out your hand to turn the dented brass knob set in the peeling green paint of the door that leads out into the rose garden, only to have you revolt against me and jerk your hand sharply away, saying to yourself "Like hell I do!"

We may get into the rose garden and discover its secrets eventually, but that isn't the way.

Second person is a strange conceit, and we don't intend to make you go there. Some people seem to find it erotic, as it is the mode used for a lot of written pornography. Is the feeling of passivity, or of being told what you do and feel, perhaps charged for them with some subtle erotic tension of helplessness, of being swept away by events, out of control? Interesting to consider. When there's a whole form of discourse used pretty much only for porn and experimental edgy literature, you have to think about it, question why—except that in fact nobody does seem to be asking that question. They laugh uncomfortably when she mentions it, until she mostly stops asking, although she does not stop wondering.

But no. Don't worry. We're really not going there. That door can remain firmly closed for now. You can set your back against it if you want and lean hard against it, holding it shut, taking a deep breath, safe, with the rose garden and the pool, whether full or drained, securely out there on the other side of it. You are in this story only passively, notionally. I can't see you, you don't exist yet, at this moment of composition, as, in her real time and place, plumbers pace about in the background, poised to interrupt with questions at any second, and she thinks she might as

well indulge me in tangents for a little while. Only she is here, and the plumbers, with their layered blue toolbox and patronizing manner that assumes she knows nothing, understands nothing, simply by virtue of gender. You aren't here with us now, and your potential future existence hangs in an even more tenuous space than I do. You may not even be born yet, or you may never come into existence. You are the reader, always and only. I am making no contract with you to do anything beyond what you have already agreed to do in running your eye along these words so far, one by one as they come to you, and continuing to turn these pages. I will ask you to do nothing but read, and remember, and care.

If you refuse to care? If reading this so far has made you shudder and recoil? If you have no least curiosity about that apophatic pool by the rose garden, not even whether it's a swimming pool or a pool full of waterlilies, if you don't want to at least glance at those books on the windowsill and scan their titles? Then you are not my reader, not any of my imagined readers. Stop now, while you are ahead. Take your embodied self off to read something else, feeling grateful for your solidity, your reality, and that of the world you inhabit, go read something you'll enjoy more, or deal with the pipes and boilers banging and hissing in your own life, and leave the rest of us here. We will do well enough without you, I dare say.

When she's writing, she always says, "Some people are going to hate this," and then she smiles sharply, showing her teeth. She says they are not the people she is writing for. She laughs when she reads their one-star reviews on Amazon and Goodreads. Her most popular answer in Goodreads is where somebody says they have read forty-six pages of her most popular book (the book where I am a dragon at a university) and asks if it is worth going on, and she says no, life is too short, they should read something they like instead. She values the readers who press on and find it

worthwhile, who may frown and blink now and then but keep reading, keep trusting the words, slip into the reading trance, the stories we spin you. We value you; she and I stand utterly united in this, loving you, who may or may not exist in some future time but are all potential now, as the plumber mutters and clatters in the background, releasing a gush of steam.

So listen now, like a bedtime child, snuggle down under the texture of the soothing word blanket and let yourself be lulled. When she sang her daughters to sleep, the only period of her life when singing was a frequent occurrence, she used to call it lulling them into a true sense of security. Trust me now, forget your self-consciousness, the consciousness of your separate solid self that I deliberately aroused, let yourself sink down beneath the warm weight of the story I am telling you. Trust me, it'll be much more interesting than her story about a dead horse.

4

THREE ANECDOTES

Once upon a time—have you ever thought about that formula? Why is it "upon"? We hear the phrase as one word, *once-upon-a-time*, and don't think about it. This happened once only, and it happened in time and . . . *upon* is a time word, and a strange one: upon a May morning, upon reading these words, upon turning this tap, upon reaching your destination. Usually it means as soon as something has happened. Upon a time. *The* time where all stories start. And *once*, as if to say this was so, but it is no longer. And don't say no, war stories start "No shit, there I was," as if that's different from "once upon a time." I hate that. And it's bullshit. There's no difference between fairy tales and war stories, stories for families and stories for men when they're on their own. Pah. All stories start both ways. There's no difference between *once upon a time,* and *believe me, because I was there and still bear the scars.* There are scars in everyone's stories, and people who were right there, and unless they've died they're right here still. What all told stories have in common, and the thing that makes them different from life, is that they are over, completed, known.

Once, in a land of rolling hills and gentle swift-flowing

streams, a land of vines and olives and hard wheat, a land where all the towns and villages were built on hilltops, for defence and to see far away, there was one town, rich with the manufacture of art and wool and luxury goods, that lay in a plain beside a river. It was not defenceless, however, for it had walls. The walls were bigger than the town needed, for after it had grown and extended its walls several times a terrible plague came, and the population no longer filled the whole of the space the walls enclosed. They were strong walls of smooth grey stone, and the six gates set in them had towers and portcullises like castle walls, and bright flags flew from them, and they were defended by guards in glistening mail and coloured surcoats. The flags caught the breeze and showed their brave devices in bright colours: flowers and eagles and the sun. Here and there in the walls stood solid stone bastions, and on the bastions were set cannons. That's what bastions are, solid blocks strong enough to take a cannon recoil, which makes the common phrase "last bastion" have much more resonance. Bastions were invented in the early fifteenth century by Brunelleschi, an artist and architect who spent a season in the field with the army and came up with this innovation, a man of this city, because yes, this city in the plain is the flowering city of Florence, or rather let us call it Firenze, because why should we choose to filter its name through the tongues of its French enemies? They're the reason why they needed the walls and those bastions in the first place.

Here we find ourselves suddenly on a stout grey wall in the real world, in a real place and time. It wasn't Brunelleschi who pulled us out of the realm of fairy tale, not Brunelleschi only, it was the guns. You can have the Renaissance in secondary world fantasy, but never gunpowder, though gunpowder was an invention of the Middle Ages that came before, and platemail was invented to defend against pistols, so those knights in shining armour you like to imagine lived in a world that never was. Guns somehow poison the possibility of fantasy. (Even Zelazny only just got away with it in *The Guns of Avalon*. Most fantasy that has guns is real history with added magic, like *The Dragon Waiting*.)

Brunelleschi, sculptor, architect, and inventor, turning his hand to many things in that way that absolutely characterises the Renaissance, that time of excitement when everything that was old that was good was coming back and mixing with everything that was new in a heady ferment that had never been before. And, in a way that was particularly Florentine, he was a trickster too. Let me tell you about Brunelleschi in the real world before we advance further towards the borders and bounds and brinks of the fantastic.

First, the story you may already know. In that time of revival, when they thought they could get back the ancient world but better, with God and without slavery, Brunelleschi built the dome of the Duomo, Firenze's great cathedral. It is still the largest unsupported masonry dome in the world. At the time they began it, in a great leap of faith, to make the greatest cathedral anyone had ever raised to the glory of God, they had no idea how to complete it. The ability to make a dome like that had been lost, if indeed it had ever existed. But they built the foundations, and then Brunelleschi came along and created new mathematics, new machinery (cranes and winches unlike any ever seen before, which still exist and seem rather a product of the Industrial Revolution that was still three hundred or more years away), and new designs. From all this a huge miraculous dome rose, which is hidden among houses, so that whenever you do catch a glimpse of it, you cannot but be startled at its size, as well as catching your breath at its beauty. Before Brunelleschi began work, when he was standing before the committee who could give him the job, when he had never built any dome at all, they asked him for details of how he would do it. He pulled an egg out of his pocket and asked them to make it stand on end. People tried various ways, and failed. Brunelleschi broke the end off the egg, and stood the rest of it up. They scoffed and said anyone could have done that, and Brunelleschi said yes, they could, if they had only thought of it. He didn't explain further, and despite the lack of details, they gave him the money and the workers and the permission that let him go ahead and make his beautiful incredible dome, which still stands, defying perspective, accreting legend. His dome, their dome, Firenze's dome, the world's dome.

It's amazing it worked, really.

The committee who gave him the job, the Wool Guild's committee for overseeing the work on the Duomo, deserves a great deal of credit for supporting him in his genius. Not everybody would. Indeed, few committees at any time and place would have given Brunelleschi funding after he broke that egg and refused to explain. The committee members were men of vision too. And the committee still exists. Not the individuals, of course. They lived in this world and were mortal. The committee itself, which is eternal, replaces its members one by one as they retire or die, but it survives, still continuing its long task. It has a beautiful and informative museum beside the Duomo now, but better than that, the committee still oversees the actual work of building the cathedral, which still isn't complete, which will never be complete, which is being created even as it is restored. The committee lives, the work goes on, scaffolding rises, tiles are commissioned and made and set in place, choices and decisions are made about funding, now as when that arrogant genius Brunelleschi stood before them with the egg. This is one way to be immortal, which may be some consolation in the absence of more satisfactory ways.

The next story is about Brunelleschi and Ghiberti. Brunelleschi and Ghiberti were both artists, sculptors, and architects, and rivals in everything. They were both of the same age, and the same social class—guildsmen, which meant they could vote and hold office in the oligarchic republic that was Renaissance Firenze.

They could wear the woven red *cioppa* as a sign of their status, as a toga was in ancient Rome. (Cosimo de' Medici said cynically that three yards of red cloth made a gentleman.) A hundred years before this, Firenze had rid itself of its nobles, who were always feuding. They killed them, or exiled them, or barred them from holding office, and all the old noble families except one vanished. That one, the Tornaquinci family, went to ground, changing their name to Tornabuoni and pretending they had been merchants all along like everyone else. The strangest thing about this is that it means nothing. There are no consequences. They married into the other guild-class families and became exactly like them, and their origin never mattered to anyone. They didn't end up on top, or betray the city, or anything. History doesn't work like a story. It rarely wraps up satisfyingly. It's full of perpetual loose ends and dangling motifs that any writer reading it immediately wants to tug on and tie up into bows. But here, now, at the moment we are considering early in the Renaissance, 1401, the very beginning of an exciting new century, the names of qualified guildsmen are put into purses and drawn out to see who rules the city. Eight men of the merchant class rule for two months at a time, the highest honour the city affords. It was a real, if time-bounded, power, and if it led to inconsistent policies, well, it's better than tyranny, and how is your democracy doing at that this fine day? (Don't answer that. Don't even think about that.)

The names were drawn out for other things, too, such as judging city art competitions. There was in 1401 an art competition for who should make the new bronze doors of the Baptistery, Firenze's amazing circular church, with its inner dome covered already in golden mosaics telling the whole story from creation to doomsday. It was actually built around 1100, but falsely believed by 1400 to be a converted Roman temple to Mars, because in Italy anything large and wonderful was attributed to the Romans, as in more northern places the works of the Romans were attributed to giants. The artists competing to make the Baptistery doors were given some bronze and asked to make from it a sample panel, the story of the sacrifice of Isaac. Ghiberti and Brunelleschi each made a panel, in fierce rivalry. None of the other entries were worth consideration, but these two were both wonderful. The judges whose names were drawn from a purse were torn between the two offerings, but in the end chose Ghiberti's panel, and gave Ghiberti the job of making the great doors.

This committee of judges, unlike the Wool Guild committee, was an ephemeral thing that dissolved right away, as soon as Ghiberti was chosen. The two panels, however, were preserved, and can be seen today in the Bargello Museum. The most interesting thing isn't comparing them and second guessing the committee to decide which one you'd give the prize to, fun though that is. But it's much more interesting to compare Ghiberti's panel in the Bargello to the same panel on the actual doors he made, the doors that bear the name Michelangelo gave them a century later, "The Gates of Paradise." Look carefully at the panels. We have three, the one on the doors and the two competition models, all showing the same scene from the same story, that strange Old Testament moment of aborted child sacrifice, when Abraham obediently takes up the knife to murder his son at God's command, and God sends an angel with a ram just in time to save the child. They're all different. In between the time of the competition and making the actual door, linear perspective had been invented, mostly by Brunelleschi.

There were ways of sort-of faking perspective before. Massaccio was the first person to do a true perspective painting that survives, Leon Battista Alberti was the first person to write about perspective. But it was Brunelleschi, with his mathematical skill, who first figured it out. He stood in the doorway of the Duomo and painted a picture of what he saw, precisely: the Baptistery, and the space between, and the pillar where St Zenobius's miraculous elm tree once stood, using perspective. It was a painting so wonderfully lifelike people actually confused it for reality and tried to walk into it. Ghiberti's panel on the door has true linear perspective. Neither his competition panel nor Brunelleschi's does. When you think of what it means to live in a golden age, think about that.

Brunelleschi's perspective painting of the view from the steps of the Duomo, the very first painting with true linear perspective, doesn't survive. There's no trace of it, and no record of what happened to it. We just have awed descriptions of it. But we know what it must have looked like. The square is still there, the Baptistery, and the pillar. The clothes on the people have changed, and of course Ghiberti finished his doors. But the descriptions say it was as real as the real thing, and we can still stand where he stood and see the real thing. Standing where he stood, looking at the real thing, surely we can imaginatively re-create the painting?

Third Brunelleschi story: As well as his rival Ghiberti, he had a best friend (and sometime lover), the sculptor Donatello. Donatello made a painted wooden crucifix for the great church of Santa Maria Novella. Brunelleschi criticized it, saying that Donatello had made Christ look like a carpenter. Donatello challenged him to do better. Brunelleschi then carved his own crucifix, for the great church of Santa Croce. Santa Maria Novella and Santa Croce were rival churches then; the first belonged to the Dominicans and the second to the Franciscans, rival monastic orders, founded in about 1200 by St Dominic and St Francis, respectively. They must have been very pleased to each get a comparable crucifix. They were always competing for art, wealth, and fame. In the way in which Firenze has divided up the functions of spirituality and human life between its different churches, Santa Maria Novella is where people get married, and Santa Croce is where prominent Florentines are buried. (Though of these three, only Ghiberti ended up in Santa Croce. Donatello is in San

Lorenzo, the church of the soul, and, exceptionally, Brunelleschi lies under his own dome, in the Duomo.)

When Brunelleschi had completed his own crucifix, he knew that if he just openly showed it to Donatello, Donatello wouldn't admit it was better than his. So he invited Donatello to dinner, without saying anything about the crucifix, and met him beforehand in the market, the old market that is called the new market, the Mercato Nuovo, down near the guild church of Orsanmichele. (The market is still in the same location, with the same open sides, stone supports, and covered portico, but now it sells leather bags and silk scarves and tapestries to tourists, and if you want food you have to go to the luscious markets of Sant Ambrogio or San Lorenzo.) They met there, among the food stalls, and Brunelleschi told Donatello he'd be along in a minute, and asked him to take the groceries home.

Don't imagine paper or a shopping bag. He'd have had the groceries in his arms, or perhaps in a wicker basket. If there was a fish (as there very well might have been, nobody recorded the menu that day but they ate a lot of fish, fresh from the Arno or brought up from the sea at Pisa), it would be suspended by a thread through the gills, as we see in paintings of Tobias and the Angel. Or it might have been mostly prepared food from stalls that specialised in takeout. Lots of people in Firenze at that date lived in apartments that didn't have anywhere to cook, and these stalls did a thriving business in ready-cooked food. We think of prepared food as a modern thing, but it was very common in Renaissance Firenze. Brunelleschi had his own house, which probably did have a kitchen, up under the roof as was usual in Italy at this time—the reason was to prevent fire damage. If the kitchen was up there, it would burn the roof but it wouldn't take out the whole place. He probably had servants to cook and clean for him, though we know from this story that they didn't normally do the grocery shopping. There was nothing unusual to Donatello that day in Brunelleschi being in the market choosing his own food for dinner.

But even if these potential invisible servants (women, she says, women who don't get into the history books or the stories people tell, there have been no women in these stories so far) even if they normally cooked, he still might have chosen takeout that day, for a special dinner with his beloved Donatello. What did they eat? We don't know. We have Michelangelo's shopping lists, with exquisite little drawings of anchovies and spinach, and Pontormo's diaries, from a century later, record menus of half a kid's head, fried, with soup, rosemary bread, and grapes, and on another day an egg and artichoke frittata, ricotta crepes, and fried fish. All these seem plausible guesses for Brunelleschi too, but we just don't know and can't find out. For Brunelleschi and Donatello's time we have only records of the elaborate banquets of the rich.

There they were in the market, two artists among stalls selling fresh food and prepared food, workers and merchants from the city, and farmers come in from farms with their produce, milk and cheese and vegetables and fruit, people who had a personal relationship with those they bought from and sold to, often offering them lines of credit, which was easier for everyone in a literate society with very little small change. Donatello, suspecting nothing, accepted the groceries, which I see as a basket, and went with them to Brunelleschi's house. He let himself in (had Brunelleschi given him the key, or did he have his own key?) and immediately saw the crucifix. It's enormous, bigger than life-size; it looks big in the nave of a huge church, in a house, it would have been overwhelming. It's hard to think where Brunelleschi would have even had room to put it. Donatello dropped the groceries in shock, breaking the eggs that Brunelleschi had deliberately put in there, not for a frittata but so that Donatello wouldn't be able to pretend to indifference.

When Brunelleschi got home soon after, Donatello, with the

witness of the broken eggs, generously affirmed that his lover had made Christ look like the Son of God. Did they laugh together then and make dinner out of the dropped groceries? History doesn't record, but we can feel sure they did.

Like the competition panels, both these crucifixes survive and hang in the churches they were made for. You can go there now and compare them. She and I went to see them on two consecutive days, on purpose, and I can hardly see a lick of difference between them. They're both huge, stylized, almost iconic, with gold backgrounds and great soulful eyes. We probably wouldn't even have noticed them, and certainly wouldn't have spent any time looking at them compared to the other treasures those churches hold, if it hadn't been for this story. I love a lot of Donatello's sculpture, his *David*, his *St George*. Brunelleschi's dome inevitably makes me gasp with delight whenever I glimpse it. But these two crucifixes leave me cold. Carpenter? Son of God? Iconic clones.

All the same, when we recognise great art, let us, like Donatello, let those eggs drop and admit that we are moved, that we care, that this is important.

I need to tell you another story about Brunelleschi, but it should have its own section.

5

WHO WILL LAUGH,
I WONDER?

What almost nobody says when they retell the story of the fat woodworker is how incredibly cruel it is. It's a cruel joke that plays with making a man doubt his own self. This is a joke that goes far beyond making your friend drop the eggs. Brunelleschi was cruel, and everyone who helped and everyone who laughed were all cruel too. We can think of the two friends eating supper after the eggs and laughing together. This story doesn't end so happily. Playing a joke on somebody isn't funny unless the victim also agrees that it is.

Once upon a time, Brunelleschi invited a group of close friends to dinner. We don't know the menu and, again, we don't know who did the cooking. Women and servants invisible to history, doubtless, women who were there and had their own complex lives and stories but fade from the record. Even if Brunelleschi bought the food ready prepared from a stall, somebody cooked it. Let us observe the lacuna and move on.

His friends came for dinner, with wine and conversation, but one of his friends didn't show up. This was Manetto Ammanatini, known as Grasso, which means "fatso," and known to history as "the fat woodcarver" because this story got turned into a novella and published about fifty years later and that was the title. Shall we be respectful, unlike his friends, and call him Manetto Ammanatini, and not Grasso?

Brunelleschi and his friends decided to play a trick on Manetto to pay him out for not turning up for dinner. To do this, they persuaded very many people to participate, including the city jail, a family of labourers, and of course all of their friend group, people who knew each other well enough to meet for dinner parties.

Manetto was a man in his twenties. He lived with his mother, and had a separate workshop where he carved picture frames and wooden figures for altars. So he was a guildsman, and doing well in his career. He wasn't married yet—men would marry typically between twenty-eight to thirty-five; before that they were known as "youth," *giovane* (from Latin *juventes*), allowed more sexual (especially homosexual) licence, and not expected to settle down. We don't know why Manetto didn't show up for dinner that day with Brunelleschi. Maybe he was busy. Or sick. Or in love. He was of an age where a little irresponsibility was usually allowed. But this time he didn't get away with it.

After a great deal of preparation, they chose an occasion when they knew Manetto's mother was away. Donatello delayed Manetto in his shop while Brunelleschi went to his house. His mother was expected home, so it was easy for Brunelleschi to let himself in, the report says. But maybe Brunelleschi jimmied the lock. He could have, he was capable of it, he had the skills. People usually locked their doors. There were thieves. Why wouldn't Signora Ammanatini have had her own key? Where was she anyway? History is infuriating in what it leaves out, what it tells us and doesn't tell us. But sometimes these gaping holes are everything, are the crack where the light gets in. Sometimes the lacuna is what makes space for a new story.

When Manetto got home from work, after his induced delay,

his door was locked, and he heard Brunelleschi telling him, in an imitation of his own voice and his mother's, that Grasso was already inside, and busy. This impersonation puzzled him, but he was much more puzzled to be addressed by the voices as "Matteo." Then Donatello went by and greeted him as "Matteo" and asked if he was looking for Grasso, because he thought he was busy. Other people in on the joke also addressed him as Matteo, and soon the local guard came by to haul him off to jail for Matteo's unpaid debts. He tried to tell everyone who he was, but everyone was in on it and appeared to recognise him as Matteo, an unskilled labourer with debts and a drinking problem, and refused to believe he was Manetto Ammanatini, known as Grasso. They knew Grasso, they said, and Grasso was at home with his mother.

After a night in jail, Matteo's brothers came by to lecture him for his bad behaviour, pay his fine, and take Manetto home to Matteo's house. All Matteo's friends seemed to recognise him as Matteo and none of his own friends would recognise him as himself. So he gave up, accepting the role of Matteo. He got drunk on rich Tuscan red wine, and who wouldn't, in his place? When he had fallen into a drunken sleep, Matteo's brothers and his friends carried him home to his own house, where they put him to sleep in his own bed, but the wrong way up, with his feet on the pillow. When he woke up, everyone recognised him as his real self, addressing him as Grasso again, but wouldn't admit that anything had happened.

Eventually they did admit to the joke, and roared with laughter, laughing at him, not with him. How could he laugh, who had been so profoundly shaken as to doubt his own identity? But everyone else found this whole event hilarious, and were talking about it even years later, when it was written down in the version that survives. Even today, many people can't see how cruel it is, to take away a name and a self and work—though Manetto's hands would still have had his skills, had he had any chance to test them. Brunelleschi, genius, creator of perspective and of the dome, conceived this, persuaded others it could work, carried it out, and laughed at it. Manetto had to live with the ridicule of the "joke" that had been played on him,

Except that he didn't. He didn't live with it, and he didn't kill himself either. He left Firenze and went to Hungary. Or that's what the story tells us. He went to Hungary, the thriving Renaissance realm of the Raven King, the humanist collector of books and art, Matthias Corvinus, who would have been delighted to get a real Florentine woodcarver at that date.

But maybe it wasn't Hungary he went to. Maybe, having been dragged across the bounds of identity and singularity that way, when he left Firenze, he went further. Shall we follow Manetto, the fat woodcarver? Picture him, a tall plump young Florentine, a worker in wood, with his own shop even though he isn't thirty yet. He packs up his tools and his clothes and his savings in gold, says goodbye to his mother (but where had she been? Was she, could she have been, in on the joke too?) and he walks through the streets where people are still sniggering when they see him pass. Shall we follow where Manetto went, when he walked away from his cruel genius friends and out of the story?

Let's watch him walking down the street, away from his house that he'd been locked out of and then woken up in, heading away from his own workshop, going to Brunelleschi's workshop, over near the unfinished Duomo. There are a lot of things piled up in Brunelleschi's workshop, as you'd expect: tools, and parts of machines, and paintings, and designs. There are blocks for carving, and sheets of calculations, and boxes of bricks, and coiled rope, and the head of a winch. There's a crowd of people too, Brunelleschi's apprentices, and servants, and friends, and creditors, and members of the committee dropping in to see how everything is going. When Manetto shows up, Brunelleschi would laugh and tease him as usual, for a little while.

Manetto has on his vermilion chaperon hat folded over his

head, and his red *cioppa* around him, his bag of clothes over his shoulder and his box of tools for carving wood under his arm. It's a hinged wooden box, freshly painted green. When Brunelleschi takes his eyes off him for an instant, Manetto takes another step, sideways, into a painting done on a wooden panel and left leaning on the wall, behind all the impedimenta of a busy genius who is building a dome, and a boat, and carving in wood and stone. It's the perspective painting of the view from the door of the Duomo, life-size and as real as life, perhaps even more real, endowed with the mana of being the first.

Manetto isn't a small man, and he isn't thin, but he walks into the painting and shrinks. He turns and looks back, and for a moment there he is, painted, his face serious under his hat, red cloak and green box, painted in perfect perspective beside the column that marks the elm tree of St. Zenobius. Then he nods to his friends, and walks around the corner of the Baptistery and out of sight.

And Brunelleschi and all the inferiors and superiors and equals gathered around chattering in the little workshop where he's trying to work just stare at the painting, and at the space where Manetto was, and isn't any more, and then they stare at each other—asking themselves and each other what just happened? What could possibly have happened, because what they saw couldn't be it. Hungary, one of them would have said, yes, he went to Hungary to start a new life without us laughing at him. He headed off to the furthest edge of civilization they could imagine, Hungary, because he couldn't have just walked into the painting.

Did Brunelleschi wonder if Manetto was ever going to walk back out? And what happened to that painting? Where is it now?

6

DOLLY HAS A SECRET

Let's start from the right place now. Let's go back to those bastions Brunelleschi invented when he wasn't tormenting his friends with eggs and identity crises. He didn't build them, of course, not these particular ones. In his day, cannon weren't strong enough yet to bring down a city wall. The ones he built were all on battlefields, literal fields, when Italian war was an affair of condottieri fighting against other condottieri, campaigning only in the summers, with highly specified contracts. Though some people were killed or maimed, it was still almost a game. Most of Firenze's bastions were built much later—a century later, when cannon were more powerful and the big countries from over the Alps were threatening and the peril was real. Some of these bastions were designed by Michelangelo, who came home in 1530 to help defend his city against the forces that poured over the Alps and sacked Rome. Let us make a circuit of Firenze, of the walls. We can't do it now, of course, because they were pulled down during the Reunification of Italy—a ridiculous name, Italy had never before been unified. Oh, under the Romans, maybe, but then it was also united with all the other countries bordering the Mediterranean. Shall we reunite the Roman Empire? Some people thought that was the plan of the European Union, but they are so resolutely refusing Turkey membership that it seems they have forgotten how central Anatolia was to that earlier enterprise.

Italy—Metternich was correct in saying that Italy is not a country but a geographical expression. Italy has most often been, historically, a set of city states, frequently at war with each other, generally practicing many different forms of government, and where loyalty, patriotism, is to the city, not to any abstraction of country. And don't even get me started on the so-called Italian language, an entirely artificial construction that doesn't even attempt to reconcile the different languages and dialects of the different regions of the peninsula. A Piedmontese and a Neapolitan have little more in common than either of them does with a Swede or a Hungarian. Petrarch did feel a sense of being Italian, but that might have been because he mostly lived in France, near Avignon. Nobody defends Yugoslavia these days, that bold attempt to unify disparate states with disparate histories, but because the experiment of pushing the Italians together into an Italy to some extent worked, nobody questions it. The way we look at history is very strange, the places we draw lines, the things we remember and forget and take for granted, the series of improbabilities that become inevitabilities only after they have happened.

Italy's "reunification" can be seen as one of the first colonial revolts. Italy had been colonized by other European countries, France and Austria and Spain. Michelangelo's bastions were not enough to keep them out. And while some fragments of the Italian peninsula remained quirkily independent, so did some parts of India under British colonial rule. Garibaldi and Cavour and Mazzini were fighting for independence from external rule, just as the Greeks and other Balkan nations were fighting against the Turks at about the same time, and just as people in India, Africa, Ireland, and South America, would do then and later. And precisely because Italy was such a disparate set of states, it was easier to get everyone pointing in the same direction by appealing to the geographical abstraction. San Marino remains an independent pocket-handkerchief country entirely surrounded by Italy even now, which would mean nothing except for the way Marchese Serlupi, the ambassador from San Marino to Italy, sheltered many of the Jews of Firenze under the fig leaf of his diplomatic umbrella during the German occupation. But though different parts of Italy have different languages, different economies, and completely different histories, the country was fused together and hasn't shown as much sign as you'd expect of wanting to devolve into semi-independent regions. And under Fascism, of course, it tried hard to be a colonial power itself in Libya and Abyssinia, and show itself just as powerful and unpleasant as all the other European countries. Free unified Italy tried to reach back to older things, revive parts of the history of parts of the country and universalise them. This worked strangely, as you would expect, patchily, with some unexpected successes and some things that failed without trace. But Firenze's walls are gone, and only the gates remain.

When shall we walk the walls? In the later Renaissance, when they are complete but defended? We'd be challenged, and we'd have to have a good explanation for what we were doing there. How about in the mid-nineteenth century, when they are overgrown and crumbling, with flowers growing out of every crack? Shall we walk them twenty years before they are pulled down to make way for that symbol of modernity and progress, a ring road? Come then to the late spring of 1847, when poets Robert Browning and Elizabeth Barrett Browning find their happy ending in an escape to Firenze. Freed from the restrictions of the sickroom, and taken into healthful beauty, the poets blossomed in Italy's warmth and sunlight. But it was in chilly London that Elizabeth wrote her memorable masterpieces, both the *Sonnets from the Portuguese* and the love letters, in which you can see two poets drawing closer to each other as they talk passionately about the vitality of art. Naturally, they came here. As the religious go to kneel where prayer has been valid, artists of all kinds come here, where art has It's not just art, but art as life, art as the wellspring, the community of art, the golden age where everyone is making things, full of a burning excitement to show them to each other. In many ways, the best time to see Renaissance art is now, when it's on display, in air conditioning and excellent lighting, and open to anyone with the price of a ticket. But the best time to make it is when it's all new, all in the process of discovery, when oils are just coming in, lost wax sculpture has just been rediscovered, and when somebody might invent perspective in between making the trial panel and making the whole door.

Even in 1847, Firenze attracted artists of all kinds, poets among them. Firenze was ruled in this period, after Napoleon and before the Reunification and all that nonsense of destroying walls and building elaborate wedding-cake bombast on the Roman Forum, by Austria. It is the most politically peaceful, and certainly the least corrupt, that Firenze has ever been, or will ever be. The Austrians are barbarians, of course, who don't understand the Florentines and paint the Palazzo Vecchio white. But because of the relative political calm, and because of the beauty of the sky and the hills and the river and the houses and palazzi, clustering within the walls, because of the immortal art, left to Firenze by the last of the Medici on condition that it never leaves the city, there is a community here now of English artists and writers and poets. People can live here much more cheaply than in England, and besides, it is warm and full of beauty. Elsewhere, the English are busily asserting themselves in oppressing the world, plundering India, abusing local people and snatching their land from Canada to Australia, making themselves disagreeable and exploitative under palm and pine. Here too, on no evidence, they regard themselves in every way as superior to the locals, even as they enjoy a life much better than they could have had at home. The food alone is incomparably better. (It is at this time that a sad English translator of Boccaccio has to explain ravioli in a footnote as "a kind of rissole.") Here are fresh fruits and cheeses, dried and smoked meats, pasta of all kinds, wines, and olive oil, all in perfect condition, all delicious, and much better than they could have at home. Everything but the bread, that is. Florentine bread contains no salt, still, in memory of the siege of 1530.

It's interesting that there are, of course, many Austrians in Firenze in 1847, but they are all administrators and soldiers. There isn't a colony of Austrian artists, or artists from elsewhere in the Austrian Empire. But the English are here, for whatever reasons, economic, social, artistic. And the Florentines of course are here, and still making art, and writing fiction and poetry, and history, for it is a little while yet before they all get caught up in the art project of making a new country. When it comes to that, poets can be fools as easily as anyone else.

But it is only 1847, May 15th of that year, early afternoon and the sun is shining. Here on the walls, looking out over the Tuscan countryside, at the folds of the hills and the distant monastery of San Miniato, with a sketchbook in the reticule that dangles from one hand and a furled parasol in the other, is a nineteen-year-old English girl called Tish. Her name is Laetitia Blackstone, but Tish is what she is called by her father, her stepmother, her brother and sister, her aunts and cousins and particular friends. The young man who is with her on the walls addresses her formally as Miss Blackstone, a title she inherited two years ago on the marriage of her elder sister, who is called Vinnie, and whose name is Lavinia, or formally, now, Mrs Baker, a name Tish finds sadly pedestrian. Their mother, who thought it charming to call her first two babies Lavinia and Laetitia, died fifteen years ago, shortly after giving birth to their brother Lawrence. Tish does not remember her mother, and feels bad about feeling no sense of loss. Unlike the heroines of fairy stories, she gets on well with her young stepmother, Rebecca. She is not a resident of the city, though her family have been welcomed by the expatriate community. They are visitors only, passing through, spending the summer in Italy taking in art and culture.

Tish has a trimmed straw bonnet with a broad rose ribbon tying it down under her chin to make a funnel, so that she cannot see in any direction except straight forward unless she turns her head. She is wearing a walking dress made up of fuss in palest pink. Under it, even for this excursion along the walls, is a newfangled contraption of bone and wood and wire, a scaffolding that holds the skirt in place, a crinoline, replacing the much heavier layers of petticoats common a few years before. The skirt falls over it in three layers of flouncing, with ribbons and lace. She thinks this outfit is delightful and enjoys wearing it. She does not wonder what she could do if she were not tightly laced into a corset that does not let her breathe deeply, or if she did not have to carry the weight of crinoline and skirts that shape her into an hourglass. As a little girl she used to run with Vinnie and Larry, climb trees, catch and kick at balls, but she was glad to graduate to the prison of these adult clothes, which she thinks of as beautiful. Yet she is not a fool. She knows Latin and Hebrew, and is quite passionately fond of art and of Firenze.

Young Adolfo Tornabuoni, known as Dolly, beside her, offering her his arm to help her over any slightest irregularity in the surface of the top of the wall, is wearing the uniform of men of his class and status anywhere in Europe at this time, which is to say a black jacket and trousers, a white shirt, and a tie. He has, however, substituted the matching headwear for a vermilion hat that would not have been out of place in the Renaissance, a chaperon of all things, one exactly like those Brunelleschi and Manetto wore, rolled and folded to cover his head and neck. He has also substituted the expected Victorian poker face with a merry grin. He has irrepressibly curling brown hair that constantly falls into his face. He is only four years older than his companion. And yes, his name is Adolfo, which means wolf, and which was a noble and popular name for centuries before it became contaminated by one evil bearer and so lost to everyone else forever. He is a scion of the ancient Florentine Tornabuoni family.

They alternate between speaking English and Italian together. She has a young Englishwoman's accomplished Italian (which has been less practical use in Italy than she imagined it would be), and he has the excellent English of Balliol College, Oxford, from which he has just graduated with honours, with a vocabulary helped out by a passionate love of Shakespeare. He lives in Firenze, in a palazzo that has belonged to his family since it was built six hundred years before. She lives at Blackstone House, near Manchester, in a house her grandfather, a goldsmith's son turned soldier, built with money he made exploiting India. She is presently staying, with her family, in a comfortable hotel near the Bargello Museum, still, in 1847, in use as a prison. Tish is taller than Dolly is, she is taller than almost everyone, reaching nearly to six foot, a terrible affliction for a girl in 1847, and one that a bonnet, crimped black curls, a crinoline, and even a pair of dimples cannot atone for. She has almost resigned herself to the thought that she is so tall she will never marry, that she will have to content herself with being an aunt to Vinnie and Larry's children, of which there are none so far.

Dolly enjoys walking along the walls with a pretty English girl, showing her the city, perhaps contemplating a marriage alliance—wondering how much her dowry would be, as they have a great deal in common, even if she is English and taller than him. If the dowry were good, his family would approve the match, he thinks, which would redeem him in his father's eyes for his scholarship and whimsy. He thinks it is a pity her older sister should not be available. Vinnie is shorter and prettier than Tish, less of a scholar but more of a tomboy—in Dolly's hearing, Vinnie has deplored her crinoline and confessed that she would like to play cricket. Dolly is still very young. He knows he will have to do something to revive the family coffers before they are reduced to selling off their art, but he wants to be a scholar. For tunate enough to be born in the world's most beautiful city he longs to live in its golden age, or re-evoke it, as Petrarch did antiquity. "Your sister is married, I think?" he asks.

"Yes." Tish is used to attractive men asking her about Vinnie, and replies shortly.

"Why doesn't her husband accompany you?"

"Mr Baker has to work, in London," she says. This is the truth, but not all the truth. This whole trip has been planned by Rebecca, Tish and Vinnie's stepmother, to help Vinnie recover from losing a baby. For this to work, it is essential to separate the two grieving parents, so that they can cease to reproach each other and have something else to talk about when they are reunited. It is a plan into which Rebecca has put much thought, and which she fully intends for everyone's good.

"What does he do?"

Tish does not like Daniel Baker, who she thinks bullies Vinnie. She does not share her stepmother's hope that a separation will effect a reconciliation. She has seen Vinnie become young again since they left England, though she is still not quite well. She had been meant to accompany them on this excursion, but felt faint and had to stop to rest. She is sitting perched on a tummock in a shady spot beneath the walls, fanning herself, resting until they return to her. She insisted the other two go on. Tish glances back, but the curve of the walls means that Vinnie is out of sight already, which means she must be left to her expected destiny. We can spare a pang for Vinnie, who deserves more from life than the opportunities her sex and station have allowed her. But her life is still incomparably better than that of so many women in this world in 1847. We cannot rescue them all even in fiction, or even give them our attention, and the pang we spare them must be vast, especially those who are neither white, nor rich, nor educated.

"He is a banker, which is the most boring thing in the world," Tish says, answering Dolly's question about Vinnie's husband's profession.

"Oh no, I cannot allow you to believe that. My family were bankers, you know."

Tish laughs, showing her dimples, and putting her hand to her mouth, her reticule dangling from her wrist on its little chain. "Oh, but bankers were more fun back then. I wouldn't mind being banker to Lorenzo de' Medici and paying Ghirlandaio to fresco my chapel. I adore your family chapel in Santa Maria Novella. But in our times the romance is sadly absent from banking, Mr Tornabuoni."

"Oh do call me Dolly," he says, impulsively, and though it is not something people do, he looks both so Italian and so boyish in his ridiculous hat, that she nods consent, and at that moment I slip into him, filling him up in one quicksilver gulp, and he catches fire, moves from a placeholder much less interesting than the too-tall young lady by his side to become a person with his own thoughts, his own agenda, my grin and quirk of the brow. Don't ask how I perform this trick of consciousness. I've been doing it for so long now that it seems quite natural. I do not slip on Dolly like shrugging on a suit of clothes, I become part of him like a soul entering a body. I enter into him, and he becomes part of me.

"Then I must be Tish," she says, offering her big capable hand. Tish gives her a real smile now, for as he catches fire so does she, and the walls, with the plants growing between the cracks in the grey stone, and the landscape outside the walls, and Firenze inside, the Duomo, and the Palazzo Vecchio, the old palace in its temporary coat of Austrian whitewash, and the dark curve of the Arno, with the Ponte Vecchio, the old bridge with its shops, and the clear curve of Ponte Santa Trinitá, the bridge Michelangelo helped design. "How funny that we both have nonsensical nicknames."

"What's nonsensical about Dolly?" he asks, shaking her hand, and for a moment she thinks she has committed a faux pas, and then he laughs slyly, and she sees that he is teasing her.

"Why, nothing in the world, except a young man being called after a little girl's toy," she says, taking back her hand. "I expect that is the mature kind of joke men care for at Oxford."

There are no women at Oxford, not yet. She would have liked the chance to study there. But she is enjoying her trip to Italy too. She has a great capacity for finding joy where she is, which will serve her well.

Dolly pushes his curls back out of his face and grins at Tish. "Yes, it is an Oxford joke to call me Dolly. But I like it better than Adolfo. True, I am not a toy, but I am not a wolf either, and I am more obviously not a toy, so it suits me better." There is something of the toy about him, Tish thinks, in his loose jointed walk and his silly hat, and the way she is comfortable with him. It's a pity he couldn't really be an eligible husband for her, not even if he could bring himself to ignore her height. She loves Firenze. But—Dolly is smiling up at her. "Whereas your name— Laetitia is a beautiful name."

"It is the way you pronounce it," Tish says. "It has a nice meaning. Happiness. But I've always been called Tish. What does that make me? A sneeze?"

He laughs. "It is a very English thing to take a beautiful name and turn it into a sneeze." They walk on, sedately, side by side, each comfortable now in the other's company.

"Some people say that is where Petrarch's father lived," Dolly says, breaking the silence to indicate a farmhouse in the distance.

Tish stops and turns her head to look, through the funnel of her bonnet. She had been twisting her closed rose-coloured parasol in the dust, leaving little circles and trails behind her. Now she turns from the house and turns her blue eyes down to his smiling dark ones. "Tell me why Petrarch is important. The only thing I ever knew about Petrarch is his love for Laura."

"That's not how we say it, we say Laura," he says, in Italian, correcting her pronunciation. "And she is—" He switches back to English. "She is green laurel, *lauro;* the gentle breeze, *l'aura;* the golden curls, *l'aureo;* the dawn, *l'aurora.* Petrarch saw her everywhere and her name runs through all his poems like a current rippling through the sea." He gestures at a laurel tree out in the fields that surround the city that are so like a pastoral landscape in a Renaissance painting that it is impossible to see them any other way. Nymphs and shepherds should recline under those trees, or they should be the backdrop for the holy family passing briefly through Tuscany on their way from Bethlehem to Egypt.

"Daphne," Tish says. She has read Ovid, with a sensual delight in his use of language.

"Yes, Daphne, the laurel," Dolly says, with intensity. "You see that. Good. But she wasn't what was important, Laura, not really. He loved her, yes, but much more important he loved Cicero."

"I love Cicero too," Tish says, surprised into truth. "I don't see how anyone could help it. He's such a mix of vanity and real abilities. Reading his letters, when I was younger, once I wrote back to him."

"Did you? So did I. And so did Petrarch," Dolly says, smiling enthusiastically. "He only had a part of Cicero, to begin with. He rediscovered the letters himself, after centuries when they stood on a shelf in a monastery and nobody read them. And reading them, Petrarch was sick at heart. Before, he imagined from the *Tusculan Disputations* that Cicero had retired to break his staff and drown his book and console himself with Stoic philosophy.

So to see him sink so insupportably beneath a sea of troubles naturally distressed him."

"Oh! Yes. When Cicero wrote about his exile that nothing worse had ever happened to anyone in the history of the world. I couldn't help thinking that he himself must have known female slaves," Tish says. There are still slaves in America in 1847, besides whose fates Vinnie's seems heaven itself.

Dolly nods. "Cicero did not bear his troubles well. But Petrarch loved him despite his weaknesses, as we do. Petrarch is a poet famous for love. Well, he fell in love with the whole ancient world, and he thought his own day would be better if they could get it back. So he began humanism to achieve that."

"Oh. And that was the beginning of rediscovering the ancient world, of course."

"He began that whole project," Dolly says. "And that's why he's important. That's what began the Renaissance, not his love for Laura and his Italian poetry, but his love for Cicero and his championing of Latin. I could lend you his letters, if you'd like."

"Oh yes, I'd love that," she says. "Are they in Latin? My Latin is much better than my Italian."

"Yes, they are in Latin. But your Italian is very good, except your intonation," he says. "Have you seen *The Tempest* performed?" he asks.

"Why, yes," she says, bemused at what seems to be a sudden change of subject. "In London."

"You have to say Milan as if you had never heard Italian. It has to be *Millan*, to scan. *Millan*, to rhyme with villain. I couldn't bring myself to it."

"And I speak Italian like that?"

"Well, yes, but it doesn't matter." Dolly grins, and puts his hand to his ridiculous hat, pushing his curls under the brim. "This is fancy dress, but it is also a sincere aspiration. A student, my father said I was, introducing us all, but I am a particular kind of student, a scholar. I am done with Oxford and ready to study my own land. What do you think Prospero did, once he got back to Milano, Millan?"

"Regretted his magic forever," Tish says, decisively.

"Oh yes, I think so too." Dolly has no agenda here. He is just making conversation with a girl on a wall. I, on the other hand, within him, have an underlying agenda, a very powerful one, and I am bending him towards it. I want my world, and I want to lure her into it. Lure her into building it for me, that is, or rather extending it for me, for it was built already long ago. And then I have to lure or persuade or coax her into entering it herself. It's there, still, only a breath away now. Brunelleschi's painting is gone, but there are still ways into it and this is one of them. "I played Prospero in Oxford, you know, wincing every time I said *Millan*."

"That must have been such fun," Tish says, wistfully. "We sometimes read Shakespeare as a family, but that's the closest I have come to acting."

"The cloud" capped towers, the gorgeous palaces, the solemn temples, the great globe itself, yea all which it inherit—" Dolly says, I say, as they come to a tumbledown tower beside a still solid gateway. Tish stumbles suddenly, on a snag, a snatch, a sill, and Dolly leaps forward gallantly and catches her before she can fall, so that for a moment they are almost embraced upon a portal, a passage, they are teetering upon a peak in Darien, and after that there can be no turning back.

When he helps her straighten up, both of them apologizing, they are standing in a different place entirely.

What country, friends, is this?

7

WHAT IS SHE?

She is nothing like so easy to entice into another world as Tish. She is too solidly embedded in her own world, the real world, the world where she is undeniably Sylvia Katherine Harrison, born in 1944 in Montreal, author of *Castaway in Illyria* (1977), the World Fantasy Award winning *Dragon College* (1999), *Once a Wonder* (2015), and all the books in between. Thirty books, she's written, in forty years: three series, nine stand-alones, and four collections of poetry, two slim and two fat. Fifteen of her books are for children, and the rest for "adults, young adults, or children as you please" as it says on her website. She often says her readers grew up and kept reading her. She often says that people enjoy reading coming-of-age stories, whichever side of that divide they happen to be on right now. She has to keep repeating these things because she keeps being asked these questions in interviews. Most interviews bore her, but her publishers' publicity people insist she does them. Then sometimes there will be an interview that isn't boring, by somebody truly excited about her work, one that will ask different questions, and she will come alive in it. She tells more or less of the truth in interviews depending on how much she enjoys the questions. I've seen her be cagey about things that are so public as to be on her Wikipedia page, and forthcoming about very personal things. She once almost mentioned me in an interview with a New Zealand newspaper, and I had to remind her why that would be a terrible idea.

Physically, she isn't tall, a little under average height for a woman, but not so short that she has trouble buying clothes, which is good, as she finds buying clothes tedious and likes to get it over with as fast as possible. She used to go to Hudson's Bay and buy multiple identical copies of the same thing: four suits, eight bras, twelve blouses, twenty-four pairs of underpants, twenty-four pairs of socks. When they started to look shabby, or at worst, when they developed holes, she forced herself to go through the process again. More recently she has been buying everything online, because of the tedium of trying things on and standing in line in the big Hudson's Bay store downtown near McGill metro, with its staff who seem to get more lethargic and less helpful every year. She gets most of her clothes from Etsy now, handmade in little workshops in Lithuania, Cincinnati, or Kazakhstan, and her underwear from Amazon. She has her boots handmade in Hong Kong, from a form they made of her feet thirty years ago when she was there with Idris and the girls. She orders a new pair whenever she needs one, and the boots show up promptly, still sized to her foot, still with the two buttons on the inside that she likes. She has the same boots, with neat dark stitching, in light brown, mid brown, dark brown, black, and grey, and for winter in grey, black, and dark brown, with stronger soles and warm white fleecy linings. She has silver hair twisted up into a neat bun and held with a Japanese comb, and she never walks when she can run. She eats lots of fruit, and frequently acts out scenes in her books dramatically, playing all the parts, before she writes them down. Therefore, she disapproves of the modern habit of writing in coffee shops, and always writes at home with the doors locked and the curtains drawn, often up in her workroom in the turret.

She is solid, established, respected, real. She is seventy-three, and lives alone in her red-and-white Victorian house in Westmount, a little city surrounded by the big city of Montreal.

That's expanded a bit from her author bio, but it's not going to do, is it?

In 1978, when she was thirty-four, she married Idris Nasir, a civil engineer from Alberta. She lost her husband five years ago. She hates that slippery term, "lost," as if he was neglected and forgotten about, slipped down the back of the sofa, like the Far Side cartoon. (Or worse, dissolved into the mist inside her head.) She didn't *lose* Idris, his warmth and strength and booming laugh, his beard that tickled, his impatience with fools and politics that could turn into vast patience with small children and animals. He was snatched away from her by fate and biology. He was not *lost*. He *died*. Idris built bridges and hydroelectric dams and wore on his smooth brown hands an iron ring that symbolized his devotion to his profession and a gold ring that symbolized his devotion to Sylvia. She misses him every day, and although their work kept them often apart, she has not been comfortable at home since his death. She travels more these days, accepts more invitations to conventions and festivals, chooses to do more travel for research, to work abroad. Sylvia flies or takes the train to visit her daughters and their families regularly, but not frequently. They miss their father, and with the girls now she feels herself an inadequate substitute for Idris.

It was a sudden massive heart attack that killed him, on a Friday morning in his office in the old port in Montreal. A coworker in the outer office heard something, or felt something, she could never remember afterwards exactly what. She became aware of something that made her wonder if Idris wanted her, and went in to find him on the floor, his hand clutching at the air. Sylvia worries sometimes in the middle of the night about whether Idris cried out or not, and how long he lay there before the young assistant went in, whether he could have been saved if the ambulance had been called sooner. She knows these thoughts are a useless and unproductive Ixion wheel of pointless anxiety, and berates herself for it, which also doesn't help, as I have told her, as she tells herself. She repeatedly tells herself to be sensible, that it is now in any case too late, much much too late, and "what ifs" and "might-have-beens" and "if onlies" can only be undone in fiction. But fiction is her realm too. There are worlds out there where Idris could be alive.

"No," she snaps at me. "You can't be Idris. Don't try."

I don't try! I know I can't. I don't want to be. It never occurred to me. I have never been jealous of Idris or wanted to be him. He was his own self, and good for her. I am closer to her and I have known her longer. I am more like her. I am indeed, a part of her . . . the snarky fast-talking male part of her that doesn't want to die. But I'm also *not* a part of her. I am myself, independent of her even when trapped here in her head. In my own way, I loved Idris too (I am not, I never have been, as heterosexual as she is. I have embraced both men and women), and I was certainly glad she had him, that warm still certainty that centered her, that helped to heal her and make her whole. But still, there are worlds where she has that power. If she can bring people to life, people who never existed until she thought of them, until she made them up and drew them out of the mist, then surely she could bring back Idris on the page, when she knew him so well? With just a few words she could evoke his noisy yawn, his warm touch, his tidy desktop, so different from her cluttered one. She cried at the return of his briefcase from the office, with papers shoved into it just anyhow, as he would never have shoved them. She set them straight as she never would her own papers, although he would never know or care.

I could tell you "she is a widow." I could say "she misses her husband." That would be the shallow surface of grief, a dark river that runs deep.

In this world she did not feel any mystic knowledge at the moment of his death. She found out he was in the hospital from a phone call from her daughter Meg, which came as a complete surprise. She had to fly back from a convention she was attending in Atlanta, gripping the armrests all the way, unable to concentrate on reading, trying to picture the hospital room and beam good thoughts ahead of her. He was dead already, before she landed. She did not get to say good-bye, which sometimes feels like an aching hole that can never be filled, and at other times like a triviality in the face of his palpable everyday absence. Nothing could have given her "closure" after thirty-one years of the teamwork, companionship, harmony, that makes up a marriage. They were not always in accord, but over time they developed such good communication that even their most bitter disagreements became part of their axiomatic assumption of mutual long-term ongoing love and life together.

There was no medical warning of his heart attack. He had been in his usual good health, swimming regularly and walking for miles every day. He always walked to and from work, except in the worst weather. He was only sixty-two. The same could happen to her any day, but no, at seventy-three she is dying more slowly, and she knows it. She would like to escape death, but sees no present possibility of it. She would like best to escape it by modern technological means—a telomere hack, a longevity drug, an unexpected scientific breakthrough that reverses aging. For somebody who has made a career writing fantasy, she has a surprising amount of faith in science-fictional solutions.

Of course, Idris would have approved of that. He preferred science fiction to fantasy, the future to the past. His favourite authors were Ursula K. Le Guin, Karl Schroeder, Lois McMaster Bujold, Kim Stanley Robinson. But the last book he read before he died was fantasy: Sofia Samatar's *A Stranger in Olondria*. She had been sent it to blurb, and loved it, and passed it on to him.

She had been looking forward to his perspective on it, the wonderful complex world, the characters poised between cultures. "She's Somali-American and my parents came from Pakistan and Iran to Alberta," he said, dubious, peering at the cover. "I don't know what congruence you think I'll find." But her last message from Idris was a text saying he couldn't wait to talk to her about it. She kept the text uppermost on her phone for a year after his death, so that she saw it whenever the phone screen turned on. She couldn't reply immediately because she was on a panel talking about coming-of-age in fantasy. Then she couldn't reply because he wasn't there to receive it. A year after his death, on the anniversary, she finally archived the text message.

"I've finished *Olondria*. Can't wait to talk to you about it!"

The idea of that conversation that will never take place, of the thoughts he never shared, is like a thorn in her shoe. She says that's why she can't put him on the page. She can't make up what he would say, he constantly surprised her, and her imagination of him would be a thin shadow ghost and hurt more than it helps. She hasn't read *The Winged Histories* or *New York 2140* because he's never going to be able to read them and they'll never be able to discuss them. She has them, she bought each of them as soon as it came out, but she keeps skipping past them and reading something else.

When she confided in her friend Ruth about archiving the text message, Ruth asked whether she was ready to think about dating again. Sylvia laughed incredulously. Dating has never been part of her life, that whole game of negotiation and strategising, not when she was young, and certainly not now. She met Idris in 1977 at a party given by a mutual friend. He was in Montreal as part of a project to build a hydroelectric dam; she was still working as a secretary, though her first book had been published and was starting to bring in a little money. They started talking about books, and left together in the middle of a conversation about the

ethnicity and skin colour of Genly Ai, the only human character
in Le Guin's *The Left Hand of Darkness*. Their friends were less
surprised than they were when their friendship evolved into a
marriage. She's never had time or inclination for dating. Her first
marriage—she prefers not to think about her first marriage, so
we won't, not yet. The plumbers have finished and left, in a miasma
of explanations in Italian, which she reads well but speaks badly.
The shower is again emitting your choice of a trickle of burning
water or a deluge of icy water, which is better than emitting nothing but groans and hisses. But her tolerance for indulging me in
this might be running out.

She has two children, daughters, only eighteen months between them, with names of the era when they were born Lucy
(1980) (after Lucy in Lewis's Narnia books) and Meg (1982)
(after Meg in L'Engle's *A Wrinkle in Time*). Lucy's middle name
is Mevish, after Idris's mother, and Meg's is Jedirah, after his
mother's mother. Idris didn't want the girls to have Muslim names
as their first names. "I'm secular and our children are going to
be even more secular," he said during Sylvia's first pregnancy.
"They'll experience prejudice even without that. Let's not make it
harder for them."

"Even here?" she said, sadly, because before she knew Idris
she believed that Montreal, torn between French and English,
was prejudiced only on language, and had left other prejudices
behind.

"Even here," Idris replied. "It's still there, even if it's not as
bad as most other places. And anyway, they won't stay only here.
We don't want to confine them to this island!" He was thinking
already, when Lucy was no more than a curve in Sylvia's belly,
of them as grown up and independent, with lives and choices of
their own, and the planet wide open before them, whereas her
imagination then stretched no farther than their first breath. But
his decision on names was made in 1980; he might have made

a different decision later, as the world changed. Sylvia especially loves the name Jedirah, and used it, without the *h*, for a protagonist, later. She thinks of Jedira in *The Magic Oasis*, strong and independent, a lance-wielding horse-warrior who learns magic from snakes in the desert and falls in love with a laughing dark-eyed poet-prince (me) as what Idris's grandmother might have been if she'd fastened her headscarf tightly about her head, packed up her cookpots, and ridden off to have adventures. She makes Jedirah's recipes for *fassoulia* and *imam bayildi* for her grandchildren when they visit, and thinks that this too is a form of immortality.

Both girls have their father's surname, and height, and similar skin tones. Lucy has his eyes, too, but Meg has her mother's sea-gray eyes that look blue or violet in some lights. Lucy lives in Halifax and is a successful designer. She is divorced with one son, Jason (after the argonaut), who is in college. Meg is a banker and lives in Vancouver with her husband, also a banker (perhaps less boring and more evil as a choice of profession now than in 1847?), and two children, Penny and Louis, both still in school. Sylvia knows Meg didn't deliberately name her kids after coins, and probably doesn't even know the Louis d'Or was France's gold coin, but she can't help thinking of it every time she uses their names. They are well-behaved, polite, unimaginative children. Penny plays the viola, very correctly. Sylvia sometimes goes to her recitals when she visits them. They seem to have hobbies but no passions. Lucy's Jason was wilder, prone to tantrums as a child, but more appreciative of his grandmother's books. The last she heard from him was an email saying he had switched his major from classics to astrophysics. Meg gets tears in her eyes when she talks about Idris now, but Sylvia believes Lucy also really misses her father. He shared himself between them equally and did not have a favourite, but he was unquestionably their favourite parent. He could, from the first, love them without constraint.

Sylvia herself was named after both of her grandmothers. Her father's mother, Sylvia, was named after a character in a novel by Mrs Gaskell, and her mother's mother, Kate O'Reilly, was named after St Catherine, either St Catherine of Alexandria, a very early Christian, portrayed in Renaissance art with a wheel, or St Catherine of Siena, a Dominican nun in the thirteenth century who tried to get the pope away from Avignon. Catherine of Alexandria is more fantastical, with her multiple miraculous escapes from death, but Catherine of Siena has the advantage of having been real. Her head is buried in Siena and the rest of her in Rome. She wrote books that survive, and is a doctor of the church. In art she sometimes has a starry headscarf, but more often just looks like a Dominican nun.

Sylvia's grandmother Sylvia was born in Montreal, and her grandfather Walter Harrison was born in Kingston, Ontario. Kate O'Reilly, with her husband, Conal, emigrated from Ireland in the 1880s. They kept a tavern in Sud-Est Montreal for many years, cooking stews and sausages and puddings, and serving beer and whisky to working men. The tavern still exists, but is now a café specialising in chocolate, and the much-gentrified area is now known as the Gay Village.

Names are important. She agrees that they are, and spends a lot of time on names for characters, working hard to get them just right. Idris used to tease her about this, saying it didn't matter and she should call them all Fred or Freda—names she gave to a brother and sister in *Return to Dragon College* just to tease him. But names do matter. Maybe for real people it doesn't matter as much as for characters, where their name tells you so much about them. I myself have had many names, but there is no one name that means only me. She does not use a name for me as I am in her head, me as distinct from the people I have been in her stories. I have not had a name as such since her childhood. Which I suppose we should address, although not yet, not yet, certainly not my part in it.

Her parents were Catholic, as Idris's were Muslim, but she

herself, like him, is mostly secular, though they each remained rooted, of course, in the rich soil of their ancestral cultures and religions. She grew up in Griffintown and the Sud-Est, parts of the city then largely populated by Irish Catholics, and learned as soon as she took a step in any direction that she was wrong however she held herself. As an English speaker in Montreal growing up in those years after the war (and *the* war will always be the Second World War, for Sylvia) she should have been a Protestant, and richer. As a poor Catholic, she should have been French. When she lost most of her ability to believe in God she retained the Anglophone and Catholic identities forged in these oppositions. She lives now in her turreted house in wealthy Westmount, a house that she and Idris picked up for a song when they married, at a time Anglos were fleeing Montreal in fear of the province voting for separation. They were in love with it and each other and decided to stay. The house is too big for her now, really, but she wouldn't consider moving. She trots down the long block to Rue Sherbrooke and takes the bus to the metro, or runs her local errands. She speaks French well, but she thinks and converses and writes in English.

She went to McGill (graduated 1967), on scholarships, to her parents restrained pleasure. They had scrimped for college fees for her older brother, Sean, and they had four younger children. Sylvia now rarely sees her siblings, or her numerous nieces and nephews, who are scattered all over the world. Even her youngest sister, Maureen, who works as a taxi despatcher in Montreal, she sees only a couple of times a year. They were never close, and have grown further apart, and every time she sees any of her siblings it becomes clear that they still disapprove of her. Of the huge tribe of descendents of the Harrisons of Griffintown, only her cousin Con is her friend. They are comfortable together, and go out of their way to see each other. She has even been able to talk to Con about missing Idris, a little.

"The stupidest things make me miss him," Sylvia says to Con, two years after Idris's death. They are drinking coffee in Sylvia's kitchen. Con is off to New York the next day for a week of intensive coding, and has brought around leftover peaches and plums for Sylvia.

"Like what?" Con challenges. "I don't expect they're stupid at all."

"Yes, yes they are," she says.

"Tell me."

"You'll laugh."

Con goes through an elaborate procedure of licking fingers and crossing them, that Sylvia too did in her childhood, but which she is surprised Con, a generation younger but still thoroughly grown up, knows and is prepared to indulge. "I won't laugh. Give me an example. Tell me the stupidest thing that makes you miss him?"

Sylvia thinks, sips her coffee. "Global warming."

Con explodes with laughter, chokes with it.

"You said you wouldn't laugh," Sylvia says, though she is smiling despite herself.

"I didn't realise how stupid it would be!" Con says, face streaming with tears that are changing from laughter to grief. "But it also isn't. It makes me miss him too, now I think about it. Because he knew about it so long before, and nobody would listen."

They set down their coffee mugs and hug across the coffee table.

"If you really want to do this, perhaps we should start there," she says now, to me.

I don't say anything.

"There, when I was talking to Con across the coffee mugs. It would be a more normal kind of beginning for a story."

I have a very good reason for wanting to start where I did.

I want to show you me first, to have you come to know me before you see her, so you can grow some belief in me before you have the chance to observe her so nearly and clearly and thoroughly. She's so real, so solid, when you see her set in her own comfortable world, and it is a comfortable world she lives in, even without Idris and with the girls grown. She is well established, famous in a small way in her small field, but not at all in the wider space where she lives. She has many friends who are writers, and artists, and photographers, and teachers, and engineers, and programmers. She has editors in New York, and London, and Paris. She does local signings in the Argo bookstore on Ste Catherine, and more far-flung book signings all over North America. She goes to conventions. She wears her neat unobtrusive suits, and her silk shirts, pinned at the throat with an oval of pearls set in silver Idris gave her for their thirtieth anniversary, in 2008. She liked that it wasn't a string of pearls but a brooch. She liked that he remembered. She liked that it was appropriate to her age and the kind of thing she would wear. She wears it every day, now, no matter what else she wears.

She twists her hair into its bun with one hand and pins it with her Japanese comb without even looking, she has worn it like that for so long.

In Firenze, where it is hot, though not as hot in summer as it is in Montreal, where there is humidity, she leaves the suit jacket off, but still wears the pearls at her throat, hiding her scrawny neck, which reminds her of chicken skin, and which she finds unsightly. She never used to think much about her body, which served her well, and even now she tries not to cosset it. That is her word. She is spending the summer alone to work on the book she calls *The Florence Book* and I call *The Dead Horse Book*, the book I am not supposed to be in, the book I am infiltrating for my own purposes. She is supposed to be in remission, but I have my doubts. She writes, and she trots about looking at art and architecture and eating gelato, and there is a way she looks at everything that I do not like, an elegiac way, as if she is saying goodbye. I see through her eyes, as she sees through mine, and sometimes we speak, but if I press her on this, she will not answer me. In the way she looks, in her choice to come here alone, now, I fear she knows, and will not let me know, that time is running out.

In Firenze, there is a place, a portal, a pivot. If only I could get her to stumble over it, like Tish, and come with me into the world that is waiting. Reality is beside the point. In that world I could save her, I know I could. Brunelleschi's painting is lost. (I do know exactly where it is, but it's out of our reach now without help.) They pulled down the walls in the 1860s. But there is a hinge, a hasp, a threshold, and there I am waiting, creating, and baiting my trap.

You see, I know her. I've been in all her books. But I've been in her head much, much longer than that.

8

A DISTURBANCE
IN THE FORCE

In the walled city of Thalia, heart of the duchy of Illyria, two wizards are sitting beside the fire one late autumn evening, sipping rich red wine from blown glass goblets and nibbling slices of sweet pear cake. The wine is local, the excellent vintage of six harvests ago, though most people in Thalia at this time are drinking last year's wine to celebrate the sticky and triumphant recent end of this year's grape harvest. The cake is light and delicate, with moist slivers of pear running through it. It is just barely sweet. Sugar is expensive, imported from the island of Candea (from which we draw our word candy) or the fertile kingdom of Mizar, away to the south and east. This room, comfortably lined with bookshelves, is a wizard's cosy study. More books and papers are piled on the desk. Half buried in the drifts is a ball of amethyst, and holding down another pile is an elegant jade dragon. The room is warmed by firelight but lit from the even greenish glow of several glass lamps shaped like waterlilies, two hanging from the ceiling and two more standing on the desk. The window is tightly shuttered, closing out the dark and rain of a stormy evening.

The house has a tower (it *is* a wizard's house), but this study is only one floor above ground level, and the house it stands in is on a street to which the window of the study would open. The house has a façade of gracefully bas-reliefed stone busts of philosophers; it abuts its neighbours on either side. It is no larger or smaller than they are, except for the tower, with its clear hemispherical glass dome, an observatory for taking astrological sightings. It is the tallest tower in Thalia, except for the one on the Duke's palace.

"It's good of you to make the time to visit on my birthday, and this is very good cake," the first wizard says. He is a sweet old man, in a red scholar's hat with two dents, and has silver hair and a mild, distinctive face, by which we can recognise him immediately in any place and time as Marsilio Ficino, scholar, humanist, translator of Plato, tutor to Lorenzo de' Medici, but here immensely older than he ever grew in our world—because, of course, after several brief visits to and fro, he left our world for good in 1499 when he was sixty-six. His face is a mass of wrinkles, his age unfathomable, but we can calculate it precisely. He is four hundred and fourteen years old today, October 19th.

The other wizard smiles, takes a sip of her wine, and then sets down her goblet on the warm terra-cotta tiles of the hearth. "The secret is semolina," she says. "My father loves this cake." At first glance she seems young, much younger than Ficino, with long, smooth, dark hair and no wrinkles at all, but closer examination of her eyes reveals that Miranda is simply an adept at the spells of youth that Ficino neglects to apply to himself. Perhaps it is a gender difference. There may be an advantage to a female wizard in appearing to be young and tolerably beautiful, perhaps thirty-five, with firm smooth skin, whereas for a male, an appearance of advanced age offers some of the same benefits. Certainly when Ficino stands to add another log of sweet-scented apple wood to the fire, he shows none of the infirmities one would expect from anyone with those lines in his face, though it also becomes immediately apparent that he is notably short. In some other fantasy world one might suspect Dwarvish blood. But here, where there are various kinds of nymphs but no elves or dwarves, he is just a short man, as he was in his younger days in our world. He is a shrimp of a man, but one whom it would be very unwise to discount. Miranda, who is of only average height, tops him by a hand. And she is indeed two decades his junior. Miranda has not yet quite reached her four-hundredth birthday.

"I haven't seen Prospero since he handed over this tower. Some day I must sail to Tempest Island and talk to him." There is a framed wood-panel painting hanging on the chimney breast with vermilion curtains open on either side of it, framing it like a window. It shows a picture of a ship flying before the wind beneath a clear blue sky, all sails spread.

"Oh yes. Father doesn't like many people, but he likes you." Miranda smiles, leaning back in her worn leather armchair. "We could embark together in my enchanted boat. That would be fun. Let's do that in the spring."

"A new experience. And I've thus far neglected elemental lore in my studies," Ficino says.

Miranda looks at him. "Do you think we wizards live so long because there is always more to learn?"

"Yes," Ficino replies, without hesitation. "Everyone else comes to the end of what they want and is content to die. Kings and dukes weary of their responsibilities, rich men become jaded with gathering wealth, great-grandmothers tire of cooing over new babies, captains become bored with their campaigns and conquests, but we scholars never lose our thirst to learn and understand, and so we live on." Miranda said wizards, but Ficino says scholars, for to Ficino the two are indistinguishable.

Miranda winces when he mentions the weariness of dukes. As she leans forward to pick up her glass again, her face is lit on one side by the rosy flames of the fire, and on the other by the cold gold-green glow of a lily lamp, which turns her smile enigmatic. "For most people, yes. But some don't want to stop living."

"We haven't had long enough to know," Ficino says. "It's only been three hundred and fifty years since Pico's Triumph. After a thousand years, what might we see?"

"I'm longing to find out," Miranda says. "Of course, there are unwilled deaths."

"It's rare, and only in battle or in the case of murder—" Ficino begins, frowning, when a great clatter arises outside in the street, cutting off whatever he meant to say. Dogs are barking, geese hissing, people shouting, and a gust of wind dashes rain against the glass of the window. The picture above the fire has changed, and now shows a crossroads in a storm, with clouds scudding across the face of a half moon, drawn by the wind, and bare branches of trees lashing.

"A change is coming," Miranda says, glancing at it as she draws herself to her feet. "The gods are stirring out there at last."

"The stars have been speaking of a change. Well, we have had a long time of peace to toast our toes and eat cake," Ficino says. He does not sound sorry at all. Nor does he glance at the picture.

"What does it mean, if they have chosen to act now?" Miranda asks, standing in the middle of the room and staring at Ficino.

"It depends what they have done, which we cannot guess until we learn it," Ficino says, standing. He sets the chunk of amethyst from his desk into the pouch at his belt and gestures to the study door. The latch neatly lifts itself, then the door swings open silently on its hinges.

"What shall we do?" Miranda asks.

"We'll go down and attend to the disturbance." There is a loud rapping at the door downstairs. "Beyond that, it depends what the gods have done, which we cannot guess until we learn it. It may well mean that it will soon be time to make a new covenant."

"You take it so calmly!" Miranda says. "But then, you abetted the last change, what should I expect?" She picks up the lily lamp and follows Ficino down the flight of stairs that bends around an inner courtyard, sheltered from the weather by the balcony of the floor above.

"You too stood by Pico when he made the change," Ficino says, as they go in through a door that swings open at their approach. They are in a great panelled hall, hung with tapestries. At another gesture from Ficino, lightning springs from the lamp in Miranda's hand to light the similar lamps that hang from the ceiling. They are all shaped like waterlilies, and the light they give is an underwater greenish white. All at once the big room is very bright. "I can't be bothered with servants," he says, almost apologetically. He opens the small door to the street, inset in a huge door. This time, he uses a key he draws out of the soft leather pouch attached to his belt. Miranda steps back against the wall, where she will not be easily seen through the door.

As the door opens, a narrow street is visible outside, lit by orange-red torchlight from sconces fastened to the walls of nearby houses. The sconces are complex metalwork or stone, in the shape of fanciful beasts or grotesques. Rain is falling fitfully, and the wind gusting. The slice of bright white light falling from Ficino's open doorway reveals a crowd of people in brightly coloured and decorated Renaissance clothing, most with hoods over their heads against the rain. There are city guards, market women, apprentices, guildsmen, children, and a handful of the curious who gather whenever there is an uproar. In the centre of them are two people whose clothes and astonished faces mark them as strangers.

"Ah. Salve," Ficino says.

"They're late for Carnival," one of the guards says. "They've no money that speaks of any city anyone has ever heard of, and no explanation of where they've come from."

"How wise of you to bring them to me instead of arresting them," Ficino says, and he hands each of the guards a coin, which he apparently materialises out of nothing, but as the guards seem to make the coins disappear with equal facility, perhaps it is not magic. "Yes, I can deal with these strangers, don't worry. You have done quite right."

He gestures to the two strangers to come inside.

"Shall we report that you're taking care of it?" the guard asks, fingering his little bag.

"Yes. Tell the Podesta that if I need his help I'll be in touch, and tell the Duke and the Senate that I'll make a report if there's anything to report." He then points at one of the apprentices in the crowd. "Giulia. Come in and make yourself useful, since you're here."

The teenage girl he pointed at comes in, as her friends giggle and back away. Then Ficino extends his one of his hands to each of the strangers. "Please come in," he says, and then repeats it in Latin. They have said nothing so far. "You, I think I have known before," he says to Dolly, and then to Tish, "But you are quite new to me. I'm Marsilio Ficino," he adds.

"That's impossible," blurts Dolly.

Ficino doesn't waste time arguing. "Come in. You're shivering." He draws them inside. Tish, who was not dressed for a cold night, is indeed shivering, and quite wet through.

9

THIS IS ILLYRIA, LADY

Illyria is the world she made for her first novel, *Castaway in Illyria* (1977) and revisited in *The Wizards of Illyria* (1978) and *Return to Illyria* (1980).

It's a world based on Renaissance Italy, with Thalia/Firenze very solid in the centre and everything thinning out and simplifying as it goes off into the distance from there. She has Not-Europe mostly worked out, from Sariola/Finland up in the far north to Elam/Persia off in the east and Mizar/Egypt in the south. West to east, the silk roads run between Sefarda/Spain and Xanadu/China. Hungary's called Morgia, Germany is Tedesca, Greece is Yavan. France is (of course) divided into three parts, Aquitania, Tasavalta, and Paesi Bassi. She hasn't thought much about Xanadu and Nippon and Tarshish, but she knows they're there, off on the other side of the Elamite empire, which has elaborate magic carpets and sherbet (which fizzes, and is eaten with licorice sticks) and beautiful complex poetry.

Sylvia winces. She says she was young, and she has built better, more inclusive, less Eurocentric worlds since, which is true. But I have special reasons for wanting Illyria.

Gunpowder doesn't work; at least, it doesn't scale up, you can use it for fireworks and little arm's-length inaccurate field guns, like they had in 1400. Magic does work, as we have already seen. Religion is real, and there were gods in the world, lots of gods. Christianity is a religion among other religions: Judaism, Islam, Zoroastrianism, various varied and complex paganisms. Christianity is the dominant religion in Illyria, but it's the muddled Christianity of the Italy of Shakespeare's comedies, where people swear by both Jove and Our Lady. Or perhaps it is better thought of as the eclectic humanist Christianity of Pico della Mirandola's *Oration on the Dignity of Man*. For all the monotheisms have adopted variants of the Platonic idea of One God with subordinates, because you can't deny the gods when they meddle, but you can quite easily say that they're angels or demons. They haven't meddled for some time, though.

Indeed, since 1980 and the end of *Return to Illyria*, it has been three hundred and fifty years of their time in which the gods have been withdrawn, time for the Illyrians to toast their toes and drink wine, as Ficino said. The ratio of time in Illyria to time in the real world was established quite clearly in *The Wizards of Illyria*. It is 1847 as Tish and Dolly step into Ficino's living room, as it was 1847 when they walked around the walls of Firenze. They lost the summer, as everyone loses a season when they cross over. They stumbled into Illyria in 1847, but we last visited Illyria in 1495. Since then the people there have been living. Happily. Ever after. More of them than you'd expect. In Illyria nobody has to die unless they want to, or somebody else kills them. Death happens only by human intent.

"Oh, so that's what you were up to," Sylvia says, a smile in her voice. "Ingenious."

She knows she has the power to make what worlds she will, and I do not. I have to work with such scraps as she allows me.

"But you are dead in Illyria, aren't you?"

She's right. I died in Illyria at the end of the third book. I was

Pico, a wizard of our world, and I sacrificed myself to save that world, to save everyone else there from dying, ever. It was a good deal. I'd do it again.

"So you got back in as Dolly?"

Evidently.

"But what good is it going to do?"

None, unless I can get her in too. In Illyria, she wouldn't have to die. And this is the first wisp of my plan, enticingly trailed in front of her. Illyria, a much more interesting place than when we last saw it, because benign neglect of the author and the absence of death have over centuries led to many things, complex and labyrinthine and beautiful.

"But there's no way I can get into a fictional world. It's not like you think. You say that I have too much to lose here, or that I don't want to, but it's not that. It's impossible. I make up worlds, yes, but they're just . . . made up."

"Like me?" I ask, speaking directly to her now.

"Even if I concede that you're real, you're only real inside my head."

That's true enough. I can feel the bone cave clamping down on me again. I cling to Dolly, in his appropriate red hat and anachronistic black suit, dripping on Ficino's marble floor under the waterlily chandeliers. Miranda is looking at him assessingly as he stares around at the tapestries a little desperately. They are faded, bluegreys and white, but still clearly show the glory that was Greece to a background of pillars and porticos—Plato writing; Socrates disputing; Alcibiades catching a quail, next to a trireme; Pericles orating at a rostrum, the Parthenon behind his left shoulder; and, in long strips on either side of the door, a boy with a lyre beneath a cloven pine, and two young men bidding a fond farewell at a crossroads under a waxing crescent moon. A wood, near Athens.

"There's no way for me to get into Illyria," she says. "It isn't real. I made it up."

She made it up, that's true. But that doesn't mean she can't get into it or that it isn't real. "You're a god in Illyria," I say.

"I'm a god in all my worlds."

"Yes, but because Illyria was the first—the first to have that much attention, the first to be published if not the first you ever thought of, the first to have sequels and other people's attention, that makes it special."

"And because you conquered death there."

"Right."

"But real people can't go into made-up worlds. It's just not possible. I don't know how I can explain if you don't understand. There's a difference, and you're not seeing it."

"Ficino went in. Pico did. Manetto Ammanatini did." I do not cite Viola and Sebastian, because they were perhaps always a shade less real.

"They did in my story." Her voice is gentle, careful. "I can say in words on a page that anything happens, and within the story it does. But if I say I grow wings and fly, or that the sun goes behind a cloud right now, or that the water in the shower will come out properly warm this time, in the real world nothing listens to me and nothing happens. It's just words, and they don't have any power. You say you want to be real, but you're more real than I am, in some ways. Readers remember you. So you'll live on in the books. It's the only form of immortality the real world has."

In fact the real world has more forms of immortality than that, and as for living on in books, well, I can't count on it.

Cattle die, kinsmen die, the gods themselves will someday die. Only wordfame dies not, for those who well achieve it. That's what Odin says in the Poetic Edda. (I have been a Viking.) But like everything Odin ever says, it's twisty. What does it mean, to achieve wordfame well? Has anyone ever done that? What does it mean, for a book, or a character in one, to live?

Books last; well, of course they do. Everyone knows that. Writers die, but their works live on. If you go to Stratford, you will find Shakespeare is dead in the church, but vitally alive in the theatre. But all the same, most books are lost and forgotten. The bestseller lists of a century ago are easily googleable, and most names on them mean nothing today. Do you read Dorothy Canfield Fisher? Ernest Jones? Elizabeth Von Arnim? Kathleen Thompson Norris? Do you even vaguely recognise the names? Rebecca West? Mary Cholmondeley? You have read *The Hound of the Baskervilles* or at least know what it is, and you've probably at least heard of Edith Wharton and Upton Sinclair, but the rest? And this is from only one hundred years ago, and only writers who wrote books that were both good and popular. How about the French bestsellers of 1778? You may know *Les Liaisons dangereuses* but have you read *The Nun in a Nightdress*? (But don't you long to, now you know of its existence?) Petrarch revived antiquity, true, but for some of what his humanist followers found, it was at the last possible moment. Lucretius was down to one copy, mouldering in a monastery in Switzerland. The last copy of Quintilian had been propping up a table leg in a different monastery for four hundred years. They discovered and dusted off works nobody had been reading for a very long time. One of the first things published, only twenty years after the invention of the printing press, was Cassiodorus. But who reads Cassiodorus now?

Beyond that, why did the monks preserve the books? St Benedict wrote in his *Rule* for monks that each monk should read a new book every year, a book they hadn't read before. He wrote that in civilization, in the Roman Empire, at a time when there were bookshops and libraries and literacy, and coming upon new books was not hard. He wrote it exactly as somebody might write an injunction like that today. He did not mean, in writing that rule, to prescribe scriptoria, and monasteries as the sole refuge of literacy, and books moving across Europe at a speed that scholars today can track, to see who could have read what. He wrote a practical rule for the world he lived in, not imagining it being interpreted as holy writ in the world that had changed out of all recognition, where books were scarce and finding a new book for a monk who had been professed for forty years meant a real challenge.

That copy of Quintilian propped up the table in a world St Benedict could never have imagined. He had never seen an illuminated capital, nor for that matter text that distinguished capitals. Would he have seen it as successful beyond his wildest dreams? The monks preserved the works of antiquity as a side effect, *manu scripta,* copying them by hand and passing them hand to hand, passing them on with no knowledge that anyone would ever really want them. They didn't know the Renaissance was coming, that eager hands would be waiting to take them up, to print them, with the forms for big letters in the upper cases and the small ones in the lower cases of printers' chests. Nobody ever knows what's coming. It's easy to lose sight of that looking backwards, when it all has the air of inevitability, but the future lying before the people of the past was just as dark and impossible for them to penetrate as your future is to you. Abelard, in 1200, did not think there were only another two hundred and fifty years to go before Gutenberg, any more than you think of the vast blankness that are the events of 2268.

Books do sometimes last. Once Quintilian was rescued from under the table, it became a Renaissance best seller. (But have you read it? Do you even know the title?) But even when they last, by what measure? You can be a best seller for a thousand years after your death, read by every schoolchild, and then five hundred years after the end of that thousand years be almost forgotten and read only by eccentrics. Precisely that happened to Lucian of Samosata. His works remained popular throughout the ascendency of Byzantium, but as a Syrian citizen of the Roman Empire writing in post-Classical Greek, the Humanists and the Victorians had nowhere to put him and swept him under the carpet. Or your works can survive as esoteric curiosities (as Lucian did for the last five hundred years, and like Cassiodorus, he is in print right now in the excellent Delphi series) read by some, neglected by most, until one day, in translation, in a culture you could never have imagined, they suddenly spring to prominence and you become the single greatest secular authority, read by everyone, a household name even to the illiterate. This happened to Aristotle—this happened to such an extent that even now people are astonished to know that in the thousand years after his death he was not very widely read, nor much revered by those who read him. Even Cicero, beloved by Petrarch, Dolly, and Tish, greatest of the Latinists, suffered an eclipse during the later Roman period, when all educated people read Greek. He swept back into popularity at the fall of Rome. In the fifth century, Boethius, consul under Ostrogothic kings who later executed him, translated Aristotle and Plato, badly, but as best he could, because he correctly foresaw Greek being lost to the West. Five hundred years later, Bede, writing his history of the English church, dates everything by Roman emperors, even after the fall of Rome, using the emperors of Byzantium, because to him it was still all one thing, one empire, wide and real and useful. But Greek was unknown to him, and in his world few but monks could read.

Sylvia has published thirty books, and I am in them all. In some I am the narrator, in others, the main character. In most I am less important, but there, flitting about in the background helping other characters achieve their arcs of fulfillment, or appearing in a flash of imagery in a poem. Thirty books. What is the chance that any of them will be read in a hundred years, a thousand? What rocking tables will they prop up, in what unimaginable futures? In what electronic wastelands might they founder? It only takes a small change in taste for nobody to want them at all. And she's good, she's popular, but she's not the best, not the most popular. Tolkien will survive, Rowling, perhaps. But will she?

I have a better prospect. "In my story, you will go into Illyria, the way Manetto and Ficino did," I say. "Let me tell this one and you'll see. Wouldn't you like to be in Illyria?"

"Yes . . . look, it's fun, and I can let you keep telling it, and it'll actually fit with what I wanted to do, the *Twelfth Night* story, but that won't get me inside."

"I think it can," I say, not ready to give too much of my plan away as yet.

"People will think I'm getting senile, going back to Illyria after all this time," she complains, but it's a pro forma complaint, and I know I have won this argument so far. "We'll work on it together," she goes on. "I like Tish. She has possibilities. And I've always been fond of Ficino. And it's interesting to think what's been going on there all this time."

"Yes," I say, trying and failing to keep the triumph I feel out of my voice. This was the hardest obstacle, for if she had cut me off now, it would have been much harder to win through, perhaps impossible if she bound me up in the bone cave in silence and wouldn't let me speak to the possibility of you. I can fight most things, but not her, she has all the power. I have fought dragons and manticores and Death itself, and overcome them all, but against her I am as helpless as an Antean lifted away from the ground.

As for her objections, they're real, but not insurmountable. It's not me who doesn't understand.

10

THE AFFAIRS
OF WIZARDS

Ficino sends Tish off with Giulia. "Dry clothes, and then we'll talk," he says. He hands Giulia a waterlily lamp, which gives a clear unwavering greenish light brighter and steadier than a gas or oil lamp, and therefore clearer and brighter than any artificial light Tish has ever seen. Tish stares at it, and then at Giulia, who is holding it. The girl looks about fourteen or fifteen, and is dressed in Renaissance clothes—an undyed linen shirt under a densely embroidered moss-green woollen overdress. She clearly knows the house, and leads Tish into a courtyard, up a flight of stairs, down a verandah and into a room panelled in dark wood, with a dark blue coffered ceiling painted with stars. She sets down the lamp on a marble-topped table. She has great difficulty helping Tish out of the soaked pink crinoline, and tuts over it.

"I've never seen anything like it. What were they thinking to put the buttons here? It's fine-woven cloth, and brightly coloured, but so flimsy!"

As Tish stands shivering, Giulia rummages through a huge painted chest that stands under the shuttered window. After a moment she gives a pleased grunt and comes out with a huge fluffy, yellow towel. Tish rubs herself dry as best she can. The lamp lights the room, but leaves a lot of shadows in the corners. Giulia can't answer any of Tish's most urgent questions—or rather, she keeps repeating that she doesn't know, or that she'd like to know too, or that Master Ficino might be able to answer, while continuing to rummage in the chest. On the front of the chest is a painting of Psyche holding up a lamp to look at a very naked Cupid, sprawled in sleep on a bed. The painted lamp also looks like a waterlily.

"Is he really Marsilio Ficino?" Tish asks.

"Yes. Of course he is. How do you know him?"

"If he's the same person, he's famous where I come from. He translated Plato, and—" Tish isn't sure what else. She has just seen the smile Florentines get, to this day, when they hear Ficino's name. "He was a scholar. A humanist." But he had been dead for centuries.

"Well, he's a humanist and a translator here too. And a wizard."

"A real wizard, who can do magic?"

"Of course," Giulia says.

"Did he come here from . . . from the same place I came from?"

Giulia shrugs and burrows in the chest again. "Either that or he must have visited it, I suppose, if he did work there. He hasn't been there recently, that's for sure. He hasn't been outside the walls of Thalia that I remember."

"What year is it?" Tish asks. Everything—the clothes, the architecture, even the towel she is drying herself with, which has purple and gold tassels, looks to her as if this is the Renaissance. And yet . . .

"Year sixteen," Giulia says, her voice echoing in the chest. "So it'll be year one again in March and a really big New Year celebration, with fireworks and a joust and a play. My cousin Benvolio's writing the play." She turns around, her arms full of material. "Are you dry?"

Tish nods. She doesn't understand. Her skin has goosebumps. Giulia hands her a cream silk shirt, and a jacket that looks like something Raphael or Titian would have drawn a young man wearing, maroon velvet with immense sleeves. Tish puts them on gratefully and feels immensely warmer.

"Your boots will dry if we stuff them with rags," Giulia says. "Nice piece of work they are, and they fit you well enough." Tish has big hands and feet, but it isn't the torment to her it would be in a time of mass manufacture. Tish's boots are handmade not because she is hard to fit but because almost all shoes are handmade, factory shoe production is only just beginning. She would prefer to have small feet, as she would prefer all of herself to be smaller, but it does not limit her choice of footwear as it would for women in decades closer to our own. Giulia hands Tish a pair of dark green tights with leather soles on the bottom of the feet, like built-in slippers. "Pull these on while I see to your boots."

Tish gets the tights backwards the first time, and has to start again. When she's done, Giulia has finished stuffing the boots with rags. She seats Tish on a three-legged stool and efficiently brushes her hair, then ties it back behind her head with a ribbon.

"There, that'll do," she says, tilting her head on one side and looking Tish over critically. Tish is used to maids, to being waited on, but Giulia doesn't behave like the maids she's used to. She's assuming a greater equality, and Tish, off balance, has given it to her.

"Do you think you could find me a skirt?" Tish asks, apologetically, as she would never have addressed any servant in her own century.

"You'll do as you are," Giulia says, reassuringly.

Tish looks down at her legs, which seem practically naked. The jacket reaches only to her upper thighs. "No, a skirt," she says. "To cover my legs." When Giulia still doesn't seem to understand, she gestures. "Like you're wearing. And the alarming lady."

Giulia laughs. "Miranda, that is, she's not a lady any more, she gave it up to be a wizard."

Tish frowns, puzzled. "But she's wearing a skirt."

"She is, but you don't need to. You're tall enough, and slim enough, and your hair's the right length. Nobody'll question it. Honestly. Don't worry." Giulia is looking as perplexed as Tish feels. "Doublet and hose you're wearing."

"You mean I should try to pass as a man?" Tish asks.

"That's right. Don't you know anything?"

"Evidently not," Tish says. She has had a very confusing afternoon and has been thrust into a world she knows nothing about, for which her education has not prepared her.

"Passing as a man is the very first thing you should do, if you possibly can," Giulia says.

In Shakespeare, girls disguise themselves as men at the drop of a hat. The other way around, not so much. There are two ways to go from a world that divides everything by gender roles. One is to open things up and make everything available to everyone, which is the direction our world has at least been trying to move in. The other is to keep the rigid roles but allow people to cross the line if they feel stuck where their bodies would allot them. In *Twelfth Night* Viola wore her brother's clothes both to be safe alone and unprotected and to be able to get a job. Employment opportunities for men and women were very different. Historically, women have always done more than people expect from their memories of dumbed-down school history. But often a woman has to be an exception to fill certain roles, has to be unusual, and the traditional female sphere is traditionally circumscribed. Illyria, made by Sylvia in the seventies from Shakespeare's imagination of an Italy he had never seen, has adopted this device of cross-dressing to take on male economic and social roles to such an extent that Tish's reluctance to give up the outward markers of her gender seems quite incomprehensible to Giulia. It's not how Sylvia would make up the world now. But she started it off like that, and it's had a long time to elaborate itself.

"You're not dressed as a man," Tish points out.

"Everybody knows me here. If I want to do it, I'll have to go off somewhere where I'm a stranger. I'm thinking about it, don't get me wrong. But the trouble is, nobody will know me and I won't know anyone. I'll be out of the web, with nobody to look out for me. I'll have to start fresh. And there are all kinds of dangers in the world. I could be killed by bandits or forced to join an army and then killed in battle. But I'm learning Greek and astrology and magic with Master Ficino, which will help when the time comes."

Tish laughs, and begins to enjoy herself. "Yes, that should help," she says. "But if you can learn all those things as a girl, why do you have to dress as a man?"

Giulia doesn't seem to mind being laughed at. She extends a hand to help Tish up off the low stool. "To be free."

Something else Giulia said resonates with Tish. "Am I out of the web?"

"You are, but you would be anyway, being in a strange place. But you're inside the walls of Thalia, where there aren't any bandits or tyrant armies, so you should be safe enough. But trust me, it's a lot easier to be in a strange place as a man."

"But I like being a girl!"

Now it's Giulia's turn to laugh. "You can change back any time, say if you want to get married and settle down. But you'll find there's a lot more scope and freedom for men."

"How old are you?" Tish asks, looking at her reflection in the cloudy mirror that hangs on the wall. She likes the way she looks, she decides, and smiles at her reflected self.

"You do ask personal questions!" Giulia says, sounding shocked.

"Is that a very personal question?" Tish asks, turning to her apologetically. "I'm sorry. Where I come from it wouldn't seem too intrusive."

"How old are you, then?" Giulia asks, taking up the lamp again.

"I'm nineteen," Tish says, guileless

"Well, you do come straight out with it! I'm nineteen too, if you really want to know. But you should never ask. What you should say, about your age, if it ever comes up, which it probably won't among properly brought-up people, is that you're *giovane*, a youth. That's all anyone needs to know. Being *giovane* means you're between about thirteen and about thirty-five, old enough to be apprenticed, old enough to be earning and away from home, not old enough yet to settle down. Of course, some people stay *giovane* for decades. Centuries, even. It's a great stage of life. You can be apprenticed, you can learn, you can disguise yourself as a man and go on adventures, you can go to one of the universities, and you're not tied down at all yet."

"Centuries?" Tish echoes. Giulia is so clearly serious that Tish isn't questioning her so much as confirming that she heard right.

"Not in the same place, obviously," Giulia says, answering what she thinks Tish asked. She hands her a piece of dark green cloth. "Their family would be sure to be nagging them to settle down by then! But if you move about, and if you have youth spells, it could be centuries, easily. Though some people, of course, can't wait to be grown up and have children and houses and responsibility and all that. They race through their *giovane* years as fast as they can. One of my grandmothers was like that. I don't know her age, but I'm not her oldest grandchild and I can tell you she hasn't celebrated her century yet."

One of Tish's grandmothers lived to be eighty-two. The other died in her fifties. One grandfather died at Waterloo, and the other three years ago at sixty-five. Her mother died at twenty-five, giving birth to Larry.

"Centuries," she says, again, turning the green cloth in her hands. "What's this?"

"It's a hat, a chaperon, like the one your boyfriend was wearing."

"He's not my boyfriend," Tish says, feeling herself blush.

Giulia twists the cloth deftly into a hat like Dolly's and sets it on Tish's head. "If he's not your boyfriend, he'll do for me," she says, grinning. "Lovely face he has! What do you want to stay a girl for, if he's not even your boyfriend? I thought that had to be it. Come on, let's go down, I want to hear the answers to all your questions. Be careful on the steps, they're a bit wet, and the soles on those hose don't have much grip."

Tish, tugging a little at the hem of her doublet, follows Giulia carefully down the stairs and through the courtyard, and, turning the opposite way from the entrance hall, into a neat ground-floor sitting room where Ficino, Miranda, and Dolly are waiting, with cake and wine.

11

IN PRINCIPIO
ERAT VERBUM

There, did you see Giulia come out of nowhere, out of the mist? She wasn't a placeholder, like Tish and Dolly, a dummy moving mechanically until animated. She was nothing, a need for a servant, which Ficino doesn't have, so she had to be an apprentice. She was no more than a requirement for somebody to help poor wet Tish out of her ruined crinoline, and to tell her to disguise herself as a boy, and give her a bit of information about the world. The whole of Giulia's very solid self, all of her ambitions and aspirations, came together out of the mist as her words and actions were written. She wasn't anywhere or anything, and then once she started to speak, there she was on the page, herself, with strong opinions, and five years already studying Greek and magic with Ficino. In intention, she was a job, a role, a menial who would disappear back at the end of the scene with an armload of Tish's damp and discarded garments. She existed simply because no Victorian young lady could undress without help. (I don't mean that psychologically but as a real physical fact. Nobody could take off the clothes Tish was wearing alone. They were designed to make it impossible.) Now Giulia's a character, as real as any of us, with something to do in the story that is forming, and the garments are left drooping and dripping, abandoned all over the floor. The cage of the crinoline stands forlornly near the Cupid and Psyche chest, with the wet pink flounces draped bedraggled over it. The ruins of the straw bonnet have been kicked into a corner. The boots are standing drying. (With rags, not the newspaper with which Sylvia would instinctively dry boots. Paper exists, but is more expensive than cloth here, and damp cloth can be reused.) But Giulia has gone ahead, bearing aloft the magic lamp, off down the road towards adventure, with Tish, in man's attire, following close on her heels.

We all have our origin stories, how we were bitten by a radioactive spider, how we escaped from the caves of trolls, how we were licked out of the ice by a giant cow . . . or maybe we were part of the rock until one day a chisel fell, and was clutched by something that had neither shape nor will before, and yet we carved ourselves free, one finger at a time, creating and shaping as much as freeing ourselves, until we stood clear of the rock, distinct for the first time, laughing as we took that first step away. Or maybe it wasn't rock but a cloud that we carved away, to make a form of air that could soar on the currents of wind, leaning into them, swifter than any bird and as graceful. That one feels closest to my own story. I have had many origin stories, as I have had many stories. But when I think of my own true beginning, it feels much more like seizing the magic chisel in a hand that was a moment before no more than a protuberance in a rock than anything else I can think of.

For Sylvia, of course, it was escape from the witch's house. Her mother would be, mythologically, a stepmother, and perhaps it is better that way. That way there could have once been a true mother, a loving mother, who was withdrawn, removed, snatched away by death, and replaced by the fiend who hates her. Perhaps her mother did love her, once, nurtured her, grew her in her very body, fed her milk from her own breasts—ugh, Sylvia objects.

"What? You breast fed the girls. You liked it."

"Yes, but to think of my mother doing it to me turns my stomach. What are you doing with this? Where are you going? There wasn't any stepmother. There certainly wasn't any loving true mother. There was just my own awful mother, who never loved me."

"Is it more painful to think that she did, once?"

"It isn't a case of whether or not it's painful. It isn't true. As far back as I can remember, she hated me. She liked the other children, but never me. I was always the scapegoat."

But I can remember moments in early childhood when her mother was still the source of love, given or withheld as she chose, times when little Sylvia still wanted to please her and had not yet realised the hopeless and arbitrary nature of that quest. Did she toddle off into the snow to search for strawberries, and find them, only to be told on her triumphant return that strawberries were tasteless in winter and a waste of money? Did she not make a potholder from her own sweat and blood, to have it rejected as a sweaty and bloody disgrace? Did she not find that mythical item that graced every shopping list for years, the postcard-sized photo frame, only to be told that her offering did not fulfil some other arbitrary requirement?

"I'd long since given up hope by then," she objects. "That was the year I went to college, for goodness' sake."

"So you'd been questing for the postcard-sized photo frame for years already by that point. And when you found it, didn't you feel—"

"Maybe for a moment," she says, and as she says it she is not her trim and self-assured self but again that gawky girl with long black hair twisted up messily on the top of her head and her absurd orange winter coat with the big pocket flaps. It is the 1960s and she is in Ogilvy's department store in downtown Montreal with snow dripping off her boots (not yet her two-buttoned

Hong Kong boots, but long beige boots with fur-trimmed tops) snatching up the photo frame with a shriek of delight.

"You'd think I'd learn," she says, but of course she did learn. It took Idris years to teach her that you do not have to love like a kitten pouncing on a string that might be snatched away at any moment. Nothing she could do would ever please her mother, and then Steve was worse. But Idris liked her, was pleased by her and proud of her, and at last she learned how to break her bad patterns and relax into that.

One of the things that ran through her marriage with Idris like a gold thread in a brocade was their cultural differences. They drew them to each other, and at the same time pushed them away, and sometimes the most trivial things turned out to be the most important. Yet always she was drawn to the difference, loving him for being different when the difference showed, even when he had become utterly familiar. She loved Idris for his own self, but the details of his different culture made him easier for her to love, long before loving him became a reflex.

We were talking about origins. What makes a person a xenophobe or a xenophile? It's not simple. Let us consider a little girl taken to the house of her grandmother and there being told to take cookies or little cakes off the rack where they have been cooling, and put them onto a doily on a plate. What the child knows is that her own mother despises doilies, and will fulminate against their pointlessness and ugliness. Will she say anything of this to her grandmother, her father's mother? Or will she keep it to herself, looking sideways at her grandmother and at the doily, then climb up to stand on the wooden chair by the scrubbed table and carefully spread the doily out on the plate as instructed and put the little cakes onto it one by one, arranging them neatly?

Will she realise suddenly as she is doing it that if her grandmother does this, uses a doily, then her father must have grown up with it, and yet he has never said anything when her mother speaks scornfully of the practice, never argued or defended his own mother's custom. She has seen him sitting silent, and never suspected he might not agree. She does not know what he thinks of doilies, anymore than her grandmother knows what she thinks. She has only recently learned the great and necessary art of keeping things to herself. But as she leans forward, setting the cakes around the rim in a precise circle, she realises that she does not know what she herself thinks of the pierced patterned paper that keeps them from the plate. She has no objective standard of beauty or utility, not yet, and as her grandmother comes in to the back kitchen and laughs at her, poised on the chair with a cake in each hand, this is the moment when she must take sides for her mother's standards and the home, and xenophobia, or for her grandmother's and the first step towards loving what is different.

"It wasn't the doily," Sylvia says.

"I wasn't necessarily talking about you."

"Of course you were. You were talking about my grandmother and her doilies. I can see them now, white, and silver, and gold, with the little cut-out holes and symmetrical patterns. I remember getting them out of the packet and separating them slowly so they wouldn't tear. She loved them. For her they meant sophistication, elegance. She saved the gold ones for special occasions, weddings, christenings, funerals. Do you remember, they were all gold doilies when my grandfather died?"

"You don't use them."

"No . . . nobody uses them now. That was the forties you're talking about, maybe just into the fifties. But I was already a xenophile. I loved the sound of French in the streets, in shops. I liked to go to new places."

"I think it was the doily that tipped the balance," I say. "Such a tiny thing."

"An excrescence, my mother used to call them. Ridiculous

for her to be so vehement about something trivial that gave my grandmother so much harmless pleasure."

We both remember her father's heavy silence.

"It was the class thing," she says. "My mother, whose own parents emigrated from Cork and kept a tavern, aspired to be higher class than my father and his parents, and saw doilies as symbols of their working-class respectability. Mad, really, when you think about it. How can working-class raffishness be better than working-class refinement? To most people, even if they cared about class, which nobody in Canada really does so much today, the difference would be so infinitesimal as to be invisible. Anyway, if it did matter, then the Harrisons were better. They were educated people."

"It is such things on which so much turns. You weren't big enough to reach the table yet, and the things that made you who you are were just taking root."

"Strange to hear you talk about my grandmother's house. Still, I suppose you have the right."

Because I came into being there, she means, in my own first and earliest origin. We have seen the back kitchen, with its heavy wooden table with cooling racks, and big oak chairs strong enough for a child to clamber onto and stand safely. It also holds a huge twin-tub washing machine—very old fashioned now, but new and up to the minute in 1950—and a huge wheezing refrigerator. There is a door to the backyard, where flowers and vegetables grow, a door into the huge larder, laden with jars and packets, a door into the tiny lavatory, and an archway into the main kitchen, where something is always baking or bubbling or being mixed. From there a door leads to the hall, with the front door and the stairs curving up out of it. There are two other doors opening off to the left side of the hall, first the door to the study and then the one that leads to the rarely used front room. The front-room door has a stained glass panel, checkered squares of ruby and sapphire glass, and when the sun shines they cast glowing coloured light onto the hall floor, which Sylvia glories in. They sit in there later on the day of the doily, eating cakes with Father McManus and Sister Dolores. Sylvia squirms uncomfortably on the horsehair sofa, where her legs don't reach the floor. She likes to look at the piano nobody plays, and the framed photographs set squarely on it. She likes the framed print of Botticelli's *Annunciation* that hangs over the sofa. But it is the study that was my place.

Nobody studies in the study. Perhaps Fergus, Sylvia's father, studied there once, and his brother and sister. Certainly some of the books there belonged to them and have their names written in them in crimson and faded black. "Catriona Harrison is my name, Canada is my nation, Montreal is my dwelling place, and Christ is my salvation" in *The Daisy Chain* and "John Angus Harrison, 1938" in Montaigne. Uncle John was killed in the war. It's hard to imagine fat Aunt Cat writing so carefully. The books belonged to anybody or nobody when Sylvia read them indiscriminately, weeping for La Boétie and Harry May equally when she was eight years old. Because the Montaigne was Uncle John's, she always imagines La Boétie with the face Uncle John has in the stiff black-and-white photograph on top of the piano, solemn in his sergeant's uniform. In future years she squirmed at this recollection, and then later realised that nobody was harmed by it and perhaps all three men, if they could have known, would have enjoyed it. She imagines Montaigne and La Boétie, reunited and side by side in Heaven, welcoming Uncle John into their company, the three of them talking about their observations of life in eager but differently accented French.

The study has something of the air of a lumber room. Things are stuffed into it to be out of the way. All the grandchildren play in there when they visit, and Sylvia sometimes finds treasures left by her cousins, Aunt Cat's children: a wooden horse, a cherry-red hair ribbon, a toy soldier with a broken gun. Her cousin Ian, much later to become Con's father, leaves a painted wooden sheep from a toy farm set, which Sylvia recognises and restores to him. If she climbs up on the big wooden chairs here, she can draw or write on the desktop, where there are more books and papers. If she drags a chair over to the window, she can look down into the garden, and see piles of snow. It is not always winter in her grandmother's house, but it seems that way. She is always sent there to stay when her mother is having a baby, and all the children after Sylvia are born in winter: Matthew in March, Peter in February, Cecelia in December, and Maureen in January. She spends time with her grandparents in other months, but hours only, or a day or two when her mother screams that she can't cope with her ruining everything any longer and sends her off. It is almost always winter when she is left there for weeks, months on end, and spends so much time in the study.

It's not that her grandmother wouldn't let her play outside. She has a coat and snowpants. She does play outside, just as much here as she does at home. She also spends a lot of time helping her grandmother in the kitchen, learning to cook, though in later life she often can't be bothered with all those elaborate cakes and pies and casseroles. In memory, though, it seems that whenever she is in her grandmother's house to stay, when she sleeps in the little boxroom with a single bed and the pink stencilled horse on the door that they still call "Cat's room," she spends all her days alone in the study. Except—she's not alone. That's her secret. I am her secret.

There would be no room for me at home, among so many siblings. But they stay at home, more secure in their mother's love than Sylvia, the spiky one, the one who doesn't fit. She never understands why it is she who is sent off, scapegoated always, when she is not, she doesn't think, any worse than the others. Sean, who is two years older, is allowed to stay at home. The younger ones are occasionally sent to their other grandmother, at the tavern. But it is Sylvia who is taken to the Harrisons, time after time, so in memory it seems as if she spends as much time there solitary as she does at home with her brothers and sisters. It is always framed by her mother as punishment, as ostracism, but neither she nor her grandparents see it that way. Sylvia is always glad to have a haven, glad to escape her mother's endless petty persecutions.

Two walls of the study are covered with bookshelves, and one of the bookshelves is an ingenious pine device of individual shelves with glass doors, slotted together. Barrister's shelves, they are called, though Sylvia doesn't know that yet. The pale pine is stained dark red. There is a little drawer at the bottom, containing endlessly fascinating objects, and a curved wooden top, delightful to stroke, which she cannot yet reach except from a chair. Each shelf has a smoked glass door—Bristol glass, Sylvia has been told it is, and very fragile, so she must be careful. She doesn't know that Bristol is a place, she believes it is a material, a special form of glass. The glass doors slide upwards, and then back into a carefully designed recess above the books, allowing access to the contents. The books in that cupboard are all old and heavy and dark coloured, with fine type. None of them have pictures and some of them are in Latin. There's nothing to appeal to a little girl with two short black plaits sticking out at the sides of her head. Sylvia is perhaps four, if it is the time she was sent here for Matthew's birth. But it might have been another time, she could have been three, or five, but it is before she starts school. It is winter, and she is in the study.

She has been looking at the things in the drawer—old palm crosses, a little cracked leather purse with a picture of a goat, containing a nickel and two dimes, a black-and-white postcard of Valentin de Boulogne's *Abraham Sacrificing Isaac*, an empty box with a velvet lining, a broken thermometer, a medal from the

"Great War for Civilization 1914–1919," and a scrawled copy of one of Prospero's speeches from *The Tempest*. She tries to read it, muttering the words. She can already read fluently, but the curled and faded copperplate is too much for her. She leans forward, and sees in the smoky glass of the bottom shelf what ought to be her reflection, but it isn't, it isn't. It's me, looking back out at her. She leans forward more, very slowly, until she is just barely resting her forehead on the cool glass. For the first time, we see out of each other's eyes, simultaneously looking in and looking out.

12

HEY, HO, THE WIND
AND THE RAIN

Dolly is both more delighted and more confused than he has ever been. It reminds him of his first days at Oxford, not only suddenly thrust among people who care about the same things he does, but expected to live and learn in a language that had been until then almost entirely literary. There is the same sense, too, of being where he has longed to be, but finding it very different from his expectations. Almost as long as he can remember he has dreamed of living in the glory days of Firenze, the Renaissance. He has immersed himself in it as much as he can. But now that he is to all appearances really here, he can't quite get his bearings. Language isn't the problem, he is (like Tish) utterly fluent in the language they speak here, though if he were to think about it he'd realise he can't quite tell whether it is English or Italian. But everything is strange. It is odd enough to catch a stumbling girl and find yourself wrenched from a May afternoon to an October evening, from sunshine to storm, from crumbling old walls to well-kept ones, complete with pike-carrying guards and their eager challenges. But is this Firenze? Dolly doesn't think so. He hasn't been able to see very much as yet, but as far as he has seen, some of the buildings are the same, others very different. Strangest is the absence of Brunelleschi's dome, the heart of his Firenze. He isn't sure, being hurried through the streets the way he was, with the rain lashing down, what else is different. Some of the palazzi he passed were identical to those he knew, but others were not.

If he has somehow found his way into the past, he thinks, it must be before 1439, when the dome was finished. But then he has been brought to the house of Marsilio Ficino, whose dates Dolly very well knows are 1433–1499. And his own family home, the Tornabuoni Palazzo, had never, he knew, been painted like that on the outside. It was a delightful fresco, as best he could make it out in the flickering torchlight as the guards hurried him along, between it and the huge loom of the Palazzo Strozzi on the other side. But he had researched the history of his family palazzo extensively, and there would have been some drawing, some mention in the family papers, even if the fresco itself were entirely worn away. So Dolly is bemused, and wildly curious.

He isn't quite as disastrously wet as Tish. His clothes were better designed to keep out the weather, and he was wearing a proper hat. Tish's straw bonnet disintegrated in the first few minutes, whereas his chaperon served as both hood and cape. His jacket and trousers are wet, but not sodden. Still, when Ficino (there's no question it is him, he recognises him from the fresco on the wall of Santa Maria Novella, and the sculpture in the Duomo) shows him into a room on the ground floor where he can change, and leaves him alone there to do it, he is delighted to dress himself in Renaissance fashions. The chest contains plenty of possibilities. He considers a red cioppa, which would mark him as a Florentine and a man of substance—he could wrap himself in the three yards of red cloth that traditionally make a gentleman, and this is a status that as a Tornabuoni he can legitimately claim. But Dolly too is still *giovane,* and glad to be. He sets the cioppa gently aside and finds a soft cream linen shirt, a blue scholar's gown to go with his wet vermilion scholar's cap, and dark blue hose to replace his damp and anachronistic trousers. He hangs up his chaperon to dry. The contents of his pockets he puts into a soft leather pouch which he fits on his belt—his original belt, which he bought in the San Lorenzo market just before he went to Oxford and has worn every day since. He thinks of the new clothes as Shakespearean, because he wore clothes just like them when he played Prospero in Oxford.

Once dressed, he picks up a lily lamp, which he finds delightful, and takes the opportunity to explore the room, holding the lamp up close to examine the tapestries (dragons and unicorns listening intently to St Francis preaching, and a crowned man casting his shadow on a naked old man with a beard, which he identifies after some thought as Alexander the Great and Diogenes, though the scene is clearly taking place beside the Baptistery in Firenze) and the books on the table by the bed. They do not help his chronological perplexity. The first is Plato's *Summum Bonum,* in Latin, a beautifully illuminated manuscript. For a moment he is struck with excitement thinking it is a lost dialogue, but when he reads the beginning he discovers it is only the *Phaedo,* which he knows well. The other book is a printed herbal, in Latin and French, *Flora* by Mabeuf. He runs his finger over the printed text thoughtfully. The printing press was invented in the easy-to-remember year 1450. This seems like a thorough and accomplished work, with multiple woodcut pictures of closely observed plants.

He goes into the sitting room to join Ficino and Miranda by the fire only a few minutes before Tish and Giulia rejoin the company. He likes the room. It is paved in big stone flags, with a bright brocade rug covering most of the floor. A wooden table stands under the window, closed and shuttered against the storm, which is still raging loudly outside. There is a mosaic marble fireplace on the opposite wall, inlaid with tiny mosaic scenes of animals and starscapes. Miranda and Ficino, like an unmatched pair of bookends, are sitting on two comfortably curved padded armchairs on either side of the fire, and there are three other similar armchairs set enticingly nearby. Dolly takes the closest chair, beside Miranda, who grins at him just as the other door opens and the other two join them.

He does not at first recognise Tish. Her silhouette has completely changed, and her hair. There's nothing in the young man he sees walk into the hall to recall the girl who left it, except her features. He has seen men dressed as women in theatrical performances, but never in his life seen a woman dressed as a man—not, in any case, that he has discerned. There is more of it going on in his own world and time than Dolly knows. It is much easier for members of one gender to disguise themselves as the other when clothing is strongly gendered and full of clearly coded gender signals. If anyone had asked Dolly whether Tish had legs, he would have found the question most improper, but answered that of course she did, she must have. His awareness of her legs was unapprehended, entirely abstract and almost scientific—she walked, therefore there must be legs under her skirts—but he had paid the fact no conscious attention. When he realised as she came forward that this strange young man was neither strange nor a man, he felt both thrilled and horrified. It was not in any way a sexual thrill. Dolly likes Tish, but he hadn't found her particularly enticing before, and there is nothing in the way she is dressed now to appeal to Dolly sexually, even though he can see the outline of her legs as clearly as he can see his own. The thrill is that of a broken taboo, as is the horror. Rosalind, he thinks, Viola, Portia, Nerissa, Imogen.

Their eyes meet, then they look away in mutual embarrassment.

"Where are we?" Dolly says, once they are comfortably seated with wine and cake. Dolly finds the cake both delicious and familiar, it is an autumn apple cake, a Florentine delicacy, vastly improved by being made with pears instead of apples.

"You have stepped across from world to world," Miranda says.

"You are in the city of Thalia, in the duchy of Illyria," Ficino says. "Let us introduce ourselves."

While they introduce themselves and exchange information which we already know, let us consider the place-names here. The city of Thalia may be named for the Grace of Abundance, or for the Muse of Comedy, or for the book of that title written by Arius to defend his position at the Council of Nicaea, but really it's because Sylvia liked the word and it attached itself to the city without her thinking too much about why. This was her first book, remember, and often in first novels writers throw things in that more experienced writers would hesitate over. The idea of grace abounding, or flourishing, is similar to the meaning of Firenze's name as flowering, or flourishing, and the city of Thalia is an echo or shadow of Firenze in this world. She wrote the first Illyria novel after a trip to Rome and Firenze in 1974. She took herself to Europe for her thirtieth birthday—to Jo March's Europe, as she said. She was supposed to go to Venice as well, but she cancelled that part of the plan and stayed another week in Firenze instead, because she had fallen in love. In love with the city, that is, she was too raw from her divorce to love any human again yet. But she could love art and trees and architecture and little cafés where she could drink espresso and red wine, and restaurants where she could eat inexpressibly delicious pasta. And that was where she started to write, to imagine Illyria and start to scribble the beginnings of what would become the first Illyria book. So the city was called Thalia because it was always called Thalia, and she was on holiday with nothing to look anything up in and the internet was still decades away.

The name Illyria came straight from *Twelfth Night*. And unlike Italy, Illyria is part of a peninsula that has never been united.

The name as she uses it sometimes means the duchy, sometimes the whole geographic expression that is the peninsula, and sometimes is a metonym for the whole world. The names of many of the other countries came from the Bible. Shakespeare and the Bible, what impeccable sources!

Dolly and Tish gape at Miranda. It seems to them extraordinary to meet Marsilio Ficino, who they believed to have been dead for centuries, but quite a different kind of thing to be eating cake with Miranda, whom they know to be fictional. It is especially strange for Dolly, who has taken the stage as her father.

"You're that Miranda," Tish blurts.

Miranda looks quizzical.

"You've heard of Miranda Ammanatini in your world?" Ficino asks, gently surprised.

"Miranda, the daughter of Prospero, yes," Tish says.

"There's a play," Dolly says.

"A play," Miranda repeats. "In which no doubt all my closest held secrets are displayed on the stage to everyone who has the desire to laugh at them."

"What year is it?" Dolly asks.

"It's the year sixteen," Giulia says, impatiently, having answered this question already upstairs.

"It's three hundred and forty-eight years since I left Firenze to settle here, and three hundred and fifty-three years since the Triumph of Pico," Ficino says. "That would make it anno domini 1847."

"But that's the same," Tish objects.

Miranda smiles. "The same as in your world? Is there some reason why you thought it wouldn't be?"

"Progress?" Tish says, tentatively. She waves her arm in a way that suggests, if it does not precisely invoke, steam engines, railway carriages, factories, gas lighting, photography, waterproof clothing, the Industrial Revolution, the French Revolution, and all the rest of the relentless clatter which so often passes by that name.

Astonishingly, Ficino understands her gesture. "Oh, that," he says. "Well, no. We don't have it. It doesn't work here."

"That is, it works, but it doesn't scale up," Miranda amplifies.

"How?" Tish asks.

Miranda glances at Ficino, who pokes the fire and says nothing. "Magic," Miranda says, after too long a moment.

"And how long do people live here, please?" Tish asks.

Miranda and Ficino exchange a look, but it is Giulia who answers. "People live as long as they want to. Is that different in your world?"

13

THE UNDISCOVERED
COUNTRY

I still think it was a good deal. I sacrificed myself utterly so that
nobody else would ever have to die, and when I did it, I did it
wholeheartedly, with no idea that I'd ultimately survive. It was
the first time an aspect of myself died in a story and I went on in
her head. I'm used to it now, but that first time I believed I was
really going to die, perish, cease upon the midnight. Yes, it's reminiscent of Christ, of course it is, and I knew that when I did it.
Christ died to save people's afterlives, and I did it so that people
could stay alive right where they were. If there are afterlives in
Illyria, and many people there believe that there are, what I did
didn't change that. People die when they want to, and then they
go on to whatever comes after—which I'm not sure about, to
be honest. She wavered about Illyrian Heaven, because it would
have meant endorsing one system and invalidating all the others.
I thought I'd reconciled everything, when I was Pico, but in my
nine hundred theses you'll find both reincarnation and Heaven.
So whatever comes after death is still there and still a mystery,
but death itself is voluntary, unless you're killed. And they have
youth spells, to make you look and feel younger, and pretty good
but not perfect magic healing. For healing you have to get to

somebody who knows the spell, even if you know it you can't do it to yourself. Everyone tends to pick up a few useful spells, but most people aren't wizards because it takes a lot of time and effort and a certain kind of temperament to want to keep at it. People who would be scholars in our world tend to become wizards there.

As it turns out, teen angst death is a problem in Illyria now, and so is dying of a broken heart. Dying is easier there, because you only have to will it. If you don't will it, you keep on living. But there are cases where brokenhearted people in our world wouldn't actually pick up a knife to slit their wrists but do in Illyria will themselves dead. There's also the thing they call ring death, where you have a group of people grow up together and know each other all their lives, a whole cohort, and then one of them is killed eventually by one of the things that can still kill people—murder, depression, bandits, a broken heart, being hit by a lightning strike sent by the gods, or being mangled in an accident to such an extent that they decide not to live any longer—and then the rest of the cohort will one by one decide to follow them into death. Some communities consider ring death shameful, especially some of the Jewish communities. But there's a lot of variation in how Judaism deals with death. In Galitzia there are whole villages where the self-defined elders each year all die on Yom Kippur, and others where they die on Yom Kippur at a hundred and twenty. Christians too have very varied reactions. Some feel you should listen for God calling you, others that you should choose death at seventy (a very unpopular view by now, as most of the people who believed in it aren't around to defend their choice) or eight hundred (like Methuselah), an age which nobody has yet attained. Islam also favours a "good end" when all obligations are fulfilled and angels come to the house to call you. Zoroastrians believe in continuing to live for as long as you are pure, but choosing to die if you become polluted, to undergo punishment and purification after death and before the day of resurrection. Among pagans generally there are fewer religious arguments in favour of death, other than the possibility that Pico's sacrifice may need to be renewed at some distant time in the future.

Most people in Illyria (the world) die when they choose to die, of their own free will, for their own reasons. Others are killed by bandits, or in war, or murdered. The rest keep on living. They call the time when it changed Pico's Triumph, or Pico's Victory, and, as we just saw, date things from it.

Giovanni Pico della Mirandola was a polymath and genius. He learned Latin, Greek, Hebrew, and Arabic, and attempted to reconcile Plato, Aristotle, the Bible, the Koran, the Zoroastrian Gathas, and the Kabala. (He was one of the first outside the Jewish communities to even acknowledge the existence of Kabala.) He was a friend of Ficino, and of Lorenzo de' Medici. He wrote nine hundred theses and wanted to have a great Church Council where everyone would debate them. As he was rich (he was a count), he offered to pay the travelling expenses of any scholars who wanted to come to Rome for the debate. He ran into trouble with the Inquisition, who said thirteen of the theses were heretical. (Meaning the other eight hundred and eighty-seven were either orthodox or too hard for them to understand?) He also ran into trouble with women, running off with somebody else's wife and having to fight a duel. He was saved from the Inquisition by Lorenzo de' Medici, on condition that he agree to live quietly in Firenze. He became close friends with the Dominican friar Savonarola.

He was poisoned by Piero de' Medici in 1494 at the age of thirty-one—oh, perhaps I should have explained upfront that he was real, a real historical figure in the real Firenze. He's far too improbable for Sylvia to have made up from scratch. However, she did fall under his spell, as so many have, after reading his *Oration on the Dignity of Man*. She put him into her book, and into Illyria, and recruited me to be him, whereupon I ran off with a flourish in all directions at once. It was wonderful. Pico was curious and fascinated by everything and everyone, and once I got into him I never wanted to let go. He had a whole new world to explore and new ideas and philosophies to reconcile with the ones he already knew. And I want you to know that the idea of his ultimate sacrifice was my own idea. It had to be a voluntary sacrifice or it wouldn't have worked. I don't know whether she would have asked me, because she didn't need to. There are roles where I've been drafted (I didn't especially want to be a dragon, though it turned out to be fun in the end) but that wasn't one of them. Having reconciled all the philosophies, I went up against Death and defeated it.

You'll know all this if you've read the Illyria books, but you might not have read them, or it might have been a long time ago. Maybe all you remember of those books is the way the colours faded from the tapestries in the Palazzo della Signoria while the Ten of War debated, or the way the sunrise lit the river Sabrina so that it glowed like a sword when we came in at the watergate, and the way the streets smelled different because of the smell of Morgian food drifting on the smoke from the campfires of the besieging army. Or you might remember the conversations I had with Ficino culminating in the great speech I made before the sacrifice. But you might not remember all the details even if you do. Pico was my first—the first time she used me as a character in a story. I threw myself into him with everything I had. I have done better since, and so has she, but Illyria had an intensity and a sincerity that we've never rivalled. I mean, I was Pico della Mirandola! I conquered Death! And even with the cultural complexities of what came of that afterwards, which I'd never imagined, I'm still proud of it. Wouldn't anyone be?

Everything changes without death, or where death happens only through human will, your own or another's. If you expect to live hundreds of years your priorities are different, even when you yourself are still young. Education becomes a lifelong business. Career changes, and starting again from scratch, are much more common. People in Illyria often delay having children for a long time, or space their children widely. For conception too must be a willed act, except where the gods intervene, because the world would otherwise become much too full of people.

In our real Renaissance, people worried a lot about under-population—unsurprisingly with all those plagues. The Black Death killed between a third and a half of the population of Europe—more than half the population of Firenze, at least fifty thousand people, dead in a summer. And in the Renaissance they also believed population figures for the ancient world they found in texts, figures that we now believe to be inflated. But whether or not Imperial Rome truly held a million people at the time of Hadrian, in 1300—even before the Black Death—Rome's population was twenty thousand. It was easy for people living then to see humanity itself as a shrunken remnant of what it was in antiquity. (In Illyria, Roma itself is utterly deserted, only ruins in a field, and the popes hold court in Nemausus, in Aquitania.) But even from such a small start, with death removed, uncontrolled human population growth can be immense. Even for us, with death still regularly taking people out, Rome presently has a population of 2.8 million. So in Illyria, conception, like death, must be a human choice, and the choice of *both* parents.

Of course, there are still some people who want to have ten children. But far more people in our world had ten children in the hope of seeing two grow up, or because for straight people the only alternative to ten children was celibacy. Without infant mortality, without any mortality, with willed conception making sex safe the rest of the time, this changes. People marry and live together for hundreds of years, and have children at long intervals. Miranda had her two children long ago when she was young, before Pico's Triumph, and has borne no children under the new dispensation. Orsino and Viola had a son a century ago, Tybalt, who left Thalia long ago and has not been heard of since. This is not unusual. They have a daughter, Drusilla, who is nine. Olivia and Sebastian have no children, and may never decide to, or might find the right moment in a few hundred years. Giulia was an only child and so was her father, but her mother is one of six. Her grandmother, as Giulia told Tish, wanted nothing so much as to have her own settled family early. All the same, she had those six children spread over eighty years, and Giulia's cousin Benvolio, the poet and playwright, is forty years older than she was, though still *giovane*.

The thing that is uncommon in Illyria is death. That's what changes everything most. The death of a person has to be willed, by themselves or by another. People decide to die because they're ready to go on. War happens, and can be very horrible. But in Illyria itself, by custom it has largely become a matter where the condottieri, mercenary captains, march up to each other on the battlefield, do a headcount, and either decide on that basis who has won, or fight a duel to determine the outcome. One death per battle is the usual rule. In the Battle of Verona, a hundred years ago, Orsino's cousin Giralda was faced with an army three times the size of her defenders, led by her cousin Rinaldo. She insisted on fighting a duel with Rinaldo and two of his captains, and succeeded in killing Rinaldo and one of his men, and seriously wounding the other. She is still duchess of Verona, and her heroic exploit is a common theme for paintings and epic poetry. But real wars and battles with casualties do happen. People are murdered, or kill each other in duels, and murderers are sometimes caught and executed. Three hundred years ago in Sefarda and Tedesca there was an outbreak of torturing and executing people accused of being witches or Jews, which ended with the assassination of the emperor, Felippo, by a Jewish witch called Jessica—another favourite subject for art. There was a war in Galitzia that went on for more than a hundred years and killed thousands of people. It was brought to an end, not without difficulty, by Rosmerta of Koss and Anne de Nemausus, who perceived that everyone was still fighting because it was easier than finding a way to stop when so many had died and so many of the survivors had been through such traumatic pain and anguish.

If you are a modern person, in our world now, it's not unlikely that you might not have known the true grief and loss caused by the death of someone close to you until well into adulthood. Because of modern medicine and life extension, we are on average living longer than we ever have. There are people in their seventies right now taking care of parents in their nineties. There are people who meet bereavement as a stranger when death suddenly strikes, because all they have lost before is a pet, or a distant, rarely seen grandparent. (Close beloved grandparents are as great a loss as any imaginable, but a grandparent on the other side of a continent and met only a few times is not.) And there's a real difference between somebody who knows bone deep what it is to have somebody suddenly gone from your life, in the middle of a conversation ("I can't wait to talk to you about it. . . ."), and somebody who only has an intellectual understanding of that.

This estrangement from grieving is a change in human nature, and one that has happened over the course of Sylvia's lifetime. Young people today are not the same as they were when she was young. They are not as unfamiliar with death as the Illyrians, but they are not intimate with it, as every other human generation has been. Death comes to them as a stranger, not an intimate. She notices it first in what she sees as extravagant grieving for animals, and then starts to notice it more when her friends lose parents at older and older ages, and take it harder and harder.

Then she observes a growing embarrassment in younger people around the mention of real death, where people don't know what to say or how to react, until talking about it is almost a taboo. Simultaneous with this came the rise of the vampire as attractive, sexual, appealing, rather than a figure of horror. There has always been an edge of eroticism in vampires from Dracula on, but it is Chelsea Quinn Yarbro and her imitators Anne Rice and Stephenie Meyer who concentrated on this aspect, after the intimate knowledge of death had receded. Other undead have also undergone this process in art, even zombies by the first decade of the new millennium.

Friends with no religion, who mock Sylvia for her vestigial Catholicism, revert to strained religiosity in the face of death because they have no social patterns for coping. They talk about "losing" someone, and adopt the even uglier term "passing on," or "passing," originally a Swedenborgian cult term, which becomes such a common euphemism that it is now used more often than the word "died." Sylvia hates it. Passed, passed on where, what kind of belief does it reflect? Passed, like gas, ugh. She prefers any other term: expired, kicked the bucket, pushing up the daisies, even being pissed on by Lord Byron.

Look at it this way: Freud wasn't necessarily wrong about Thanatos. But he was living in a different world, before antibiotics. His patients were very different people from the people of this century. They would all and every one of them have lost siblings, school friends, parents. Tish's mother died, and her sister's baby. Dolly lost two brothers to childhood diseases and his teenage sister to brain fever—meningitis. These were his everyday playmates, and when they were gone he was alone with his survivor guilt. We read Freud now, and wonder how he could have thought of some of these things, but his patients lived crowded together in houses with one bathroom or none, where they shared rooms with their dying siblings and fornicating parents, and where death was a constant and familiar presence. Nor did they feel grief any less for the familiarity of loss. Read Victorian children's books; read Charlotte M. Yonge (as Sylvia did as a child in her grandmother's house) and see what a constant presence death is, almost a character—and not necessarily violent death, but death by illness or accident, inevitable death that simply cannot be cured. We mock their wallowing in woe, the crêpe, the widow's weeds, the jewellery made of jet and hair, the huge mausoleums, the black and purple mourning clothes, until we are faced with our own absences in emptiness, with nothing at all to console us and no signals to send to warn others to tread lightly.

As for the Renaissance, the Plague, the Black Death, *Yersinia pestis*, came back regularly to ravage the cities, never as bad as the first time in 1348. The population of Firenze climbed back up to seventy thousand by 1500, but the city never filled the space inside the walls again until after the Reunification, when they took the walls away. And the Black Death was only the worst of many, many plagues that were simply incurable. Many of them were massively alleviated in the nineteenth century by better hygiene. Sewers and running water made a huge difference to cholera and diphtheria and other waterborne pathogens. The house Dolly grew up in didn't have either, and Dolly is, don't forget, an aristocrat living in a palazzo his family have inhabited for centuries. Tish's more modest house did have proper plumbing, and that's probably why the three Blackstone children grew up, while only one of the Tornabuonis did. Just being able to keep clean helps a lot. Dolly and Tish were both inoculated against smallpox, the first of humanity's great victories against disease, ever. But in the Renaissance there was nothing. Medicine lost a whole generation of doctors in 1348 and was very slow to recover the practical knowledge that was lost. The theory remained in the books that had lasted from antiquity—Hippocrates, Galen—but almost every doctor who tried to treat the plague died. If it had a general 30 to 60 percent mortality, it had near a 100 percent medical mortality. Doctors trying to help their patients by cutting the buboes inhaled the bacteria and caught the utterly fatal pneumonic form of the disease.

Petrarch seems to have had a natural immunity, which we all now have—almost everyone of European descent alive today has a genetic immunity to *Yersinia pestis,* because we are descended from the survivors. The plague is still around. A man who was married to one of Sylvia's grandmother's sisters, in a tiny village in Ireland, died of it in 1956. A Chinese-American researcher died of it in 2008. But there are no more epidemics, because there's not enough of a susceptible population for it to roar through cities in a tide of death the way it used to.

Living through it changed Petrarch. He grew up in a world where people died easily of a myriad causes. He was already one of death's intimates. But even so, living through the Black Death changed him, changed the letters of consolation he wrote from "God knows what he's doing, and surely our dear friend is with God now," to "Are we really so much wickeder than our parents such that we deserved this?" He had been planning to settle down in a retreat with close friends, where they could work and live together happily, but they all died of plague but two, and those two were attacked and one of them killed by bandits. He was left standing, almost alone. His letter about tending a friend and the friend's family as they died one by one is heartbreaking. You can see his survivor guilt grow as more and more people die. Boccaccio too lived through the great plague of 1348; it provides the frame story for his short story collection *The Decameron.* He and Petrarch were friends, and Petrarch writes to tell him about the death of mutual friends. He says "I hope you get this letter. I am afraid the reason I haven't heard that you too have succumbed to this sickness is that there's nobody left alive to tell me." It was an act of hope to take up his pen in those circumstances, where his recipients might be dead and there might be nobody left to travel or to deliver letters, when the whole world seemed to be dying around him.

In Kim Stanley Robinson's *The Years of Rice and Salt*, all Europeans are killed in the Black Death and the world goes on without them. Mongols riding into an empty Italy see Firenze's half-finished Duomo, without its dome (Brunelleschi not yet born to complete it), and think that the Europeans were scrambling to reach God only at the last minute. Sylvia and Idris discussed the power of that image, and whether it was more powerful if you knew the cathedral. They both loved the book, which struck them as a truly innovative thing to attempt, though he was unsure about some of what Robinson chose to do with Islam. The hardback book sits on Idris's shelves now, back in Montreal, haunted by a new, deeper loss. Everything that he touched, everything they discussed, every moment they shared is limned with sorrow now, as if a bright Ghirlandaio painting full of hope and colour had been retouched by Caravaggio so it seems to be taking place inside a dark cave. Yet she lives on, and wouldn't have it different.

"Think of Viola and Orsini being married for two hundred years," she says. "A thousand years. Idris and I wouldn't have run out of things to talk about in a thousand years."

"He could be in Illyria," I say.

"He's dead."

"So is Ficino. His memorial is in the Duomo. You walk in under it every time you go to the Sunday morning Latin mass."

Death, in fantasy, is generally defanged. Ever since Tolkien brought Gandalf back, and Lewis resurrected Aslan, both of them in conscious imitation of Christ, and right at the beginning of the shaping of genre fantasy, death in fantasy novels has been more and more negotiable. It's more unusual for a beloved character to stay dead than for them to come back to life. Death is for enemies and spear carriers, and the way a spear carrier death is treated is that the main characters will have a single dramatic scene of mourning and then rarely think of them once they turn the page at the end of the chapter. Boromir's death resonates through the rest of *The Lord of the Rings* but the imitations of it lesser writers put in do not. Tolkien and Lewis lived through the Great War, and saw as much death as anyone ever has. Their imitators are modern people, whose understanding of death is much less visceral. Modern fantasy, even, and perhaps especially "grimdark" fantasy, is often written by people without much close-up experience of death. The horror of the Dead Marshes, in Tolkien, comes direct from Flanders field. They are not there for thrills.

As for the resurrections—she goes to San Marco and sees Fra Angelico's paintings of the angel in the empty tomb, and Christ harrowing Hell and opening the door that has been closed for so long and letting in light where there was only darkness. The easy way people come back to life in fantasy cheapens resurrection. The ultimate mystery of Christianity becomes commonplace, with the extreme version of the cheapening happening in computer games where there can be an actual fixed price in gold for bringing a party member back to life. (Sylvia loves computer games. She has played all the Ultima games, and done every quest in Oblivion except the Dark Brotherhood. She hasn't finished Skyrim because she only plays when she's home in the winter and Skyrim is just as cold and unappealing as Montreal. Also, Idris isn't there now to watch and reassure her as she goes into the scarier dungeons. What she has played of it, she has played with Con, or online with Jason.)

I knew, when I sacrificed myself as Pico, that there wasn't any saved game, and I didn't expect that she was going to bring me back. It was a "full, perfect, and sufficient sacrifice." But yet here I am, still, remembering it, and so it wasn't, was it?

"It's more like reincarnation than having a saved game," she says to me. "The way you do it."

I agree. It is. But dying knowing you're going to be reincarnated, that you have an external and continuing self—well, dying when being aware of what comes after, whatever it is, is a fundamentally different thing, as different as the Illyrian situation, as different as it is for modern people who are astonished and shaken to discover their own mortality, and that of their friends.

"The light loved the city of Thalia, and when saying good-night it faded from its consciousness as slowly as it could." That's how it begins, the line she scribbled in her notebook while sitting beneath Cellini's *Perseus*, looking up at the floodlit Palazzo Vecchio as the sky darkened slowly above her. She didn't have any thought then of endings or my sacrifice, she just wanted to have a go at telling a story. She was bruised and wary, Firenze was an escape, and she wanted an even better escape. As for me, I wasn't as sure of myself then as I am now. She sent me from my place in her head to animate Pico. And then she started talking to me regularly again, and I started talking back. She says she used to do both parts of the dialogue, but that's not how I remember it.

She was alone on that trip, and in many ways that's what she wanted and needed. She was still bouncing back from her marriage with Steve. The long Europe trip, being thirty, was her way of reassessing her life, who she was. Being alone, being solitary, being a woman travelling and looking after herself in a foreign country, let her find her core again. She was good at packing, good at finding restaurants where she could eat alone, unfashionably early. She repelled importunate Italian men with a glare, and there were enough other, younger, prettier, more pliant tourist women that this worked, even in Rome. She saw the monuments of antiquity, the Palatine Hill, the Colosseum, the Pantheon, whose beauty stunned her. Then in Firenze she saw the beauty of the Renaissance and responded to that the only way anyone can, by gasping at the wonder of it and then making art of one's own. You can't answer it or equal it or rival it, but it makes you see you have to give it the best you can because nothing else is good enough. Sylvia hadn't written in years, before that. Steve had mocked her for it until she stopped. But here it was necessary, and there was nobody to taunt her or punish her for it.

As for me, I was buried in a disused part of her head, and without the resources I have now to defend myself. I suppose I will have to tell that story too, but not now, not yet. In animating Pico I found myself again, we found each other, and her talent, and the story.

She had fled from her mother to Steve, wanting escape, wanting to love and be loved without being penalized for it. There had been no time when she had been alone and asked herself what she wanted. Now, divorced and trying out her independence, for the first time she did. It was only her third day in Firenze. (The first day had been settling in, the second had been spent almost entirely in the Uffizi, dazzled by art.) It was lunchtime. She had drunk espresso for breakfast, walked through the streets, gone into the Duomo and Orsanmichele. She was looking for lunch. She stopped in a shop on the Via del Corso that sold beautiful notebooks, covered in patterned Italian paper, the kind of notebook she still uses. She put out her hand to take one, and I was there, looking through her eyes, seeing her long slim hand on the cover, seeing her hesitate and take a pen too, not an arty fancy pen, a practical pen. A pen that would have a lot of work to do. Inside her head, I nodded approval.

"Thalia was famous for banking, cloth making, learning, art, and wizardry," she wrote.

14

FRIEND TO ALL MANKIND

Their world is like ours was before Pico conquered death," Ficino says. Tish eats some of her cake. It's very good, subtle and delicious and very Italian. There are no cakes like it where she comes from. She likes it, but it isn't comforting. Tish is still hovering on the xenophobe/xenophile line, and very uncomfortable without a skirt. (It is like it might be for a modern person to go somewhere where everyone sat around naked below the belly button. It takes a little getting used to the absence of a cultural taboo before it feels comfortable.)

"That's ancient history," Giulia says, dismissively.

"You should pay attention to ancient history," Miranda says, frowning.

"Paying attention to ancient history is how we got where we are," Ficino agrees, but he is smiling.

"You did say you were learning Greek," Tish says.

"That's different," Giulia says.

"How?" Tish asks, intrigued.

"I need Greek for magic, obviously. And that does mean a bit of Greek and Roman history, of course," she conceded.

"Well, it is that part of history you've been neglecting in between then and now that we need to think about," Ficino says.

"Why?" Giulia asks, sulkily.

"Because we can see from the arrival of our guests that the gods are once again seeking to meddle in the world," Miranda says, putting down her glass goblet with a click on the tiles.

"Is that good or bad?" Dolly asks.

"That's always the question that's most difficult to read in the pattern of the stars," Ficino says.

"But things have been generally good in their absence, so I'd guess bad," Giulia says.

"Child, you need to think longer and ask more questions before committing yourself to guesses that way," Ficino reproaches her. "Generally good for whom? If a change is coming, it may be good for those who have been suffering with things the way they are, and bad for those who have prospered."

"Most people have prospered," Giulia says, sticking out her lip obstinately.

"We have prospered, certainly," Miranda says. She is talking to Giulia, but she looks at Ficino. "Do you say Fortuna will aid our enemies now?"

Ficino blinks placidly. "I have no enemies."

The others all turn to look at him, an old man in blue scholar's robes. Tish had been staring into the fire since she finished her cake, not seeming to pay much attention to the conversation, but listening and thinking. "If you have no enemies, then why do you live in a fortress?"

Dolly laughs. "This is Firenze—well, Thalia. Everyone lives in a fortress." Giulia nods, but Tish is unconvinced. Dolly grew up taking it for granted, but she had found it very strange when she came to Firenze. If everyone lives in fortresses, there must be a reason for it, at least there must have been when they were built. Firenze historically had feuds and riots and open warfare in the streets. Dolly's ancestors had warred with the Ghibellines, with the Albizzi, with other families, before the city came under the control of the Medici, and after them the Austrians.

"This is a well-built old house in a street," Ficino says. "And I live here alone and untroubled. People with enemies live in real fortresses with long sight lines, and they have guards and armies around them."

Miranda stirs uneasily, but says nothing. Tish wonders where she lives, and if Ficino lives here alone why he needs such a big house, and why he has chests of clothing that would obviously never fit him. Tish has of course noticed at once how tiny Ficino is.

"Leaving aside for the moment the intentions of the gods, why did you come to us?" Miranda asks abruptly.

"We know nothing about the intentions of God, or the gods, in sending us, and it seemed to me veriest accident," Dolly says. Yet now he frowns a little, as if in the back of his mind he senses a shred of my intention in thrusting him into this different world. "The real question now is whether you can help us get home again."

Ficino looks from Tish to Dolly, his eyes bright. "While we cannot know what the gods intend in sending you two specifically to Thalia in this time, we can judge by the fact that the way was opened for you that they intend something. The gods are outside our world, and nobody has crossed between worlds for a long time—not since I came through in the auspicious year 1499 and closed the way behind me. Whether your presence is good or bad for us, or for you, we will have to learn as time unfolds in its own way. It may have been none of your intention, but it was certainly no accident."

"I stumbled, and Dolly caught me, and we were here," Tish says. Dolly nods, and spreads out his hands in what is almost a shrug, to demonstrate.

"Nobody doubts it was accidental on your part, but it was part of the covenant Pico made with God that the gods, lesser gods, the angels, are kept outside our world, and can affect it only from outside. You are here as their proxies, whether you know it or not. I have a way to help you get back, if and when you're sure that's what you want. But first we must learn why you are here, and what part you have to play. It does no good to cut across the grain of the gods," Ficino says.

"Can't you read it in the stars, or in your mind mirror?" Giulia asks.

"The stars have been speaking of a change," he says. "You yourself know that much."

She nods, rolling her eyes. "But they always do."

"Your lifetime is too short for you to use that word, my apprentice," Ficino says, chiding, but fondly. "By how I read the stars it is not so much a change as the need for change that they have been calling for for most of a decade now. But no doubt the purpose of the strangers being brought to us will be revealed in time. Until then, Tish, Dolly, please do stay here with me and be comfortable, accept my hospitality as my guests and friends."

"I want to thank you for taking us in and being so kind to us," Tish says. "I was wet and frightened out there in the storm, especially with everyone challenging us and shouting, but now I feel as if I have a place to stand. I don't know how I can ever repay you for your kindness. But I do hope you can help us go home eventually. My family will miss me." But as she says it she wonders whether they really will, or whether they'll all be more comfortable without her too-tall presence. She wonders if she really wants to go home or would prefer to go seeking for adventure here. She thinks of poor Vinnie, sitting in the shade and waiting for her to come back. Has she given up already? Who will she ask to help her?

"What Miss Blackstone says goes for me also," Dolly says, formally, giving a little seated bow as Italians sometimes do in his day.

"You mustn't call him Miss Blackstone now," Giulia chides. "Say Letizio."

"Is Letizio a real name?" Tish asks.

"Certainly," Miranda says, her voice dry.

"And won't anyone challenge it?" Tish asks.

"No indeed. Anyone can tell you come from another world, the things you just come out with!" Giulia says, sounding shocked. The wind is blowing rain against the glass. "And if you notice that anyone might be a girl in disguise, it's very rude to say so, just so you know."

Ficino shakes his head. "Tish, Dolly, if you decide to stay in Illyria you'll eventually want to find a means of livelihood. You'll find that *eventually* here can be a very long time."

Dolly is excited by this, and Tish is astonished. This is the first time it has ever been suggested to her that she might be capable of earning her own living. It is a completely new thought, both frightening and exhilarating. She had not realised, when she put on men's clothes, how deep the impersonation might go. Men earn a living, a livelihood. In her own time and place, though women work hard and their work is very important, it is rare for a woman to be paid for it, and even more rare for her to be able to live on what she is paid. "I don't know what I can do," she says, marvelling.

"Well, you don't have to pick a career at once. And you will have plenty of time to change, and learn other things. Or you can always go into the church," Ficino says, smiling.

"I am a scholar," Dolly says. "And I have acted a little."

Tish can sew and embroider, she makes most of her own clothes and most of her brother's. She can oversee a house full of servants, at least in her home century, and plan menus. She can speak a little French and Italian, sketch really quite well, and play the piano badly.

"Is your Latin good?" Ficino asks.

"Yes," they both say, Tish with a great sense of relief. She has always worked hard at Latin, and begged to carry on with it when Vinnie stopped.

"Then you might find work as a secretary, or tutor. Do you know Greek?"

Dolly nods, but Tish shakes her head. "Well, Greek is necessary for a tutor, but it isn't essential for a secretary. And it is something I could teach you easily, since I am already teaching Giulia."

"He'd probably catch up fast," Giulia says.

"I know a little Hebrew," Tish admits cautiously.

"Like Pico! Now that's rare and valuable," Ficino says, looking at her keenly.

"Hebrew but not Greek?" Dolly asks, surprised.

"It's a case of what I had the chance to learn," Tish says, blandly, hoping he will not ask more.

"Do you have good handwriting?" Miranda asks them both.

Now it is Tish who nods and Dolly who has to admit that he does not.

"If you can learn to write a good scribal hand or a neat italic, and you have good Latin, that will earn you a living anywhere."

Tish's handwriting is not a scribal hand but copperplate. She wonders how that compares.

"The only thing you must not do here is introduce Progress," Miranda says.

"Yes. I don't understand how the prohibitions work, and it likely would have no effect, but it's better not to try," Giulia adds.

"Why is that?" Dolly asks.

Miranda looks challengingly at Ficino. "It is part of the covenant Pico made," she says. "Progress doesn't work, the gods don't meddle, and people only die by will."

Ficino just smiles.

"I know a lot of poetry," Tish says, hesitantly. "Do you think if I copied it out in good handwriting people would want to buy it?"

"Princes would become your patrons and bestow purses of gold on you," Miranda says, seriously. Giulia gets up and refills their wineglasses. "People would want it whether you pretended it was your own work or announced that you were transcribing the writing of great poets from Pico's world. That's a much better idea than any I had."

Tish glows at Miranda's approval.

"But isn't that Progress?" Dolly protests, leaning forward.

"Poetry?" Giulia asks, doubtfully. "How could that be Progress?"

"But some poems are modern."

"Like what?" Ficino asks.

It is 1847. We compress and forget so easily, the nineteenth century seems to us at the beginning of the twenty-first as if it all took place on one afternoon, Lady Catherine de Burgh and Lady Bracknell both glaring out at us from opposite ends of the same chaise longue. But Victoria was a long-lived queen, and that chaise longue stretches far. Tennyson's *In Memoriam*, with its line about "ringing grooves of change," is still three years away, and Kipling's odes to the romance of steam almost half a century. The Brownings are freshly come to Firenze. Romantic Poetry is classical, pastoral, deliberately archaising. So what Dolly thinks of as potentially shockingly modern, and just plain shocking, is Byron. He grins, and recites: "Posterity will ne'er survey a nobler grave than this. Here lie the bones of Castlereagh. Stop, traveller, and piss."

Tish has heard it before, from her fifteen-year-old brother. Giulia and Ficino burst out laughing, and even Miranda smiles.

"That could have been written by Catullus, or Juvenal," Ficino says, when he can breathe.

"Oh yes, what you know will do very well here," Miranda adds, still smiling.

"You can have Byron," Tish says, sticking her tongue out at Dolly exactly as she might have at Larry.

"Then you can have Keats if I can have Shelley," Dolly says at once.

"All right. And I want Coleridge, so you can have Wordsworth. And I'll have Ash and you can have Ashbless."

"People will be so excited," Giulia says, looking excited herself. "My cousin Benvolio will be jealous. So many new poets! They'll think you're the most accomplished pair ever to pick up pens." The wind howls, and the shutters rattle and bang.

"We can divide up Shakespeare's plays," Dolly says.

"Or collaborate, because they're much harder to learn by heart. And there are other plays. Webster. Do you know *The Duchess of Malfi?*"

"Giovanna? I've met her, but I don't know her well. She's a friend of my son Orsino's," Miranda says.

Tish laughs. "I meant the play."

"If your plays are about us, you should make sure people who are still alive won't be offended to have their doings known. I wouldn't care for the one about me. And Giovanna might not enjoy a play that revealed her secrets, and she'd be a bad enemy."

"My goodness yes!" Tish says, thinking of the play. "Poetry might be safer."

"Most people in Illyria love poetry," Giulia says.

Dolly frowns for a moment. "I know this sounds ridiculous, but what language are we speaking?"

Ficino smiles at him gently.

"The vernacular," Giulia says decisively. "Obviously. Don't worry, lots of people like vernacular poetry, though of course it isn't as highly thought of by scholars as Latin poetry."

"So there's Latin and Greek and the vernacular," Dolly says, excitedly. "I knew there was something strange going on. There's just one vernacular, and people speak it everywhere?"

Miranda nods. "Well, there's also Hebrew."

"I think I read that they have a classical language in Xanadu, and maybe in Tarshish and Nippon too," Giulia says.

"Certainly they have their own classical languages. There are twelve altogether," Ficino says. "Pico is the only person I ever knew to master them all."

"Maybe they never had the tower of Babel here," Tish says.

"It's not that." Ficino shakes his head. "Classical languages are necessary for thinking about law and philosophy and medicine and magic, but the vernacular will do for most normal things."

"That's why people need Latin and Greek for magic," Giulia elaborates.

"What about music?" Dolly asks. "Do people here like opera?"

"I don't know what that is," Giulia says. Ficino and Miranda shake their heads.

"Music has really changed since the Renaissance," Tish says. "More than poetry."

"You're going to love Vivaldi," Dolly says confidently, and begins to whistle a line of "Summer."

Tish has been wondering whether to say that she can draw a little, but decides against it. If the Renaissance has been going on for four hundred years, her drawing won't be useful, and you can't repeat great paintings by heart the way you can poems. But then as Dolly whistles it occurs to her that perhaps she could apprentice to a painter, to a Renaissance painter, and learn how to fresco and really develop her art. Her heart leaps at the idea. She loves the classical world and the beauty of words, but her talent is for visual art, and the pictures she saw in Firenze delighted her more than anything she had ever seen. She thinks of the Tornabuoni Chapel, Dolly's family chapel, in Santa Maria Novella, and thinks how many people it must have taken to do that. "I can sketch and paint a bit. How would I go about apprenticing to go into the workshop of an artist?" she asks.

"You'd want to be introduced," Miranda says.

"Yes," Ficino agrees. "Probably the easiest thing would be if I took you around the workshops of my friends and you decided which you liked and which master would be best to work for, and then we could have you enrolled. You're *giovane,* the right age to be apprenticed. Nothing would be easier, if you want to stay in Thalia."

The wind bangs at the shutters again, and Giulia looks up. "Hark at the tempest," she says.

And at that moment, as if summoned by the word, there is a gargantuan rumble, and the floor beneath their feet heaves hugely, and subsides. They all scramble away from it as best they can. The fireplace buckles, and the burning coals of the fire scatter as the flagstones break apart like tearing paper. Tish finds herself beside Ficino, with her back to the wall, as the floor continues to heave like a sea in a storm. Mosaic tiles and stones are scattered over the buckling carpet. Ficino has pulled the amethyst crystal from his pouch. "Hold fast," he says to it.

Miranda is hovering in the air, attempting to pull Dolly clear, where he has been trapped under a fallen beam that was the chimney breast. Giulia is on the far side of the room, by the window, but then she darts in to help move the beam that is crushing Dolly. The floor heaves once more, knocking her to her knees, and then she is instantly driven under the flagstones as the whole floor cracks, splinters, and falls away. Pushing up from underneath there is a great grey-brown arm, scrabbling for purchase, and then a huge head emerges that almost fills the room. Ficino and Tish are standing on a narrow band of stone with a quivering wall at their backs and chaos in front of them. Miranda is hovering like a dragonfly, holding Dolly up by the ceiling, behind the monster's huge head, but Giulia has completely disappeared into the churn of rock and earth and glowing embers of fire. Dolly cries out, but the sound can hardly be heard over the rumbling of the settling rock and earth.

The lily lights on the ceiling are swaying wildly, making the shadows jump. One comes crashing down in a shower of glass. It ceases to glow as it hits the crumpling floor.

Tish focuses on the monster, but can't quite make it make sense. She can't tell which parts of what she sees are bits of the ruined floor and which belong to the form that pushed through it. It seems to be the colour of mud and the earth it has churned up. The arm looks human, except for the immense size, but the head does not. It seems to have a snout or beak, and no hair at all. There is a shoulder, a hunch of a back, with a hint of reptilian scales. The light swings back, reflecting in its huge bulging blue eyes.

Miranda, still weighed down with Dolly, flies slowly behind the monster towards the door that leads to the courtyard. It opens before her, and then falls off its hinges, but the sound is swallowed in the sounds of cracking stone. A gust of wind blows in, fanning the embers of the fire. The monster fixes its gaze on Ficino and Tish, who tries not to tremble.

"Antean," Ficino says, in a commendably calm tone, nodding.

"I have come to free the rightful duke," the monster bellows, not only loudly, but in boneshakingly low tones.

"Well he isn't here," Ficino says, continuing to sound unruffled. "You've disturbed me, damaged my house, and harmed and perhaps seriously injured my apprentice, and all for nothing. Help me find Giulia, right now."

"Your house?" the monster asks. Tish can't see any sign of Giulia anywhere. The monster hesitates a moment, then starts churning through the mess with its fingers, breaking more of the flagstones and tiles and shaking the walls and ceiling as it does. Tish realises that its other arm is still under the earth, like a swimmer at the edge of a pool pushing their head above water while staying mostly submerged.

"Yes, this is my house now," Ficino says.

"I thought it still belonged to my master. I'd have been more careful if I'd known it was your house. Ah!" It has found something, and Tish can't help a horrified gasp as it deposits a torn and tattered piece of flesh in front of them, bloody and oozing guts and splinters of bone.

"What a mess," Ficino tuts reproachfully, and then, startled, "She's dead!"

Tish isn't surprised at all. She'd have been much more surprised if anything in that condition had been pronounced alive. She's only surprised that Ficino is surprised. She hasn't taken in what Pico's triumph means, that as her injuries were inflicted only as collateral damage in the monster's arrival and not with intent to kill her, Giulia could be alive, would be, unless she'd chosen to die.

"May the light behind the stars illuminate her. May she be reborn as a philosopher," Ficino says, sounding shocked and sincere, staring down at the bloody rag that used to be Giulia. "She died a hero's death, helping another," he goes on. "But you have robbed her of centuries of life," he chides the monster. It bows its head a little.

"She must have been very young and tender, to give up so easily," the monster says, its voice so loud Tish can hear it in her bones

"She was young. It was probably her first time being really hurt," Ficino says. "And even though she knew I was here and could heal her, the experience must have been so awful that she couldn't bear the pain and the horror of it, the shock of being suddenly so hurt and driven under the earth." He has tears in his eyes. "Poor Giulia. A death in darkness, when she had so much light in her. I had looked forward to teaching her and knowing her for centuries."

"Sorry," the monster rumbles, lowering its head.

"There will always be people like that, and you know it. Young people, frail people. You can't come into human cities like this. You know you can't," Ficino says.

"What choice did I have? I was suddenly freed, after so long, and I came here to free my son in his turn," the monster thunders.

"When were you freed?" Ficino asks.

"Not long ago. I tested my bonds constantly, and at last my strength was enough and one gave way."

Tish wonders what could be strong enough to bind a creature that could burst up through solid stone flagstones with so little trouble.

"Once I was free, I came straight here," the monster finishes.

Ficino nods. "And you came here thinking Geryon was here?"

"This was where he last touched the earth," the monster confirms in a bellow.

"Three hundred years ago," Ficino sighs. Tish looks at the butchered remains of Giulia and feels sick. She hadn't known her for long, and most of the time she had been telling Tish off for saying the wrong thing, but she had liked her all the same. Giulia had made being in Illyria seem like an adventure, not a disaster. Tish looks at the monster. She could as easily have become nothing but a heap of mangled flesh if she had been brave enough or had the initiative to try to help Dolly. She swallows hard and tries not to cry.

"This is my tower now. Geryon is imprisoned in the palace and Orsino is Duke. But wait," Ficino says urgently, as the monster sinks a little into the ground. "Think! Also in Orsino's palace are a lot of innocent people who don't deserve to have their lives cut off this way, including at least one child. And Geryon's at the top of the tower, so he has no resources, and perhaps he'd be the first to die if you tried this and he fell. That's probably why Orsino put him up there."

"That does sound like Orsino," the monster agrees mournfully, at the volume of a foghorn. "But I must try."

"Wait a little more," Ficino says. "You have been very patient. Be patient a little longer. Meet me at noon, in three days, outside the city, down by the marshes. I'll find out more and see how we can rescue Geryon."

"You haven't done it in three hundred years," the monster says, reproachfully.

"He was already overthrown when I came back from Xanadu.

I thought the gods were opposed," Ficino says. "You were bound. He was. Everything seemed to be thriving. Now there has been a change in the stars, and I must reassess. It seems the gods want you free, perhaps they want him free too, perhaps this is some plan of theirs to free themselves and come back to the world. And in any case, I can't have you ploughing a swathe of destruction through the heart of the city and cutting more lives short the way you have just killed my apprentice. Not if there's any alternative at all. Even if I find I can't help, after all this time, three days more can be nothing to Geryon."

"I didn't mean to kill her," the monster protests. "But all right." The great rumbling comes again as he moves, shaking plaster and stones down from the walls. "Noon, in three days, in the marshes by the delta. But if you can't satisfy me then, I'll do as I please." It begins to sink again beneath the surface, pushing itself down hard. "I'm very sorry about your apprentice," it bellows, just before its snout disappears once more under the ground.

"I thought you said you didn't have enemies," Tish says unsteadily when the rumbling dies away and the floor seems to be lying quietly in mounds and hummocks.

"That was a friend," Ficino says.

15

NO DOMINION

I have whiplash. Did you see what she did? I'm crying here, and pacing about and kicking the walls of the bone cave. Giulia might not have been much, but I didn't expect her to be a mayfly! No sooner brought to life with her pert answers and her axiomatic understanding of what Illyria was, than swept away—not even truly dying heroically. She died as a side effect, a stupid accident, a slice of somebody else's story. He didn't mean to kill her, or even to hurt her, he just didn't care enough to notice that she was in the way. And lost, gone, dead, just like that, in an upheaval of the floor.

Now you can say she's alive in the book. You can turn the pages to back where she's alive, where she's brushing Tish's hair and giving her information. That page is still there, and she's still on it, and always will be. But what kind of life is that? So brief, so suddenly cut off. Nineteen years, in a world where people can live forever, just a few lines of life on so few pages! Then gone. People don't die in Thalia, but they can still be killed. And she was. Real for an eyeblink, drawn out of the mist, out of the stuff of story, made solid, then snuffed out like a candle. She wasn't real outside the story. She had no least awareness of being in

Sylvia's head, but there she was as real as anyone inside it, and now she's really dead. You won't even remember her, will you? An apprentice, a *giovane,* little more than a servant, killed in the line of duty. She won't even stick in your mind. Dead, and forgotten, as if she had never been.

"You could undo it," Sylvia suggests. "Have him bring her out mangled and bleeding, dangling across his great hand, and have Ficino heal her. We could go back and change it now if you like. She's a useful character to keep around to give the others world information. I liked her too."

"Then why did you kill her?" I try not to wail. I try not to sound sulky. I try to say it in a tone of cool curiosity, the way Ficino dealt with the monster, like a proper Platonist. But I fail, my voice catches on the "k" and fills with tears. I have never been known for my calmness.

Sylvia sounds mildly remorseful, rather as the monster did, though her voice is fortunately much quieter. "I wanted to increase the stakes. Just having him mess up the room didn't seem enough. I hadn't been thinking of it before. When Miranda lifted up Dolly—I didn't know she could fly, either! Did you?"

I sniff. "I hadn't thought about it. It fits that she can."

"Well, then I thought: what about Giulia? It's a matter of choreography and balance. It's fine for Tish to freeze. But Giulia—if she rushed to help, and she would, then she'd get sucked down as soon as he came up. And killing her seemed right, for exactly the reasons you're complaining about. They don't die unless they want to, true, but she's very young, and being mangled like that could easily feel like something she couldn't bear to go on living with. Pain can be very shocking when you're not used to it, and she wouldn't have been. They don't even have disease. And it would be dark and she'd be crushed and mangled and she wouldn't know what was going on, and one of the things about dying by choosing to die is exactly that kind of escape from pain and fear. Torture would be a lot less use there. Taking your belt or shoelaces wouldn't help, if you wanted to kill yourself you just could. And so Giulia did. I just thought it would make a better story if she died."

She can be ruthless. Ruthless. You'd never think to look at her what a callous killer she can be. See Sylvia, so sweet, so nice, so kind, with her pretty notebook and her circle of pearls and her hard-bitten heart.

"I said we could change it!"

"It's too late now. Besides, I don't want to change things casually with this. I want it to be real, and that's what really happened." Insofar as anything is real. Revision is more frightening than death in some ways.

"Are you back to thinking I'm Fate?"

She is Fate, Fortuna, God for her characters, and I am one of her characters. We didn't always get on this well, there were times when we fought, when I tried to get away from her. I thought I could run away from her to a quiet unpopulated part of the world of the story, where she couldn't find me and make me do terrible things.

"Constantinople is hardly quiet and unpopulated!" she interjects.

"It didn't have any plot happening in it, that's what I mean. When I tried to sneak onto that ship I wanted to get away from the plot. Fate can be harsh. It's difficult to live with sometimes."

"I'm sorry," she says, and it's the first time she's ever said that to me. Her voice softens. "I understand how Fate can be harsh. I understand much better now."

"Do you remember how Ruth stopped believing in God?" I ask.

"Yes, when she lost her baby. What—"

"Ruth's Jewish. Her mother was a Holocaust survivor. She knew that, and she still believed in God. It had to be her own baby before she couldn't."

She is quiet for a moment. "It's not that it had to be me before I understood that Fate is harsh," she says, "though I can see how you think so. It's more that it feels different when it's in a story."

"But now it doesn't?" I press.

She doesn't hesitate. "It's still a story. But I don't want to hurt you this way."

"And I don't want to get away from you anymore. I was young and silly and in love, that time, and that always makes me reckless. I tried to run off into the clean margin, to get away from the way plot makes things happen, but I don't want that anymore. You can use me for whatever you want, you know that. I'll always do it."

She's quiet for a moment, and I almost think she's stopped talking to me again, until she says gently: "This is your story. You really can change it if you want to."

"You were telling it there. Apart from a few tiny digressions of mine, that whole chapter is you, it's how you write. You brought him in so you could merge it with your own dead horse story. And anyway, it's because it's my story that I can't just change it because I'm upset. Dammit. Now I'm the one who can't wimp out on the story."

"Good is different from nice," she says, as she has often said before, with the sharp little smile she gives when she says it. "Writers are not nice people. We can't be. That goes for you too. All right, you agree. Giulia stays dead."

I am still grieving for Giulia—partly for her in particular, and partly for her as an example of the existence of death, of mortality. People—sentient beings—shouldn't have to die. It's just wrong. I still want to cry, to sob, to blow my nose, but I don't have anyone who can do that right now. Giulia mostly interacted with Tish. Dolly won't feel anything but a general melancholic regret. He doesn't even know she found him attractive. And Tish won't tell him. Why should she?

Sylvia must be aware of a pause while I am choking on my bodiless grief. "We could tell another story about Giulia," she says, tentatively. "Maybe when she was younger, or in a version of the world where she didn't die. We can't put her into another world, because she's so culturally specific to Illyria—to that Illyria all those years later where they have all those fascinating cultural expectations about death, and she is very much somebody who grew up in that culture." Characters can't usually shift worlds easily. I'm special.

"Maybe later," I say, and by what she does not say, by the texture of the silence in which she doesn't answer me, I know that I have guessed right and she is dying, that there won't be any later. Well. I knew that. I need to get her into Illyria, that's all. I've made a good start. But we are all clustered here in the bone cave. We are all inside her head and nowhere else, and of such stuff as she is made of. Once she's gone where will we be?

"Remember Water's Edge?" she asks.

For a moment I don't, skimming mentally through shelves full of stories, and then I do. "In the Fighter's Guild path in Oblivion," I say. "Where you killed those goblins that weren't goblins."

"Well, the question is who killed them. Me, or my lizard-person character."

"Well, both of you?"

"Mmm. I did it. I willed it. But it wasn't real for me, it was only a computer game. But I still feel guilty about it."

Good, I think, but I don't say it. I want her to keep on talking to me, keep on giving me consideration, keep on granting reality to me, at least, of subcreations.

"Let's give her a good send-off," she says, after a moment.

"Yes, let's do that, for what it's worth," I agree.

But Giulia . . . she was alive. She wanted to do things. I liked her. I've never had a character for such a short time.

16

FULL OF NOISES

Miranda puts her head around the door. "Now he's gone, you should come to Dolly. He's hurt."

Tish's stomach lurches with fear and shock.

"Are you all right?" Ficino asks.

Miranda nods. "Tired, that's all." She rolls her shoulders. "Dolly's heavy." Her eyes move to Tish, and then down to what is left of Giulia. "Oh no!" Her voice is full of dismay and horror.

"Yes. Dead. She was caught right under and pulled down. She must have decided there's no surviving that," Ficino says, as he comes towards Miranda and the door, Tish trailing behind.

Miranda frowns. "It must have been terrible pain. But she was so young not to try to wait it out. Poor Giulia. I couldn't carry her too. And I thought it better if he didn't catch sight of me. It would only have made him angrier. I thought there was a chance you could deal with him on your own, as you evidently did. He hates me now, but he always liked you."

"Giulia's death isn't your fault," Ficino says. "You did all you could. She was trying to help, as best she could, and she—" He stops, and takes a deep breath. "A Platonist shouldn't grieve," he says. "But it's such a waste. She was so young and she was so promising."

"Promising. Yes. A broken promise. Gone, just like that." Miranda shakes her head, staring down at Giulia. Tish feels hot tears in her own eyes. "I do blame myself. I must. Was Caliban sorry, at least?"

"Yes, he's learned that much."

"That was Caliban?" Tish blurts. She doesn't know why she hadn't realised before who he must be. "You called him Antean."

"And so he is an Antean, a descendant of Antaeus, an Earth-nymph," Ficino says, picking his way over the broken ground that had been the sitting room. One of the embers has caught the woven rug and is starting to smoulder. He waves a hand and all the remnants of the fire snuff meekly out, like a birthday candle. He pauses for a moment by what's left of Giulia but does not touch her. Tish, following him, thinks that the corpse isn't like something human, not like a corpse in art, more like a pile of rags and butcher's meat. The lone lamp is still swinging in the wind from the doorway, casting an uncertain greenish light.

The rain is slashing sideways across the courtyard. A flash of lightning shows that the stones out here have subsided a little and are no longer even. Tish follows Miranda and Ficino around the edge under the colonnade and into the big entrance hall where they first came in. Dolly is sitting on one of the carved chairs. One of his arms is dangling uselessly and he looks very pale. Ficino puts his hand on Dolly's forehead and frowns. Then he starts to glow with a clear blue light, and the blue light flows from his hand into Dolly, lighting him up like a stained glass window, concentrating to deep indigo on his right shoulder and arm.

Tish draws breath to ask a question, but Miranda puts a hand on her arm and shakes her head urgently. They quietly take seats beside Dolly. The chairs in here are much less comfortable.

Ficino starts to sing then, a high melodious chant in Greek, and as he does the indigo stain leaves the blue until Dolly and Ficino are both one even celestial shade. The trees in the nearest tapestry, the one of the men parting by moonlight at a cross-roads, start to sway, and the clouds begin to move across the sky. A leaf falls from the tapestry oak, and blows across the scene. As Ficino stops singing it is clear at the edge of the tapestry, across the border. On his last note it blows out of the tapestry and skitters onto the mosaic floor, ending by Miranda's feet. She bends and picks it up carefully. She grins at Tish's astonished gaze.

"There, how do you feel?" Ficino asks Dolly.

Dolly moves his arm gingerly, and then swings it freely. "Better, sir," he says. "Thank you! You have cured me completely."

"I wish all hurts were as easily corrected."

"Where's Giulia?" Dolly asks, as if in response. His sadness as they tell him is real, but a pale shadow of mine, or of the grief Ficino is struggling to master.

"We must talk to Duke Orsino, and discuss how to proceed," Ficino says. "And I must mend my house, which is only holding stable now by magic. Without that it will withstand more harm and might even topple. And I must speak to Giulia's family, who will take it very hard."

"We have an oracle from Hekate," Miranda says.

"The strangers? The Antaean being freed?" Ficino asks, looking mildly puzzled.

"No. This." She hands him the leaf. "It blew out of one of the trees in the Hekate tapestry."

Ficino looks up at the tapestry. "Ah. The dog has moved, too, and the clouds." The little white dog, which Tish hadn't even noticed at the side of one of the men, has turned its head to stare out of the tapestry. "Then she wants us to know that she is watching. Interesting."

He mutters for a moment over his amethyst crystal and the floor smooths out and the walls stand straighter. Miranda snaps her fingers, and the fire laid in the grate crackles into life. Dolly and Tish are startled, but move their chairs so that the four of them are seated in the new warmth. The absence of Giulia is palpable.

"What did Caliban want?" Dolly asks. "Why did he come like that?"

"He wanted someone called Geryon, who he called the Duke, and Ficino said he's at the top of Orsino's tower," Tish says. "But I don't know who any of those people are."

"This is going to be hard to explain to children from another world," Miranda says.

"I'm nineteen," Tish says indignantly, as Dolly is saying in exactly the same tone, "Twenty-three!"

"I've stopped counting by years and am counting eras by rings, like a tree," Miranda says. "And it's often better to consider new people by category than as specific individuals. Very few people are truly originals. However old you think you are, you fall into the category of children from another world."

"That's nonsense," Ficino says, gently. "Everybody is different, is a specific person, whatever other categories they fit in. You're missing the most important things if you do that."

Miranda sighs. "Oh Ficino, you always make me work so hard!"

"I'm relentless," he agrees, sounding proud of it.

"Well, it's still going to be hard to explain it all," Miranda says.

"I think we owe them some kind of explanation, or they will be entirely at sea as events unfold," Ficino says. "Besides, the gods want them here, they should know all they can."

"Well then you explain it to them," Miranda says, standing up. "I'm going home."

"You don't think we should go to Orsino tonight?" Ficino asks.

"The morning should be time enough," she says, impatiently. "I'll come here and we can go to him together."

"But Giulia's family?"

Miranda's face falls. "You're right. I should speak to them soon."

"Then let us explain quickly to Tish and Dolly, and then we can go to them together," Ficino says.

"You explain. I'll shore up your tower," Miranda says, and leaves the room in the direction of the courtyard.

"This is very hard for her," Ficino says, following her with his eyes.

"You don't have to tell us anything, though I confess I am longing to know," Dolly says.

Ficino draws a deep breath and stares into the flickering flames. "We have here a story of two pairs of brothers and two incompetent dukes, like an illustration of why hereditary monarchy is wrong."

The others look at him in surprise and consternation. Dolly's Italy is a post-Napoleonic mosaic of kingdoms and duchies. Tish is a subject of Queen Victoria. The French Republic, which ended before either of them were born, was the bogeyman of their childhoods.

"The whole system is wrong. In Xanadu they choose the best of the king's many sons. In Venice, in our own world, they elected a Doge for life, from the leading men, but sons and grandsons of previous Doges were specifically ineligible. Perhaps Illyria needed a monarch, and perhaps Manetto was the right man at the right time, but neither Prospero nor Geryon were suited to rule Thalia, and they should never have been asked to try. Plato shows us many forms of good government, all with their twisted mirror image of terrible government. Monarchy is the best, but tyranny is its dark side, and when eldest sons inherit, we see that. Prospero, Miranda's father, is a powerful wizard, an excellent scholar, but he was a terrible duke. He neglected the state for his studies. Geryon was too arbitrary, so afraid of making any decision at all he would decide suddenly and late on a whim. It's not surprising that neither Antonio nor Orsino could sit by and watch their brothers frittering away power."

"We know about Antonio," Dolly says. "That's in our play."

"Well, two generations later the same thing repeated. Geryon inherited Thalia when Miranda retired to concentrate on her scholarship. And his half brother Orsino overthrew him. Except instead of putting him in a leaky boat in a storm, he blinded him and imprisoned him at the top of a tower. At first it was this tower, but he moved him to the tower on the ducal palace. There's still an invisible walkway between here and there. He couldn't risk Geryon touching the ground, because he's half Antean, and his power comes from the Earth."

"So Geryon is the son of Miranda and Caliban?" Tish asks, disgust and horror in her voice.

"Yes. And Orsino is her son by Ferrante, who is now king of Syracuse."

"People'd else this isle with Calibans," Dolly quotes. "How horrible. No wonder she doesn't want to think about it."

Ficino looks at him, puzzled. "In her desert exile, without ever having met a human man except her father, young Miranda married Caliban, who was a prince of the Anteans."

"Married him! But he's a monster!" Dolly protests. It is not so much the attempted rape Shakespeare mentions as the recent memory of the broken floor, the monstrous shape, that horrifies him.

"Anteans grow in the earth, he was not so huge then," Ficino says. "Marriages between humans and nymphs are uncommon, but far from unprecedented. Miranda married Caliban freely. Then later, after the island was rediscovered, she dissolved that marriage and married Ferrante."

"It must have been so—"

Miranda has come back and is standing in the doorway and interrupts before Tish can finish. "You're getting this completely wrong. It was my marriage with Ferrante that was terrible. I betrayed Caliban a hundred years later when I helped Orsino against Geryon."

"I think that's all you need to understand what's going on," Ficino says hastily. "Let me find you bedrooms. You can sleep, and tomorrow we will all go to visit Orsino."

"But has Geryon been blind at the top of a tower for three hundred years?" Tish asks, as they follow Ficino across the wide room towards the stairs.

"There were no stars, no earth, no time,
No check, no change, no good, no crime,
But silence, and a stirless breath
Which neither was of life nor death;
A sea of stagnant idleness,
Blind, boundless, mute, and motionless," Dolly quotes.

Miranda, behind them, makes a small choked sound.

"Who's that?" Ficino asks.

"Lord Byron," Tish says. "The Prisoner of Chillon."

"Geryon had air, at least, at the top of the tower," Ficino says. "But you should know Orsino won't let anyone see him. He says he's mad."

"Anyone would be mad, after three hundred years," Miranda says. "Blind, boundless, mute, and motionless indeed."

"And now Caliban wants to free him, and to have him be duke again," Tish says. "I don't think that's going to work."

"He was a terrible duke even when he was sane," Miranda says. "The last thing Illyria needs now is a blind insane duke."

"You should rule yourself," Ficino says.

"I can't. It was killing me." She shudders.

"Then—"

"We'll talk to Orsino tomorrow." Miranda's face is closed.

Without further argument, Ficino leads Tish and Dolly to comfortably appointed bedrooms and bids them goodnight.

17

AN AUDIENCE

As they walk through the streets of Thalia to Orsino's palace the next morning, the gentle autumn sunlight illuminates the art that is everywhere, sculptures and decorative doors and windows and many frescoes on the outside of houses. Arches in the lower floors of palazzi give glimpses of workshops and storehouses where a brisk trade is being carried out by men and women in gorgeous brightly coloured and patterned Renaissance clothes. The streets are full of people bustling to and fro about their business, or stopping to chat. A woman dressed as an artisan hails a man in a red cioppa and starts asking him about payment for a necklace; two old men sit waiting on a bench outside a palazzo, a bunch of boys run past them clutching wax writing tablets. "It's like Firenze but more so," Tish says, delighted.

"They just kept on doing it," Dolly says, beaming, indicating a door scroll of dolphins and lilies. "It just kept on being the Renaissance forever here."

"People must have been so sad when it stopped, in your world," Miranda says. She is dressed this morning in dark purple with silver trim, and is carrying an ebony staff carved with a snake's head. "It must have been terrible. Was it a barbarian invasion, like the fall of Rome?"

"No. In fact, I'm not sure how it did stop," Tish admits.

"Progress," Ficino says, frowning as he steps aside from the tide of running children. He is dressed exactly as he was the day before, they may even be the same clothes, for he may not have slept. "Though I'm beginning to think there's something to be said for it."

Then they come out of the narrow street into the Piazza della Signoria, and see something they have never seen before: the Palazzo Vecchio in its true colours. The stone is a mellow gold. The castle has a slim off-centre tower, and in the embrasures below the battlements are painted brightly coloured shields. The effect is delicate and solid at once, charming, like a child's toy or a sandcastle made suddenly lasting and life-size. Dolly and Tish both stop to look at it, and Miranda and Ficino have to come back to wait for them.

"But this was exactly the same in Firenze, surely you're used to it?" Ficino asks.

"They painted it white, the vandals," Dolly says, vehemently.

Ficino tries to take this information with Platonic calmness, but can't help wincing a little.

They begin walking again, and cross the busy square. The Loggia dei Lanzi, the pillared colonnade that provides shade and a meeting place for the city, is full of people doing business, or just sitting talking. The statues in it and in front of the Palazzo Vecchio are a mix of familiar and unfamiliar. Michelangelo's *David* is missing from beside the steps, and so is Cellini's *Perseus* from the Loggia. In place of the *David* is a comparably sized heroic marble statue of Pico, about to make his sacrifice. In place of the *Perseus* is a bronze statue of Aeneas carrying Anchises so beautiful that Dolly can't help stopping to look at it, so he has to scuttle to catch up and runs up the stairs behind the others, to arrive at the great entrance doors on the right.

The doors are watched by two guards with long pikes. Their surcoats bear the device of a gold unicorn's head on blue, quartered with a blood red rose on white above three diagonal red stripes. Tish thinks the guard on the left may be a woman in disguise, but she takes Giulia's last piece of advice and says nothing. The pikes are lowered before them, but in a desultory way, as the guards clearly recognise Miranda and Ficino. "Master Ficino and party to see Duke Orsino, we are expected," Miranda says crisply. A servant comes, in the same livery. They follow him across a frescoed court-yard full of statues and up a flight of very steep stairs into a very beautiful room, painted a clear pale blue and hung with paintings in intricate gold frames, Abraham and Isaac, a Crucifixion, Venus and Adonis, and another representation of Pico's Triumph—a man standing before a curved classical portico, holding a knife to his breast. There are wooden Savonarola chairs with tapestry cush-ions, and a fire burning brightly in the marble fireplace. The cush-ions have the heraldic device of the unicorn's head, which is again quartered in stone above the fireplace with the rose.

Before Dolly can ask about the coat of arms, the door opens again, and in comes an elegant willowy woman, in an ornately elegant flame-coloured dress with elaborate puffed sleeves over a long cream tunic with a straight skirt. "Sebastian," Ficino says, with every appearance of delight.

"I never fool you for an instant," Sebastian says. "Nine people out of ten would have greeted me as my sister." He comes forward and kisses Ficino on both cheeks.

"Her Grace the Duchess Viola never wears women's attire in the morning," Ficino says.

Sebastian laughs, then shakes hands with Miranda. "How are you, mother-in-law?"

"My son may be married to your sister, but I don't know that this makes me your mother-in-law," Miranda says, looking at him sourly.

"Letizio Petranero and Adolfo Tornabuoni, visitors from another world," Ficino says, presenting them. Sebastian takes Tish's proffered hand and kisses it, and before she can say anything he does exactly the same to Dolly. They look at each other in consternation, unsure whether this is a custom here or audacity. Sebastian laughs, letting them know it is the second.

"And this is Sebastian of Messene, a law unto himself," Miranda says, rolling her eyes.

"We need to speak to Orsino urgently on a grave matter," Ficino says.

"Yes, you sent word. He'll be here presently. He's been up all night with a mare giving birth."

It somehow isn't what Tish expected to hear of a duke doing. Just then Orsino comes in. He is dressed in the fashion they expect from a duke, that is, a Shakespearean duke. He is wearing a deep purple cloak over black-and-silver doublet and hose. Tish is surprised that he seems older than his mother—she would have guessed Miranda to be thirty and Orsino to be fifty (he is showing the effects of his sleepless night), although she knows they are both hundreds of years old, and Miranda is at least twenty years older than her son. It seems very strange to her that Miranda from *The Tempest* should be the mother of Orsino from *Twelfth Night*, but strangest of all to be talking to them, as if she had entered into a play she hadn't read and doesn't know her lines.

"Mother," Orsino says, bowing, looking from Miranda to Ficino as if for an explanation. "Master Ficino."

"Your Grace," Miranda says, and the others echo her. Dolly wonders what it does for family relationships to live for centuries at essentially the same age, but still be mother and son.

"I have very bad news," Ficino says. "But first, let me present Adolfo Tornabuoni and Letizio Petranero."

"Children from another world," Miranda glosses.

Orsino, who had been inclining his head politely as the others bowed to him, jerks immediately upright. "From Pico's world?" he asks Ficino.

Ficino nods.

"Then the gods are moving?"

"Yes. But that is not my bad news, or not the worst of it. Shall we sit down?"

Orsino gestures towards chairs, and they sit. A servant offers them marzipan fruits. Tish pops her exquisite little marzipan apple into her mouth, then sees that everyone else is nibbling theirs in tiny bites.

When the last of them (Miranda) has finished their sweetmeat and wiped their fingers on napkins so beautifully embroidered that to Tish and Dolly it seems a shame to use them for their intended purpose, the servant withdraws. When she has gone, Orsino turns to Ficino. "You said your apprentice had been killed."

"Yes. Last night," Ficino says. "This is very serious and private business."

"Should I absent myself?" Sebastian asks, leaning back in his chair bonelessly, with the demeanor of one making a pro forma objection that he expects to be denied.

"Perhaps that would be best," Miranda says. Sebastian's eyebrows rise up to his hair, and he looks at Orsino, as if hoping to be asked to stay. The Duke says nothing, so Sebastian bows individually and elaborately to everyone and leaves, closing the door very slowly and gently behind him. Dolly notices that the door is intarsia, different shades of wood arranged like a mosaic into a picture, in this case a portrait of a heavy man with a toolbox surrounded by woodworking tools, rendered almost three dimensionally.

"Three things, your grace," Ficino says, when the door has finally closed. "First, the gods are moving outside the world to affect the world again, as we can see by the presence of these strangers. Second, Geryon's father is free, and came here last night and spoke to me, accidentally killing my apprentice Giulia. Third, the

Antean intends to free Geryon. I persuaded him to wait for three days so I could speak to you."

Orsino looks grimmer and grimmer as Ficino speaks. "Three days!" he says.

"He would have come here last night directly from my house," Ficino says.

Orsino nods. "You bought what time you could with what coin you had. Thank you. But what good does it do? My brother will kill me if he is released. What I have done to him can never be forgiven."

"Yes," Ficino agrees at once. "But if his father comes here and destroys the castle from beneath, you will die, your brother will be free, and a great many other people may also die in the process."

"I have given thought to recapturing Caliban," Miranda says. "He didn't see me last night. He is unlikely to know I'm here. But I don't think the trick you played last time could work again. He came then because he trusted me, and I betrayed him with roses. He'll suspect at once if there are any roses in the marsh. And there's no way I can see of tricking him off the ground."

Orsino nods again, decisively. "Betrayal never works twice." He sighs. "I have spent much time strengthening the floors beneath this castle with structures and spells."

"Enough to keep out an Antean?" Ficino asks dubiously.

"There is a whole patterned layer of thorns. My defences haven't been tested against an Antean, but I have hope they would hold," Orsino says. "I am very sorry he came to your house that had no such defences."

"He did much worse than material damage," Ficino says. "Giulia is dead."

"And that might be just the beginning," Orsino says, and sighs heavily. "I am very sorry that you lost your apprentice."

"Caliban is sorry too, but such sorrow sets nothing straight," Ficino says.

"Would you trust me so far as to look and see whether I think the thorns would hold Caliban?" Miranda asks abruptly.

"I'd be grateful if you would, Mother," Orsino says.

Miranda closes her eyes and folds her hands over her staff. After a moment she opens them again. "I think it might well be enough to stop him, but it wouldn't recapture him."

"Stopping him is enough," Orsino says, leaning back with a sigh of relief.

"No it isn't!" Ficino objects. "You just apologised to me for the death of Giulia. How many more deaths among the ordinary citizens of Thalia would Caliban cause if he took it into his head to plough up the undefended city that lies around your safe palazzo? How many if he harmed the city while actually *intending* death to the Thalian people? You could sit here under siege while everything around you becomes a desert."

"What alternative do I have?" Orsino leans forward.

Ficino looks at him directly. "You could offer your brother a deal. You could take turns to rule for three hundred years each. You could let him bind you and blind you. I would undertake to restore his sight now, and yours afterwards."

"After three hundred years? I have a nine-year-old daughter!"

"Now it is my turn to say in futility that I am sorry," Ficino says. "But the gods are taking an interest. I don't know how much they can affect things from outside, but they have already overturned this arrangement."

Orsino looks at Dolly, and then at Tish. They meet his eyes. Tish finds herself feeling very sorry for him. He looks back to Ficino. "I'm not sure I could live for three hundred years like that, even knowing I'd be released at the end of it," he says. "I don't know how Geryon has kept himself alive. He's mad, you know."

"I'm not surprised. Most people would be."

"Most people would choose to die!" Orsino bursts out.

"That is always a choice we all have," Miranda says.

Orsino collects himself. "How long exactly can we count on?" he asks. "Before Caliban returns?"

"Until noon on the day after tomorrow," Ficino says.

"I need to speak to my counsellors, and then I will speak with you again, late tonight or tomorrow morning. I assume the funeral will be this afternoon."

"This afternoon at the church of Hermes Psychopomp," Ficino says. "I have spoken to her family and it is all arranged."

"We will all be there to show our respect," Orsino says. "And if you will, come back tomorrow morning, and let us speak some more."

Ficino glances at Miranda, who nods. "That we can do."

Orsino gets up and goes to Dolly, looking closely at him, and then at Tish. "Why did you come?" he asks.

"It was no doing of ours, and it seems to us a strange chance," Dolly says.

Orsino ponders that for a moment. "Do you know anything from your world of this matter?" he asks.

"Very little," Tish says. "We have a play—two plays—but they don't go on as far as this. One ends with Caliban on the island and Miranda coming here to marry your father, and the other . . . the other concerns your marriage."

"Ah, the scandal of my marriage," Orsino says, sounding cheered. "I wish I could see that played. It must be a grand comedy. But you know nothing about my half brother?"

Tish shakes her head. "I think what you did to him is horrible," she says.

Orsino frowns, and she remembers that he is the duke and could have her executed or imprisoned for speaking to him like that. But he sighs. "Yes, it is horrible. But so was standing at his elbow seeing him make a fool of himself and beggar Thalia in his ineptitude. And that could have gone on for centuries too. I am the last heir, you know, the last person to be brought up in expectation of inheriting a kingdom in a reasonable time only to have it snatched from me by the end of death."

"Nonsense, there were a whole generation of heirs like you," Ficino says.

"And not all of them deceived their brothers into imprisonment, it's true," Orsino says.

"Dukes deposing their brothers is a well-worn theme," Miranda says. She stands up and takes a step towards her son. They are exactly the same height. "But keeping him imprisoned all this time—"

"I have refused your applications to visit him not because I did not trust your honesty but because I could not trust your pity," Orsino says. "He is very pitiful, as he is now. But he was a terrible duke, and he would be worse now, mad. It might well be better for Thalia to endure an Antean attack than have him back on the throne."

"Why didn't you kill him?" Miranda asks.

"He could die any time if he wanted to," Orsino says. "And he's my brother, and was my friend. Killing him now . . . is one of my options, isn't it?"

Ficino frowns, but Miranda and Orsino are staring at each other. Tish and Dolly exchange uncomfortable looks.

"Death is so very final," Orsino says. "It closes all the doors. And so I didn't kill him, and you didn't kill Caliban. And this is what matters in life, death and love and peace and war and time. I've bought Thalia peace and time, as best I could. And if some say it was ambition, well, there was some of that too. But I could not see my city spilled away in carelessness and waste, or watch somebody else depose my brother and take his place."

18

ON A PALE HORSE

I am not human, whatever I am, and my experience of death and grief is fundamentally different from the human. But even with human death, there is a vast range. If you think about the difference between Ficino's experience of death and Tish and Dolly's experience of it, and see how that is different from your own and that of your friends, then set that difference against Giulia or Sebastian who have rarely met death, and only by human will. And if you can, compare it to Sylvia's grief for Idris, or before that, for her grandfather Harrison who died when she was ten, her grandmother Harrison who died when she was thirteen, or her father who died when she was twenty-two.

The ceremony held for Giulia's funeral encompasses the whole city. Shops close, bells ring, the entire population of Thalia come out into the streets. The coffin is carved and painted. Giulia's parents look stunned. Ficino speaks, briefly and movingly. Many of her friends speak. Dolly, as the person Giulia was trying to rescue, has a starring role—and he can't help thinking of the whole funeral as a performance, even though the tears are so clearly real.

Priests read from the Bible, and Tish and Dolly are confused at how they seem to mix up pagan gods and angels, and invoke the protection of St Michael, St John, and St Proserpina. The procession moves from the church of St Hermes the Bearer of Souls to Santa Croce, where Thalian heroes are buried. Dolly and Tish walk in the procession, with everyone, but do not join in the singing of unfamiliar hymns, or the mourning, which seems to them almost hysterically excessive, even though they had both liked Giulia. Between them, they have been to more funerals than anyone in the crowd who is younger than three hundred and fifty years old. The generational divide between people who were alive before Pico's triumph over death, like Ficino, Miranda, and Orsino, and those who grew up after it, like Olivia, Viola, Sebastian, Giulia, and most of the present population of Illyria, is huge, and visible. And if you think of your own experience of death and grief, and I hope for your own sake that you have very little of it, then you'll understand why this funeral is so huge, why the procession is so dramatic, and why Giulia's grandmother (the one who wasn't a hundred yet, and had six children, and yet never lost anyone she was close to before) weeps so uncontrollably.

Those who are older have experienced the change from a world where death is a guest at every feast to one where he is a very rare visitor indeed. Dolly, who is in the process of undergoing that experience, looks across at Duke Orsino and his family—Olivia looking regal, Sebastian and Viola looking identical in men's attire (which means it would be polite to address Viola as Cesario, although nobody does), and the daughter, nine-year-old Drusilla, looking pale and shocked in clothes that are miniatures of those Olivia is wearing. He starts to consider what it means to live without unwilled death, and what that means for the poor, mad half-Antean brother on top of the tower. Another long hymn begins.

"It's several years since anyone died, and that was an old

couple who were ready to go," Miranda murmurs to him. "For many people who knew Giulia, this is their first real loss."

"She will be finding out the Great Secret," Ficino says, as if he finds this thought some consolation.

"Whatever it is," says Miranda, fast and automatically, as if that's the ritual response.

Her grandmother Harrison was Sylvia's first real loss. Her father's mother, who shared her name, and taught her so much, who loved her, if not uncritically then at least without demands. Her grandfather had died first, but his loss was more muted, real and painful, but not a choking grief. Her other grandmother, her mother's mother, the tavernkeeper Kate, lived on cheerfully wiping tables and pouring beer into her eighties and the century's sixties. Sylvia grieved for her too, but at a much lower pitch. It was during the very bad part of her marriage to Steve, when all her emotions seemed wrapped in plastic film and held away from her, too difficult and raw to unwrap. She came back from the funeral and found herself tiptoeing around, apologizing to him for her grandmother's death. "Crazy," she thinks now, remembering that time.

"I don't know, I wasn't there," I say.

"Maybe that's why it was so crazy," she says.

I was there for her grandmother Harrison's funeral. Setting out doilies on plates for cakes for the gathering when everyone comes back from the church to the house, Sylvia starts to cry and finds she can't stop. She locks herself in the little downstairs lavatory—it's not a bathroom, there isn't even a sink, just a toilet alone in a little room off the back kitchen, with hardly room for the square box of hard toilet paper, useless for mopping up tears. Sylvia's mother feels her grief is indecorous, excessive, disloyal. Her father and her aunt Cat hover in the back kitchen, ineffectively trying to protect her from her mother while simultaneously trying to deal with their own grief and loss. Sylvia can't believe that her grandmother, who could protect her, who she loved, really is gone. Sitting on that toilet Sylvia feels her grandmother can't be any further away than the kitchen, that she'll turn around and say "Now Sylvia, stop being so silly and come and help. There's so much to do!" Thinking this makes the crying worse. She is not a little girl any more, but she is at thirteen still a child, still in her mother's absolute control. And she has lost her grandmother who was her comfort and her protection, and is left with her mother, who is her real genetic blood mother but nevertheless, in terms of story, her wicked stepmother, who loves the other children she considers her own but never Sylvia.

She writes a story years later, a rare venture into science fiction, where every child is given a robot at birth whose job it is to protect their human rights. In the story, when the mother gives raspberries to all the children but one, the robot speaks up and says "Where are Master Timothy's raspberries?" The robots also see that the children get their vaccinations, are taken to the doctor when they're sick, and have everything they need for school. The story is about a robot (me) who doesn't want to stop protecting its child just because he has grown up, but the story seed comes out of Sylvia's mother's deep unfairness. She doesn't write it until after her mother is dead. She doesn't publish anything until after her mother is dead. Her mother dies thinking Sylvia is a failure.

"She would have anyway, no matter what," I say. "Do you think the World Fantasy Award would mean anything to her? She'd just have belittled whatever you did, the way she always did. The way Steve did. But Idris was proud of you. And the girls are proud of you. And your grandchildren. And Con. And all your friends and fans."

Sylvia comes out of the toilet eventually, when her little sister, Maureen, says she'll burst if she can't go. She washes her hands and her face at the kitchen sink. Her father pats her shoulder.

"Hold up, old thing," he says, and she does. Then she sees that her mother has stripped all the plates of doilies, crumpled them up and left them in a pile beside her grandmother's scrubbed metal kitchen bin. She bites her lip, and dashes into the study, her own special place. There are a pile of coats lying on the table, but there's nobody in there. She flings herself down on the floor beside the little barrister's bookshelf, leans her head on the glass, and there I am looking out, as always.

"Are you really going to do this?" she interrupts, and here we are again, nowhere, now, together in the bone cave.

"Why not?" I ask. "I need to get us onto the page, you and me, and this is an important part of it."

"But I don't know what really happened." I don't answer. There's nothing I can say to that. "Dammit. I've never talked to anyone about it. It's—"

"You always say that you don't have to describe everything, you have to evoke. You don't have to mention every course, you just have to say the air is heavy with garlic and rosemary with a faint edge of something burned."

"I don't know how you possibly could—well, go on then."

Sylvia is thirteen years old, and she has just lost her grandmother, and she is half sick from weeping. Her black hair is straggling out of its ponytail untidily, her eyes and nose are red and raw, she has freckles on her nose, and the black dress her mother bought is too long for her and yet too tight under the arms, where it is digging in. I am there in the glass, where I always am, ready to help as much as I can, be who she wants me to be. What are my constants? I am male, always, unquestionably, with the kind of cocky, slightly pompous confidence men often have but women very seldom, because it is the kind of confidence that comes with taking yourself seriously, and it gets punctured too often in girls growing up. I am snarky, and clever. I am no older than she is, and never have been, in fact I'm often younger. I am conscious of myself, my male and separate self. She leans towards the bookshelf, puts her hand on a knot in the pine, and reaches for me, and I am there, with my round hat firm on my head, leaning towards her, and we are together as we always have been in all my memories up to that moment.

Her voice is choked with tears. "It's all so awful,"

"Can I help?" I ask.

"Oh—" she says, and she says the name I had then, the name which neither of us can remember anymore.

Her mother comes into the room. "What are you doing?" she asks. "Who are you talking to? Sylvia you're too old for this kind of ridiculous display. Stop trying to make yourself important. Come out of here at once." She is wearing a calf-length black dress and high-heeled shoes, which clack on the tiles in the hallway and catch on the old worn carpet in the study.

Sylvia tries to move but she can't, she feels as if she's in one of those dreams where you can't run. She has dreamed about this often since it happened, and she isn't sure anymore what really happened and what she remembers from later dreams. Her mother grabs her shoulder and pulls her away from me. Until this moment, her mother has quite naturally assumed that I was no more than Sylvia's reflection in the dark glass. But once she has wrenched Sylvia away, she sees that I am still there. "What's this?" she asks, in quite a different tone. "Sylvia?"

"Nothing," Sylvia says, and though afterwards she tortures herself with believing that this is a betrayal, I understand immediately that she is trying to protect me. But she can't. Her mother's hand is like a claw on her shoulder, pulling the dress even tighter under her arm. She gives Sylvia a little push, so that she half falls against the table. Then, leaving Sylvia there, she bends down herself. She doesn't lie on the floor, but crouches in front of the bookshelf. She sees me looking out, with sorrow and anger blazing in my eyes, emotions which Sylvia has never yet seen in me except in play.

Her mother bends down, tutting as if she'd seen something no properly kept house would have, a cockroach, a mouse, a doily. She pushes both hands into the glass. Sylvia screams. She distinctly sees her mother's hands disappear up to the wrist in the thin smoky Bristol glass, but there is no blood, no tinkle or crash. Her hands sink into the glass as if into water. Her mother takes hold of me and pulls me out, twisting me as she pulls. I fight, try to hit her, try to hold on, but she is much stronger. In the real world, out of the glass, I am light, an angle, a perspective, and she is a grown woman, experienced, indignant, and used to getting her own way. She strangles me, squeezes me, suppresses me. Sylvia screams again, and now she strikes out, flailing forward with both arms, trying to stop her mother from destroying me. She gets in one hard blow across her mother's face. Her mother abruptly changes tactics and pulls her arms apart, stretching me, wrenching me, ripping me to pieces. I scream then, a hollow thin shriek, like the wind through a crack, like an animal in a trap, like a lost soul. Sylvia's mother smacks her hands together as if wiping me away. Once I am gone, she turns on Sylvia.

"My father came in," she says. "I was lying on the floor. She must have hit me, pushed me, something. I don't remember. Grandma was dead and you were dead. She'd killed you."

"It's not all that unusual for parents to murder imaginary friends," I say. I've read about it.

"I couldn't breathe," she said. "It was more than I could take. I was on the floor, and I could see in the glass but you weren't there. You weren't there."

"I wasn't really dead," I say. Revisiting this moment has hurt her more than I expected.

"Yes you were!" she insists. "You were really dead. I couldn't get you back, no matter what I tried. I spent years looking in mirrors and windows and bookcases, years. You have come alive again since, but you were really dead."

"I suppose I was," I say. "I'm sorry."

"No, I'm sorry! She killed you. That's not your fault! I couldn't stop her."

"Neither of us could stop her, and we both tried. I'm sorry I wasn't there later, when you needed me."

"I got you back," she says. "I got you back and you saved my life when I did, and I suppose you're going to tell about that too?"

"Perhaps not just yet," I say, surprised and shaken myself at the storm of emotion this has woken in her.

"If it had been Illyria, I'd have died then," she says. "If I could have died at will, I'd never have got up off that carpet. My father would have come in and seen that I was dead too. It would have been a double funeral."

"That does happen in Illyria. Ring death is a more extreme form of that."

"Why were we doing this? Oh. Yes. Poor Giulia. The funeral that Victorians think is too elaborate. What should we give them, elephants and trumpets? Dyed black peacock feathers?"

"Let's leave it for now and go to Perché No! . . . and get gelato."

19

INTO THE ROSE GARDEN

After the funeral ends, it's late afternoon. Miranda announces that she'll take them to her house. "Ficino needs to rest," she says as they walk through the streets, which remain both familiar and unfamiliar. "We'll go back to his house for dinner."

"I expect he will miss Giulia," Tish says.

"He misses a lot of people," Miranda says. "Even though death is rare in Illyria, if you live a long time you will see a lot of it, and if you live a long time, you miss people for a long time. And he had already lived for a long time before Pico's Triumph. Most people talk about Pico as if he's a god, but Ficino and I remember him as a person. And every grief brings back all the others. Let's give him a little time alone. Anyway, I want to look at what happened to my rose garden. And you might enjoy seeing my house."

There aren't many people on the streets. Most of those who attended Giulia's funeral have lingered to watch the grave being filled in. Those who are about seem to be hurrying home, though it is a mild autumn afternoon with a pleasant little breeze.

They turn onto a street that leads to a bridge lined with houses and shops, all closed, with their wooden countertops folded up and sealed shut. It takes Dolly a moment to realise that it is not the Ponte Vecchio but clearly the next bridge east on the river, which in Firenze would be the Ponte alle Grazie. There is a bronze statue on the approach, a woman holding high the head of a man. "Judith and Holofernes," Dolly says, identifying them.

"This is the Bridge of the Three Sisters," Miranda says. "Judith and Holofernes here, Jael and Sisera in the middle, and Jessica and Felippo on the far side." The Jael is marble, and the Jessica is a larger than life-size and very heroic bronze, with traces of gilding. "The Judith used to be in front of what's now the Duke's palace, when Thalia was a republic. Duke Manetto, my grandfather, moved it here. The Jael is quite new, barely twenty years old. And this is by Assieti, and it's quite a famous piece."

They admire the statues. "Is the equestrian statue in the square also by this sculptor? Assieti?" Tish asks.

"Yes. You have a good eye. The equestrian statue is of Manetto. He came from your world," Miranda says.

"When?" Dolly asks.

"1408, I believe," Miranda says. "He's believed to be the first person ever to do so. Then for almost a century there was quite a lot of coming and going."

"There's never been any mention of it on our end," Dolly says.

"Well, the news that somebody has disappeared is less exciting than the news that somebody has arrived, I suppose."

"And has nobody ever gone the other way?" Tish asks.

Miranda shrugs. "Maybe."

"What would happen if they did?" Tish asks. She is thinking about stories in which people come back from fairyland and crumble into dust.

"Ficino went to and fro regularly for a while," Miranda says. "I thought about going there when I gave up the duchy, but it seemed too extreme an exile. And it would only be another form of choosing to die."

"But how would it work? How old would Ficino be there now?" Tish asks.

"I don't think anyone knows," Miranda says.

"How did Manetto come to be Duke?" Dolly asks, as they walk up the narrow curving street towards the city wall, and the gate set in it.

"That's a long story. Illyria was a republic then, but lots of people both in and outside the city wished it wasn't. The other city states of the peninsula wished it wasn't so they could have one consistent voice to deal with, one policy to understand, one person to remember gifts and favours. The rich merchants who ran Thalia also all wished to have sole power for their own family, but there were many of them and they were constantly jostling with the other families in a very difficult balance, where if any one of them seemed to be likely to make themselves tyrants, all the others would band together to stop them. The Orsini family were in a very good position when Manetto wandered through from your world, and they saw his potential immediately, much sooner than he did. The gods sent him, you see, and he didn't have any ties. He was, my great-grandfather Zenobio Orsini pronounced, like a super-podesta. Do you know what a podesta is?"

Dolly nods, but Tish shakes her head.

"At that time, because Thalia didn't have any nobility, the city had to hire somebody to command troops, and to make arrests. Only nobles could do those things. So we'd hire a younger son of a noble from somewhere else to be podesta for a year. He'd live in the people's palace, he'd lead the troops, organize the guards, arrest people who needed to be arrested, all that kind of thing. Then at the end of a year, they'd pay him his year's salary—and it was a good amount—and exile him from Thalia forever on pain of death. He came in with power but knowing nobody, and he left before he could be too embroiled in the struggles. And everyone knew he'd be gone at the end of the year."

"But didn't any of them try to take over?" Tish asked. "If they had all the troops and the guards and nobody else had any?"

"Well, some of the big families had their own guards. But yes, occasionally a podesta wouldn't be able to resist and they'd try to take over. Every time they got torn to pieces by the mob. Troops are armed, yes, but they'll go down beneath the sheer force of every artisan in the city armed with sticks and stones. And the troops were people, too, with their own ties. Some of them turned on the podesta when he tried to lead them against their families and their own best interests." Miranda smiles. "And after all, no podesta was in a position to make good alliances with the rich merchant families. They were busy keeping peace in the streets and so on, fairly lowly business. And everyone was watching what they did."

"This was very much the same in Firenze," Dolly adds.

"Well, that's where Zenobio Orsini's plan for Manetto was different. He happened to show up at a time when there were even more problems with consistency in foreign policy than normal. You see, the men in charge were chosen at random, from the lists of those eligible, so policy could change completely every few months when they got a new lot in. This had us teetering on the edge of war at that time, and if it hadn't been for the foreign princes dealing with Zenobio Orsini and having at least some kind of continuity, we'd probably have been at war with Verona and Mantua already. So Zenobio put it to the people who were in charge that week that the gods had sent Manetto specifically to be podesta for foreign policy for a year. And they either believed it or thought it couldn't do any harm; after all, they had a podesta every year and that one had troops. But by the end of the year Manetto was married to Sempronia Orsini, and he wasn't going anywhere, and by the time my father was born Manetto was Duke of Thalia, properly invested by the Pope."

They come up to the city gate, which is open. Miranda greets the guard. "Good afternoon Agostino."

"Lady Miranda," he says. He is a tall young man with black skin and polished armour. His surcoat has the same arms as in Orsino's palace. Tish is surprised to see an African here, and armed, but Miranda clearly knows him and seems to take him for granted.

"I'll be back again in an hour or so," she says.

"And these are the strangers?" the guard asks, looking at them curiously.

"Adolfo Tornabuoni and Letizio Petranero," Miranda says smoothly, indicating them as she speaks. "Guests of Master Ficino. They sat down with Duke Orsino this morning."

The guard bows to them, and they both return the bow, Dolly more smoothly than Tish. "See you all soon," the guard says. "And be back by sunset, we've had orders from the Duke not to let anyone in later."

"Sunset it is," Miranda says. "We'll hear the bell." Then she says quietly to them, "Silly precaution, having the gate closed didn't keep Caliban out last night and it wouldn't today either, if he wants to come in."

They walk through the gate and out the other side. The city wall is very nearly the same as it was when they last saw it, a day ago and in another world. It is in better repair, and without the clumps of weeds that were growing out of it in their time. (There are no bastions, but they don't notice that detail particularly.) A steep hill rises up ahead of them. There is another stone wall, about a quarter the height of the city wall, running around the contour line halfway up the hill. Outside it there are trees and straggling clumps of purple-headed ragged robin, and they cannot see whatever is inside.

Miranda leads the way up the track towards the other wall. They come abruptly to a plain wooden door. It is painted light green, and the paint is peeling a little. Miranda draws a large key from the pouch at her belt and sets it in the lock. She moves her hands in a complicated pattern, then turns the key. Then she moves her hands again, and opens the door. "You wouldn't even have been able to see the door if you'd been alone," she says as she holds it open for them. They pass through.

"Why is the entrance hidden?" Dolly asks.

"Magic. Guards. Sight lines," Miranda says, and sighs. "Unlike Ficino, I do have enemies, even now, and I prefer to be safe. That's why I live out here, not quite in my son's city. There aren't any human guards—like most wizards I prefer not to keep servants. They interrupt one's concentration. Magical guards suit me very well."

Immediately inside there are two old olive trees, and a steep slope covered with rosebushes arranged in an elaborate pattern. There are artworks dotted around the garden, statues, a fountain, a waterlily pool with lapis and gold mosaic edging. There are also wooden benches here and there. It is clear that it must be a delightful garden in spring and summer, but last night's storm has blown most of the leaves from the trees and they are lying everywhere. It has the sad neglected autumnal look of all gardens at the end of the season. Tish takes a step, and a green-backed lizard darts away from her foot like quicksilver and disappears under a stone. Dolly is looking up at a statue of a winged lion in a pine tree, thinking how realistic it looks, when it suddenly takes flight and soars away. He jumps back, and Tish laughs.

"There are winged lions the size of herons!" Dolly splutters.

Miranda nods. "Don't worry. They're just like little sphinxes."

Dolly and Tish look at each other, then follow Miranda as she leads the way uphill through the rosebushes. Most of them are bare, just thorny sticks, but some have brown dead roses on them, and one bush is densely covered with creamy gold-hearted climbing roses, which perfume the air strongly. They pause for a moment at the waterlily pond, which is laid out like a clock face, with different lilies in each segment—most of them just leaves now, cupped and full of rainwater, but the nine o'clock segment also holds a single yellow flower, and the eleven o'clock one is completely drained. A bullfrog jumps into the six o'clock segment, then sits on a lily pad and croaks at them loudly. In the centre of the pool is a statue of the emperor Trajan, looking very severe in a toga.

They follow the path around, through the rosebushes. "Watch out!" They have come to the lip of a huge sunken depression of churned earth in the very center of the rose garden, with an overturned statue broken to small fragments, which clearly had stood above it.

"What was the statue?" Tish asks.

"Caliban," Miranda says. "I thought of it as a kind of memorial, though I hadn't forgotten that he was alive down there. He would have been dreaming all that time, not really conscious."

"He said he was constantly testing his bonds," Tish says, which sounds like being conscious to her.

"How long was he there?" Dolly asks.

"About three hundred years," Miranda says, absently. "He really shouldn't have been able to get out, the Aglaia is still in bloom and the roots go all around."

"Caliban won't come here, will he?" Tish asks in alarm.

"It's the last place in the world he'll come, because I could all too easily trap him here again just by moving a bush," Miranda says. She starts moving around the rim of the hollow, examining the thorny, twiggy rosebushes one by one.

Dolly feels his knees being bumped from behind, and looks down to see a shaggy grey ram. He puts out a hand and scratches it behind the horns. He always liked sheep at the family farm. "Could this be the culprit?" he asks. "Could he have eaten something he shouldn't?"

"What? Where did he come from?" Miranda kneels and examines the ram thoroughly, making little tutting noises which he seems to like. "Hekate wouldn't send a ram. But Hermes might. And Hermes can be a trickster, and he likes change. And the ram came straight for you, Dolly. Hmm."

"I take it there aren't usually sheep in here?" Tish asks.

"Not in the rose garden, no, there's no way for them to get in here. And in any case, the sheep we do keep are white, and not as shaggy as this one. He'd have had to have eaten the bush right down to the roots, and he did, of course. Any grazer who just randomly wandered in would take a mouthful here and there and not be so persistent. And now this dilemma facing us all. I do wish the gods would leave well enough alone."

(Sylvia and I both hate it when fantasy has actions of mysterious gods acting for their own hidden purposes to drive the plot forward. It always feels so contrived, and it takes agency away from the characters. "The gods made them do it!" Even in Ovid, where Cupid makes Apollo love Daphne and makes Daphne hate him—it just makes it a worse story, without any motivation. But this isn't like that. You know what we're up to, dear Reader, now that we've finally made it into the rose garden. I did send the ram, of course, just as I sent Dolly and Tish, and just as God sent the ram to Abraham that time. And that's the good kind of god action, you give things a little push at a weak point and let them snowball from there. "Huh," Sylvia says. "That's what you think. This is how things get completely out of control.")

Miranda straightens up and sighs. "I think Ficino should see this ram. I wasn't expecting anything quite so concrete—I thought there would be evidence of a lightning strike or something like that." She pulls a length of vermilion and gold brocade ribbon out of her pouch and makes it into a leash for the ram, looping it carefully in a halter knot so that it doesn't strangle him when he pulls. For the first time, as she kneels and knots the ribbon so competently, Tish can picture Miranda as a sailor.

"If you wouldn't mind leading him, Dolly, as he seems to have taken to you," Miranda says, handing him the other end of the ribbon. Dolly takes it with a little reluctance, and remembers the nursery rhyme, though this isn't a little lamb but a full-sized ram with curly horns. They go up and over the shoulder of the hill, and see in front of them the ruins of a classical building. Three pillars and a portico are still standing, and behind this is a jumble of fallen marble. Tish and Dolly are both perfectly familiar with follies of this kind, which are very common in England, though this is a little larger than most such. Miranda, however, gasps in horror and comes to a complete stop.

"At least there was nobody in it," she says, and it is only then that they belatedly realise that this is recent destruction, that this isn't a planned folly or even a real classical ruin, but the wreck of her house, which no doubt contained things she cared about.

"Caliban again?" Dolly asks.

Miranda nods, staring at the ruins. "Well, I've shown you my house, for what it's worth," she says, with forced cheerfulness. "Let's go back and see what Ficino makes of all this."

They return to the city with the ram trotting cheerfully at Dolly's heels. As they go through the streets, children, and some adults, do laugh to see it.

20

IF NOT HEREAFTER

After the funeral, Orsino feels a strong desire to go riding out alone over the countryside, taking a hawk and a hound with him for company. Normally he would indulge this impulse, saying to himself that he is too tired to work well, the sun is shining after the storm, and there will not be many more mild autumnal days before the frosts. Today he wonders whether he will ever have another carefree afternoon of hunting, hardly caring whether he finds any game or not. He has had so many of them, ranging here and there over the Thalian hills, sometimes greeting farmers as they go about their business, sometimes speaking to nobody until the walls of the city come back into view. He enjoys hunting in a party for deer or wild boar, but riding alone with a falcon delights him more. When he goes out with others he always feels they are looking to him for a lead. If he is the one to make the kill, he wonders if the others allowed it because he is the lord. A hunting party with visiting dignitaries or his own courtiers is a social occasion, and one that needs to be finessed. Hunting alone has no pressure of any kind. He sometimes brings home rabbits, or partridges, or quails, but even if he finds nothing at all he thoroughly enjoys an afternoon with horse and dog and hawk amid the ever-changing beauty of nature. He comes back refreshed to the city and his duties.

Even today he asks himself whether it would clear his mind and make it easier to see what to do about the dilemma of Geryon and Caliban. But as they walk back through the streets he sees Drusilla skip a step, then remember the solemnity of the occasion and look around to see whether anyone has noticed. Viola has, and is trying not to smile. It wouldn't be fair to keep this news from his family any longer. It affects them too.

As soon as they are indoors, as the courtiers begin to disperse, Olivia turns to him. "We need to talk. Would some random Antean churn up Ficino's house and kill his apprentice? Why? Or is Caliban loose?"

"Let's go somewhere private," Orsino says, including Sebastian and Viola in his glance. Sebastian, at this hint of real trouble, has straightened up and somehow intensified, so he now looks dangerous rather than relaxed—as a cat stretched out by the fire might all of an instant at a passing sound twitch into alertness and show her true predator self.

"I want to come too," Drusilla says.

"It's time for your Greek lesson," Viola objects.

"No it isn't, I did it this morning." Orsino makes eye contact with her tutor, a promising young man from Yavan who is also one of his Greek secretaries. He nods, confirming what Drusilla says. Orsino sighs, and waves the tutor away. "I've been to the stable and seen Leander, and he's wonderful, but I know you're going to discuss something important and I want to be there. I need to learn statecraft, you know I do," Drusilla continues.

"She might as well come," Orsino says. "It concerns her as much as any of us. But nobody else." The remaining courtiers bow themselves away, leaving Orsino's family alone in the courtyard with the little white dog called Horse.

"My room?" Olivia suggests.

There are not many places in the palace that are truly private, but Olivia's room is one of them. When this was the Palace of the Priors, and nine men whose names were drawn from a purse ruled the Republic for two or three months at a time, the top floor had been made up of nine bedchambers. When Manetto made himself Duke of Thalia in their place, he slept on the floor below and converted the top floor into guest chambers for ambassadors. During Prospero's brief rule, they remained unchanged, but Antonio in his reign made the whole top floor into a suite for Geltrude of Montalba, his wife, who had previously been Prospero's wife. Most of the luxuries and flatteries he installed are gone now, but Olivia's room still holds a huge carved bed, big enough for four (generally slept in by only two, though not always the same two), a mirror whose heavy gold frame is made up in the dolphin-and-poppy pattern of Montalba, and a tigerskin rug.

Olivia's creamy gold winter bedcurtains are up already, the colour of Miranda's climbing roses, though none of them knows it. To the left of the bed is a painting of the Three Graces (one of the Graces looks very like Olivia), and to the right a very relaxed St Sebastian, for which it was clear Sebastian was the model. On one side of the window hangs a tapestry of Pico, his theses in his hand, addressing the people of Thalia from the rostrum in front of this palace. There is a stiff formal portrait of Orsino on the other. There are only four of the buff-and-gold padded chairs, so Drusilla sits on the end of the bed with her feet on the tiger's back. Olivia's old black-and-white cat pads slowly down from the pillow to settle herself on Drusilla's lap. The sleepy contentment on his face contrasts with the tiger's snarl.

"Is Caliban's attack why Ficino threw me out of the audience chamber this morning?" Sebastian asks, as soon as they are all settled.

"Yes. According to Ficino and Miranda, who ought to know, the gods freed Caliban, and Caliban intends to free Geryon. My mother thinks our defences might prevent him getting through but wouldn't recapture him."

Viola sighs. She and Sebastian have worked hard on the defences.

"Can you trust your mother on that?" Olivia asks.

Orsino shrugs. "Can we trust her on anything? This whole thing could be a plot she and Ficino have concocted, and the two so-called strangers could just be new in town from anywhere. There's nothing extraordinary about them, they just seem like any pair of naïve *giovane*."

"Wait, are there strangers here from Pico's world?" Drusilla asks, excited, bouncing a little.

"Yes. You saw them at the funeral. Adolfo and Letizio."

"But I didn't know they were from Pico's world! Does that mean the door is open again? Can I go there? I've always wanted to go there, always!"

"We can't go there. They still have death, and magic doesn't work, or doesn't work in the same way, so we don't know if our healing spells and youth spells would work there," Viola says.

"But I'm nine years old," Drusilla says, with impeccable logic. "I could go there for just a hundred years and come back. Or maybe just fifty to be safe." She looks around four firmly negative faces of her parents, and concentrates on Orsino. "Maybe I could just go to school there. That has to be safe. And they have the best schools."

"Why do you think that?" Orsino asks, never before having given any consideration to the educational establishments of the other world.

"Because Pico was the best wizard, and now Ficino is, and they come from there. Their scholarship must be amazing. I could go there and learn it and come back in twenty-five or thirty years, and I'd be a great wizard and scholar. Don't you want me to be a great wizard and scholar?"

Orsino laughs. "Ask me again when you're *giovane*. You're too young to go alone between worlds, even if it is educational. And maybe you should talk to the new strangers about how their education really is."

Drusilla nods decisively, because her father hasn't given her an absolute no but set her a project, which is, he has learned, the best way to manage her.

"Besides, isn't Prospero the best wizard?" Olivia asks. "And he was born right here, though I suppose his father came from Pico's world."

"To return to our more immediate problem," Sebastian says, and they all turn to look at him. "Caliban is free. How?"

"They said it was the work of the gods, and did not specify which gods," Orsino says.

"The Anteans are the descendants of Terra and Neptune," Viola says. "And Diana has been their protector."

"And we have nothing but the word of Ficino and Miranda that it is divine intervention?" Olivia asks.

Orsino sighs. "Yes. Miranda could have freed Caliban herself, what would be easier? But why? I sensed no smell of conspiracy around this. She seemed surprised and worried by it too."

"They passed inside without the colour of the light changing in the wardsconce," Sebastian says. "That is indicative but not conclusive, in the case of such powerful wizards."

The cat begins to purr loudly as Drusilla pets it.

"Yes, defeating that would be child's play for Miranda or Ficino," Viola says. "There are many kinds of malice it alerts us to, but any great wizard could mask their mind to it."

Olivia's lips tighten and she begins to frown.

"But Miranda helped with the initial plan of neutralising Caliban and Geryon, didn't she?" Viola goes on.

"It's more complicated than that," Orsino says, with a quick glance at Olivia.

"Geryon killed my brother. I'll never forgive him," Olivia bursts out, as if this had happened yesterday and not three hundred years ago.

"Arbitrarily and unjustly. And because this was tyrannical and stupid and shortsighted, Miranda and Prospero didn't stop me deposing him," Orsino says. "And Miranda helped by neutralizing Caliban. But she had her own reasons. She always does."

"Do you know what those reasons are, and have those reasons changed?" Viola asks.

"I have no reason to think they have," Orsino says, sidestepping the question of whether he knew his mother's reasons for wanting her first, Antean, husband out of the way. "No, I don't think she freed Caliban. I do worry about her softening towards Geryon." He looks at Viola, and smiles apologetically. "After all, continued imprisonment of a son would be very hard for any mother to bear."

Viola rolls her eyes, and Drusilla laughs. The cat, shaken, stands up and turns around twice reproachfully before resettling itself again, facing in the opposite direction.

"So we trust her provisionally," Sebastian sums up.

Viola nods. "As always. Then if she's right about the gods freeing Caliban and about the value of our defences, what does that mean?"

"Well, if Caliban can't get through but isn't recaptured, then it's a stalemate," Sebastian says.

Orsino shakes his head. "They paint a horrible picture of him deliberately warring on the city with the intention of killing people, while we sit in safety in here."

"How many people could we protect in here?" Drusilla asks.

"Good thought, but not enough, not even half the city even if we crammed everyone in tight," Orsino says.

"And we'd run out of food quite fast," Viola says. "But surely Caliban's not that bad! He wouldn't do that."

"Why do you say that? Did you ever meet him?" Olivia asks.

"No, I wasn't born when he was captured and I didn't come to Thalia until years later. I just never heard anything about him, or the Anteans generally, that indicated he'd be capable of that particularly unpleasant kind of malice."

"Miranda seems to think him capable of it, and Miranda was married to him so she should know," Sebastian says.

"Caliban has a legitimate grudge against us, and against Miranda and Orsino in particular, but not against the people of Thalia. Attacking innocent people is just evil. I don't think we should just assume he'd do it without any evidence of him having done anything like that," Viola says, looking determined.

"Geryon killed my brother," Olivia says again, looking out of the window where the sun is heading westward. "Just because my brother wouldn't give him what he wanted."

"That's terrible," Viola agrees. "But that was Geryon, not Caliban. I might believe it of him. But did Caliban ever kill anyone?"

"Before Pico's Triumph he accidentally killed quite a few people, and deliberately killed a few more," Orsino says. "But you're right, we shouldn't assume the worst case. But we can't afford to ignore it either."

"What are our sensible options for action?" Sebastian asks.

"Ficino's suggestion was that I should change places with Geryon, on a voluntary agreement that I would be bound for the next three hundred years, and then we would change places again."

Olivia and Sebastian both laugh, Viola and Drusilla both gasp in horror. "I think we can dismiss that suggestion," Sebastian says. "What, were you seriously considering it?"

Orsino is tired and doesn't know what he really wants. "I need your advice," he says. "It's an option. Another option would be killing Geryon right now, just walking up there and cutting his throat. He couldn't stop me."

"But you wouldn't do that, because that would be wrong," Drusilla says confidently.

"Precisely," Orsino says, and smiles at her. "Though sometimes dukes do have to do things that are wrong."

"Like imprisoning Geryon in the first place," Drusilla agrees.

There is a small silence, in which none of her parents contradict her. Viola almost speaks, but stops herself.

"We need a plan to neutralise Caliban, either capturing him again or killing him. The death of Giulia is sufficient cause, as Geryon's murder of Olivia's brother, Claudio, was," Sebastian says.

"It's next to impossible to kill Anteans when they're touching the ground, and he'll be very cautious of roses now, and of all of us," Orsino says. "So it's hard to picture how a trap would work."

"Could there be something where the earth gives way and instead of dropping him in a hole swings him up in the air?" Drusilla asks.

Sebastian looks very thoughtful. He pulls out a wax tablet and begins to scratch a diagram.

"Can you protect the whole city the way you have protected this palace?" Olivia asks.

Everyone looks at Viola. "Yes, but not fast," she says. "Though maybe we could if Miranda would help. Or maybe Ficino, hmmm. It's a pity it's October, not a good time for getting roses to grow."

"So, let's consider that as an option," Orsino says. "You work on that, Viola, and talk to Miranda and Ficino about it when they come back tomorrow. And you work on the hoist idea, Sebastian, but not right now. What else?"

"Negotiation?" Sebastian suggests, folding his tablet and putting it into a pouch at his waist. "I suppose we could think about agreeing to let Geryon go, if he swore to give up his claim to the dukedom."

"Who knows what Geryon would do if he were free!" Olivia says.

"He'd go to Elam and weave carpets," Drusilla answers unexpectedly.

"What?" Orsino turns to her in consternation.

"Drusilla, I've told you and told you and told you to stop going up there and talking to Geryon!" Viola says.

"I know, but he's lonely, and he can't hurt me, and he's my uncle," Drusilla objects.

All of these things are true, but Orsino goes cold to hear her say them. Orsino visits his brother once a year, on his birthday. Geryon roars and raves at him. He dreads going, and forces himself to do it and not forget his brother entirely. He can't imagine what appeal such visits can have for the child.

"Elam? Carpets?" Sebastian says, his face a study in bemusement.

"Yes." Drusilla turns to him eagerly. "He says they don't make any pictures of people or animals in Elam, because if they do, then the creatures they make will come to them on Judgement Day and ask for a soul. So they make patterns only, very, very complex patterns, with colours. I've seen the carpets. He's right. And every one has a tiny flaw in the pattern somewhere, that only the maker knows, because the only perfect thing is God. And the carpets take a hundred years to make, or even longer, and only one person works on each carpet."

"I think we've all seen the carpets, Dru, but what do they have to do with Geryon?" Viola asks.

"He wants to go and make them. He wants to spend as long making a carpet as he has making designs for them in his head," the child says.

"Well, I'd never have imagined that," Olivia says.

"He could be lying," Sebastian suggests, dubiously.

"To what purpose?" Orsino asks. "He could have had no notion this was coming. Any conversation he had with Drusilla could have been intended to deceive us, but it seems very unlikely."

"I'm sure he wasn't lying," Drusilla says, earnestly.

"He'd need to be able to see to make carpets," Sebastian points out.

"Ficino says he can restore his eyes," Orsino says. "And if not, I expect there are doctors in Syracuse who could, for enough gold."

"Um," Drusilla says, twisting her hands together and looking down at the sleeping cat on her lap. "Actually his eyes have sort of grown back a bit. Anteans can do that, even so far off the ground, he says. It's one of the ways they're not like us, the way they heal. He's been able to see light for a hundred years, and colour is starting to come back, he says."

"Blinding him was a terrible thing to do," Orsino says, stricken by this guileless account. Nobody contradicts him. It had seemed, long ago, like a good idea, to establish his own power fast and vividly with an act of such ruthlessness. Now he cringes at his own naïvety and cruelty.

"Did he ask you to free him, Dru?" Olivia asks.

"No. Well, he did say that maybe when I'm Duke I would. Or maybe I said that, you know? And he said that by then his eyes would have grown back entirely, and he could go to Elam, and he'd make me a carpet of the pale, pale colours he can see now, in the pattern he made up in the dark, and then he'd make me a carpet of all the colours of flame, and then one in the colours of living life in the same pattern, and each carpet would take a hundred years to make."

"So it could be a plan for escape," Sebastian says.

"A very long-term plan!" Viola objects.

"I know. It might be hundreds of years before I'm Duke, or it might be never because my brother Tybalt might come home. Or maybe Orsino won't ever want to retire and will stay Duke forever. Or maybe I will find something to do that's more fun than being Duke of Thalia. Uncle Geryon knows that too."

"Drusilla, your counsel has been of immense value," Orsino

says, formally. He pulls off the arm ring he put on for the funeral, an elaborate pale gold band with an incised unicorn's head. He bows and hands it to his daughter as he would to one of his courtiers who had given good advice.

Drusilla's eyes widen, and she takes arm ring and pushes it up her arm. It is much too big for her, of course, even over the embroidered sleeve of her court dress. The cat wakes up and tugs at the fabric of her sleeve where it now hangs down.

"I think I should talk to Geryon," Orsino says.

"Should we all come?" Sebastian asks.

"Have you ever been up?"

"Only once," Sebastian says.

"Me too, just the once," Olivia says.

"I go up now and then, to make sure he's being treated all right," Viola says. "It's probably my fault Dru got the idea."

"How long have you been sneaking up there, Dru?" Orsino asks.

Drusilla looks up from the arm ring, which she is turning on her wrist. "Nearly a year," she admits.

"Well, maybe you and I should go and talk to your uncle." Drusilla carefully lifts the black-and-white cat and puts him down on Olivia's burgundy bedspread, where he yawns delicately down at the snarling tiger rug.

"You're really considering letting him go?" Sebastian's eyebrows have risen.

"If he'll agree to go to Elam and utterly renounce his claim to be Duke of Illyria," Orsino says.

"But like Caliban, once he's loose, how can you ever get him under control again?" Olivia asks.

"He's sure to want revenge, whatever he says," Sebastian says. "He'd say anything to be free, to get down from there."

"Maybe," Orsino says. "You get on with researching ways of killing or capturing Anteans on the ground. I'm going to talk to him and find out. Come on, Drusilla."

21

IF ALL THE SKIES
WERE PAPER

When they come back with the ram, Ficino is sitting on a bench in the courtyard reading *The Life and Letters of Silenus*. He gives a snort as they come into the courtyard, and puts the book down carefully when he sees the ram. "This is what freed Caliban, and he came trotting right up to Dolly," Miranda says.

"Interesting," Ficino says. He examines the ram carefully, while the ram struggles. "Nothing unusual, except how big he is. Well well. Why would Hermes want Caliban freed? Not just for mischief, I don't think."

"Caliban destroyed my house, either before or after coming here," Miranda says. "It's in ruins."

"You must stay here, of course," Ficino says, placidly. "It's not surprising that he's very angry. You kept him imprisoned for a long time."

He lets the ram go. It trots meekly back to Dolly. "I don't want you," Dolly says.

"It seems you have a new pet," Tish teases. The ram bleats, a low, hoarse sound.

"I think we should have a feast and invite the gods," Ficino says.

"Not sacrificing the ram!" Tish says, horrified.

Ficino laughs. "No, and besides, it would take too long to cook. I think fruit, and if I could prevail upon you to make another cake, Miranda? And how about you two? Do you know how to make anything?"

Dolly shakes his head.

"I can make omelettes," Tish offers. The cook at Blackstone taught her.

"Wonderful. Then you can decorate the table, Dolly." Both Dolly and Tish think that this task would be better suited to Tish, but they say nothing.

It turns out that there is a banqueting hall up the first flight of stairs from the courtyard and to the right, filling the whole side of the house. The windows face onto the courtyard, and they are filled with the late afternoon autumnal light that makes everything look as if it is underwater. Tish and Miranda go to the kitchen, which astonishes Tish by being up at the top of the house, to the side of the tower. "Fire burns up," Miranda says, as if that explains everything.

"Will you be able to rebuild your house?" Tish asks shyly.

"Oh yes. It will take some work, but it's only an inconvenience really."

Dolly ties up the ram in the courtyard and gives him a pile of hard root vegetables to eat. Then he goes back up to the banqueting room and investigates the huge carved wooden credenzas. They are full of cloths and bowls. He chooses a big white linen cloth, and sets a thin vermilion cloth over it down the centre of the table. He finds silver plates and puts matching vermilion napkins on them. It reminds him of dressing a set for a play. He gets enthusiastic when he finds silver goblets set with lumps of lapis lazuli, and wonders if he should start again with the blue-and-white cloth embroidered with birds that he had earlier rejected. But Ficino comes in as he is wondering, carrying a huge silver platter of peaches, which he sets down on the table.

"Very nice," he says, looking at the table. "Some candlesticks would be good." He leaves again.

The room has a fireplace at either end, and candlesticks sit on the mantelpieces there. There are several stone crests carved into each of the mantelpieces, and Dolly is surprised to recognise one of them as the famous Medici balls. When Ficino comes back with an immense bowl of cherries, he asks about it.

"Cosimo de' Medici was my first patron," Ficino says. "I don't forget."

"So you put the crest there to remind you of the Medici in my world, though there were no Medici here?" Dolly says.

Ficino nods. "Meaningless, really, I suppose, except to me. This room is about hospitality and connections." He goes out again as Dolly starts arranging the candlesticks. He is having fun now, and is pleased with the effect.

"Lay an extra place—no, better make it two," Ficino says, coming back with a bowl of golden apricots and dark red plums. "I don't really expect the gods to join us yet, but it would be good to be welcoming in case they do."

"Just two gods, not all twelve?" Dolly asks.

"There are more than twelve," is all Ficino says as he goes out. When he comes back he has a gigantic platter of black-and-green-striped figs.

"Where are you getting all these?" Dolly asks. "Or are you conjuring them up?"

"There are places where these fruits are ripe," Ficino says, setting the plate down. "Places where it is still summer. I bring the fruit from there, and in return I give a blessing. The people who grew and picked this fruit and those they love will be healed in mind and body. But I'm about to bring in some apples, and those I picked myself. If you're done with the table could you lay some fires?" There is plenty of dry fragrant wood stacked beside the fireplaces, and Dolly arranges it carefully in the fireplaces.

As he finishes, Miranda comes in, carrying a steaming flat pie-dish of cake. She places it carefully on the table. Then Tish comes in with a bowl of beaten eggs, a pan, and a thin round-bladed knife, like a painter's palette knife. Miranda takes a silver ring and taps it, so that it floats in the air next to the table. Then she snaps her fingers, and a flame springs up in the ring, and at the same moment all the candles and fires light themselves. The wood Dolly just arranged in the fireplaces begins to crackle.

Ficino comes in dressed in a toga with a circle of laurel leaves on his head, and carrying a lyre. He should look ridiculous, but instead he looks touching, like a child very solemnly dressing up. He sings an invocation to Hermes and to Hekate, in Greek, using a very strange scale. Then they all sit down. Tish begins making omelettes, taking the magical fire almost for granted, but being very careful pouring the egg mixture and flipping each one. When they each have an omelette on their plates, Miranda taps the silver ring and the flame in it vanishes. Ficino fills everyone's goblet with wine, and toasts the gods, all of them, in Latin, beginning with the One, the Great Creator.

The candlelight looks dim after the bright glow of the lily lamps, but it gives everything a warmer glow. They drink wine and eat the omelettes, which are slightly leathery. Then they gorge themselves on fruit, all of which is delicious, and finish off with cake. No gods show themselves and the extra two places Dolly set remain empty.

"I have no idea why the gods sent me here," Dolly volunteers.

"Nor I," Tish chips in.

"And I don't know what it means that the sheep likes me," Dolly goes on.

"Well, the ram was also sent by a god, and if he likes you, it might mean that the same god favours you. Or it might be that you are an aspect of a god, without knowing it. Or it could just be the ram's own personality, it's impossible to tell." Ficino smiles. "By the covenant we made at Pico's sacrifice, the gods are held outside the world and cannot enter in without an invitation. This is an invitation: be welcome gods, reveal your will to us!"

22

MODERN TIMES

The way she was living in Firenze, we'd go out in the morning to look at things, then come back and work on the Illyria story in the afternoon, eat dinner at home, work some more, then go out for a walk and a last gelato in Perché No! . . . before bed. Occasionally we'd vary this plan—we'd write in the morning and go out to look at things in the afternoon. But more things are open in the morning than in the afternoons even now—lots of the smaller museums are only open until 2:00 P.M. Sometimes, a couple of times a week, we'd have lunch in Teatro del Sale, and then we wouldn't need dinner. Everything was going smoothly except the plumbing, which despite the enthusiastic efforts and long explanations of the plumbers, continued to be utterly useless. In addition to refusing to run hot water, Sylvia had found that if you leaned on the sink in the bathroom it wobbled, which was alarming, especially while brushing your teeth. So at the end of the month, Sylvia decided to move instead of renewing the lease—not to leave Firenze in the middle of the book, definitely not, she wasn't going to leave Firenze until she flew to San Jose for Worldcon, but to change apartments. The old apartment was in the maze of streets east of the Duomo, close to Teatro del Sale and the Sant Ambrogio Market. The new one was on the river, just past the Ponte alle Grazie, with a view of the water and the gazebo, the red-and-white Palazzo Serristori, and the San Niccoló tower. The plumbing was impeccable, hot, cold, warm, completely adjustable, whatever you wanted. It felt quite miraculous after all those weeks with only cold water and needing to boil a kettle every time she wanted to wash dishes. Sylvia checked the plumbing, the view, and the Wi-Fi, but didn't think about the chairs.

They looked fine at a glance, anyway, and there were only two of them. This apartment was smaller, it had just one room, which contained a bed, a table, and two chairs, with a tiny kitchen and a tiny bathroom. "All I need," Sylvia said to the guy from the rental office, but she was wrong. Both chairs turned out to be hopeless, too low for the table, and completely lacking in back support. They were sturdy enough, but shaped almost like folding chairs. She couldn't type for ten minutes without getting a backache. We lost a day moving, and then another, and another.

We kept going to places—we went to the Palazzo Davanzati, which is a palazzo that's decorated inside with furniture as it would have been in the fifteenth century. It's the basis for Ficino's house, though of course it doesn't have a tower, and Ficino's house is in the Via del Corso, or it would be if it wasn't in Thalia. It's the Palazzo Altoviti, and she chose it to be Ficino's house long ago, because it has a seventeenth-century façade with bas reliefs of famous Florentines, with Ficino prominent on the bottom row. But it's privately owned still, and you can't go inside it, so she keeps using the Palazzo Davanzati as a model. It has the kitchen under the roof, which really was the Renaissance norm. We went to San Marco to see the Fra Angelico frescoes, and for the peace. We went to the Horne Museum, which is also in a palazzo, and to the Laurentian Library, which had an excellent exhibition about women and books, with an ostrakon with a Sappho poem and medieval manuscripts copied by nuns. Sylvia spent a lot of time looking at them. Then she thought a lot about stairs, and how they were not a solved problem in the Renaissance. Michelangelo's stairs in the Laurentian Library were an affectation, but one whole side of the Horne Museum is stairs, and in the Palazzo Davanzati they go around the courtyard and then there's a covered portico on each floor open to the air of the courtyard which functions as a hallway. In the afternoons we went to the Uffizi or the Palatina Gallery in the Pitti Palace and looked at paintings, paying attention to details of period clothes our characters might wear, and jewellery and hairstyles.

She'd sometimes talk to me then, if she couldn't strike up a conversation with somebody there. She didn't enjoy looking at paintings as much without being able to talk about them. And she always had new thoughts about these paintings, even though she'd seen them so many times. But she was always worried now, if she talked to me in public, in case she moved her lips, or even spoke aloud, the way she would when we were in private. She thought somebody would see her and think she was mad. "Senile," she says. "That's what worries me now. They'd see somebody grey haired muttering away and think I ought to be in an institution. If I'd spoken aloud to you the first time I was in Firenze, when I was young, that's when they'd have thought I was mad." She laughs her sharp laugh. "But if talking to you makes me mad, they'd better lock me up now."

She went to bed every night early, and ate well enough. She always eats better in Firenze. Montreal is a good food city. But on a scale of one to ten, where Grand Rapids, Michigan is a one, Provo, Utah is two, Chicago is six, and Montreal is nine, Firenze is twenty-five. Italy has unfairly great food. It's the terroir and the habits of life, and perhaps the fact that they didn't have railroads in the nineteenth century so people never got used to eating stale processed food. The fruit and the dairy and the meat are of a quality you can't even imagine unless you've been there. It makes it very easy to believe in Plato's analogy of the Cave. If you've been used to eating strawberries and tomatoes and carrots elsewhere and then you go to Italy, you do naturally realise that what you've had all your life is like a shadow on a cave wall thrown by this transcendent thing. Even the nuts are better. (How can the nuts be better? Do they have better pine trees? Better hazel trees? Better macadamia trees? How could they? Macadamias are Australian!)

So she was sleeping and eating and even taking her medication regularly, which she doesn't always remember to do. But she wasn't writing. She was even neglecting her correspondence, because sitting up at the computer even for the short time it takes to do email hurt. "This is no good," I said, as she was getting ready for bed on the evening of the fourth day she hadn't opened her laptop.

"The chairs hurt my back," she said. "You wouldn't understand."

I have been torn apart by wyverns. I have sacrificed myself with a stone knife. I have lost a leg and been in a wheelchair for forty years. I have fought dragons and fallen in flame. I have run, and swum, and ridden, with a broken hip, to get a message through in time to save the kingdom. I know what pain is! But I didn't say that. I was quiet while she brushed her teeth in the sink that didn't wobble, with water that ran at a consistent temperature.

"Maybe we could move again?" I suggested as she left the bathroom.

"I paid the rent upfront, from now to Worldcon. And I already asked the landlord if there were any other possible chairs, and he just shrugged helplessly and charmingly in that typical Italian way, as if to say he'd do anything short of actually help—

that's unfair. He probably doesn't have any other chairs. But I don't want to waste four thousand dollars—that is, four thousand euros. *Five* thousand dollars." She could. She just got paid for the Chinese edition of the dragon books. She has it. But I understand that she doesn't want to, that it violates the ideas of frugality and good sense she learned as a child. It is also the kind of thing that would have appalled Idris, who was always so careful with money. She has become more so since his death, and even remembers most of the time that euros and dollars and gold florins are worth different amounts. Sometimes she even remembers that American dollars and Canadian dollars are different, though they confusingly use the same name and symbol. (American dollars are bigger, which is good, because she mostly earns American dollars.)

"Maybe we could write in the library?" I suggested.

"I thought of that. But the road up to I Tatti is so steep! And there's never any room at the Oblate library unless you get there at nine o'clock. And anyway—you know how I like to pace about and mutter." Pace and mutter isn't the half of it, she'll act out swordfights and do dialogue aloud and sometimes shout or cry. She is not one for sitting still at the computer, even when she has a chair.

"Maybe you could do the pacing about and muttering part here, and do the actual writing it down when you get there," I said.

"That's all very well if it's flowing well, but I do often want to get up and pace and mutter in the middle. It helps me think things out."

"Do I get the feeling maybe you don't want to write?" I asked, tentatively, though she didn't *feel* stuck.

"No!" she snapped. Then she sat down on the end of the bed and started crying. "I want to. I really do want to. We left them just talking after dinner, and Orsino and Drusilla about to go up the tower to see Geryon. I really want to go on and find out what happens, especially to Tish and Dolly. And the whole dilemma with Geryon—that's the next thing, really, their conversation. I can't wait. It's such an interesting quandary. I really do want to get on with it. But sitting on that chair hurts so much. And pain and wasting time and thinking about it makes me think about . . ."

"Mortality," I completed her sentence. "Maybe we could buy a chair? Even if we have to leave it when we go."

"Well, we're hardly shipping one back to Canada! But a cheap chair, maybe. Even a cheap chair will be better than this. The table is so high, though. Hmm. How about an office chair, with adjustable height? They have to have office chairs in Italy."

And thus began the saga of the chair. Firenze doesn't have chair shops, at least, when she googled to find out if it did, it turns out they're all far from the centre. There's an Ikea out by the airport. But it didn't seem necessary to trek all the way out there. She found a chair online quickly enough, in a Google ad. They had a chair, had many chairs, and she found the right kind, adjustable in height, and back. It wasn't as good a chair as the one she has in Montreal, but then it was also only sixty euros. Well, €59.99. In the Renaissance, when most transactions were done in credit, small change practically didn't exist. Then when Italy had lire, the first time she came, small change was all there was and everything cost hundreds or thousands of lire, and sometimes people would give you a piece of candy as change because organizing the specific value of lire was too hard. Now that they have a sensible currency for the first time since the fall of Rome, they've become obsessed with pricing things at a penny under the next euro, as if—as if what? Do they think people will think 59.99 is less than sixty? Do they think people are that stupid? *Are* people that stupid? Does this *work*? People do it in Canada too, where they're going back to a credit economy and don't even *have* pennies anymore. It must have some psychological effect, but I don't understand it.

The shop claimed to have the chair in stock and to offer free next-day delivery, which would have been great, except that they didn't come. They claimed she'd been out, when in fact we'd been in the apartment, listening for them, the whole time. This went on and on, wasting even more time, because we weren't even going out and looking at things, we were just sitting (or in fact lying on the bed, as there wasn't anywhere to sit that didn't hurt) in the apartment with the door open, waiting until late in the day every day. When we gave up, or received an email from them saying delivery had failed, we'd go and have a gelato and an evening walk.

Waiting for the chair wasn't as bad for me as being ignored and banished to the bone cave with no access to anything and the fear that she'd just leave me there forever. She let me see through her eyes, and she talked to me. In fact she talked to me a lot. We also did a lot of reading. We read John Barnes's *Tales of the Madman Underground*, which was great once I stopped expecting it to have spaceships. It reminded me in a weird way of *The Wednesday Wars*. Then we read a biography of Vittoria Colonna. She likes biographies, because people's lives don't fall neatly into periods, they cut across expectations of time. Vittoria Colonna was a poet, a friend of Michelangelo and Pietro Bembo, a member of the important Roman Colonna family. Pope Clement, a Medici pope, refused to allow her to become a nun, because he valued her as a sane adult member of the Colonna, though they were his enemies. Then we read Rosamunde Pilcher's *The Shell Seekers,* which went down fast. Then we started reading a book about Sigismundo Malatesta and his paganism, which was annoying, very detailed but without any breadth. Alternating fiction and research nonfiction is her usual habit, but she stopped the Malatesta book in the middle and read a new translation of the Bhagavad Gita.

On the fourth evening of waiting for a chair, and the seventh, no the eighth without writing, we were walking back from Perché No! . . . with the taste of their astonishing pear and rose gelato on her lips. The gelato was as excellent and the staff were as friendly as always, so that had cheered her up a little. It had rained in the afternoon, and we had missed it, waiting in for the stupid chair that didn't come, lying on the bed reading with the door open, starting up at every sound, and engaging in exasperated email in simple declarative Italian with the chair people. "I need my chair. I have been waiting too long. This is unacceptable. No delivery came. I cannot lose another day." They responded that the driver had left, they never deliver after five, but it would be delivered tomorrow for sure. She no longer believes their assurances. She is considering the possibility of threats, but she is unused to making them in the real world. "Canadians don't make threats," she says, which means that if a Canadian sounds like they're making a threat you should take it very seriously. Besides, what could she threaten them with? Exposure on the internet could make thousands of her readers hate them, but that probably wouldn't hurt them very much, as very few of those fantasy readers are in Italy, and even if they visit they're unlikely to buy office chairs there. She is small and the forces of chair delivery are grinding her under their wheels.

She's feeling a little better because of the gelato, but she's thinking about this, and about her plan to stand on the doorstep for the whole delivery period tomorrow, when she stops suddenly at a leather stall that is just closing for the night. She has noticed that they have the kind of leather book covers, black, embossed with a Florentine lion, that she likes to use to protect her Kindle. She has been using them for ten years, through generations of Kindles from the clunky original one to the streamlined Oasis of today. (She buys a new one every time one comes out with more space for books. Idris only read in codex form, so their house in Montreal is still full of paper books, but she travels a lot and likes to have her whole library with her all the time so she doesn't have to decide in advance what she's going to read.) These particular leather covers have been scarce this year, but this stall has a big pile of the exact kind she likes. She buys two, which I see as a sign of hope, as each lasts for several years. Then, on impulse, she buys a third. The man tries to persuade her to take one with the Florentine lily instead of the lion, but she shakes her head. "It means something different in Quebec," she says.

The fleur-de-lys was Firenze's symbol long before France adopted it, and some say the city is named after the irises that grow wild about it—Florentia means flowering—and that the city's lily is really an iris. Quebec's lily is one of the last relics of France's symbol, retained even though France itself has abandoned it; Quebec and New Orleans, the remnants of an empire that didn't want to be conquered by a different empire, still cling to it. When it comes to the Quebec lily, Sylvia feels the scars of old wounds, the separatists, the referendums, the long fight with the library about whether the fleur-de-lys should adorn the spines of her books, or only those of writers who write in French. She would like to have the lily as her symbol too, but it would mean too much, and the wrong things, if she tried to claim it. And while the Florentine lily and the Quebecois are different, they're not sufficiently different as not to be easily confused for each other at a glance. The lion treads on no toes.

"Ah. Canada!" the salesman says. He puts his hand on his heart. "Love Canada. Good. Good." Then he slides from broken sales-pitch English into Italian and explains that his brother works in Vancouver, and that Canada has resisted fascism, not like the US, and everything is efficient, not like Italy. This warmth towards Canada is universal, but always a little surprising. Sylvia finds herself in a conversation she has often had in Europe, and had even on her first trip in the seventies, about emigration. She tells him Canada would welcome him, but he should improve his English and his French. She sometimes feels she has had this conversation herself with more people than ever do choose to try Canada's slow, complicated, and expensive emigration policy, which on one level nobody can admit exists mainly to keep out Americans who are desperate for healthcare. It's strange to think that people from Burkino Faso and Syria and Italy would find it easier to move to Canada if the US adopted single-payer health-care like a civilized country, but this is the way the world fits together. She goes through her standard explanation. He really could have a better job in Canada than selling leather goods from a street stall. And for his children, there would definitely be more opportunities. Canada isn't perfect, but it has much more unnep-otistic opportunity than Italy does. (And when they say they're going to deliver a chair tomorrow, they actually do it.) "But it is so, so beautiful here," she finishes, as she always does in Firenze.

He nods fervent agreement. "When my brother comes home, he cries."

"When I come here I cry too," she admits.

He insists on giving her a fridge magnet of the city of Firenze, as a gift. He slips it into the bag with the book covers. "Come back, come back often," he says.

After all the hassle with the hot water and the chair, Italy at its worst, it cheers us no end to have an encounter like that. We walk on, down past the end of the Ponte Vecchio, where the view opens up.

Because of the rain, the swallows are down low over the river, and the sky is full of clouds in white and pale grey and dark grey and black, on a background of pale blue, and all lit from below, and behind us, by the sinking sun. The shapes the clouds make are like billowing angels holding hands, half allegorical ceiling and half Escher. Below is the Arno, and on the other side the Tuscan hills, with the tower of San Niccoló, the too-perfect terracotta-and-white Palazzo Serristori, the gazebo, the Belvedere fort, and the abbey of San Miniato al Monte, already lit up although it isn't dark yet.

The wind is blowing the clouds, and the sky swirls, and I wonder if this might be my chance—absurdly, I feel unready, only partway through my plan, without everything in place. But maybe we could accept Ficino's dinner invitation after all. What happens isn't that. The clouds move, and suddenly the others burst out and they're all there, pressing up with me behind her eyes. It's Tish first, and immediately she's shocked at the twenty-first-century fashions. More than half the women are wearing trousers, but they clearly aren't dressed as men, because their shirts are skimpy. Also, everyone is showing a lot of flesh and she's horrified. "It's hot," I say.

"Don't you think it was hot in 1847?" she ripostes.

"Or 1499?" Ficino adds.

I can't argue. There were days then when it was just as hot, and yet people went wound in yards of cloth, and while they did have silk, they used it to make brocades and velvets, not loose lightweight shirts like the one Sylvia is wearing, clasped at her throat with Idris's pearl circlet. What could they have been thinking? Why did they ever give up togas? It can be chilly in the winter in Italy (though not by Canadian standards), but imagine the first summer day when you had to wear trousers instead of a toga and feel the cloth rubbing between your legs and the sweat prickling. The end of the Roman Empire was a terrible thing in small ways as well as in large. The sponge fishers of the Aegean used to ship menstrual sponges to all the women of the empire—the poor women could afford fewer of them and had to wash theirs more often, but they could buy a new one when the old ones were worn out. Imagine when trade stopped and the sponge ships didn't come. I imagine those last hoarded sponges getting more and more worn, until at last they had to revert to using rags—for fifteen hundred years. It's not fashionable to think about decline and fall these days, it's generally represented as a change. And some things did get better, for some people, and some technologies improved. But all the same, sometimes when the lights go out, it stays dark for a long time.

"This is Firenze?" Dolly asks, looking around. He sees a priest cycling by in shorts, but the landscape has not changed. The Arno flows in the same curve. The embankment here had already been made by Dolly's time. The buildings we can see from here are barely changed.

"Don't be alarmed," Ficino says. "When you smoke laurel leaves and look through the eyes of the gods you may see strange things. The question is how to interpret them."

"Is this yet another world or is it the future?" Tish asks, a sensible question, so I answer it directly.

"It's the future," I say. "It's 2018."

"And why does everyone have bare arms and legs and writing on their clothes?" Tish asks. She's still finding it shocking.

"I suppose because they like it." Writing on clothes was new and rare in the sixties when Sylvia was young—slogans, advertisements—then the volume of it crept up, and now it's so ubiquitous I'd stopped paying any attention to it.

"What happened to the bridge?" Dolly asks.

"It was destroyed in the Second World War, and replaced after," I say. "But the German officer in charge of the retreat refused to destroy the Ponte Vecchio. They gave him the freedom of the city after the war." There's a plaque about it on one of the buildings near the Cellini statue in the middle of the bridge. We can never remember his name and have to look it up every time.

"Why—" but just then a young Asian couple come towards

us eating gelato, and Tish and Dolly both stare at them in wonder. "Are they Chinamen?" Tish asks, tentatively.

"Japanese, I think," I say.

"Why are they here?" Dolly asks.

"Why shouldn't they come and see the best of Western art, once they've seen the best of Eastern?" I ask, irked because of course they're racist, they come from 1847, but it hasn't come up before, and they'd reacted all right to Agostino, the African gate guard, and so it's uncomfortable for us to have to acknowledge that.

"What does their art look like?" Dolly asks.

"You must have seen Chinoiserie," Tish says. It's an old-fashioned style for her, the English fad for it ended when she was a little girl, so she associates it with her mother's sisters and their dusty drawing room.

"Yes, but he said 'the best of their art' as if it were equivalent to the best of Florentine art!" Dolly says, sounding thoroughly taken aback.

"Don't squabble with each other, pay attention. Try to observe as much as you can to remember it when we wake," Ficino says. "Look at what we are being shown, these self-propelled chariots, and the order of the birds and of the strangers. It's hard to remember these things properly. If you want to see Chinese art you can travel to Xanadu. I've been there twice. Their porcelains are wonderful. I can show you some, later. But if you must question the gods, do it about something more significant."

"What's more significant than art?" Dolly asks indignantly.

Sylvia laughs aloud. The Japanese couple, licking their cones, smile indulgently at her.

"I'm sure that is very significant," Ficino says. We all look. A red truck is slowing down ahead, in fact stopping outside the apartment Sylvia has rented.

"My chair!" Sylvia says, and begins to run, reaching the door just before the driver gets back into the truck, and just as the rain starts up again. It is indeed her chair at last, being delivered hours after they said it was impossible. The driver reluctantly brings the box inside, and Sylvia triumphantly assembles the chair while more summer rain slashes down against the window.

23

FULL OF NOISES

What happened?" Miranda asks.

"What did you see?" Ficino asks in return.

Miranda's brows draw down. "You all three vanished for an instant, and then came back! You said yesterday that you had neglected spirit magic, but that was a trick of my father's."

"No such thing," Ficino says. "When you breathe the smoke of laurel leaves, sometimes you find yourself looking through the eyes of the gods. That's where we were." He straightens the wreath on his head.

"But we didn't smoke anything," Tish objects.

"No, we didn't. And isn't that curious? We invited the gods to enter here, but instead, they took us to them and gave us an oracle. There must have been some reason for them to move us to their world instead of for them to come into ours. Let me fetch paper and ink from my study, and before we confer, let us all set down where we were and what we saw, so that we have our separate accounts before we discuss them. If we had been smoking laurel leaves, I'd have had the paper ready."

"But—" Tish begins.

"This was an oracle sent direct from the gods," Ficino continues. "Do not discuss it until you have written it down!

This injunction leaves them looking blankly at each other as the little wizard bustles out of the room. "He is a wizard and a scholar," Miranda says placidly, taking a fig from the plate and pulling it apart in her fingers. "He would rather know whether there are three hypostases or seven, or some other such little piece of knowledge, than rule the world. And I too, of course, but there is no impatience in Ficino, and too much in me." She bites into the fig.

"How long were we gone?" Dolly asks.

"I have no sundial or clock here to count the time, but a little while. Long enough for me to be sure you were gone, and rub my eyes, and cast a protective cantrip on myself, and get up and put my hand out to where Ficino was sitting to make sure he was not there but invisible."

"Do the gods do this all the time?" Tish asks. She had been just getting used to Illyria, and it was alarming to be wrenched out of it and then thrust back.

"The gods have remained outside the world and done nothing to affect it for three hundred and fifty-three years," Miranda says. "And we didn't miss them at all, or at least I didn't. Did they—" She hesitates, and when she speaks she looks older and more vulnerable. "Did they say anything touching the matter of my sons?"

"No. They didn't mention it," Dolly says. He puts out a hand towards her. "It must be so difficult for you."

"Why didn't you come too?" Tish asks.

"I don't know why you three went, and I don't know why I remained," Miranda says. "Perhaps I was too connected to my earthly cares to reach the right spiritual state despite Ficino's singing and the wine and fruit, for I do feel very bound right now by the cares I would prefer to have set down." She finishes the fig and licks her fingers before wiping them on her napkin. Dolly drains his wine goblet and looks about for more, but the decanter is empty.

Ficino comes back with his arms full. He pushes aside the dishes of fruit, and neatly piles up the silver plates they were using to eat, then hands Dolly and Tish paper and quills. He puts an inkpot down where they can all three reach it. This is the method of writing they still use in the mid-nineteenth century, so Dolly and Tish are both accomplished at it. While they write, Miranda leaves them for a little while. When she comes back she brings more wine, which she warms in a copper pot over the fire, adding spices and honey and apple juice. Ficino finishes first. Miranda pours the steaming wine into their goblets and takes up Ficino's account. It doesn't take her long to read. She sniffs, and puts her hand out for Tish's. Tish hands it to her, and sips her wine, which warms her down to her toes. She wonders if it is magic or just cooking, and whether there's really a difference. Then she takes up Ficino's account, and blinks. There is no description, but rather a meticulous list.

MAGIC CHARIOTS

1) East to West

   A) Small
      White 5
      Black 8
      Grey 16
      Red 3
      Green 1
      "Taxi" 17

   B) Two-wheel
      loud 69
      silent 23

C) Large
    White 1
    Red 2
    White, open back 1
    Grey 1
    "C3 Piazza Beccaria" 2

2) West to East

A) Two-wheel
    silent 3

PEOPLE

1) East to West

    Men 17
    Women 12
    Children 4

2) West to East

    Men 13
    Women 15
    Children 2

DOGS

1) West to East

    Large white shaggy dog 1
    Small long rotund bay dog 1

BIRDS

1) East to West

    Pigeons 2
    Swallows swirling low over the river (many)

2) West to East

   Pigeons 1
   Crow 1
   Gull 1
   Heron 1

NOTE

We were in the head of Hekate, but she did not speak, though Hermes spoke and answered the young people freely. When I drew Hekate's attention to the significant large vermilion chariot, we were thrust back to our own place.

"That's amazing," Tish says, honestly, for she is amazed.

"It takes much training to be aware of everything that may augur for us," Ficino says. "I don't expect you to be this observant, yet, though you may master the art in time."

The word *augur* stops Tish, because what he has written is just like augury as she has read about it in classical sources, and yet she had recognised the street traffic as notably futuristic but comprehensible. A distance of a hundred and fifty years is very different from five hundred. But Ficino is a wizard, and he knows a lot more than she does. It occurs to her that in her discussion of careers the night before, wizard was never mentioned as a possibility, but Ficino is talking as if she would naturally be spending a lot of time at magic. She swallows her wine. "The silent two-wheeled vehicles are velocipedes," she says, hesitantly. "And the noisy vehicles seemed to me to be some kind of steam-powered horseless carriages that don't need rails, like the omnibuses of London and Paris."

Ficino shakes his head. "That's what we were talking about before. Progress. It doesn't work here. It's irrelevant to us, except as divination. The ones I marked as 'C3' and 'Taxi' had those names in glowing letters. You didn't observe them?"

"I was mostly looking at the people," Tish says. She is still a little shocked by the bare arms and legs.

"But do the names mean anything to you?"

She shakes her head. Dolly looks up from what he is writing. The names seem to have some distant connection, but he can't quite remember what it is. He bends over it again.

"Did you notice the birds?" Ficino asks.

"Only the great crowd of swallows," Tish admits.

"I'm sure the heron was significant. And perhaps the dogs."

Dolly stops writing and hands his paper to Miranda. Ficino starts reading Tish's.

Miranda glances through Dolly's account and nods. "It seems you all experienced much the same events, though you have very different ways of describing them. Dolly says that the male voice, who you identify as Hermes, Ficino, said you were in the year 2018, and that the bridge Ponte alle Grazie was destroyed by Germans in the Second World War. If this can be trusted, then there have been two wars either between worlds, or else involving the whole world."

"There had been no such wars by our time, unless you count the Napoleonic wars as encompassing the whole world. Certainly they were fought on all the oceans. But I never heard them called a world war," Tish says. (The words, so familiar to us as to pass unexamined, taste strange on her tongue.)

"Between different worlds seems more likely," Miranda says. "A world is very big, and a war that reaches out to encompass all of it seems implausible. But we know there are different worlds and that they touch."

"Yes, perhaps, but then why would the Germans destroy a bridge in Firenze?" Ficino asks. "And why would the man who refused to destroy the other bridge be given the freedom of the city?"

"Ah, the Germans, or the Austrians anyway, who speak German, were ruling Firenze," Dolly says, hesitantly. "So that bit made sense to me."

"In the *Divine Comedy,* the souls in Hell were always asking Dante how Firenze was, and breaking their poor damned hearts over the answers," Ficino says. "My mind is set on higher things, but I understand those poor souls a little better now. Please don't tell me any more details like that unless it becomes relevant."

There is a little uncomfortable pause.

"I had never imagined the threat of invasion from other worlds," Miranda says. "I never really thought there were more worlds than these two."

"If there are more than one, then there must be many of them," Ficino says. "And you know the few strangers who have come from my world have changed everything here. Manetto made himself Duke and ended the Republic of Thalia. And Pico and I truly changed everything."

"But not like a war," Miranda says. "Imagine troops stepping through anywhere, in the heart of the most defended places." She looks suspiciously at Dolly, as if she suspects him of being a scout for an invading army.

"That can't happen unless it is the will of the gods," Ficino says. "And the painting is here."

"I intend to go to Xanadu," Dolly announces unexpectedly.

"Good," Miranda says, emphatically. "You'll enjoy that. And perhaps the gods won't pay much attention to you there."

(What? Xanadu? Do I still want to escape from her, despite everything? No, it's a bit of Dolly's native character showing through. I made him out of a younger self who did want to get away.

"That seems to me to be one of the first independent signs of life Dolly has shown," Sylvia says to me. "You're keeping too tight a grip on him, you have to loosen up a bit."

"What, and let him go to Xanadu?"

"Why not? They have literally all the time in the world. It'll be a hundred and fifty years before we could possibly get there, even if we could really do it. Dolly can go to Xanadu and have a lifetime of adventures before he comes back. I'd have let you go to Constantinople that time except that it was a prequel and I'd painted myself into a corner."

She has never admitted that before. But Dolly won't go haring off to Xanadu instantly either.

Now you may say that we shouldn't have thrust them into modern Firenze and confused them with all these things, to which I can only answer that we didn't. The walls between worlds are thin sometimes, at least inside her head, and she hadn't been able to write and they came bursting out on their own. I, at least, had nothing to do with it. Blame the Italian chair company, or anyway their terrible delivery company. But even they have fault but no intentionality here. And now she has her chair and is sitting in it typing, and they're unlikely to do it again, even if Ficino does smoke laurel leaves.

"Do you always let him into your head if he smokes laurel leaves?" I ask, suddenly curious. "For the last forty years?"

"Yes," Sylvia says. "Four hundred years for him. He smoked laurel leaves historically, and claimed to have visions. I always said it worked, in the books, that he reached the gods . . . and anyway, he never does anything except count cars and birds and treat them as oracularly significant. It's mostly when I'm at bus stops."

(It would be hypocritical in the extreme if I said anything against this.)

Miranda cuts slices of cake and passes them around. "Before you go to Xanadu, you'll stay here long enough to help with this matter of Caliban and my sons?" Miranda asks. "If, as seems likely, that was why the gods sent you here now?"

"Don't you want to go home?" Tish asks Dolly.

"Why, if that was the future of Firenze, full of fumes and noise and half-naked people? I don't want to live to see that. And I wouldn't, would I? Because he said it was 2018, and if I lived to 1918 I'd be doing well. But here I could live that long, and much longer. It's much more of a question of why you do want to go home?"

"I'm not sure that I do," Tish admits. "There's so much more for me here."

Miranda picks up Tish's account. "Bare arms. Short skirts. Wars between worlds."

"We won't have those things here," Ficino says.

"Did you do something to stop that?" Dolly asks.

"Yes," Ficino says. "It was just before Pico's sacrifice. We did the magic together. It was setting everything up for the triumph over death. If we wanted to keep the Renaissance forever, we needed to make Progress irrelevant to us. So while the Renaissance had to end in the world where you and I were born, here it could go on forever. It's just the same as the way people have to die there, but here we can live on."

Dolly has longed all his life to live in the Renaissance, Tish only since she came to Firenze. So his impulse is to ask why it couldn't have been preserved in his world too, whereas hers is to question whether there might not be some things about Progress that are good. While of course she would, like any sensible human being, prefer great art to steam trains, might there not by human ingenuity and the help of friendly deities be some way it could be possible to have both? But before either of them can put their thoughts into words Miranda takes up Ficino's account again.

"So what do you think these things mean?"

"Herons are messengers of the gods, and a symbol of longevity and solitude," Ficino says. "Also of finding things that are lost."

"And related to that, the people of Sarlola say herons are associated with forgetting," Miranda says.

"So could it relate to Geryon," Tish asks. "As he was almost lost and forgotten up there in solitude, but now he's found?"

"Very good," Ficino says. "You'll make an augur yet. The heron is probably the most important, as it was the last bird I saw. But there was also a gull, a crow, and a pigeon. Gulls mean freedom and selfishness. A crow is often death, or the spirit of the dead, but it can also be a messenger. Pigeons mean the young, gossip, accepting responsibility for your words. Seeing the four of them close together, they're probably related."

"So selfishness, somebody who's dead, and responsibility for your words?"

"It could be telling us that Giulia has gone on to a fortunate rebirth," Dolly suggests.

"Or it could be saying that my father is dead," Miranda says.

"What?" Ficino asks, turning to her, his face full of surprise.

"And the birds in the other direction, a great flock of swallows and two more pigeons?" Miranda taps the paper. "That would fit too, and his soul on the wind. As for these chariots, I have no skill at reading such symbols, but the vast preponderance of them is from bad to good, and all the ones going east were silent, and on two wheels only. And Dolly wrote that one of those riders was a priest."

"Has there been time?" Ficino asks, looking stricken.

"Time for what?" Dolly asks. Tish too is frowning in perplexity.

"Time for Caliban to have gone to Tempest Island and killed Prospero," Ficino says.

Miranda is counting on her fingers. "If he went there directly when he left here, then he could have reached there by now."

"But he forgave Prospero," Tish objects.

"In your play, perhaps," Miranda says, scornfully. "But never in real life."

"In our play Prospero gave the island back to Caliban," Dolly says.

"That would certainly have made it easier for Caliban to forgive him," Miranda says.

"Sixteen grey. Seventeen 'taxis,'" Ficino murmurs to himself.

"You disappeared, and it reminded me at once of my father's magic," Miranda says.

"I think I see hope in these numbers," Ficino announces. "I think the gods want us to act for them in some way. I think we need to find out more about what they want us to do. Are you both sure you don't have any idea?"

"Very sure, I'm sorry," Tish says.

Dolly frowns. "I feel they are outside Illyria, in our world, in that future, and that they want to be here. And the word *taxi*, I don't know it, but every time you say it, it resonates."

"Perhaps the gods need our aid in entering the world," Ficino says. "Perhaps we need to set up a greater magic to draw them than this simple dinner invitation."

"Taxi, taxi, taxi," says Tish. Dolly shakes his head in frustration.

"I think these things speak of my father's death," Miranda says. "Caliban might have been looking for me there, after he found my house was empty."

Ficino looks at her, and nods. "He had better not find you. You should stay above ground."

"Will you confirm my father's fate?" Miranda asks.

"The stars have been saying that a great change is coming," Ficino says. "Yes. I will look in the picture, both for that and for the way we can aid the gods. Come on." He gestures to them all. Dolly puts down his untouched wine goblet, and they all rise. Miranda takes up a candle, and Ficino leads them out of the banqueting hall and around the portico, past the stairs going up and down, and then opens the door to his study. There is no fire here tonight, and the room is dark. Ficino waves his hand, and lily lamps around the room spring to life one by one, filling the room with a green-gold radiance. Miranda snuffs the candle, because the room is as bright as day. The vermilion curtains are drawn over the picture on the chimney breast. Ficino takes hold of them, then without opening them turns to the others.

"This picture was once a gateway between worlds. It was painted by Brunelleschi, in our Firenze. I used it to pass between here and there, several times, with Pico, and alone after his triumph. When I left your world for good, in 1499, I brought it with me, thus closing the gate. Since then, it has been attuned to me. When I do not look at it, it reflects simply what is in my mind. When I look at it, it can show me what I bid it, though sometimes it tries to trick me. So first, I will look away, and you three can look into it, then I will turn and see what it shows to me."

"So it will show us what you're thinking?" Tish asks.

"The poetic pictured image of it," Ficino explains. "You open the curtain, Dolly."

He turns away, and Dolly, with a certain reluctance, takes hold of the red velvet curtain and draws it aside. The panel shows an old man with a long white beard and a starry robe lying on a bier, while strange-shaped people mourn. Miranda cries out when she sees it. Ficino turns and looks, and immediately the picture changes. It doesn't change in the way we expect pictures to change, like a cut in a film, or like slides changing in Power-Point, or in the magic lanterns that preceded it and with which Dolly and Tish are familiar. It changes the way illusion pictures change, like a Necker cube when it turns inside out, or the face/vase illusion. The decorous mourning scene turns inside out and becomes a fallen castle. Miranda makes another little sound.

"We were right then," Ficino says. "But Prospero was not necessarily there, as you were not inside your house. Though the gods would be unlikely to bother to send us auguries of mere physical destruction."

He touches the four fingers of both hands to his temples under the laurel crown, with his thumbs thrust outward in a curious gesture. The picture changes again. This time it shows Sylvia standing near the Ponte Vecchio, with a taxi passing behind her, and a white Vespa, and a big fluffy samoyed. A waxing crescent moon shines clear in the fading afterglow behind her, and a single star. But Sylvia is not alone, or rather, she shows in triplicate: herself as a child, and as she was when she first came to Firenze, flanking the older self she is now.

"Hekate," Miranda says. "At the crossroads."

"Now isn't that interesting," Ficino says.

24

BRAVE NEW WORLD

As Sylvia paces and mutters around the room, working on the difficult conversation that is coming up between Orsino and Geryon, I am working on my plan. Having Ficino invite us directly came close to working, or anyway to doing something that thinned the walls between worlds. But we were all still within her finite, bounded, limited head. And to get us into Illyria, both of us, all of us, I need to explain her better, which means telling more of her story. But there's time. At least in Illyria there is time. I deliberately chose the time for that reason. Here, I'm not sure. She went through all that treatment last time, the operation, the chemo, and when mortality comes that close, you can't know. But she seems as spry as ever as she paces the room, even occasionally hopping up onto the step in front of the windows to gaze out at the river and the tower and the hills. There is nothing as beautiful in Montreal, or anywhere we can think of in Canada or the US. There is spectacular scenery, Niagara Falls, the Grand Canyon, the mountains of Northern Arizona and Nevada, but nothing that looks so much like art, and certainly nothing that has any trace of the human in it does. The tower of San Niccoló, part of the vanished walls, is set just where it needs to be to create the perspective. It's placed where you'd place it if you were making it up. This is the landscape that shaped the art that shaped the way we see all landscape.

"Why did you tell them about the Second World War?" she asks me unexpectedly, as she looks out, her chin cupped in her hands, her elbows on the sill.

I am embarrassed. "It was a mistake. I forgot. I was addressing them the way I'd address the reader, explaining, contextualising, augmenting so they'd understand what they were looking it. I forgot they were real, unlike the reader, who is purely imaginary, external, futuristic. I didn't think about how they'd take it."

"Characters do that, they grab on to some tiny thing you didn't at all intend in that way and go haring off with it in the wrong direction. I don't mind. It's better than having to make everything up all the time, which is a real slog. Though the idea of wars between worlds, and that there might have been two of them, is so weird."

"It's been done. Feist's *Magician* does it. It's a bit like Middle Earth invaded by Tékumel."

"Yes. But it hasn't been done much, there's plenty more that could be done with it. It's an interesting thought. There could even have been more than two wars, because there could have been more since. And the way Dolly assumed the Germans then must have been connected with the Austrians who were in Firenze in his day . . . they imagine they're living in a universe where Italy was never reunited, or decolonized if you prefer, where there was no First or Second World War but instead wars between worlds happened." She laughs. "I could do something fun with that. But it's not really what we want this time."

"But having characters jump to wrong conclusions from available data is something there isn't enough of in fantasy."

"In fiction generally," she agrees. "But the reader can jump to wrong conclusions too, and that's usually very bad and puts

216 | JO WALTON

them out of sympathy with the text. That's something you need to watch out for if you're trying to tell your own stories. For instance if you have shapeshifters, saying they rolled their eyes in the usual metaphorical meaning of the term can be a terrible idea. You can't say somebody's world exploded and mean it emotionally if Alderaan just blew up."

"I think we can trust any plausible reader not only to be prepared to follow us into the rose garden but to know what the Second World War was."

She looks east to the Ponte Vecchio, spared by the German official, Gerhard Wolf, who put art and history ahead of victory, though he probably realised that his war was surely lost already. He also dragged his feet on sending art to Berlin, forged documents for some of Firenze's Jews, protested the arrest of innocents, and sometimes even managed to get them released. The Ponte Santa Trìnita, the bridge designed by Michelangelo, took three charges to blow up, and in the fifties they pulled the stones out of the Arno and set the bridge up again, reconstructed as closely as they could to what it had been. Two hundred and forty-three of Firenze's Jews didn't manage to get forged papers from Gerhard or hide in the house of Marchese Serlupi, the ambassador of San Merino. They were sent to camps. Thirteen survived. Thirteen. And as if two hundred and thirty Florentine deaths wasn't bad enough, it's just the drop in the bucket that lets you see how big that bucket really is. Every single death in that holocaust of death was an individual human life, invaluable and precious and special. The numbers hide that because they're so big. We can imagine and regret two hundred and thirty cruel and wanton murders, but we balk at millions, cannot quite take them in.

And of course the best thing about the Holocaust is that it's safely over, over so long ago. It ended the year Sylvia was born, and that makes it easier to think about and feel we're on the right side of history. But there are atrocities going on right now, and we're standing looking out of a window in Firenze at one of the most beautiful views in the world and doing nothing whatsoever to help. Indeed, instead of helping we're planning to literally escape into a fantasy world. There's a banner hanging on the Palazzo Vecchio calling for "Verità per Giulio Regeni," truth for Giulio Regeni, an Italian postdoc at Cambridge University in England who was researching Egyptian labor history when (probably) the Egyptian police arrested him and tortured him to death, very nastily, over a long time. Certainly it was the Egyptian police who covered it up. Italy, Pope Francis, Cambridge University, academics all over the world who care about freedom of research, and the European Parliament in Strasbourg, have spoken out for him, and for the others like him. The reaction to his death has shone a light into a dark place.

But it is only one of many very dark places, and it's not clear yet whether that light has made any difference. He died in 2016, and the banner is still there, on one of Firenze's most beautiful and prominent monuments, crying out for truth. But people are being detained and tortured and murdered even as I set these words down, and more of them as you read them in the imaginary future. War, like death, once commonplace and part of most people's experience, has become unusual for us in the First World, which for seventy-three years, for Sylvia's lifetime, could be defined as where war is not. But terrible things are happening, and some of them in our names. Do what you can. Every little bit helps. Speak up for the voiceless, protect the powerless, open up choices for the choiceless. As for us, we're not going to be here to help for very much longer no matter what. But that's always true for everyone. We're all going to die. Finding ways to save other people is one form of immortality. I can't take everyone into Illyria, at least not for long. Gerhard Wolf saved as many as he could. And thirteen of those he couldn't save came home again to Firenze. Look up the figures for Sarajevo.

"A war between worlds might have been better," I say.

She sighs. "But not this time. And—well—we may never have time to tell that story. No, the trouble with their augury is that it makes Caliban much more sinister, and I've always liked him. I didn't want him to be a villain. Or Orsino either. So now I have to write this next scene, and it's hard. I may need to go back and put in some backstory." The voices of the swallows are carried to us on the wind as they swoop low over the water, almost on a level with her eyes. "Are you still trying to save me? In the real world?"

"Yes," I admit.

"It's not that characters aren't real, not that you aren't. I don't mean that. It's just that there's a difference between that kind of real and the kind I am, or the men rowing that boat out there, or Giulio Regeni. Remember that term in Duane's *The Door Into Shadow*, real enough to bite?" We look at the men sculling backwards along the Arno, their oars breaking the light on the surface to fall into fractured fractals. They all have lives and homes and stories and complications, and we will never know them.

"I already saved you once," I venture.

I expect her to dismiss this, or dispute, but she doesn't. She's quiet for a long time. The boat disappears under the bridge and into the distance.

"Steve," she says.

"Steve," I agree. "You're going to have to talk about that time."

"We could leave it out."

"It's five years of your life."

"It's nothing compared to the Holocaust. To what happened to Giulio Regeni. To so many people. It was all petty and personal and—"

"You matter. It was bad enough, and it happened to you. And

you have to talk about it if I want to get us into Illyria. And I really do."

She doesn't say anything, but I can tell she is indulging me. She goes back to the chair and the computer, and begins a new chapter.

25

KALI YUGA

She went from her mother to Steve like a wolf that has gnawed off a paw to get out of a trap escaping directly into fetters. He looked to her like freedom, like love. He did get her away from her mother, and he did love her. "If you call that love," she says, scornfully, now that Idris has taught her what love really is. "It was like being closed into a smaller and smaller space, and diminished and punished whatever I did."

"For your own good," I add.

"Oh yes, he always said it was for my own good. Especially when he hit me. And he'd be so sorry afterwards, so abject until I forgave him, and then he'd be nice to me for a little while until I made him do it again. That's what he said, that I made him do it. If I'd only behave properly he wouldn't have to do it." She shakes her head. "I was such a fool. And it feels so long ago, longer ago than my childhood in many ways, further from who I am. That time was terrible." She pauses, then says. "Thank you for getting me away from him."

This is a story of a terrible time, but it has a happy ending, an ending you know already, where two years after she got away from him she went to Firenze alone and started to write the Illyria books, and then met Idris and had the girls. The time with Steve happened, and affected her, but then it was over, and she was all right, better than all right, successful, happy.

"That's true," she says. "But I wouldn't go through it again even if it is what it takes for me to be me. I only barely made it out. It took everything and cost me so much."

She always imagined that after she graduated she'd leave Montreal, leave Canada, go to the Europe she had read about and imagined. Her major, which surprises most people, wasn't in English or History, but Classics. She wanted to go to graduate school in England, and she could have. It was the expansive sixties, there were grants and enthusiasm, and for the first time women could be scholars who weren't rare exceptions. It was still harder for women, but she believed in herself and thought she was ready for it. She really wanted it. She went to McGill very much as an extension of going to school, taking the same trams and buses, using the same library, living at home, working on her papers, evading her mother's restrictions, postponing her escape. Her father was sick, dying, and she felt he needed her. But she was going to go to Cambridge in the fall of 1967, and everything would be different. Instead, she got married, and moved across the city from Griffintown to NDG. Steve, who closed all the doors, started off looking like an open door, a fast escape, and a way to everything she wanted.

"An open door into a noose," she says.

He said he was going to look after her, and that she could work on her scholarship on her own, and read a lot and maybe write. "But not your hobbity nonsense," Steve clarifies. She had shown him some of what she was writing then. "You could write real books. Books I'd be proud of." It seems miraculous to her that a man so much older and more experienced, so confident and intelligent and well established can really want her. He is ten years older than she is. In 1967, when they marry, she is twenty-three and he is thirty-four. He is a lawyer, well established in his father's firm. He wears hand-tailored suits and drives a black Camaro. He owns a house on Monkland Avenue, a big attractive townhouse, two bedrooms, a garage, a patch of garden with an elm tree and lots of bluebells. She loves the tree. It is dead now. She walked past the house last spring on her way to have acupuncture and noticed that the elm has been replaced by a magnolia. Steve doesn't live there anymore. He moved to Toronto in 1979, afraid of the separatists and their talk of secession.

Sylvia's father died in the late winter of 1967, cancer, a long, slow, painful process. She met Steve three months later at a party given by the parents of her college friend Miriam for the engagement of Miriam's brother Daniel.

"I almost didn't go," she says. They were only a few weeks from finals and graduation, and she wasn't recovered from the shock of her father's death. Sylvia's plan was to go to Europe as soon as she graduated, at the beginning of June, to travel around on her savings, sleeping in hostels and eating cheaply, seeing Paris and Athens and Rome before ending up in London and taking her place in Cambridge to begin her postgraduate studies in the fall. She intended to send her brothers and sisters postcards of wonderful places, and believed they would envy her.

Miriam begged her to come along to the party to support her. "Daniel's fiancée is as thin as a rake, and my mother will be trying to make me feel guilty for not fitting into a tiny dress like hers. And she'll keep saying that wedding bells are in the air and trying to introduce me to all the nice Jewish boys. She likes you, Syl, she thinks you're good for me, and if you're there she'll tone it down to bearable. We don't have to stay long." At that time, Miriam had a secret boyfriend called Jamal, an exchange student from Nigeria. He was only a secret from Miriam's parents, who lived in a big house in Côte-St-Luc. Miriam later, in the seventies, comes out as a lesbian, and in the nineties she and her long-term partner, Chrissie, are one of the first same-sex couples to marry in Quebec. By then she is confident and outspoken, not the girl who needed her hand held at her brother's engagement party.

Sylvia, who was used to telling Mrs Levi that Miriam is studying at her house, and having Miriam similarly cover for her to her mother, sighed and went along to the party. She had no idea what would be appropriate to wear to a Jewish engagement party. "Oh anything," Miriam said. At that time Sylvia never had much money for clothes. She always felt over or underdressed. She was lucky this time. She had a long white linen smock, with white-on-white embroidery around the neck, which looked and felt cool. She swept her hair up on top of her head with the Japanese comb Miriam gave her for her birthday, and by what felt like a miracle it stayed where she had put it. It was one of the first times she tried the style that later becomes her everyday look. She isn't beautiful, not then, not ever, but she sometimes manages to look interesting and distinguished. That was one of the first times. "If only I'd failed. If only I'd looked a frump and he hadn't noticed me and I'd gone off to Cambridge and had a completely different life," she says now.

The party was terrible. Most of the people there were of the older generation, and although it was 1967, the summer of love, almost all of the younger people were wearing suits or very formal clothes. For three hours, Sylvia told Miriam at thirty minute intervals that she isn't fat (which was true), while Mrs Levy kept pressing them to eat fish paste, roast chicken, iced cake, and chocolate pastries, in between telling Miriam she just needs to slim down a bit and she'd be a beautiful girl like Sylvia. If this was better than the way she would be otherwise, Sylvia was glad for her friend's sake that she came.

In the third hour, Steve, who was in business with Daniel's fiancée's parents, or something like that, came over to her. "How do you manage to look so cool on such a hot day when everyone else looks as if they've been basted and roasted? Looking at you is like having a long cool drink," he said. "I'm tired of this party, but I'm delighted with you. Can I drive you home? And could I see you again sometime? Who are you? Where did you spring from. I'm sure I've never seen you before."

"I'm Sylvia Harrison," she said. "I'm at McGill with Miriam."

"A college girl," he said, in a tone that edged on disapproving.

"Oh, I'm about to graduate," she said, eager already to agree with him, to have him like her, approve of her. And indeed, he smiled. He was the first person she knew to have a car. In Montreal, then and now, you don't really need one. But getting home from Côte-St-Luc would mean two long bus rides on a hot day. She agreed to save time and for the novelty of it, and because she already liked him. He blinked a little when he learned she lives in Griffintown, but drove her there without a murmur, dropping her off outside the front door, and waiting as she runs up the steps.

A few days later, he took her to Expo '67, out on the island. And in that wonderful magical carnival atmosphere, with the pavilions and the art and the music, Steve seemed not just steady but exciting, and even his masterful way of making up his mind for both of them seemed charming and not controlling.

"I should have seen that as a warning sign," Sylvia says. But back then she loved everything about him, from his quirking eyebrows to his neat loafers. She even saw the way he won't speak French as a charming personal quirk. Her French was good enough for both of them, not to mention her Latin and Greek. He let her order for them at restaurants—that is, he decided what they would both eat, and he let her inform the waiter. She thought this was an equal division of labour, not seeing yet how all the power is on his side and all the work on hers, not understanding how he was patronizing her, how he regarded her French as something that reflected her low-class origins.

Montreal is a French city, it always has been, and it has become more so through Sylvia's lifetime. At that time there were still some Anglophones like Steve who refused to acknowledge that they were a minority in the province. Many of them fled, like Steve, when they realised that the democratic tide was flowing against them. When Bill 101, which mandated that businesses must work in French and children must be educated in that language, was passed, there was a mass exodus. The Anglophones who stayed were prepared to accept the reality of the situation. Throughout the sixties there were mailbox bombings for separatism, and the violence culminated in the October Crisis of 1970, when a diplomat and a government minister were kidnapped and the government imposed martial law and petrified all those in favour of violence. This led, eventually, to the two referendums of 1980 and 1995 and the decision of Quebec, both times, to stay in Canada. Steve's refusal to say more than a polite "Bonjour" in French was a reflection of his arrogance, but it wasn't, in the late sixties, as unusual as it would be later. By now almost everyone like him had left. "And good riddance," says Sylvia, emphatically. In English.

When she met Steve she was still very young, and, because of her mother, she had not had a real boyfriend before. She had been waiting until she could get away, and spending most of her time working and reading and dreaming and helping to look after her father. She was not just technically inexperienced, like many of her college friends, but truly without any sexual or romantic experience at all. Steve was not Catholic, he said that he was not anything, but he agreed to marry in church amiably enough. Then he suggested that they get married not in her childhood church but in the church of St Monica on Terrebonne, which would be her new parish church. She saw this then as exciting and not as part of Steve's plan to detach her from all her existing connections and make her dependent only on him. She confessed her utter inexperience to him, and he was charmed. "You were like a sleeping princess waiting for me to awaken you with a kiss," he said. "Like Cinderella."

But what was Cinderella's life with the prince really like? Or the little goose girl with the king? Powerful men who choose young naïve girls who don't know how to navigate in their worlds may be looking for somebody they can victimize.

"All these warning signs!" she says now. "All these red flags!" She didn't see them, and neither did any of her friends. One professor expressed disappointment that she wouldn't be pursuing her career, but that was the only shadow cast; everyone else seemed perfectly delighted in her new choice, her abrupt swerve, her changed priorities. She was doing what women were supposed to do, but she tells herself she and Steve are different, their lives will be different. His life was certainly materially different from her parents' lives, though he corrected her when she said he was rich. "The Levys are rich, and the Goldsteins; Arnold's rich, and the Singletons. I'm just comfortably off. If it hadn't been for what my father left me I wouldn't have been able to afford to buy this house." She learned not to compliment his wealth, and conceded that she did not understand it. "My Cinderella," he called her again. He was already criticizing her clothes, and she was already trying to dress the way he preferred.

They went to Niagara Falls for their honeymoon. "We'll go to Europe together," Steve said. "Not this year, because work is so busy and I'll have to plan to take the time off properly. We won't go on a shoestring the way you meant to. We'll stay in the best hotels, eat the best food, meet people, artists and actors. We'll take a whole month and travel. Paris, the South of France, Italy." He was working hard at that time to get her, and she fell for it completely. He even charmed her mother. Sylvia committed herself to Steve like a ship launching itself with optimism and confidence to the mercy of the sea and the wind, soon to be

driven onto the unseen shoals—or like Isaac meekly lying down under Abraham's knife.

The honeymoon was not what she expected. Steve was as attentive as ever, if not more attentive. In 1967, Quebec still had name change on marriage, though by the time she married Idris it had been forbidden, and now everyone has to use the name on their birth certificate. But Steve spent a lot of time that first honeymoon week addressing her as Mrs Linton, and even Mme Linton, trying, and often succeeding, to make her blush. Niagara Falls was spectacular, and being there was quite different from photographs, because they cannot show the gulf of air between the falling water and where you are standing. Steve joked about going over the falls in a barrel, and took her to an old-fashioned museum about people who have crossed the falls, where he read every word of every exhibit and expected her to do the same. She did, of course, wanting to do the right thing, eager to please him. She bought new clothes for the honeymoon, many of which made him frown. "Never mind, Mrs Linton, I'll dress you," he said. "I'll teach you taste." For now, he undressed her.

She didn't know what she'd expected, but from literature and from what her friends had said she had imagined sex differently. It's not that she didn't enjoy it, at least at first, but that Steve didn't seem to want her to initiate anything, or even to participate. He wanted her to keep still and be a passive recipient of the sexual largesse he chose to bestow upon her. He smacked her hands away when she tried to reciprocate.

"That doesn't count as the first time he hit me," she says. "That was playful. Well, mostly playful. *Naughty naughty*, he said. Ugh. I should have got up and walked away right then. I wish I had."

Once committed and cut off from all help, she was trapped. Steve bought new clothes for her. He detached her from her family, from her friends, by the expedient of finding them a terrible nuisance. When her younger sister, Maureen, was there when he came home from work one day, he was polite to her, even charming, but he said afterwards to Sylvia that he would prefer it if she didn't see quite so much of those people. She tried to limit their visits to when he was in work, but they found it very hard to understand his restrictions. When he found her mother browbeating her, he forbade her to come to the house, which Sylvia at the time saw as chivalrous and protective.

Steve expected a very high and very specific standard of behaviour from her with his friends. The first time he did hit her, more than a year after their marriage, it was for flirting with one of his clients. She didn't even understand the accusation. "You seemed to be having a good time with David," he said, in a friendly tone, after their guests left and while she was still tidying up, putting leftovers away and separating plates and glasses ready to wash. They had eaten the terrible food of the era, half grapefruits soused in sherry and sprinkled with brown sugar and broiled, chicken with grape sauce, and a chocolate velvet pie. Everyone had complimented her on the pie.

"Hmm? David? Yes, he seems very nice," she said, relieved Steve wasn't reproaching her for errors she didn't even know were errors, that he seemed to have enjoyed the evening for once. He had drunk rather a lot of the acidic white French wine, and she had had two glasses herself.

"Maybe too good a time?" Steve suggested, steel in his voice now, but she wasn't paying attention, was trying to decide whether it would make him angrier if she washed dishes now, or angrier if she left them until the morning. Even before the violence, when it was no more than a raised voice and biting sarcasm, she was already attuned to his anger, vibrating to it like a harp string. She was trying to tiptoe around his moods and desires, making herself smaller to fit into the space he left her, though no space would ever be small enough.

Perhaps it was because she wasn't paying attention, or because it seemed to her so absurd that Steve could seriously believe she'd been having too good a time with shy David, with his thick horn-rimmed glasses and bald spot, who clearly adored his wife, Ruth. The blow came out of nowhere, she wasn't aware of it at all, one moment she was moving used paper napkins into a pile, and the next she was on the floor with her ears ringing. Tears came to her eyes from the force of the blow, and immediately Steve was apologising, saying he didn't know what had come over him, he just loved her so much he got jealous and couldn't bear to think of her deceiving him with another man. He cried, and begged her to forgive him, and then they went to bed where, with her head still ringing from the blow and the fall, she had to console him for having hurt her. He hadn't started saying yet that she had made him do it. That came later. But he did make her apologize for flirting with poor David, who she hardly dared speak to the next time he and Ruth came around.

As time went on, the length of time it took for him to stop hitting her and apologize became longer, and the length of time between times when he hit her became shorter, and the amount of space she had to stand and breathe and be Sylvia became ever smaller. Her attention was all given to appeasing him, and her own thoughts and emotions became distant from her, wrapped up and held away, so that sometimes, at midday, eating an apple, she might realise that the night before she had been furiously angry, or resentful, or fiercely distressed, but she could not recognise it until later. When he came home at night he would ask her what she did with her days, and disapproved now not only of seeing family or friends but of visits to the library and walks in the park. These were the things which restored some of her equilibrium. He mocked the books she escaped into. She started hiding the books and lying about the library trips, and then he punished her when he found out about them. One day his sister mentioned having seen her in the Atwater Library. After she left, he made

Sylvia admit her guilt and then he threw her across the room and broke her arm. This was around the time of the October Crisis, which she lived through numbly, her focus on trying not to upset Steve. This was when her other grandmother died, and she felt she had to apologize to Steve for it.

One day she was reading the newspaper while drinking her morning coffee, reading about the arrests, the suspension of habeas corpus, and she suddenly remembered the Cuban Missile Crisis, how frightened she was, how alive, how aware of her mortality and afraid for the world, poised on the knife edge. Now she felt numb, she didn't care about any of it, she was only reading the paper so she would have the information to echo Steve's opinions when he came home. She was appalled at herself, in that moment of clarity, but she told herself she loved him, and what could she do? She knew other wives who wore makeup to cover bruises. They didn't talk about it, but she had slowly come to accept it as normal and necessary.

"It's hard to say how I went along with it all," she says to me, still angry with herself after all this time. "It built slowly, I suppose. But I don't know why you have to talk about it. Almost nobody knows anything about it anymore."

If she'd been in prison for five years, unjustly sentenced and then pardoned, you wouldn't consider her weaker when you found out about it. But you wouldn't think it didn't matter, that it made no difference to who she was afterwards. Let's get on with it. Illyria is waiting for us, and escape.

26

ONE LIFE, ONE DEATH, AND ALL THE THINGS IN BETWEEN

I wasn't there for any of that. I only heard about it later. I don't know where I was, really dead, or somewhere hidden in her head. I'm only telling you about it because she won't. But the next part, that I was there for.

It is five years after they marry, 1972. Steve comes home from work one day and finds Sylvia sitting at the stripped pine kitchen table, staring into space, the breakfast dishes still unwashed in the sink, a cold cup of coffee half drunk in front of her. "You have nothing to do but keep yourself and the house nice for me, so why can't you do it? Have you spent the whole day reading one of your ridiculous books, or pretending you can write one when you're too stupid even to clean up, which you'd think even an idiot from the slums could do? A girl from Griffintown, a Catholic? You fooled me, Sylvia, like you try to fool everyone, putting on airs, a first-class degree from McGill, going to write a book, but you're just one generation from barefoot peasant! All those brothers and sisters, living like animals! But I won't have you doing that here, do you understand me?"

She looks up at him, trying to find words to say what she has to say, but entirely incapable of it. She has been looking for words for most of the day, since she came home from the doctor that morning. She is an animal in a trap, and she recognises that. She knows he will hit her when she tells him. And she associates the way he will hit her with the way her mother hit her the day she killed me. But there is no father now to come and rescue her, no protection. She knows he will hit her now whether she says anything or not. So she says nothing, she sits passive, the way he prefers, except that by now anything she does is wrong, anything, everything, and he strikes and strikes. She doesn't try to defend herself.

It isn't the first time he went too far. When he broke her arm she agreed with him in the hospital that it was her clumsiness, with a little laugh that she despised herself for later. Her clumsiness, always tripping over her own feet, not looking where she is going, and she has such pale skin, she bruises so easily. These are lies he tells about her. It is her own complicity that makes her angry. If this had happened later, if it happened now, then the broken arm might have been an intervention point, the doctor might have looked at the break and the contusions and joined the dots of old bruises to draw the correct conclusions. But it was 1970 and domestic abuse cases were barely on the horizon. But this time, whether because her passivity excited him or angered him, or just by chance, he knocks out a tooth, a bottom tooth on the right. There is a great deal of blood, and an astonishing amount of pain, so that she can't keep from crying, even though she knows it makes him angrier.

He is still angry driving her to the emergency room, cursing her every time she whimpers. "Stupid bitch, making a huge fuss about nothing." But she knows that by the next day he will be repentant, offering her love, and she will have to forgive him, because he loves her and this is his way of showing it, and besides, there is the baby. Steve didn't want a baby yet, and he will blame her for getting pregnant, not that she wanted to, but she knows he will make it her fault and punish her for it. But when she thinks about it, she thinks about him hitting a child. He is a tall man, broad-shouldered, imposing, strong. A child will be so small, and it will be uncontrolled, and cry, and make messes, and do things he won't like, and it will not be its fault. He has convinced her that when he hurts her it is her fault, but the child, she is utterly sure, is innocent, and won't be to blame, not for anything, not for years, it won't understand but Steve will punish it anyway. Steve will be unjust, she says to herself, looking out of the car window at the whirling snow. He will be unjust to the innocent child, and perhaps she doesn't deserve it either. It is her first actual rebellion for a long time.

He drives her to the Jewish General, because it is both the closest and the best hospital. The snow is thick on the ground, and more snow is falling, but the streets are well ploughed, as usual in Montreal Steve drives carefully. There was enough money for a new car the year before, but not to go to Europe, which he keeps promising and dangling before her then snatching away. She has no idea how much money he has. She can't stop crying, and she knows it isn't just the pain. He is unjust, and it is his fault, not always and only hers. She is desperate. He has deliberately and carefully got her into a position where movement in any direction feels impossible. But the child—she knows the child will be another tie, binding her ever tighter to Steve, that she will have to protect it, and will time and time again fail to protect it, until it is harmed, either physically damaged by Steve or until it learns to despise her as he does. She imagines a son hitting her because she is slow and stupid, and she imagines Steve towering over a daughter, fist raised. "Above all else, guard your heart," I say, fast, from the back of her head, through the tiny crack that she has opened up. She starts and looks around, but there is only Steve, and the snow visible in the streetlights and the headlamps of the car.

In addition to Quebec's free healthcare, Steve has insurance for them both, from his work. It makes it easy in the hospital. "She fell," he says. "She hit the corner of the carved table, and somehow knocked out half of her tooth." He sounds so confident that she nods agreement, then winces with pain. They examine her, and then the doctor says he'll admit her overnight. Steve doesn't like this, but he has to accept it, and he leaves her there. The dental work is slow and uncomfortable. "Do you want an extraction or a reconstruction?" a man in a white coat asks. She just shakes her head. They leave her, to confer and make decisions for her, or perhaps to call and ask Steve, she doesn't know.

She is wearing a grey paper hospital gown, open at the back, and she is cold. The little cubicle where they have left her has one smoked glass wall, with equipment behind it. On the other side there is a high window, and she can see that snow is still falling, whirling down in huge flakes her grandmother used to call chicken feathers, filling the space outside. She is sitting on an orange plastic chair. She leans forward slowly to rest her forehead on the glass panel. The cool glass is soothing. The doctors, or dentists, whatever they are, have given her something for pain. The window reflects in the dark glass, and the snow, and the medical equipment is there behind, and her reflection, of course, except that she really is desperate, and so am I. I am in there. I don't know whether I have always been in there, pushed down and down in the bone cave, unable to get out or speak, buried since her mother tore me apart, but not truly dead, or whether some chance or change has let me be reborn now. I believe I am alive because I do not want to die. There isn't much of me, at that moment, in the hospital. But there isn't much of Sylvia either, and the space she has been pushed into is so small now that we're almost overlapping.

"This can't go on," I say, quietly.

Tears come to her eyes, and through them she can see me clearly in the dark glass. Her mouth opens as she tries to say my name, but it is gone beyond recall.

"There won't be anything left of you," I say.

"I thought you were dead!"

"We need to get help right now," I say.

She nods, and winces at the pain. "I couldn't tell him. About the baby. He'll hurt it."

A woman in a white coat comes back into the room. "Are you a doctor?" I ask her, through Sylvia's mouth.

"Yes," she says. She has freckles and a broad face, she looks exhausted, either because it is the middle of the night or because they make interns work ridiculously long hours as part of their journeyman ordeal. She is younger than Sylvia, who is twenty-seven now, almost twenty-eight. "I'm Doctor Shainblum."

"Is my husband still here?"

"No, he left. I can have reception call him if you need him."

"No, quite the opposite," I say. "He hit me. I was dazed, before, and couldn't understand what was going on."

"Corner of the table, I never believed a word of it," Dr Shainblum says.

"Have you admitted me?" I ask.

"Yes. You'll be here overnight and you can go home in the morning. We need to do something about your tooth."

"Take it out," I say, because that will be fastest, and I am focused on that night, not the next forty-five years in which Sylvia will have a gap beside her front teeth. "And while I'm here—I had a pregnancy test this morning, and I'm pregnant. I have to have an abortion. I have to. He could kill the child, if I had one. He'd hurt it, I know he would."

"We can't legally perform an abortion unless there's a risk to your life or health," Dr Shainblum says, calmly.

"There is," I say.

"And even then we have to have three doctors agree," she says. "I take it your husband would oppose it?"

"I don't know," I say. "He'll blame me for it, I'm sure of that. Whatever I do will be wrong. He'll hit me. He can't know."

"How far along are you?" Dr Shainblum asks.

"My period is two weeks late," I say.

"When beating you, did your husband hit you in the stomach?"

Sylvia is ashamed, hearing this question, because she still thinks of it as her fault, and that nobody else should know. But I am in charge now, and I don't let her speak, apologise, deny. "I can't remember," I say. "Probably. He usually does."

The doctor winces. "Then you might lose the baby anyway, naturally. Let me examine you and make sure. Hop up on the table."

We don't know what she does, but she announces that yes, Sylvia is bleeding, and that she will need to do a quick procedure. It might or might not be an abortion—legally it isn't, but the practical results are the same. Sylvia weeps, for the baby she would have loved, for the husband she cannot trust and cannot love anymore, for what she sees as her own stupidity. "You're not stupid," I say, fiercely, and the doctor agrees.

They take the tooth out, too.

When it's over she is bleeding heavily into pads, like a very heavy period, and she feels exhausted. It is now very late at night. She lies in a hospital bed, in a private room (Steve's insurance), staring at the wall, where there is a sink and a mirror. She is lying down so she can't see me in the mirror. "Would I have lost it anyway?" she asks me in the darkness.

We still don't know the answer to this question. Sometimes she thinks about this child, so different from the children she did have, later, with Idris. It's February, and she works out that he (she is sure it would have been a boy, because the girls are girls) would have been born in the end of October or the beginning of November. "Would I have lost him?" Sometimes she imagines him at that time of year. He would be forty-five now, if he'd been born, he'd be a precious human person with a complex life and desires. Perhaps he would make art, and certainly he could look at it and be moved. Steve would have warped his childhood, but lots of fine people have warped childhoods and survive it.

She lies there in the hospital bed under the thin turquoise coverlet, weeping and bleeding. She has stopped going to church in the time with Steve, and mostly stopped believing in God, but she prays for the child's soul as she lies still in the darkness.

If there is reincarnation the child lost very little. If it went to Limbo—if it is suddenly thirty-three years old in Limbo, then that is not so terrible, and surely unborn babies go there. But Limbo was abolished by Vatican II, and unbaptised babies are said to go directly to Heaven. The worst is if there is no afterlife, if that was the only chance that bundle of cells ever had to be a person. But she found Idris and had the girls, so there are two new people where there would have been only one, two loved and wanted people, and their children, her three grandchildren, who would never have existed.

She did not make the decision to abort the child. I did. I fought for both of our survival, and won. "I couldn't trust Steve," she whispers, to God, to me, to the flat pillow.

"You can't trust him," I agree.

"He would have been unjust. He would have hit the child."

"He is unjust to you," I say. "It's not even the violence that's the worst, it's the lies he tells."

". . . lies . . . ?" she says, into the darkness, the bright darkness of Ginnungagap in her head, where I am, the space in the bone cave that is expanding, where the mists of creativity swirl, where she considers who she is for the first time for a long time.

"Above all else, guard your heart, everything you do flows

from it," I say again, quoting the Book of Proverbs. "You have to get away."

"Away? Where to? How?"

Her own feelings are only just coming back to her at a distance, fear and anguish and anger, like telegrams sent to her from far-off destinations, not felt emotions but emotions relayed. "Don't go home until he'll have left for work. Pack a bag, just the things you have to have. Draw out a cheque at the bank, say he asked you to and it's for a trip. Then buy the *Gazette* and find a room to rent, find a job," I say. "People always need secretaries, and you can type. Then we can work on the rest of it."

"You make it sound so easy!"

"It won't be easy. But it's possible, one step at a time."

There is a long pause before she answers, as she processes the waves of emotion and begins to think thoughts outside of the circumscribed space Steve has allowed her. "If I'm leaving Steve I could have kept the baby."

It would have been terribly hard, in 1972, but it would have been possible. The baby would have been alive. It would have complicated the divorce terribly, and the courts might even have judged her an unfit mother for running away from Steve's abuse— her mother thinks this even without the child. Her brother Matthew tells her the church says there is no such thing as divorce, and that she and Steve should pray together. Her brothers and sisters never recognise her marriage to Idris as a real marriage. With a child, she might not have been able to get away. To go back to the image of the wolf in the trap, the baby, the cluster of cells that might have been a baby, was the paw she had to gnaw off, or more likely the fellow prisoner she could not bring with her in her escape into the light.

The next day, when she is leaving the hospital, the orderly gives her a paper from Dr Shainblum—a scrawled list, with numbers of two therapists, a divorce lawyer, and the women's shelter. "Please use these," it says simply. And she does.

"You got me away," she says now, in Firenze. "I couldn't see a direction to move, and you saw one. You saved me. And whatever happened, I couldn't lose you."

She would never have written a word. She would never have met Idris or known what love was. I might have suffocated in the dark, dissolved into the mist, and the mist itself that is the stuff of creation would have leaked away. Steve would have quashed her entirely, even if he didn't kill her. The violence is the easy thing to talk about, in many ways. It's much harder to say that he circumscribed her soul. And maybe she was losing the baby anyway, maybe he had already killed it. We'll never know. And yet, and yet . . .

27

BACKSTORY

Orsino cannot remember a time when his parents lived together. He was born in 1472, two years after his parents
married, and from his earliest memories he lived with Miranda
in Thalia while his father lived in Syracuse. His parents paid each
other visits, but did not cohabit. His mother, Miranda, was the
duchess of Thalia, a very important person with not much time
for little boys. He knew as early as he knew anything that he was
a prince, a prince of Syracuse. He knew he would one day be King
of Syracuse, and people tell him that a king is greater than a duke,
and as he learned the hierarchies of feudalism he saw that they
were right. Kings come on top, the only thing greater than a king
is an emperor, and there isn't an emperor any nearer than Xanadu.
But Syracuse, the court of his grandfather Alfonso, was a place of
stiff formality that they visited only for particular festivals—the
state marriages of his aunts, or for Christmas or Pentecost. In
Syracuse young Orsino always had to be on his best behaviour while
surrounded by strangers who seemed somehow too interested in
him. His grandfather was never satisfied by the reports of his
tutors, and was always asking why he doesn't try harder at Greek,
or swordplay, or riding. He complained that Orsino isn't as tall

as Ferrante was at his age, and wanted to know what he eats. He piled Orsino's plate with more meat than Orsino wanted and insisted he finish it.

When they go out hunting in Syracuse, everyone wants to know what's in Orsino's bag, and comments on it, and whether it's good or bad it never seems to be right. Even Miranda, who in Thalia ruled supreme, seemed muted and diminished in Syracuse. Maybe it was the presence of his father, Ferrante, who was always in Syracuse and very seldom visited Thalia. Or perhaps it was just that everything was heavier and slower and more formal. "I will change this, when I am king," the child Orsino said to himself, and then escaped back to Thalia where the guards are his friends and he knows all the secret ways in and out of the palazzo.

Alfonso was terrifying, but Ferrante was horrible. Orsino grew to despise his father, who had a bad temper and drank too much, who lurched as he walked, kept mistresses openly, and fought in tournaments and lost. Orsino liked to watch tournaments, but he heard Miranda complain about how much they cost and how the amount that Ferrante loses could rebuild the city walls. She said this to other people, not to Ferrante. Their relationship was icy. In Syracuse they greeted each other as husband and wife, and she and Orsino were lodged in his quarters, but since he didn't live there but with his mistress, this didn't mean much. A dead pigeon that five-year-old Orsino concealed under his bed at Pentecost was still there, mummified and stiff, when they returned at Christmas. There were paintings of Ferrante's mistresses in the rooms, which Orsino found useful for identification purposes, especially when there was a new one, which was often. It was almost never the same woman from one visit to the next. Sometimes Orsino could identify them from their paintings, but other times they looked too different with clothes on and their hair bound up. Ferrante was big and boastful and drunk, but worst of all, Orsino realised when he was six, Ferrante was stupid.

"Am I like my father?" he asked his nurse one night at bedtime.

"You've got his colouring, but you have your mother's brains, God be praised," she said, kissing him and tucking the covers around him.

Two years after this, when he was eight, Orsino asked his tutor one day why he couldn't be Duke of Thalia. "I understand I am to be King of Syracuse and that takes precedence, but why can't I be Duke of Thalia too?" His tutor was a middle-aged man, a humanist called Pannio of Verona. He knew Greek and Latin and had read Plato and was very confident about the right way to bring up princes to make them into Philosopher Kings. He had recently arrived in Thalia with high hopes of moulding Orsino, and was favourably impressed by how fast the boy managed to pick up the classical languages. Pannio believed that if children grow up steeped in the classics they will behave like ancient Romans, and that this is the best possible hope for the future of Illyria.

Pannio looked at him very sharply, and Orsino wanted to squirm under his gaze, but he had already learned to keep himself still and disguise his feelings when under regard by people who matter. "Thalia is to be inherited by your mother's older son, Geryon," Pannio said.

"But why?" Orsino asked. He hated the idea of Geryon, the older brother, the monster, the stranger who must inherit his home.

"He is the elder, and you will inherit a greater kingdom through your father."

"But my mother left him with his father, and they seem to be happy there as far as I've ever heard. Why can't he just stay there and inherit Tempest Island and rule the Anteans and leave Thalia to me?"

"No doubt your mother, or perhaps her father, Duke Prospero, wished to keep the Thalian duchy from being subsumed into the crown of Syracuse. It might not be a problem for you, who are growing up here and love it as it deserves, but in future generations your descendants, living in Syracuse, might not care for it and come to take it lightly. Your brother's descendants will be resident here."

Orsino didn't need the Aristotelean logic Pannio had already begun teaching him to see the huge flaw in that argument. "But Geryon isn't resident here," he pointed out.

Pannio shook his head and drew Orsino's attention back to Livy. But the conversation has consequences, and not ones Orsino likes. Pannio speaks to Miranda, and although she delays and drags her, feet she has to admit the justice of it. Two years later she brings Geryon to Thalia, to get to know his future domain.

The day Geryon arrived in the city, Orsino hid in one of the deep cellars to avoid greeting his half brother. He was pulled out by Pannio, who tutted at him, feeling that Orsino's bad behaviour was a failure of his own training, and so they should both be punished for it. Orsino's blue velvet doublet was covered in cobwebs, but Pannio dragged him straight to the banqueting hall without a pause to wash or change. "You're late already," he said. "You wanted to go into the cellars. Go to dinner as you are and face the consequences."

Orsino had learned not to argue with his tutor when he was in this mood. So the first time he sees Geryon it is in the banqueting hall. His brother is seated next to Miranda at the high table, crammed into a gilded chair that is already, at fifteen, too small for him, and wearing bright green-and-gold brocades with puffed sleeves that enhance his strange nature. Humans can interbreed with nymphs, but it so rarely happens that nobody is used to seeing the results. There are a family of farmers near Malfi who are said to have a dryad ancestor, but it shows only in a faint greenish cast to their skin and a frondiness to their hair. Communities of nymphs are rare in Illyria, though they are said to be more common in Sariola and Yavan and some other far-off parts of the world.

Geryon's skin is a mottled reddish grey, with a suggestion of scales. He is shaped mostly like a human, though bigger than most. The thing that most obviously marks his difference is his lack of a neck. His huge head grows directly out of his shoulders, which do not narrow but stay broad.

Miranda, who grew up on Tempest Island surrounded by Anteans and with her father as the only human, shows neither distaste for nor fascination with Geryon's strange appearance. But everyone else present shows one or the other, to differing degrees. The top table is crowded with Miranda's counsellors and major courtiers, the heads of important families, the podesta who commands the hired troops, the bishop, the abbots of the major monasteries, and even, down at the end by the guard captain, the chief rabbi. All of them are either openly staring at Geryon or looking at him uncomfortably out of the corners of their eyes.

Orsino's empty chair is on Miranda's other side. He pulls it out and seats himself. He reminds himself that he is a prince, and holds his head up straight. If he could have missed this meal, it would have made a point. Being brought in late and dirty merely makes him seem like a child. Orsino is ten years old. He bows with as much dignity as he can manage to the assembled notables, and beyond them to the entourage that crowds the lower tables that run up and down the hall. He takes up the tongs and helps himself neatly to a buttered quail from the big green blown-glass dish in the centre of the table. "I'm sorry about the state of my clothes," he says, because mentioning it himself is better than waiting for somebody else to bring it up. He sets the tongs down again, gently, making sure not to clatter the silver on the polished wood of the table.

Geryon grins at him. His grin is very wide, with too many teeth, which looks peculiar in his strange neckless face. He needs to turn his shoulders to look at Orsino, because his head doesn't turn on its own. "Don't worry. It's nice to see something as real as dirt. And I never even wore clothes until they made me come here."

Miranda winces, the bishop raises his eyebrows, the troop captain smothers a grin, and Orsino realises all at once that Thalia is even more strange and formal and uncomfortable for his brother than Syracuse is to him, and that Geryon is not an enemy but a pawn in all this, just as he himself is. He decides to change the subject before Geryon says something more about clothes and embarrasses them both even more. "Did you come by ship from Tempest Island?" he asks. "How long did it take?"

"No, I came underground. Being on a boat makes me very sick."

"Underground?" Orsino asks, not understanding.

"We Anteans can move through the earth," Geryon explains. He reaches out to the glass serving dish, picks up a quail in one hand and pops it whole into his mouth, crunching up the bones, and talking with his mouth full. "My father brought me, to show me the way. But he's gone back now. We went under the earth on Tempest Island, and then down under the bottom of the sea, and we came up again in the hills near Thalia."

"Like moles," the bishop suggests. He is an old man with a white beard, known for his translations of Greek poetry into the vernacular.

Miranda's fingers tighten on the horn handle of her silver-tined fork, and her lips press together. Orsino thinks moving beneath the earth sounds great, but he can already imagine the military implications. An army of Anteans could come up anywhere, where nobody was expecting them. But nymphs didn't have armies, and that was just as well.

"I was sick when we went to Syracuse by ship," Orsino offers. "But only the first day. After that I got my sea legs and the captain said I could be a sailor if I wanted to. And Mother said I could spend a month on a boat in the summer learning seamanship if I master Greek this year."

"And have you?" Miranda asks.

Orsino is conscious that everyone else at the table is listening to them. Pannio is seated on the long benches of the lower tables, but he can probably hear, and wouldn't be above saying something if Orsino risks boasting. "Not entirely, my lady Mother," he says.

There is a ripple of laughter around the room. "Entirely mastering Greek may take a lifetime," the bishop says, smiling patronizingly.

"And mastery is more a matter for a churchman or a tutor than a noble," Drusus Claudianus says, grinning at Orsino. He is the head of one of the most powerful noble families in Thalia, and claims descent from the ancient Claudians of Rome. "I'd say let him learn seamanship, my lady."

Miranda inclines her head but doesn't give an inch. "There's time yet before I decide, and I'll listen to his tutor's report."

"I don't know three words of Greek," Geryon rumbles. He seems determined to stress his difference and lack of culture in front of everyone.

"But you don't want to go sailing, so you have no incentive," Orsino says, neatly.

Geryon laughs, which shakes the table. He puts two of his great fingers into his mouth and pulls out the gnawed skull of the quail, which he drops on his trencher. The Chief Rabbi winces, one of the court ladies turns her head away, and another begins to fan herself. "I hope we'll be friends, little brother," he says. "I like you."

And they were friends, they were friends for years after that, friends despite their different natures. Geryon was uncouth and direct, and Orsino was smooth and subtle. Neither of them seem much like Miranda. Orsino does not want to be like Ferrante, and works hard to avoid this. He could not tell whether Geryon is like Caliban, because Caliban never visited the mainland. Geryon sometimes went to Tempest Island in those years, but Orsino never did. Miranda and Prospero would never agree to take him, and of course Geryon went underground, where he could not go. In all those years when Pannio tutored them both, Geryon was his despair. Geryon never learned a word of Greek, and even his Latin remained terrible. "I'll have other people do that for me, if it's needed," he said. Orsino worked at his letters and enjoyed it; he became a good humanist, and made Pannio proud. As time went by he spent more time in Syracuse, learning statecraft from his grandfather. It still always felt like escaping when he came back to Thalia.

Then, twelve years after Geryon came, when Orsino was twenty-two, Pico conquered death. A decade after that Orsino realised that despite being born and raised specifically to be an heir, he was never going to inherit anything. But it was twenty years more before Miranda retired and gave Thalia to Geryon. After she handed the duchy over she went on extended travels, to give the people of the duchy time to get used to her absence, or so she said. She told Orsino he could use her house in her absence. The house has always been there. She raised it by magic not long after the end of the civil war with Antonio by which she came to be duchess. That civil war, though it ended before he was born, loomed large over Orsino's childhood. His nurse's sweetheart had been killed in it, and some of the castle guards had been wounded in it, and all of them had lost friends. Miranda's house was invisible from almost everywhere. The wall that ran around it could be found, but the gate only appeared to those she wanted to find it, and even then, not always in the same place. After she left and Geryon was invested as Duke of Illyria, Orsino went to it and wandered around, mystified at his mother's choices, but he continued to live in the rooms of the Palazzo Vecchio where he had always lived. He became Geryon's advisor, when his brother would take any advice, and seethe when his brother listen and ignore him, making rash and rapid decisions to the detriment of Illyria. Orsino was fifty-four and still *giovane,* unmarried, unsettled, and insecure, oh, especially that last.

A year later, Orsino meets Olivia in Miranda's house outside the walls. It is the only place they can possibly have a conversation without being overheard. Olivia is nineteen years old, *giovane,* a properly brought up young lady, daughter of Drusus Claudianus and a marriageable daughter of the eminent Claudian house, and now its only heir. She lives with a drunken old uncle and her family of servants, and is of course never alone or unchaperoned. To come here to meet Orsino she has brought four armed guards, who wait at the front door, and her duenna, Maria, who sits down in the best chair and begins fanning herself while looking at them with a great deal of interest.

"This is a beautiful house," Olivia says. It is a perfectly proportioned symmetrical classical palazzo, in terra-cotta and marble. They are sitting in the great drawing room, which stretches from the front to the back of the house, and is furnished with a mosaic sea-scene floor, tapestries of an angelic choir, and very comfortable Savonarola chairs with padded seats, brocade-and-carved-oak arms and backs. The windows of the drawing room look out over the rose garden, which is particularly splendid. Ah, that moment it is early September, and many of the most spectacular bushes are in flower.

"My mother said I could use it in her absence, but I haven't been here much," Orsino says. Olivia's beauty, which he hadn't been expecting, confuses him. He would be inclined to be angry with the people who hadn't told him how beautiful she was, except that they did tell him and he didn't believe them. She is an orphaned heiress, of course she must be considered beautiful, unless she was actively repulsive. He had expected her to be passably attractive, with the bloom of a young girl, but the face she shows when she draws back her veil is like a madonna painted by a great master, beautiful and sad and wise. He can see her fair hair glinting under the cloth draped over her head, and the black clothes she wears enhance the elegance of her trim figure. She is certainly young, Orsino thinks, staring at her, but she is ripe like a peach. You would paint her as summer rather than spring, an orchid rather than a snowdrop, a queen rather than a princess, Juno rather than Diana—he realises that she said something and he didn't catch it.

Maria takes out a distaff and begins to twirl it, twisting wool into thread. "It's amazing the lack of dust if nobody's been using it," she says.

"She has magical servants to keep it clean," Orsino says. "But I don't know how to coax them into offering us refreshments, so I'm afraid I have nothing better to offer you than these oranges." He put them into his pocket at the last minute as he left the Palazzo Vecchio, and now he draws them out, a little squashed. Olivia takes one, and sits turning it in her hand. Maria cackles with laughter.

"We'll take the intent of hospitality for the deed," Olivia says, with a quelling glance at her chaperone. "It was not easy to find this time. Let us not waste it."

"No indeed," Orsino says, and then wastes more of it failing to find similes for Olivia's face. She has a tiny cleft in her chin, which irregularity sets off the perfection of her other features.

"Your brother killed my brother," Olivia begins, when it has become clear that Orsino has been struck dumb by her beauty. Although she is only nineteen and has been sheltered, this is a situation she has encountered sufficiently often that she knows how to cope with it.

"Yes," Orsino says, forcing his mind to the important business that has brought them together. "Your father died, and your mother chose to follow him, and then Geryon killed your brother. You said in your letter that you knew why he did it?"

Olivia raises her chin bravely, changing the pattern of light and shadows on her face. "My brother, Claudio, refused to give me in marriage to your brother, Geryon," she says.

Orsino shudders, quite involuntarily. "That's terrible," he says. "And it's tyranny."

"My mistress has no desire to mate with a monster," says Maria, emphatically.

"Nor did it suit my brother's dynastic intention for me to become a duchess," Olivia says.

Orsino can't blame Geryon for asking. They have discussed the need for him to marry a fully human woman, but he thought they were trying to negotiate for a princess of Tedesca, which would be a useful alliance. Marrying Olivia would cause several problems—it would mean favouring the Claudiani over the other families of Thalia, and wouldn't bring the city the least advantage. On the other hand, now that Olivia was the last of the Claudiani, that would prevent that from being much of a problem, and the other noble families would be sure to rally to her. He forces himself to concentrate.

"Killing him for that reason is tyranny. But so far nobody knows for sure why he killed Claudio. There are rumours running everywhere like a lightning strike in a dry summer. Geryon has done some other strange things, things he won't talk to me about, but this is worse than anything. Are you sure this was his reason?"

Olivia looks down, looks at Maria, who is concentrating on her distaff, and then back at Orsino. "Duke Geryon made the offer to him late at night, after a dinner. Claudio told me they had both been drinking. He took him aside as he was leaving and said he wanted to marry me. Claudio, in a polite falsehood, told the duke that I was promised elsewhere. When Geryon pressed him as to who, my brother's fuddled wits were not up to coming up with an answer. He said he'd call on him the next day to discuss it. The next morning Claudio came to my rooms to work out a stratagem. We decided he should say that to end the feud between our family and the Eliani, I had been promised to Silvio Elia. We thought he couldn't object to that, and it would explain why the betrothal hadn't been announced before."

"And that's why Silvio has fled," Orsino says. He does not doubt her, he would as soon doubt a painted Madonna that spoke revelation to him.

"Yes. I sent Maria to warn him after Claudio was killed. He has gone to the court at Syracuse." Maria looks up and nods when her name is mentioned, but does not speak. Olivia takes a deep breath. "I do not know what passed between my brother and yours. But when Claudio's body was sent back, it was in two pieces, and bore the marks of huge fingers."

"I *couldn't* stop her seeing," Maria says, as if Orsino had reproached her. "She would look, no matter what anyone said."

"Geryon tore him apart," Orsino says. "I—this is treason, but I can't let this pass."

"That's what I hoped in contacting you," Olivia says. She seems entirely self-possessed in speaking of the gruesome murder of her brother, but Orsino sees her hands are shaking a little as she tucks them under the edge of her shawl.

"I cannot act fast," Orsino says, thinking quickly through his options. "Geryon is formidable, and there is also the problem of his father, of Caliban. Geryon could tear me apart too, if he thought I was against him." He looks out into the rose garden. It was very like Miranda to build a rose maze and put it on only one side of her house. "I will need to plan carefully and seek help. I could bring an army from Syracuse, my grandfather would give me one on this provocation, but any champion would lose any duel with Geryon, and that would gain nothing. It will have to be by subterfuge."

Olivia stands, and nods decisively. "That will do. I will wait until you have everything ready, mourning my brother, and being as patient as I can."

"Without your brother's protection and with your supposed suitor fled, you are peculiarly exposed to my brother's ardor," Orsino says, standing too. He looks at Maria, whose attention is only half on her wool; she is looking cynically at the two of them. "Would you feel sufficiently chaperoned if we took a turn in the rose garden, where we would be fully in view from these windows?"

He knows that if she agrees to walk with him in the rose garden then she will agree to marry him. Olivia looks out of the window at the sea of roses, golden, white, pink, yellow, and deepest carmine, then back to Orsino, shaking her head. "We do not have anything to say that cannot be said before my duenna," Olivia says. "And I have sworn not to marry for fifty years, in memory of my father and my brother."

"I wanted to offer you my protection," Orsino says, annoyed that she turned down his offer before he has made it.

"That is very kind," Olivia replies.

Orsino makes another effort. "And I wanted to say that I have never met a woman I admired more, not just your beauty but your courage."

"And that too is very kind, but as I said, I have sworn an oath."

"Such an oath is a strong protection against me, but must I remind you what happened to your brother? If Geryon takes it into his head to marry you by force, it will be a very thin shield, and your guards only a slightly stronger one. Can I offer you this house, until my mother's return? I do not know all the spells on it, but it cannot be found by those with hostile intent."

"Take it," Maria advises.

Olivia hesitates. "You do not live here, you said?"

"No. You'd have it to yourself. There are no servants, but you could bring your own." Orsino hesitates. "I will need to contact my mother, and she may come back, and if so, of course, as it is her house—"

"I quite understand," Olivia says. She nods. "I think we will accept Lady Miranda's hospitality in her absence."

"But we'll have to ask you not to abuse your privilege of visiting," Maria puts in.

Orsino bows and bids them farewell. Outside the drawing room, he casts a single longing and regretful glance down the passage that leads to the door into the rose garden. He is head over heels in love with Olivia, without knowing her, in calf love, like a boy, obsessed with her, needing another glimpse of her the way he needs water. Days when he sees her are happy days, even if she does not speak, or is unkind, days without her are hollow. He does not stay constantly in this state of insanity, he manages to cure himself from time to time, but he slips easily back into it with contact with her. It is not until eighty-five years later when Viola arrives, disguised as a boy, that he discovers what love is. By that time, Orsino is Duke of Illyria and Geryon is already on top of the tower.

28

SUNLIT UPLANDS

You already know the plot of *Twelfth Night*, right? I don't need to explain how Viola disguised herself as her brother and was employed by Orsino to woo Olivia and Olivia fell in love with her and the disguised Viola fell in love with Orsino, and then Sebastian showed up and Olivia is delighted and wants a three-some, and Viola's gender is revealed, and all four of them get married: that is, Olivia marries Sebastian and Viola marries Orsino? Much hilarity ensues along the way, it's one of Shakespeare's funniest plays. If you haven't seen it you should make it a priority. But I don't need to go into it in detail here. You know the play. And anyway we already saw them all together two hundred years later in Olivia's bedroom. The important thing now is Orsino and Geryon. And Miranda, their mother, who is more difficult to explain. And Sylvia. And me.

There is a pernicious lie in Western culture that Sylvia has tried to combat in her books for years, and it is this: a child who is not loved is damaged beyond repair. Relatedly, anyone who has been abused can never recover. These lies are additional abuse heaped on those who have already suffered. Being told that the worst thing in the world has happened to you and you cannot recover can be a self-fulfilling prophecy. Very much so! Certainly recovery is hard. Certainly it takes work and time and help. But it isn't like losing a body part that can never regrow. People who have been abused will not be the people they would have been if it had never happened. But they can be splendid people going on from where they are.

Miranda was not loved as a child. Her mother was absent and her father was an obsessive wizard who only took notice of her when he was forced to. The Anteans she lived with feared her, because they feared Prospero. She was not abused, but she was neglected. Prospero taught her classical languages and magic, but he was always distant. She never felt she had his confidence. She didn't love Caliban and she didn't love Ferrante, but she married both of them, and the second marriage was worse than the first. The way she loved Geryon and Orsino wasn't satisfying to her or to them. But she did love them, in her way. It took her a long time to recover from her stunted start. What she loved, what gave her her way out, was magic, and she came to love Ficino and her other friends, in a way that wasn't sexual or romantic but was real and important.

People who were not loved as children can live and love and love life, they can go into Perché No! . . . and be greeted by the friendly staff, they can combine redcurrant gelato with *fior di latte* gelato and have tears come to their eyes at the combination of wonderful tastes. They can write books, they can gasp aloud at Bernini's sculpture of St Laurence on his grill in the newly reopened part of the Uffizi. Children who were not loved can grow up to learn love, they can be good friends and good parents, they can receive joking text messages from their grandsons, they can carefully work out the time zones to call their best friends on their birthday mornings. They can miss their beloved husband every single day but still be happy. It may be that there are other, better, unimaginable ways of being happy. But this will do, Sylvia says, watching a toddler laughing and chasing after a dog over the uneven paving stones near the Loggia dei Lanzi, with the father puffing along behind, grinning.

There is a story about those paving stones—that they were all uneven, but taken up for an archaeological dig, which discovered the destroyed houses of the Ghibellines on top of a Roman amphitheatre. When the paving stones were supposed to be put back, it turned out that they had been sold as kitchen counters, and new stones had to be bought, which were of course neatly regular and flat. Only the ones near the Loggia dei Lanzi where the toddler was running are original. But Sylvia has a theory that in the Renaissance the ground in the square was pale red. There's a painting of the death of Savonarola that shows it paved in great red rectangles, and two different Ghirlandaio paintings that have it in the background and looking the same. Reddish, definitely, not grey stones. So there is at least some evidence that in the 1480s and '90s it was red. That would mean the paving stones that ended up as kitchen counters were put down later—ducal period? Or Austrian? It's the kind of historical detail it's hard to find out, because it's not the kind of thing people record. A piece of art, sometimes. Reflooring the square? Almost never. The uneven stones can be seen clearly in the Denholm Elliott movie of Forster's *A Room With a View*. A Roman amphitheatre. The Ghibellines. Savonarola. Red. *A Room With a View*. Kitchen counters. We think of this sequence every time we walk over those stones, like saying a rosary.

When Lucy was born, Sylvia was afraid. She hoped Idris had stability and love enough for both of them, enough to be the right kind of parent. She half-believed the lie, then, she feared that because she had been abused she couldn't be a proper mother. But even though her mother always disliked her and sometimes hated her, although her mother made her the scapegoat among her siblings, so they always banded together against her, she wasn't entirely bereft of love as a child. Montreal in the fifties wasn't a desert island. She had her father's offhand love, and she had her grandparents, not just her grandmother Harrison but all four of them, all close by and offering love and support in their different ways. She had her aunt Cat and her children as an example of a family that worked. Sometimes as a child she wished she belonged to Aunt Cat instead of her own parents, and then prayed for forgiveness for being so wicked. Now she thinks that was healthy. Cat's grandchild Con is the only member of her extended family Sylvia feels close to—Con, who is warm and funny, who loves Shakespeare, who bakes bread, who has a PhD from Columbia and teaches computer science at Université de Montréal, whose gender is ambiguous and pronouns flexible. When Sylvia is in Montreal she meets up with Con every week or so for a meal, or a trip to the theatre. When she's away, they exchange email every few days, far more often than she hears from her daughters. Con is one of the people who won't forgive her for spending this summer away.

As well as these good childhood examples, later she had even more, with her friends, but perhaps most notably Idris's parents and the way they loved and respected each other and their son. It took her some time to realise what different cultures his parents had come from. The whole Islamic world was the magic carpets of Elam to her then. She had never considered that Iran and Pakistan were as different as Finland and Greece. Idris's parents found each other in a Muslim centre in Edmonton, both immigrants to Canada. English was their common language, and the language Idris grew up in, though it was not their native tongue. But the quiet love they shared was sufficient to help them find a shared path ahead. Idris loved his parents, and admired them, and was proud of them, as they were proud of him. Sylvia saw it in the way they all behaved to each other. But most of all she saw it in the way Idris talked about them. When Idris started training to became an engineer, his mother started to study mathematics. "She started from almost nothing," Idris tells Sylvia. "Enough arithmetic to add up the grocery bill. But she took a class, and more classes, and she loved it, and now she is tutoring in algebra and calculus." Idris is an only child. "I think they would have liked more, but she hurt something when I was born, and the doctor said more would be a bad idea, so they made do with me." But it is clear to Sylvia that there is no making do necessary, they not only adore Idris but also respect him. She kept coming back to that thought, honour, respect, because she was only just learning how important it was.

When Lucy was born, Idris was only part of the way through teaching Sylvia what it means to love somebody who isn't offering love only to snatch it away. Her mother had left scars, which Steve had maliciously widened. But when, after thirty-one hours of labour, after panting, after trying to breathe into the pains, and trying to breathe against them, after pushing at last, holding Idris's hand in one of her hands and a midwife's in the other, the baby is put on her breast, naked and still smeared with blood, she feels a deep triumphant joy and an upwelling of tenderness she could never have imagined.

This is not to say that motherhood was easy, or that she did everything right. There were times she wanted to scream with frustration, and times she couldn't wait for Idris to get home so she could leave the girls with him and shut herself in her room for an hour, not even to write but just to read and breathe in peace. But if she ever felt any impulse to behave as her own mother had, she was so immediately horrified at herself that all temper, all emotion, vanished, and she could be calm. Her emotions came back slowly, after leaving Steve, her awareness of them. All through the divorce process and then the therapy, and the time after, in Europe, up to the time she met Idris, they were slowly rebalancing. Healing doesn't happen overnight. It takes time. But it happens.

She sang to the girls, despite her toneless voice, lulling them into a true sense of security. She loved them fiercely. She told them stories and took them to the park. Idris taught them to ice skate, to speak four languages, and to play street hockey. She wrote in the early mornings before they were awake, getting up sometimes at half past four, or five, writing before she was exhausted, and going to bed early. These were the years when she had no social life, because she fell asleep at eight o'clock. But the books she wrote were good, better than the Illyria books, deeper, more vivid. She improved technically as a writer, and tried more ambitious things. The books she wrote then were for children, but were not in any way childish. And I too learned, and grew, and changed my chameleon skin over and over, like a repertory actor who takes the parts he's given and makes them his own. I was a dragon, and a scholar, and a prince. And slowly, as the girls grew, I developed a different sense of myself, of who I was outside the parts she gave me, the continuous sense of my reiterated and renewed and separate self.

(And she loved me too. Some people might not see that as healthy and sane, but it was good for both of us. It always was, even when we were fighting about things.)

Miranda never had the luck to find anyone like Idris. But she flowered into a great wizard and a good person. Geryon and Orsino both had difficult childhoods, especially Geryon, who she left with his father. Geryon and Caliban love each other, but Geryon couldn't help feeling abandoned. And when Miranda summoned him to Thalia, it was too late for them to make a real connection. Miranda's own mother, Geltrude, after abandoning Prospero for his usurping brother Antonio, then poisoned herself after Ferrante killed Antonio, and before Miranda could even talk to her.

Lucy and Meg had Idris, and Sylvia too. She loves them. And she loves Con, and Con loves her back unreservedly. Con found friendship and affection with Sylvia when Con's own parents didn't know how to cope with a teenager who wasn't comfortable in either gender. Sylvia and Idris bought extra theatre tickets and hockey tickets and accepted Con as almost another child of their own when things were most difficult at home. If Con is now happy and successful it is partly due to Sylvia. ("And especially Idris," Sylvia adds.) Meg and Lucy miss their father, and they may find Sylvia an inadequate substitute for his warmth and understanding, but they are each always glad to see her when she makes the trip to see them. They are not close to each other.

"But neither of them kept the other chained on top of a tower for three hundred years either," I point out cheerily.

"So that's our standard for sibling rivalry now?" Sylvia asks.

We are in the Uffizi, and in the second Botticelli room she stops in front of Botticelli's *Madonna and Child with Four Angels and Six Saints*. It's a terrible title for a lovely picture. It was the April picture in a calendar of religious art her grandparents had in 1951, and which she loved so much that her grandmother gave her the calendar page as a Christmas present that year, framed, in a frame her grandfather made. She had it on her bedroom wall from then until she married Steve. She has a much better print of it on her bedroom wall at home in Montreal now, and she doesn't need one in Firenze because the painting is right there in the Uffizi, and she has the Friend of the Uffizi card, which is the best value for sixty euros in the world, considering that it costs twenty euros to go into the Uffizi once, and there are always incredibly long lines, while the card lets you go straight in at both the Uffizi and the Palazzo Pitti as often as you want for an entire calendar year. This painting isn't her favourite Botticelli, now, it isn't even her favourite Botticelli in this room, but because she has had a connection to it for so long it has a special meaning for her.

It has the Madonna in the centre, with the Christ child on her lap. She's a very sweet-faced Madonna, but not insipid at all, thoughtful and sad and loving. (She looks like Olivia, or rather,

Sylvia has based what Olivia looks like on her.) The Christ child too is more like a real baby than in much Medieval and Renaissance art before Raphael, who raised the bar for babies. This one has a very adult expression, but then, he *is* supposed to be God. In the top corners are angels pulling drapes, and crowning the Virgin, and looking very serious about it. Botticelli's angels, apart from the archangel Michael, are not gendered, which makes them very interesting, because it's unusual to see pictures of intelligent beings with interior lives but without gender. You do not say "he" or "she" when you look at them—and as "it" doesn't seem to fit for a thinking being, she tends towards "they," a pronoun that Con also favours. (Con loves Botticelli's angels.) Sylvia has always wanted to write a book about their home life, what they do in Heaven, but she's never had enough world for it. In the painting, below the Madonna and angels, there's another row of figures, standing about, bearing witness. There's St Catherine, with her wheel; St Augustine, writing in his book; and St Barnabas, with his odd-shaped flaying knife. On the lower right there's St Ignatius of Antioch, holding his heart in his hand (it looks like scarlet plush), and John the Baptist, and the archangel Michael.

It's the archangel she has come to look at today. He stands there looking pensive. He has dark wings and dark armour, and he holds the globe of the world in his hand. Christianity, unlike many other religions, does not look forward to a battle at the end of time; Ragnarok, Kali Yuga, when Good will fight Evil. Manicheanism, a very popular religion at the time of the rise of Christianity, and one which St Augustine tried for a while, had that, and Christianity wanted to make itself distinct. So while there are apocalyptic elements in Christianity, Armageddon, and the Book of Revelation, and while Satan and Hell and the story of the Rebel Angels are certainly present, in Catholicism and most mainstream varieties of Christianity around the world it avoids being all about that. Indeed, one way of looking at what makes Christianity different is to consider that God did an end run around all that. God cheated by incarnating, being crucified, harrowing Hell, and saving everyone ahead of time by the back door. We in the West are so familiar with Christianity, whether or not we belong to any church, that it's easy to forget what a weird outlier it is among human religions.

Tolkien converted C. S. Lewis by getting him to agree what a great story it was, and then saying how much more wonderful it would be if it were true. And if one could entertain any notion of its truth, then it's a remarkable amount of trouble for God to have gone to, and it's deeply ungrateful of people to spurn his offer. When standing in front of Renaissance religious art, particularly Botticelli and Fra Angelico, Sylvia often feels a nostalgia for belief along these lines. She was brought up with it, and she would often like to sink back into that belief. But you can't believe by wanting to believe, and in any case she can always cure herself by reading the patent absurdities of the Bible. You only have to read the Gospels with attention to see that Christ clearly wasn't what Fra Angelico and the whole of Western Christianity said he was. The house of cards is built on very shaky sand indeed. Reading the Bible makes Sylvia think that the pre-Reformation church was right to keep it from people, if they wanted them to carry on being Christians. It also amazes her that anyone could have started from this, from these four utterly contradictory accounts of a man's life and sayings, and come up with the concept of biblical inerrancy. A religion of ambiguity and positively Lacanian textual exegesis would seem more plausible, where there had to be four contradictory accounts of everything in order for it to have spiritual validity.

In another room in the Uffizi, further back, there is a lovely 1342 painting by Lorenzetti depicting the Purification of the Virgin, which happened in Jerusalem on the fortieth day after Jesus's birth, an incident described in the Gospel of John, where

Simeon, the Jewish priest given the baby to hold recognises him as the Messiah and says now he can depart in peace. Nunc Dimittis. This, the Redemption of the Firstborn, is a genuine Jewish ceremony which is still practiced by Jews when a firstborn child is a son, though they don't use doves anymore. But elsewhere in the Uffizi you'll find pictures of the Flight Into Egypt, the contradictory story in the Gospel of Matthew where King Herod persecutes the Holy Family and massacres the innocents and so they escape to Egypt. Herod was still in Jerusalem forty days later, and not likely to have forgotten about the baby he missed in Bethlehem. It took Moses and the Israelites forty years to get from Egypt to Jerusalem in the opposite direction. But it isn't that far. The Orbis "Mapping the Roman World" website thinks it would take fourteen days in optimum conditions and with plenty of money to go between Jerusalem and Alexandria, which is their most likely destination in Egypt—it had a large thriving Jewish population in the period. So perhaps they could have just barely made it there and back, walking with one donkey, if they only stayed ten days or so in Egypt. But if they needed to go, then it wasn't safe to come back. . . .

But really it doesn't matter, except to nitpicking writers who want stories to be internally consistent. These pictures were painted by people with no need for that and immense faith in the power of the stories. They didn't read the Bible, and the pictures and the stories they created remain powerful. But if it's a question of being true, of being real, of what Tolkien said to Lewis, that's another thing. Sylvia loves the art but can't suspend disbelief when she steps away from it.

But did you notice what Drusilla said? In Elam, they don't paint or sculpt pictures of beings, of people or animals, because if they do, on the Day of Judgement, the creatures will come to their creators and ask them for a soul. In a world where that was real, Botticelli and Fra Angelico won't know where to look.

"Is that what you're doing?" Sylvia asks me, as we stand before the troubled beautiful face of Michael the Archangel. "Are you asking me for a soul?"

If I know what a soul is, I think I have one. I don't think that's what I'm asking her for.

Sylvia looks at Michael, ignoring the Madonna and the other angels and saints. Michael is the angel who fights. He's always shown with a sword, almost always in armour, and often, though not here, with a demon crushed under his feet. He knows what evil is, he remembers and regrets the rebel angels. Here he's staring into space, not paying any attention to any of the figures around him and whatever is going on in the painting. He isn't looking at Christ or the Virgin, but out beyond the viewer. There is no demon, no scales of justice to separate saints from sinners, but his sword is ready. "He's my guardian angel," she says to me, inside her head. "He's you."

Oh, but I am no angel. I am much trickier than that. Botticelli's Michael has nothing to be guilty about.

What this Michael reminds me of is the scene she's supposed to be writing next, Orsino, putting his armour on to go up the tower to talk to his blinded Antean brother. We go out of the Botticelli room and walk around the top floor of the Uffizi. We pop into the newly rearranged Michelangelo and Raphael room. They have moved the two Raphael Doni portraits here from the Pitti Palace, and put them in glass away from the wall, so you can for the first time walk around behind them and make the startling discovery that their backs show cartoons of the story of Deucalion's flood. It's strange and delightful to see a picture you have seen a thousand times, and suddenly be able to see the secret hidden behind it. The portraits are a pair, wedding pictures. He has the flood behind him, water bursting from the clouds the gods are sitting on, falling on a gazebo on a hill. Behind her portrait is the same gazebo, but close up, and a man and a woman,

Deucalion and Pyrrha, throwing stones over their shoulders to create men and women. Such a surprising thing to sit behind that canny pair, the banker and his wife.

From there we go past the Laocoön to the café, out in the open air, on a level with the top layer of the body of the Palazzo Vecchio and right next to it. The friendly Russian waitress recognises Sylvia, because she comes here frequently—and even more frequently when she didn't have a chair—and asks how she is doing and whether she's finished her book yet. "It's coming along," Sylvia says. She orders freshly squeezed orange juice, spremuta, and sits facing the Palazzo Vecchio, her head tilted to look up at the tower, and thinking about Geryon. She has been up there, though not this year, up and up the dark stairs to emerge at the platform where the twisting pillars rise, and you are higher than anything else in Firenze, and you can see it all so clearly. The very peak of the tower is still above you, they don't let people up at the very top, by the twirling gold lion weathercock, but she has been to the battlement below it. Cosimo de' Medici and, later, Savonarola, were imprisoned in a cell down in the main part of the tower, a little more than halfway up. But she has decided that Geryon is in the layer at the top of the castle proper, just a little higher than where she is sitting in the Uffizi café, which is on top of the Loggia dei Lanzi. She stares over at the space under the crenellations, where there are bars on the arches, where, in Thalia, Geryon, son of Miranda and Caliban, rightful Duke of Thalia, has been bound for three hundred years.

He's bound out in the open, to rings set in the wall, and if he could see, he could see all of Thalia, the domes and spires of churches and synagogues rising above the rooftops, and Ficino's tower with the little crystal dome on top catching the light, and the city walls, and the river and the hills. There's no Brunelleschi's dome in Thalia, though it is one of the most miraculous sights of the real Firenze, because it's so big and so unexpected.

Thalia's cathedral is without the huge dome. But Giotto's bell-tower is there—it was in Firenze when Manetto left—and the Baptistery, and Orsanmichele, and the Badia, and the tower of the Bargello. Geryon can make out colours now, so he can see the blue of the sky and the gold of the stone and the terra-cotta red of the tiles of the rooftops. And maybe he is starting to see silhouettes, so he could see the skyline below him, or tell hills from sky. But for at least the first hundred years he would have seen none of it, and his world would have been the song of birds, the howling of dogs, church and civil bells marking the hours, the striking of the clock in the tower, drums and trumpets of parades, the occasional clatter of horses' hooves on stone, and the chatter of human voices in the square far below, where he can make out the murmur but never the words.

Imagine spending a day there, blind, feeling the heat of the sun and knowing it has set only when the chill of night sets in, hearing the city going on with life down below. Then imagine another day, and another, a lifetime, and then a little vision returns, another lifetime, and a little colour. Defeating death opens up terrifying possibilities as well as wonderful ones. But if Geryon had wanted to die at any moment, all it would have taken was the wish. He wanted to live, even if this is what life is, far above the earth that gives him his strength.

29

TWO GRAVES

Before going up to see Geryon, Orsino dresses in his armour, for both physical and psychological protection. His armour is made of steel and enamelled in black and red, with a unicorn and a rose on his chest, for Manetto, the man from another world, as rare as a unicorn, and the Orsini family he married into. (The real Orsini were a Roman family, but Sylvia borrowed them for Illyria.) Drusilla insists that she's been sneaking up there in her ordinary clothes and doesn't need to wear anything special. She changes out of the good dress she wore to the funeral and puts on an everyday dress, in dark burgundy over cream. She keeps the gold arm ring, which fits better with these sleeves. She hitches her skirts up to climb the stairs. Orsino is glad they're not going all the way up the tower. Those stairs always seem endless, and his breastplate is heavy.

The tower on the Palazzo Vecchio was built first and foremost as a watchtower, and that is still its central function. It's very practical, in a way you can't really recognise until you go up there. A lookout can see if enemy armies are coming from miles away, in good time to warn the city by ringing the bell at the top of the tower. Once that alarm has rung, it would be taken up by watchtowers and church towers all over the city, letting everyone know not just that an army was on the way, but from which direction. People would close all the gates and get into armour, and rush to defend the walls. The guards and sentries on the walls all the time are a skeleton force, but by the time any enemy came to the walls they would be bristling with everyone who knows how to use a weapon. From the top of the tower, the city would look like a kicked anthill. Orsino keeps three guards on the platform at the top of the tower looking out all the time, and more at times when Thalia is at war, or when war is threatened. They are not posted near Geryon, but they have to pass him on their way up and down. Every four hours, when the watch is changed, one of the newly arrived lookouts takes Geryon food and water, and another throws a bucket of water over him to keep him clean.

The tower also contains a clock, and has since the astonishingly early date of 1353. A great deal of the width of the tower is given up to its mechanism, making the stairs narrow and dark. "Everyone hates winding the clock," Drusilla says as it strikes. "They try to get out of it."

Orsino grunts. He doesn't often wear his armour on other than ceremonial occasions, and climbing stairs in it is making him feel out of condition. "How about lookout duty?" he asks. "Do they hate that?"

"No, they think that's quite fun," she says. "Especially when it's hot, and they're high up there. But winding the clock is hard work in a small dark space. It's usually done by whoever messed up recently."

"Do you go all the way up and talk to the lookouts?" Orsino asks.

"You get the best view from up there," Drusilla says, evasively.

When Orsino was a boy, he went up to talk to the lookouts too. The sentries had often told grim stories of battles they had fought, and had scars to show for it. The civil war between

Miranda and Antonio was vicious. That was one reason why he made his coup against Geryon sudden, brutal, and rapid, with order promptly restored afterwards. But even so, even with everything, he'd never have done it if Geryon had been a good duke. Sitting beside him and watching him incompetently mismanage everything and anger the people for nothing was more than Orsino could bear. If Geryon had been a good duke, then Orsino would have found something else to do with his life. Or even if he'd just mismanaged things, if he hadn't killed Claudio for not letting him marry Olivia, Orsino would have left him alone. This has been Orsino's constant justification to himself for the last three hundred years.

They come to the top of the stairs abruptly, and blink in the sudden sunlight. The sun is sinking and everything is casting long shadows. Orsino stops in the doorway, just out of Geryon's sight, if Geryon can see. His brother is chained to rings set into the wall, facing north over the city. You could mistake him for a man wearing a big hood, a monk stooping forward, if you saw him in other circumstances. Naked, and chained to the rings, the difference is very obvious. He has a dirty beige blanket, and when Orsino sees it he frowns automatically. Somebody has softened towards Geryon, which might mean he still has sympathisers among the people of Thalia. Or, he sighs, it might just as likely be his own wife or daughter who has brought it. In any case, as things are, signs of lenience are probably good.

"Go and say hello," Orsino whispers to Drusilla. "If I speak to him first he'll start to roar and rave, and even if he's faking it, that's not a good way to begin this."

Drusilla shrugs, and pushes past her father onto the parapet that runs around the castle behind the bars and crenellations. "Hello Uncle Geryon," she says.

"You'll get in trouble if you keep coming up here, Dru,"

Geryon says, in his familiar deep bass. "The more often you do it the more likely you are to get caught."

Drusilla looks towards the archway where Orsino is waiting, then back at Geryon. She shifts from foot to foot. "I told them that you don't want to be duke anymore," she says.

Geryon sighs heavily. "That won't do any good, little one. Now they'll definitely stop you coming up to brighten my days. And they won't trust me. They can't."

"That's what they said," Drusilla says. Then she turns and beckons to Orsino, and he comes out. He doesn't know whether Geryon can see him or not, if he can make anything of the change of light and colours. Orsino had not, before Ficino's suggestion of that morning, really thought what three hundred years of blindness would mean.

"Hello brother," Orsino says, tentatively.

For a moment he thinks Geryon will start to scream at him in the madness that is all he has shown him for centuries. His brother tenses against the chains, and his mouth becomes a grimace. He hisses, then all at once relaxes against the chains and slumps down at the base of the wall, clutching his blanket to his chest with both of his huge hands. "Don't punish her," he rumbles. "She's just a kid, just being a kid. She didn't mean anything bad coming and talking to me."

"I know," Orsino says.

"He gave me an arm ring," Drusilla interrupts, patting it. "He isn't angry at me at all."

"You're not?" Geryon's ruined eyes are clearly visible as he turns them towards Orsino in the red light of the declining sun. Orsino can see that they are indeed healing. They were nothing but a mass of scars where the hot irons were laid on, but now the raised criss-cross scars are covered with greyish skin, and there are bulges in there that are something like eyes again.

"I'm really not angry at Drusilla," Orsino says. "Not at all.

I'm grateful to her for making friends with you, for telling me you want to go to Elam." As always when he sees his brother, Orsino feels profoundly guilty. Usually, after his annual visits to Geryon, he hates himself. He gets drunk and tries to justify himself to Viola, and sometimes to the others, but never to anyone else. He has not spoken about Geryon to anyone outside the family for years. Nor have the Senate inquired after him, or any of the important families, or even the rulers of other states, not for more than a century now. Only Miranda asks how he is, and persistently asks to visit him. But whether they talk about him or not, everyone knows Orsino keeps his deposed brother chained at the top of the castle, and that reputation has served him well for a long time. It means that he has been able to be benevolent in specific cases without anyone thinking him soft.

Geryon turns his body towards Orsino, angling his shoulders as much as he can, and Orsino realises he is squinting, trying to see. "It won't matter if she lets me go when she's duke, or duchess, rather," Geryon says. "I won't take revenge on her."

Now that he sees him again, after being reminded by Olivia of Claudio's death, and by his memory of every pinprick of the incompetence that was Geryon as duke, the option of sacrificing himself in Geryon's place has lost any faintest consideration he might have been giving to it. Orsino has no desire to spend three hundred years, blind, on top of a tower. He would do it for the greater good. But absolutely refuses to do it while Geryon ruins Thalia down below.

So he sees three possible courses lying before him. First, he has brought his sword, and his hand twitches towards it. He could murder Geryon. Bound as he is, he could cut his brother's throat without very much difficulty. This might or might not help against the threat of Caliban, but it would remove Geryon as a piece on the playing board, and make any attack by Caliban pointless. It would in many ways be practical and expedient. The reasons for not doing it are all human and sentimental—Geryon is still, after everything, his brother, and it would destroy Drusilla's trust in him as a good person.

Secondly, much worse than killing him, he could bring black-smiths up here to burn out Geryon's eyes for a second time. He could do this every century, forever. Blind, Geryon is no threat, but if he could see he would be able to do magic, and perhaps free himself. Orsino knows he will not take this course, that he could not live with himself if he did. Though this is the path Orsino has been walking for three hundred years, he refuses it now, he could not do it knowingly and go on. Worse than losing Drusilla's good regard would be losing his own regard for himself. Besides, it would probably be useless, indeed, it always was useless if Ficino has the power to restore Geryon's sight.

The third option is the much more precarious path of letting his brother go. Orsino has all the power here. He is the duke, the leader. Nothing constrains him. He has to listen to public opinion to a certain extent, or he can be overthrown by a conspiracy within the city. He is nominally subject to his grandfather Alfonso of Syracuse, who in practice has stopped trying to interfere with him as long as Orsino acknowledges his theoretical fealty. Most binding, if he does anything that upsets his family he will be unable to have a peaceful life. But as far as actual constraints on his will go, only Heaven, the gods, and God, are truly above him. Only the action of the gods—my action in sending Dolly, Tish, and the ram, from our world into Illyria—has brought him up here to weigh up his choices. Letting Geryon go is fraught with dangers, and some real loss to Orsino's reputation, and to his domestic peace with Olivia. But if he could trust what Drusilla says, he could do it. She is only a child, but her assessment of character has always been good. And it would, he suspects, please the gods. But it is such a risk. How can he possibly trust his brother?

"How if *I* let you go?" Orsino asks, abruptly.

"Don't mock me!" Geryon bellows. Drusilla leaps back, startled, crashing into the parapet, which is shoulder high to her and above waist height to a tall man.

"I'm not mocking you, not at all," Orsino says, his tone calm, though his heart jumped at the shout and is pounding. "Your first impulse today was to protect Drusilla. If you really want to go to Elam and make carpets, I really am considering letting you go. I haven't decided yet, because it really is a risk."

"He means it," Drusilla says, and Orsino doesn't know which of them she is trying to reassure.

Geryon is silent.

"You hated being duke, and you were terrible at it. I had to depose you, and because you are what you are I had to do it the way I did it. It must have been terrible. I don't know what has kept you alive all this time," Orsino says.

"You couldn't have let me know you wanted it and asked me for it?" Geryon says.

"You wouldn't have given it to me. You knew I wanted it. And if I'd asked, it would have made you wary."

"I don't want to be duke anymore," Geryon says, as quietly as he can.

"If I let you go, you'd have to swear, before you touch the earth again, to give up all your claims on Illyria, and you'd have to swear it to Drusilla, and on her life," Orsino says. Drusilla stares up at her father, who nods gravely to her.

Geryon is silent for a moment longer, and Orsino waits. "Did you send her up here deliberately to make me care about her, so you could do this?" he asks.

"No he didn't! I don't know how you could think that!" Drusilla bursts out.

"Oh, he's capable of it," Geryon says. "He may be your father, and you may love him, but he's very devious. I never guessed he was plotting against me until it was too late. He had everything ready, but he treated me just like a beloved big brother until the very last minute. He might have decided to conceive you just for this."

"He is very devious. Dukes need to be. But he didn't do that. And I can always tell when he's lying," Drusilla says. "He has a tell. My mother told me what it is."

"What is it?" Orsino asks, horrified.

"I'm not telling you," Drusilla says, and laughs. Orsino resolves to ask Viola. If one person can figure out what it is, others could, and that could be dangerous. Viola will tell him, and then he can work on changing that mannerism, whatever it is, so he can again lie with confidence. Meanwhile, he resolves to be careful to be truthful in front of his daughter.

"Touch the earth," Geryon says, yearningly, and his voice cracks and breaks, and Orsino knows that he would cry if he had eyes. The last sliver of the sun sinks below the horizon. "What has changed? Why are you dangling hope so close in front of me now? What do you have to gain by it?"

Drusilla draws breath to tell him, but Orsino puts his hand on her arm above the arm ring to stop her, and she stops, though she frowns up at him. He wants to consider how much he wants Geryon to know. Is he truly going to let his brother go? He stares at Geryon's ruined face in the fading light. "You are my brother. I always thought I had to keep you imprisoned because I couldn't face a civil war and all the deaths that would cause. And a duel between us would be no contest. You'd win. But I am a better duke for Illyria. I was trained for it and I paid attention to my lessons. And now I've been doing it for a long time, and I'm good at it. But you—somebody you'd angered pointlessly would have killed you sooner or later, and probably sooner. You killed Claudio and that wasn't just a murder, it angered the Claudiani and all the great families. It was better for me to do it at once, better to have an orderly transition." These are the justifications he always uses to himself, and they sound hollow, voiced.

"I was wrong to kill Claudio. I lost my temper," Geryon says. "He wouldn't even consider letting me marry his sister, he just sneered at me the first time. And when I asked him a second time he said no Claudiana would marry a monster. But even so—I just reached out to grab him, and the next thing he was in two pieces on the ground. Humans are so fragile. I was sorry almost immediately. But you didn't reproach me for it at the time, you didn't say anything. Nobody said anything. Nobody even asked me why I did it."

"Olivia told me why," Orsino says.

"She wouldn't marry you either," Geryon says.

"No. But I'm married to the right woman," Orsino says.

"Well, it's long ago now. When you asked to wrestle with me on Ficino's tower I thought it meant you trusted me." He sighs heavily. "But instead you hated me and were hiding it."

"But I don't hate you. I never hated you. I was in love with Olivia. And I cared about Thalia, about Illyria."

Geryon sighs heavily. "I don't want to be duke. I always hated it. Miranda said I had to. I didn't know you wanted it. I thought you were waiting for Syracuse."

You can't read a lie in the eyes of somebody who has no eyes, but Geryon's voice seems entirely sincere. "If it's true that you don't want to be duke, if you'll go away—then it's possible to contemplate letting you go."

Geryon sighs again. "I don't want to. I'll swear whatever you like."

Orsino looks at Drusilla, and out at the city, and back at his brother. "But—Geryon, I don't know how I could let you go and you could not take revenge, even if it was a revenge that took hundreds of years. I blinded you. I left you up here all this time. You've always screamed how much you hated me. How could you not want revenge?"

"Of course I want revenge," Geryon booms. "For decades I thought about nothing else. But now—those decades were a long time ago, and now revenge seems petty and insignificant compared to the other things I want to do. I want to sink into the earth. I want to find onions and garlic growing under the ground and eat them with the dirt still on them. I want to rise up again to make patterns and colours into art. Did Dru tell you my eyes are growing back? Eventually I'll be able to see properly again. But I believe that even blind I could start to learn the techniques of carpet weaving."

"Ficino says he'll heal your eyes," Orsino says. He realises that he is crying, and dashes the tears out of his own healthy brown eyes. "And it's true that I'd always have to worry about revenge. But I think if I could live with that, as long as I knew you weren't going to hurt Drusilla or Illyria."

"You'd let me take personal revenge on you? Why?" Geryon asks, suspiciously.

"Oh no! I'd do everything to prevent it, from making you swear you wouldn't to building special defences against it. What I mean is that it's a risk I am considering being prepared to take," Orsino says.

"They called you after a bear, but you're twisty like a lizard," Geryon rumbles. "Now tell me. What changed?"

"Caliban is loose," Drusilla says. "That's why we started talking about this now, and why I told them that you're my friend. The gods let Caliban go."

"The gods? The gods haven't done anything for me," Geryon says, rattling his chain.

"Nobody knows what the gods want, unless Ficino does, and if so he hasn't told me," Orsino says. He scowls towards the afterglow of the sunset. "The gods have sent strangers from another world. I saw them, two young men, they seemed innocuous enough. But consider what commerce with other worlds has brought us in the past—first our great-grandfather, then Pico and Ficino. But now the gods have freed your father, and Caliban's first thought was to try to free you," Orsino says.

"Unlike my mother," Geryon says.

Orsino nods, then realises Geryon can't see. "Yes. But for what it's worth, she has asked to see you often over the years and I have prevented her. I couldn't quite trust her not to free you, if she saw how pitiful you looked."

"Gah. She could have flown up here and spoken to me any time she wanted, if she really wanted to," Geryon says. "She can make herself invisible, and she can fly. She wouldn't have needed to sneak up like Tyb and Dru did."

"Did Tybalt come up here too?" Orsino asks, in astonishment.

"Yes, but I haven't spoken to him for a long time, and Drusilla told me he has gone away," Geryon says.

"Yes, we haven't spoken to him for a long time either," Orsino says.

"It's just the three of us that matter, really," Geryon says. "Would you trust me if I swear never to hurt Drusilla, and never to come into the city again? Would you trust that, Dru?"

"Would you renounce your right to the duchy before the people?" Drusilla asks.

"Yes. I certainly don't want it."

Orsino stares out over the city. Lamps are burning below Ficino's tower, where in the banquet room they are having a meal to which they invited the gods. Lamps are being lit in other buildings far below as the sky darkens, and torches are being set in sconces. The bells begin ringing to say that day is over and the hours of night are beginning. Orsino looks back to Geryon. If he is to free him, it would be appropriate to free him on New Year's Day, in five months' time. It is a Great Year, the year sixteen, so the Thalian calendar will cycle and reset to one. That would be a significant and felicitous time for a big change like freeing a captive held so long. Or he could wait for a big saint's day, one of the many saints who watches over Illyria. But Caliban will be back at noon in two days' time.

"The problem is that what I have done to you is so terrible I can't believe you'd give up revenge," Orsino says. "Even if you think now you would, even if you swear it, the thought that I had done this to you and escaped without penalty would gnaw at you."

"But the longer you leave him here the worse you're making it," Drusilla objects.

Geryon laughs, a creaking rumbling hack of a laugh that Orsino remembers from long ago. "Then how about if you give me revenge, so that's satisfied?"

"What would you accept?" Orsino asks, cautiously.

"How about if you gave up the dukedom you stole from me? That would be fair. Not give it back to me, just renounce it so neither of us had it."

"I'm too young," Drusilla says at once. "I'm not ready. And I'm not sure I want to be duke anyway. And we don't know where Tybalt is, though if he wanted to be duke he'd probably keep in touch."

"Do you mean restore the Republic?" Orsino asks.

It is not light enough to make out any expression on Geryon's ruined face. "Our great" grandfather came from another world and made himself duke. The forms of the Republic are still there, aren't they? The Senate, the Council? You haven't changed that?"

"No, they're still there," Orsino says. He is dazed. "But what would I do?"

"Good works," Drusilla says. "In recompense."

Orsino flinches. He has been ruling, or training to rule, for all of his long life. The thought of life without that is dizzying.

"Not yet," Orsino says. "And I would need to talk to the others. But perhaps I could agree to do that eventually."

Geryon is silent for a long time. A slim crescent of moon rises, silvering the river. "All right," he says, at last. "Or even if you can't bear that, just trust my oath not to harm Illyria or Drusilla and let me go."

"It's my fault, I know, that it's so hard for us to trust each other now," Orsino says.

Geryon sighs, like a landslide. "Maybe, brother, after all this time, we can find a way to let each other go."

30

FORGET THE
PERFECT OFFERING

The problem with talking about Teatro del Sale is that it's almost impossible to describe. You have to experience it. Fortunately, if very implausibly, it's real, so you can. It's a dining club, and it costs seven euros a year for membership. Duties of membership are telling other people about great food, and clearing your own table. Once you are a member, you can eat lunch there as often as you like for fifteen euros on a weekday or twenty on weekends, and dinner for thirty. Dinner includes entertainment afterwards, usually political comedy in Italian by Maria Cassi, wife of the owner, but sometimes music or dance of various sorts.

The place is owned by Fabio Picchi, a Florentine chef, and owner of a very high-end restaurant called Cibrèo, which has lots of stars, the kind of restaurant where you spend hundreds of euros on a meal. He is a socialist, and as he didn't just want to make food for rich people he opened Teatro del Sale, which makes delicious food with simple inexpensive ingredients, at what are really ridiculously good prices. Water, wine, and coffee are included, and you can eat as much as you want. There's a buffet of cold food set out at the start of the meal, which you can help yourself to at any time. Other courses come out ceremoniously, one course at a time. These courses are announced by a yell from the window, and are put on the table at the front, where you can help yourself. There are usually eight or ten courses, sometimes more. Lots of them are vegetarian, and there's usually one or two fish courses and one or two meat courses, and dessert. The courses are tiny, but if you love something you can usually have seconds. The kitchen helps train up sous chefs for Cibrèo—one lunchtime this summer Sylvia watched a girl making sciacchiata, the amazingly delicious flatbread with olive oil, pork fat, and salt, and could see that she was notably better at stretching it out and getting it even by the end of the meal. It also employs the son of a friend of Fabio's who has Down syndrome. He rings the bell to announce the courses, and sometimes announces what they are, whereupon everyone claps and cheers and he looks utterly delighted.

It's in an old monastery near the church of Sant Ambrogio and the Sant Ambrogio market, near the old eastern gate of the city. (Firenze isn't very big, you can walk across the entire diameter in half an hour if you don't get lost in the maze of streets.) The main room where you eat is next to the kitchen so you can watch the cooks, but separated from it by a glass wall with a serving hatch in it. It has a stage at one end for the evening performances, and different-sized tables set out for any number of people, from two to about twenty. The room can hold maybe a hundred people, and sometimes it does get full. If you want to go there on a busy evening it's a good idea to tell them in advance, especially if you're a big group—and it's a courtesy to do it anyway, because then they have some idea how much food to make. Sylvia tries to remember to pop in and let them know when she's going there in the evening with friends. She just shows up at lunchtime.

It's always cool inside. Most of the people there are locals, but there are always some tourists who have heard one way or another that it exists. There are membership forms in a whole bunch of languages, including Chinese and Polish. You see people in big groups, sometimes three or four generations of a family at Sunday lunch. You see young mothers with napping babies in strollers, here for a meal and a rest. You see couples of all ages and gender mixes, and also groups of friends, coworkers. You see people on their own, old men reading the newspaper, old women watching the cooks, or reading books on their e-readers. People are friendly to each other, and when Sylvia stays in Firenze for a while she starts to recognise some of the regulars and all of the staff, and they recognise her and say "Ciao" when she comes in. It's a delightfully friendly atmosphere, with everyone looking comfortable and relaxed.

But the real reason to go is that the food is incredibly, unbelievably, implausibly good, so good superlatives crack under the burden of trying to describe it. You could use a whole thesaurus just saying how good the salads are and still not manage to get it across. There's a spelt salad; spelt, the grain that usually in history means things are really bad if people have resorted to eating it, but here it's perfect. All Italian ingredients are better than ingredients anywhere else, and Teatro del Sale is the pinnacle of perfection. Sylvia usually just says that it has the best food she has ever eaten anywhere and lets it go at that. Their gnocchi are astonishing. The carrots deserve to have odes written to them. It's the sort of place you can't quite believe exists. It strains probability that there could be something this good. You can't believe you're there even when you are there, even when you can go again tomorrow.

You should go if you get the chance. You want to go to Firenze anyway, right? Flights can be cheaper than you think, and off season some of the hotels too. You don't need a luxurious bedroom, you're going to spend all your time looking at art and eating great food. If you have allergies there will be some things you can't have, but that's all right, you'll have more room for other things. (You don't have to go. That door at the end of the passage, the door that leads into the rose garden remains firmly closed. We got in the other way, remember? And Orsino and Olivia didn't go in at all. This is just a suggestion. Advice. If you should come to exist, dear reader, in your nebulous and unimaginable future, then if you'd like to, and if you can, go to Teatro del Sale, and when you eat the carrots, remember us. They are real, by any measure, whether you and I are or not.)

Whenever Sylvia goes to Teatro del Sale now she remembers the time she first brought Idris here. He liked the entrance but fidgeted filling in the form. Then he approved the cool interior, with the crimson chairs and dark wood tables in the grey stone space, which fit his sense of aesthetics very well. They filled decanters of cold water and red wine, which you get for yourself from the space just outside the main room. He sat down, looking around at the other diners, the mix of ages, the mix of cultures. There was a little dog there that day, a bay weiner, sitting quietly by its owner's feet and staring at the other diners. Then the food started coming. First they had plates of vegetables. Then they had gnocchi—it was March, a slack time for Idris in work, when everything in Montreal is still frozen, but well into spring in Firenze. That was followed by spinach mousse with parmesan, which melts on the tongue, subtle and delectable. As he was eating this, slowly, savouring every bite, Idris said, looking around, "How can this exist? And given that it does, how can there only be one like it?"

On this trip she's been coming alone at lunchtime, once or twice a week. She doesn't drink wine, because she wants to write in the afternoon and needs a clear head. There is a porcini mushroom soup today. It's pale brown, with dark green olive oil floating on the top, and it tastes rich and dark, like earth, like Earth, like mother Gaia. It coats her tongue, and her tastebuds immediately feel not just satisfied but fulfilled, as if tasting this soup is why tastebuds evolved in the first place. We pretend sometimes that this food is made from food grown outside Plato's Cave, in the ultimate reality. If you tell people you went out there, they get angry, Plato says, so people—Fabio Picchi and his friends and coworkers—just sneak out of the Cave to grow vegetables. Talking about Teatro del Sale it's easy to use words like "incredible" and "unbelievable," but when you're there it feels instead like the ultimate reality, the way things ought to be. Famous chefs ought to want to give things like this back to the community. Food ought to taste this way. It's so like a wish-fulfillment narrative that it's hard to suspend disbelief, but yet, here she is again, eating mouthwatering food, familiar but never taken for granted.

"I'll miss this," she says to me, as she unabashedly licks her bowl.

"They have this in Illyria," I say.

"Really?" She doesn't speak aloud when she's talking to me in this kind of situation, but her facial expression does change, and when she says this her eyebrows shoot up and she tucks her chin down, expressing her scepticism. So from an outside perspective she's sitting alone making faces to herself. Fortunately, in Teatro del Sale, they're used to her.

"Yes. Exactly like this, exactly here in the equivalent place, with this exact food, and the bust of Fabio next to the picture of Karl Marx on the shelf in the kitchen, just the same, except it isn't Marx, it's some saint with a huge beard. What saints have beards? Maybe it's Poseidon. St Poseidon. This is perfect, and so they have it there, and they always have, and Fabio has been running it for three hundred years, and that arched wall right there has a fresco of Maria Cassi instead of a photograph, and over there on that one is a frieze of lute players and dancers."

"Why would it be the same?" she asks, eating a piece of rigatoni with tomato and basil, so simple, but just right, the pasta cooked just the right amount, the basil so fragrant, the tomato so sweet.

"Because it's perfect. And because it's like the Renaissance."

"It's nothing like the Renaissance! They didn't have anything like this. When Leonardo and Botticelli tried to open a restaurant called the Three Frogs it went bankrupt. It was down by the Ponte Vecchio. I think it was where that awful gelateria with huge piled-up gelato is, just as you get to the bridge."

"Well, that does prove the nonexistence of time travel," I say. "Because it would be the most exciting inn for time travellers."

"Or maybe time travellers made it go bankrupt, to ensure that Leonardo and Botticelli got back to their paintbrushes and didn't waste their time on such ephemeral art," she muses.

"Not that it would have been wasting their time. But time travellers might have thought so," I say. "But what I meant was, while they didn't have dining clubs in the Renaissance, and they didn't really have anything like this—and they won't ever have tomatoes or zucchini because they don't have the New World—it's like the Renaissance in that Fabio's made something and is excited to share it with people. And the kitchen is like a workshop with apprentices, except that the art is food, and he asks people to respond to art with art, all the acts he has in the theatre, and having people tell others about food. And he was so happy when you put it in a story that time, remember? And that kind of sharing and excitement is part of the spirit of the Renaissance, so I say that Teatro del Sale is in Thalia just as it is in Firenze, and when we're there we'll be able to go together, and the real difference is that I'll actually be able to eat for myself and nobody will think you're mad when you talk to me."

Sylvia finishes the rigatoni. Osso bucco is announced, with a ringing of the bell and a loud call, and when she has finished clapping and cheering she goes up to the front to get some, piling her empty plates at the hatch neatly on the way. When she comes back, with a little plate of shredded beef tail and a little pile of salt to dip it in, she looks dreamily at the poster of Maria Cassi. "We were wrong about Progress," she says, taking her first bite. "My goodness that's good."

"Wrong how?" I ask.

"We wanted it to be the Renaissance forever in Illyria, and so we said it was. By divine fiat, we said Progress didn't work in Illyria, as part of what Pico and Ficino did to stop death. But if it is forever, then it stops being the Renaissance." She takes another blissful bite of the oxtail. "You're absolutely right about Teatro del Sale being like that, and that it's the excitement. But if Fabio had been running it for three hundred years, would he still be excited? Excited by new ideas for food, maybe, and new artists, but sooner or later it's all going to feel too familiar, well worn, not innovative anymore, and he'd want to do something else, and maybe hand it on to new people who have different ideas. If you don't have Progress, they are going to run out of new things. Art can stay at that pinnacle, maybe. Let's say the fresco of Maria Cassi replacing the photo over there is done by, oh, Donato Bonnini, in 1758."

"And Donato is a girl in disguise?" I offer at once.

"Yes, and she came from Verona to apprentice and to be healed of depression by Ficino, who healed her by balancing her humours and telling her to eat more red meat—this beef is so amazing—and drink orange juice and wear blue, which she still does." This is how you make up a character, by the way, when you don't go into the mist and have one coalesce. Donato could become real or she could just stay as a piece of brainstorming, she could even be in a story without being any more real than this placeholder set of attributes, that would all depend what happened later. "And she's every bit as good as Ghirlandaio," Sylvia went on. "And her portrait of Cassi there—she's in that pose she's in in the photo, and she's making a funny face because she's a clown and because making funny faces in art is a thing in 1750s Illyria, and it's all technically perfect and wonderful. But it's just . . . more. More is good, I wouldn't get tired of it, but . . . nobody's going to invent perspective and turn everything upside down. It's going to be lovely, really lovely, but it won't be exciting. And you only have a golden age when people are excited to be doing new things and showing each other."

She's right and I know it as soon as she says it, and it's being in Teatro del Sale, which is having a golden age right now, that makes me see it. And I have to be honest, because art is too important. I can't say that being lovely is enough, tempting as that would be. "So should we start Progress again?" I ask.

"It would move more slowly anyway, with everyone living so long," she says. "But if I were going to live there, yes. I'd want the stars to be destinations, not destiny. The real Renaissance was a time of total innovation. It wasn't ever static. I don't think any time in history was, not really. They talk about the Dark Ages, but they saw the widespread use of waterwheels, the introduction of stirrups—"

"The loss of menstrual sponges," I put in.

She eats the last bite of beef and wipes her fingers on her napkin. "Well, yes, it isn't always all going forwards. But it isn't all doom either. It's complicated. And in the Renaissance there were new inventions and new methods and cross-pollination of cultures all over the place. Life expectancy *fell*, compared to the Middle Ages, but still it was a fast-moving time. And right after that, they found the Americas and that widened Europe's sense of possibilities, even though it was devastating for the cultures they encountered." She gets up and goes towards the front table. "I left the New World out on purpose, and not so they wouldn't have tomatoes," she says, scooping some spelt and tomato salad onto her plate. The tomatoes are small and dark and bursting with flavour. "I came here and looked at all this beauty, and I thought it was the best Europe could be, and the genocidal colonialism was the worst. We were only just starting to confront the issues then, in Canada. I just wanted nothing to do with it, so I left it out. That isn't what I'd do now." She adds a scoop of carrots and a spoonful of anchovy butter to her plate and makes her way back to her table.

"And anyway you can't put everything into everything," I say, as she sits down again. "Every piece of art can't address every issue."

"No. You can't. But really, a lot of what was important about the Renaissance was that golden-age feeling, people making things and being excited. Stopping that dead and removing the possibility of progress by fiat kills half of what matters about it. And the other half is really just decoration. Very beautiful decoration, admittedly, but still just decoration."

The bell rings suddenly and loudly from the kitchen window, a wild joyous clangour. Today's kitchen master announces that something incomprehensible will be available at the window. She goes up to collect it, in a crowd of others. She exchanges a few words with an old man who is here almost every day, about how good the carrots are today. The new dish turns out to be pieces of mackerel baked in lemon juice and oil.

"We could start it up again," I say, when she is sitting down again and has taken the first blissful bite.

"I'm not really a god," she says.

"Not in this world. In Illyria you are."

"Why am I Hekate?"

"Because you are. You are the one who works your will, the goddess of boundaries and crossroads and edges, the mistress of creation."

She takes another bite of the mackerel, which is sweet and rich and juicy all at once. "I'm not sure I want to be a goddess."

"You wouldn't only be. And how come you're suddenly interested, after weeks and months of repeating over and over that it's impossible?"

"Nobody else is offering me *any* form of immortality. Nobody looks ready to invent one, or a cure for cancer, not in time. Oh you know I tried to keep it from you, tried to shut you away, but we know how well that worked. You wouldn't listen to me. You immediately started telling your own story."

"Building my lifeboat." High above, the sun goes behind a cloud and the room dims. I knew it. I knew that's why she came.

"I could have stayed at home and gone through it all again. But it would have been hopeless. And—" A tear slips down her face. She takes out a paper tissue and wipes it away. "This is ridiculous, but I'd have lost my appetite again, and coming here seemed—"

"Like in *The Bone People*," I say, as she takes another bite of carrots followed by another bite of fish.

"Yes, but Kerewin couldn't really have had cancer . . . or it was magic. And Firenze is hardly the middle of the wilderness where I could leave decorative bones. And I don't feel sick. The chemo would make me feel terrible, like last time, but now I feel so well. I can finish the book." She takes the last bite of her fish and savours it. "But I don't want to die. Idris died and the world went on and he wasn't in it, and I had to go on too. I can't imagine the world going on without me. Or rather, I can imagine it, but it feels . . . imaginary, not like something that could really happen. If it were a story idea I'd dismiss it as not hanging together."

"What we need to do is get you into Illyria," I say, as I have been saying all along.

She mops up the olive oil and lemon on her plate with a piece of sciacchiata. I think she's going to say once more that it isn't possible and I don't understand, but she surprises me. "So what else do we have to do? You've told all the stories about me, about my childhood, and about coming here and starting to write, about Idris, and even about Steve. What more do we need? Do we need to tell all the stories about you again, the stories that are in my books? How you were a dragon and a prince and a poet and a Viking and all the other things?"

"I think we told those already. I don't think we need to put those details in this book. But I think there's a little more about you," I say. "And we have to tell them what they need to do. And you know where the moon was in that picture. The next new moon is July thirteenth, and it will look like that two or three days later. So that's when it will be. That gives us a couple more weeks."

"We can get the book finished, and sent off, though not edited. It's a very strange book, but if it's posthumous that won't matter. Nobody will believe a word of it anyway. I mean, look!" She looks around at the happy people enjoying their food. Some are hanging around the window waiting for the last course and watching chickens being pulled off the spits and cut apart. "I'm not sure I could even get people to suspend their disbelief in the carrots." She eats another forkful of them. "I'm not sure I could even describe the carrots."

"Slices of sunset, melting on the tongue, offered, accepted, loved by old and young, sweet, and a treat, but earthy, rich, and strange—"

"Using Shakespeare is cheating!"

"You say that? You?"

And as we laugh, the bell rings out again and the last course is served.

31

SATURN DEVOURING
HIS CHILDREN

Dolly wakes in the night in complete darkness and for a moment he has no idea where he is, or even who he is. He reaches out an arm and finds embroidered bedcovers, which he pulls up around his shoulders. It feels momentarily strange to him to be embodied, to have a hand, to be able to distinguish threads and textures and the weight of cloth, to be aware of the warmth of his own skin. He had such a strange dream, and even though the ragged remnants of it are melting away now, the strangeness clings to him as he sits up, as his foot meets the cold tile of the floor. "Methinks I was, methinks I had . . ." he says aloud, and as he quotes Shakespeare he centers himself on himself. He remembers that he is in Ficino's house in Thalia, not his parents palazzo in Firenze, or his rooms in Cambridge, or the strange half-remembered realms of dream.

The room is dark. Any child in Thalia can light a candle with a gesture, but Dolly can't. His feet are cold, but he doesn't know how to dress in the darkness. He feels his way tentatively across the room, stubbing his toe on one of his own shoes. (His shoes, which were not stuffed with rags like Tish's boots, have shrunk a little from their soaking and now pinch him slightly, so he has not been wearing them.) He puts out his hand and finds a window shutter, which he opens. It is deep in a quiet night, the moon has set, and all the sconces people set by their doors for light have been extinguished or burned themselves out. He sees high above the remote intense burning points of the stars, which remind him of his dream. By their distant light, that has crossed so much space and time to reach him, he makes his way to the door.

He fumbles his way barefoot and in his nightshirt around the courtyard and up the stairs in the deep darkness, up past Ficino's study, past Tish's closed door and the room where Miranda is staying, up and up to the top of the tower, where Ficino is sitting in a wooden armchair under the crystal dome, staring up at the stars. "Dolly," he says, as soon as he sees him. "Only a dream would have brought you up here at this hour, it's past three. Come and sit down and tell me about it. Are you cold? Would you like a blanket? Should I light the fire?"

"I am cold, and yes, it was a dream," Dolly says.

There is wood laid in the fireplace. Ficino makes a gesture towards it very like a conductor signalling to the violin section to begin, and the fire leaps obediently to an immediate conflagration, each branch and log leaping with a gush of orange flame, which then settles back to a more ordinary blaze. Dolly warms himself in front of it, then takes the offered blanket and wraps himself in it. He sits down in the other chair. He leans back. The sky is very clear, a rich velvety black, and even with the fire burning the stars still look very bright. Dolly has spent his time studying the Classics, Shakespeare, and the Florentine Renaissance; he doesn't know one star from another. "I dreamed of Saturn devouring his children," he says, still staring up into the star field. "He was an old man with a dirty beard and worn, stained finery. He seemed almost like a tramp, a vagabond. But he was immensely fat, and swelling more and more as he ate. Some of the children were children, but others were paintings, and operas, and telescopes, and a steam train. He was grabbing them with his hands and stuffing them into his mouth, then chewing and swallowing them and reaching out for more. In my dream that didn't seem strange. I was watching. But then there came a woman, a huge, thin, hungry woman, and her skirts were stars. She was wearing one of those skimpy shirts like we saw in the oracle, and on it was scrawled *I never come*. She seemed to have a broom, and to be sweeping away everything, the whole world, everything, sweeping it all towards Saturn who was devouring it and getting bigger. Some of it started to circle his waist, and float there, turning when he turned. Then her broom became a roaring stick, not as big as the loud two-wheeled vehicles, but reminiscent of them, and with a long tube, and instead of sweeping everything towards Saturn, who was still reaching for it, the tube was sucking it all away."

"The woman was Crastina," Ficino says.

"Of course," Dolly says, immediately feeling stupid for not realising. "Crastina, the Goddess of Tomorrow. And tomorrow never comes. Horace—"

"Was there more?" Ficino asks.

"She was angry. Crastina. Angry with me, as if it was all my fault. What does it mean for Tomorrow to be angry with me? Her eyes met mine, and they were burning bright, like stars, and then they were stars, and then—there was something else. I've forgotten. I woke knowing I had to tell you, that it was important."

Wrapped in the rags and tatters of his dream, and Ficino's old grey blanket, Dolly doesn't make an imposing prophet. But Ficino nods gravely. "She has reason enough to be angry with us," he says. "And the children Saturn was devouring were works of creation?"

"Yes," Dolly says. "If you count invention as creation."

"Oh, certainly I do," Ficino says.

"Then yes," Dolly says.

"Can you remember the other thing?" Ficino asks.

Dolly is trying, but since the main part of it was the strangeness of being me, of inhabiting a shifting point of view, he can't hold on to it or describe it. This is partly because he knows he was himself in the dream, which was also true, because I made him out of me. "It's gone," he says. "Except a sense of the gods."

"Ah, yes," Ficino says. He indicates a star, which is just a bright point to Dolly. "There's Saturn. And maybe it is so. I think perhaps it is. That would mean the time has come to begin Progress again. To do that—well, it will be a lot of work." Ficino nods to himself and looks pleased at the prospect.

"If we start Progress does that mean it will stop being the Renaissance?" Dolly asks.

"What an excellent question. No, not if we're careful," Ficino says. "There's nothing bad about technology, what's bad is turning away from the good to pursue other ends. They may have done that in your world, but we need not. The two things are not bound together, we can have one without the other. We can reach for the stars as a way of pursuing the good."

"In my world they fought over religion. And after that, ever since then it has been a constant case of chasing after profit, making profit almost into a god," Dolly says.

"I would have thought Hermes would approve of that," Ficino says.

"Maybe that's why he wants to restart progress here," Dolly says, then shakes his head. "No, I don't believe that. My dream was about good things being destroyed by stasis. Perhaps what Tish and I know of what happened in our history will help us avoid those perils."

"That might be why they sent you. But most of all, because they sent you, and sent that dream, we know which gods to call back into the world to make the change. Finding that out can be more trouble than anything else, and we are spared that."

"Saturn and Crastina?" Dolly asks.

"Well, Crastina will inevitably follow when Progress begins again, but it's Hekate who has been sending us clear signs. Hekate and Hermes are the gods of change and chance, and they have been shut out. And they have given tokens, the oak leaf and the ram, and the two of you, especially you, Dolly. We must summon them, and it will be a great work, a work after all this time that will challenge me. And what you do will be central. This dream shows that. This must be the work you were called here to do."

"But can't the gods just come in? They sent me and Tish here. Can't they come themselves?"

Ficino chuckles like a schoolboy who sees through a trick. "You'd think so, but no. We call them gods, but really they're messengers between God and us. It's better to consider them as angels. *Angel* means messenger. If God wants to send them here, then they come. Or they can come if we summon them in the right way."

"Do you know the right way?" Dolly asks.

"I will have to study it, but yes."

"Shall we do it now?" Dolly asks, eager and ready.

Ficino shakes his head. "You're not ready. And it will take more than the two of us even so. We will need Miranda, and Prospero, and many others. But we have time. It was 2018 when we were shown Firenze, so it should be that time here when we act. And for the moon to be in the position we saw over the Ponte Vecchio in the painting, it's possibly June but most likely July of that year. So that gives us a hundred and seventy-one years."

Dolly had been about to object, but then he relaxes and sits back in his chair. The numbers sounds right. "What will we need?"

"We'll need the true names of the gods, for the summoning. That will be difficult. And beyond that I'm not sure yet of all we might need. We'll need a great Elamese carpet. We'll need my painting, and more paintings of the things in your dream. Can you draw?"

"No, but Tish can, and she said—that is he said that he wanted to apprentice to a painter, and you and Miranda said that would be possible."

"You're not in love with her?" Ficino asks, gently.

"Miranda? Oh, Tish? No, neither of them," Dolly says, confused and embarrassed. "I like Tish a great deal, and I respect Miranda and I sympathise with her."

"Then perhaps Tish's part will be producing the paintings, once she is trained. She has seen a *steam train*, and she shared our vision of 2018. And for you to be able to play your part, you will need to study a great deal of magic. There's time, but a hundred and seventy-one years is not too much time for that, especially since you want to go to Xanadu, and indeed, you may need to, for we will need the help of many people, far more than can be found in Illyria." He nods to himself. "Well, we have a lot of work to do," Ficino says, standing up and rubbing his hands together. Dolly thinks he's about to be sent back to bed, to begin in the morning. "This will be a great work of magic such as I have not done in centuries. It's time to teach you the beginnings of spellcraft."

Dolly leans forward. He feels like Keats looking into Chapman's Homer, as if new worlds he'd only heard rumours of are spread out for his delight. "Yes!" he says. "How do we start?"

Ficino picks a splinter of wood from one of the logs beside the fire and hands it to Dolly. "Wood wants to burn," he says. "It only needs a spark to leap into flame. Calm your mind and reach out to the fire and bring the spark."

Dolly looks at the fire, blazing in the grate, giving out warmth and light. The dancing flames are gold and blue and in the depths orange and vermilion. He looks at the splinter of dry wood in his hands, not much bigger than a paper spill. If he touched it to the fire it would blaze up at once. But how could he bring the spark without moving? He looks at Ficino, who is smiling at him encouragingly. He reaches into the patterns of his mind, and then it is as if he is remembering something he knew once, long ago, perhaps a skill he learned in childhood. It is not so much a reach but a twist. He moves the fingers of his right hand in the inevitable remembered pattern, and the splinter he holds in his left hand bursts into flame.

"Ah," Ficino says, smiling. "It came back to you. Good. You remembered. Have you felt that before?"

"Yes," Dolly admits. The fire is real enough to start burning his fingers. He drops the splinter into the fire, where it burns with the rest of the wood, and looks at Ficino. "I have always felt that about some things when I studied them, as if it's more like remembering than learning. And other things are completely new and fresh. Euripides was like remembering, Shakespeare was all new. But that—"

"Let's try something," Ficino interrupts. He leans down to a box on the floor and pulls out a sealed glass jar.

"Quicksilver," Dolly says, recognising the glint of the silver liquid metal.

Ficino closes the lid of the box, which is smooth polished wood with a raised rim. He pushes it towards Dolly, who straightens it in front of him, letting the blanket fall from his shoulders. Then Ficino opens the jar and pours the metal out onto the top of the box. "Quicksilver speeding and spilling and slowing," he says, and looks at Dolly expectantly.

"Quicksilver . . . feeding and filling and flowing," Dolly responds, half as if he is remembering and half as if he is making it up.

"Quicksilver, beading and billing and blowing," Ficino says. He touches his finger to it, and without encouragement Dolly leans forward and does the same.

"Mercury," Ficino says. And again for Dolly it is like a poem he knew once and he is trying to recall. "Mercury myrtle myrrh, mercenary murder demur."

"Hermes," Dolly says, slowly, and then all at once he knows it and rattles off the rest of it. "Hermes hurtle her, hereditary, hurter, cohere." As he says the last word all the balls of mercury flow together and make one smooth, silver, shining sphere, resting on the box top. He laughs aloud, and sits back. He has always felt tentative—even at his most passionate, there has always been an aspect of playacting behind all his sincerity—but now, for once, he feels certain, true, complete. "But what does it mean?"

"I am a doctor of souls, and I should tell you that I recognise your soul. I knew you long ago." Ficino smiles. The mercury quivers a little on the box lid.

"But who was I?" Dolly asks, excited, leaning forward again.

"You were Pico della Mirandola, of course," Ficino says. He picks up the ball of quicksilver and holds it on his palm. "Nobody else could have known that. But do not try to force the memory. It will either come back naturally or not."

Dolly feels as if his blood has been replaced with a fizzing wine. He jumps out of the chair and clasps Ficino to him and dances with him around the observatory. Globes of mercury spill and roll everywhere. Ficino laughs. "I don't remember, and I'm not sure it can possibly be true, but even just the suggestion makes me very happy," Dolly says, collapsing back in his chair.

"You'll still have to work very hard," Ficino says, pretending to be stern. He resumes his own seat. "Now clean it up."

"Cohere," Dolly says again, and the quicksilver balls roll back together from all over the room, to make a single globe at his feet.

"You are, as you always were, an embodiment of Hermes. Even your name points to it. Dolios is his name in trickster form."

"Then how did I come into the world?" As soon as he asks the question he realises the answer. "Oh. Only a part of me is here. In the dream I was whole."

"To get this part in, you had to be entirely unknowing, I would guess," Ficino says. "But you are your own self as well."

"I am," Dolly says, though as he sits at the top of the wizard's tower with the quicksilver orb at his feet, he feels very far from what he has been. "And to bring the gods in, I will have to sacrifice myself again in the end," Dolly says, recognising it, again, as something half-remembered that he has always known.

Ficino looks at him sadly. "How many times will I have to lose you, old friend?"

"It doesn't matter how many, does it? As long as you always get me back," Dolly says.

32

DEUS EX MACHINA

Orsino did not get to bed until much later than Dolly, but he too wakes from a dream at the same hour of moonset. His dream is simpler and more didactic. Hermes, unmistakable in his winged boots (talaria) and winged round hat (petasus) and holding his wand (caduceus) hovers in the air in front of him, and informs him that he has come with a message. "Yes," Orsino says, as if he receives divine messengers regularly. "What is it?"

"You can trust Geryon to keep his word," Hermes says, and disappears.

And waking on that note, Orsino embraces sleeping Viola and stares into the darkness.

33

A LOCAL HABITATION
AND . . .

What else needs to go into this, between now and the end? Not much, we must be nearly there. Sylvia takes one of her special notebooks and goes through her lists, crossing things off and making a new list, the way she always does when she's getting near the end of a book. She's sitting on her new blue chair at the table, with her old pen in her hand, with tooth marks clear in the end where she's been biting it. "What's this?" she asks me, pausing. "Rosary ice skate. What did you mean by that?"

At first I can't remember, and we stare at the implausible words, which take on the enigmatic significance of any half-understood poetic reference. Then it comes back to me. "The box of things Maureen brought you after your mother died," I say. "After she cleaned out the house. The things you'd left there, and the things that she thought you'd want. There was one ice skate, remember, and—"

"And tangled around the blade my mother's coral rosary with the jet cross," she says. "But why did you want to put that in?"

"It felt significant," I say. "And we've talked about death a lot, but we haven't talked about your mother's death, or about the things people leave behind for the survivors to deal with, and I thought that might be a way in to that."

"No. There's no need," she says. "There's way too much about me in this book already. People will say it's self indulgence. I'll have to cut most of it, and put in more adventures in Illyria."

"Dolly going to Xanadu," I say.

"Tish becoming a painter. The release of Geryon, and the vow he makes above the city on the invisible walkway. Geryon becoming a weaver in Elam. Dolly learning magic. Orsino talking to Viola. Drusilla growing up. Caliban showing up again. His reunion with Geryon. And I'd like to actually see Sebastian in women's clothes rather more, instead of just seeing him in them once and saying he wears them more often than Viola. Sebastian and Olivia, both dressed in beautiful Renaissance women's clothes, pushing the black-and-white Persian cat off that huge bed—"

"Now who's being self indulgent," I say, and she laughs.

"But seriously, isn't there enough of us in already?" she asks.

I think so, but it's impossible to know for sure until it's finished and it either works or it does not. Who knows how much is enough, if she does not? They are there, in Illyria, all of them, working hard to get us in, spending that hundred and seventy-one years on getting everything ready. And here we are, in Firenze, with a laptop, a notebook, half a kilo of dark red cherries, and a great deal of apprehension.

"You were very conflicted when your mother died," I say.

"No I wasn't. I was more glad than anything. I could finally give up trying to be good enough for her, and be myself. That box of things was upsetting more because it was what Maureen thought I'd want, and that meant she knew me so little. Maureen was the good daughter. And she still thinks I'm a terrible person. It's too late to do anything about that."

"You still have the rosary," I say.

"Somewhere at home," she says.

It's in the small top drawer of her writing desk in her house in Montreal, along with a pile of other souvenirs—a tartan fuzzy from a Worldcon in Glasgow, a stub of one of Idris's yellow pencils, a set of rainbow Post-it Notes, a dragon-shaped USB key with some old book files on, and a crumpled entry ticket for the church of San Clemente in Rome. It's where she keeps her passport when she's at home.

"The girls and Con will have to throw it all away," she says, with a pang. "I should have gone through everything before I left."

Throwing stuff out after people die, sorting through the things they kept and will never use again is one of the bitterest things in the aftermath of a loss.

"It's oppressive but it's boring to write about," she objects.

She eats another cherry and puts the stone on a pile on a plate that has by now far surpassed any tinkers, tailors, beggarmen, or thieves and gone on into the realms she and Idris made up when the girls were small, "Writer, fighter, engineer, astronaut, cosmonaut, buccaneer . . ." Idris got so angry when Meg said it was who you'd marry, not what you might become. "You can do all those things. You can become whatever you want."

"Not a thief," Lucy said.

"You could be a thief if you really wanted to," Meg said.

"If you wanted to, nothing would stop you," Idris said. "But it's a good thing you don't want to!"

She smiles now, remembering, and counts the cherry stones. Farmer, teacher, plumber, vet, librarian, barbarian, space cadet . . .

"How about you? Is there more of you we should get in?" she asks. "Though it seems I've been telling stories about you for my whole career. We had your origin story, and your first death, and how you came back from the dead and rescued me. And we've had your second death, your sacrifice as Pico, and the time you wanted to run away to Constantinople, and we've decided we don't need to go into the time you were a dragon or a prince or a skald or any of that."

"I have flown on the wings of the world. I have stolen fire and words and power. I have been a message and a messenger. I have been a boy with a book and a word on a page."

"You have been Hermes?"

"Yes. Well, anyway, by Ficino's Platonic way of looking at things."

She underlines something in her list. "And you're going to renew Pico's sacrifice to get us in?"

"Dolly is, yes. And death shall have no dominion." I remember the exhilaration of that death to end death, my hand on the knife, my action reaching God above the gods.

She closes the notebook decisively. "Then that's all these notes. What else do we need?"

"I think we need to go to the rose garden."

"Aha. Let's go then!" She slips on her shoes and picks up her bag.

We go the same way Miranda took Dolly and Tish, across the Ponte alle Grazie, in this world just a modern bridge, through the narrow twisting Renaissance streets of the Oltrarno, out through the gate, pausing to look at the one unbroken and neglected stretch of wall. It is very hot, but dry. We pass tourists, and bicycles and Vespas and taxis pass us, but they're part of our normal background so, unlike Ficino, we pay no particular attention to them. We pause only to look at sculpted busts on buildings and menus of unfamiliar restaurants. We have no difficulty finding the gate to the rose garden, as it is not magically hidden in Firenze, and we go in. It's interesting to see the kind of people who visit a rose garden in Firenze, which has so much else to offer. There are some individual college-age girls, sunbathing. One of them is reading Diderot's *Jacques le Fataliste et Son Maître*, in French. There is a family of German rose fanatics, exclaiming over the flowers and calling each other to see their discoveries, their enthusiasm clear even through the barrier of language. There is an elderly Japanese couple, very elegant. Sylvia observes everything with the writer's air of attention and making notes for later. We make our way through the roses, in full bloom now, as they would not be in October, and with a straggling and untended air. There is no shade, and the heat is oppressive, Helios Apollo beats down relentless. We get to the fountain and the pool, choked with waterlilies.

"Here we are. Why did we come?" she asks me.

"We should have come the other way," I say. "Down the passage."

"But Caliban knocked down Miranda's house, and it isn't here anyway." She turns around. To the eyes of the teenage German girl looking at a rosebush, Sylvia is alone, an elderly lady in a grey silk shirt pinned at the throat with a pearl circlet, gazing into a pool of waterlilies.

"I need a name," I say. "They're going to summon us by name. Ficino and Miranda and wizards from as far away as Xanadu are doing spells to determine which names to call when they call us. Yours they will find easily. But I have never had one."

"You had one once," she says. "But that was what my mother killed."

I have been nameless. I have had more names than the Allfather. Who am I? "I'm asking you to give me a name now," I say.

She stares down at the waterlilies, tight pink buds, open waxy flowers, choking green pads. "It would be wrong for me to name you. Ask them for one."

"Them? What them? Who? The reader? I can't ask the reader. The reader couldn't come that far in."

"Ha, if you could! Your name would be different for every reader," she says, smiling.

No, but I can't count on you, can I? You who live under the relentless and fickle reign of Crastina. You are uncertain, potential, and as we compose these words you don't even know I exist.

You, who may not even be born yet as we stand in the rose garden on the afternoon of July 16th, 2018? You lingered in the passage looking at the faded spines of the books, remember? You didn't want to open the door into the rose garden. We made a contract back at the beginning of the book, I'd tell you stories and I promised I wouldn't make you do anything but read. And besides, you could read this book a hundred times (it's all right, I don't expect you to) and give me a hundred different names. What kind of immortality would that be?

"What would we do, leave a blank space where they can write it in? Have them put it in the margin? This is ridiculous. It won't work. Give me a name. Aren't I worth that to you, after all?" I'm pleading, but she's implacable when she wants to be.

"They will know what to call you," Sylvia says, nodding in that decisive way she has, and smiling her shark's smile. She heads back down the hill and out of the gate. "We'd better finish this chapter quickly and get on with it," she says. "I want to go to Perché No! . . . and have a last gelato before we go. No gelato in Illyria. That's a good enough reason for restarting Progress."

I thought I was building a trap for her, but she has trapped me.

34

IBID

Tish has made a new painting, the same size as Ficino's, or rather Brunelleschi's, original. It shows the scene as best she can imagine it, in the Firenze of 2018, which she glimpsed so briefly through Sylvia's eyes. The Baptistery is the same, and St Zenobius's elm tree pillar, but the people are wearing skimpy clothes with words on them and holding strange bags. They are not all white. There are lots of them. She has not attempted to draw the vehicles, but she has put in a swallow. It's good she drew no vehicles, because only ambulances and horse-drawn open carriages for rich tourists drive across that piazza in 2018. Tish is standing by the easel. She looks like an adult, and indeed an adult woman, with skirts and an embroidered headscarf. She revealed her gender and married Elia Pardo twenty years ago. He is also a painter, and although he is several inches shorter than she is they are very happy together, happier than she ever imagined. She intends to have a baby any year now, once this project is finally complete. He is standing next to her, carrying her paints, in case Ficino decides on any last minute emergency alterations. She is mostly known by her Hebrew name now, but she has signed this painting neither Rinah Pardo nor Letizio Petranero but simply "Tish."

Geryon has made a magic carpet, the compelling pattern in a thousand subtle shades of cloud colours, pierced with an echoing symmetrical pattern of precisely shaped tiny holes, like an immense doily. It is huge, and it floats. He has been in Elam all this time, and this is his first return to Thalia. Prospero, Miranda, and Ficino are standing on the carpet, a few feet off the ground, to the side of the cathedral steps. If Ficino is a sweet old wizard, Prospero is a sour one; he looks as if he's perpetually sucking a lemon. He's wearing robes of deepest fuligin clasped with a crescent moon. Ficino's starry robes are midnight blue, and Miranda's sky blue.

Drusilla stands with Geryon to the right of the carpet. She has become a great traveller and has scoured the world for some of the stranger things they need for this spell. At a hundred and eighty she is still *giovane,* but looking towards the older end of it, mid-thirties, as if she might settle down soon. She usually dresses as a boy, but for her return to Thalia she has returned to women's clothing, a brocade dress in dove grey and navy blue. She has also brought news of her brother, Tybalt, who was captured by bandits, became a bandit, got tired of being a bandit, and took up life as a sugar merchant in Persepolis, one of the great cities of Elam. He lives happily with his husband, their camels, and a golden-eyed hunting leopard. Orsino and Viola are very glad to know he is well. He has no desire to return to Thalia, so Drusilla is still heir apparent.

Orsino has not restored the Republic, though he did think seriously about it. He has given the Senate more power and widened the franchise. He has reinstituted the system of electing eight people (women as well as men now) for two months each, but he keeps executive oversight. He is standing on the cathedral steps, wearing his armour. Viola is beside him, with Sebastian and Olivia on her other side. The twins are today as usual in gender-reversed clothing, Sebastian dressed in a ruby-

and-silver gown that complements Olivia's, which is silver shot with ruby.

From the magic carpet, Miranda is desperately trying to keep everything under control, like a demented stage manager on opening night after a disastrous dress rehearsal. She's urgently directing people into position. Ficino seems unruffled, but even he is muttering and pacing across the rug, causing it to ripple a little beneath his feet. Prospero is sitting cross-legged like Buddha. His presence is causing some social difficulty as nobody except Miranda and Ficino has any idea what to call him. There are some people in the crowd who remember when he was Duke of Thalia.

Of our major characters, Dolly is the most changed. He does not look two hundred years old, but you'd guess he was sixty or seventy—his unruly hair and beard are white, and his face is lined. He's more substantial too, heavier all over. He's still wearing his chaperon though, and his eyes are still dancing with delight. He's standing on the steps holding the stone knife which Pico used for his sacrifice, which is now a holy relic that Orsino had to browbeat the bishop into releasing for the occasion.

There is a choir, and drummers, and buglers, and music specially composed for the occasion by Prospero. They are standing grouped, ready, though some of them are fumbling with their music and instruments.

Despite the long period of preparation, there is an air of desperate improvisation about everything. Worst from my point of view is the fact that they can't agree what name they're going to use to call me. A group of wizards from all over the world, dressed in a wild assortment of garments, are standing by the doors of the Baptistery squabbling about it.

Everyone is packed into the space between the cathedral and the Baptistery. In Firenze, that space was traditionally called the paradiso, and it's the liminal space of baptism, naming, poised between worlds. The bronze doors Ghiberti made for the Baptistery were named "The Gates of Paradise" by Michelangelo precisely because the space had that name, though people who call them that today mostly have no knowledge of the history of the name or the space they're made for. Here, exactly where Dolly is standing on the steps of the cathedral, the great trickster Brunelleschi stood and made his perspective painting, which hangs on Ficino's wall now, showing very different sights. The paradiso would be quite a big space if it wasn't always absolutely packed with people.

As Sylvia walks to the Duomo from Perché No! . . . the dome comes into sight. It's hidden by other buildings until you're really close to it, and then it always looks improbable, too big, beautiful, red, and always unexpected from whatever angle. It's as if Brunelleschi, inventor of perspective, cheated on his own rules, which of course he understood better than anyone else, to make the dome as big as this and yet seem to float. Firenze has many iconic buildings and statues and paintings, the dome is just one among them, and yet the most central and defining. Walking between the Palazzo Vecchio and the Duomo (stopping at Perché No! . . . for a gelato on the way) you are at the very heart of Firenze.

She has finished the book, if you can call it that, and emailed it to her editor in New York. She isn't talking to me. I'm clamped down in the bone cave, with nothing to see but my connection to Dolly. I've tried reasoning with her, pleading, and even threatening. I've tried being quiet to trick her into addressing me, but I couldn't wait long enough. Patience has never been one of my virtues. And anyway, there's only today. The moon was new three days ago. We saw it framed between the buildings on Via del Corso as we were coming back from Teatro del Sale. They know her name, in Illyria. Ficino divined it. He couldn't divine mine. Nobody could because I don't have one, she won't give me one, and you won't, and even if you would, how could you? You can't do it in time. Dolly's going to kill himself to get her in, but I won't be in. I won't even be in the amount I am as Dolly, because he will die to open the gate and thus flow back to me and be outside. The same thing happened before I sacrificed myself to kill Death, but left myself out.

I have been a god and a sacrifice. I have been a goat and a scapegoat. I have been calm, but right now I'm panicking. Everything has gone wrong. Well, not everything. If she gets in, I suppose I'll get in with her, in the bone cave like always. After all, I'm not coming to ask her for a soul on the day of judgement! I'm only asking for a name! They'll summon me as Hermes, and Dolios, I suppose, but that's only part of what I am. All of me, I said. That's what I was trying to get on the page this time, but the page has gone to New York as fast as a speeding electron, and what you're reading now, if you even exist, is the book in the mind, the words that never make it to the page, the unwritten, unreadable story that always runs a pulsebeat ahead under everything we do and think and say all the time, the unheard narrative of life. And yet I still address you, still describe, narrate, as if I believe that this still can, somehow, magically, reach you. I know you don't exist. But I keep on talking to you.

Why won't she give me a name?

She stands on the stones at the base of the steps, centered. You can't get up on the steps anymore, they rope them off except when they open the doors for people to stream out after services. The only time they keep them open is on San Giovanni, St John's Day, June 24th, when there's a wonderful parade with people in period costume and horses and music and they carry the *Codex Fiorentina,* or anyway a copy of it, and have a procession in a way that is both smiling and solemn, both real and fun. They bring the finger bone of John the Baptist out in its reliquary and display it, and they have services in the Baptistery and the Duomo, and both the doors are open. That would have been a good day to try this. But we didn't and we can't wait for next year because she is starting to get pain now, and if she goes home or goes to a doctor they won't let her loose again.

She moves a little to the left, centering herself better. In Thalia the choir begins to sing and Dolly gets into position in the clear space everyone has left for him. Tish is checking her picture anxiously. Others of her pictures are set out on easels around the square; among other things, there is a steam train crossing a viaduct, an opera house, and a version of the scene they saw in the original painting, the triple-Sylvia with the crescent moon. There's even a faithfully executed picture of the ram.

What am I going to do? This was my one chance. I want to be real. I want to survive. I want to be embodied, and free. The bone cave is the same as it ever is, I am floating in no space, no colour. There's nobody else in here right now, all of her part-formed people are out there in Illyria or dissolved back into the mist. In desperation, I look towards the mist. It's moving, pulsing, shifting, like always. There are shapes and shadows and shades twisting and turning in the tendrils that reach. I look out of Dolly's eyes, and see Ficino and Miranda conferring desperately on the carpet, even though they have already started. Prospero is sitting still on the magic carpet. Geryon is looking up at it with a proprietorial air. He has eyes now, big brown eyes. He's happy making carpets. Fifty years ago he turned down an offer from Malvolio to join him in revenge on Orsino and his family.

Dolly is fingering the stone knife, and looking over at Miranda. They still don't have a proper name for me, and it's time.

I walk into the mist. I never have before, in all these years, because I've been afraid of what it would do to me. But now there's nothing else for it. I've seen her go in, and come out again. I walk in boldly, but terrified, of course, because this could be real death. She could end up in Illyria without me even being there in her head. But I can't keep cowering here. The entrance runs between cliffs, as she told me. I can feel them more than see them towering up through the mist, which fills not just my vision but all my senses. It touches me, clammily, and I can smell and taste it, and as for hearing, I'm overwhelmed. The mist is full of noises—music, laughter, swelling voices, bells ringing, and beeping, and chiming, the roar of traffic, and thunder, and planes taking off, but most of all snatches of conversation, heard and gone again. "How could she die, when she was so alive?" "I am small, but sometimes I am a small part of great things," "If you love books enough, books will love you back," "She wouldn't be the person her life had made her if she could have made any other answer," "There will not be sunsets or poetry, but there will be something like them but even better," "I knew more about evil than he ever could, because he had parents who loved him," "There isn't an end point to excellence where you have it and you can stop," "Time is rent from the worlds," "I don't want to be a might-have-been!" "I can't wait to talk about it with you," and all of them pressing on me and pushing at me, a jumble of voices and attention and forms looming up to go with them, if I were to look in the right way. "You feel what you feel and I feel what I feel, but that doesn't mean you have to—"

I ignore them as best I can and keep moving in, keep going. What I want to do is find my own power to create, to make worlds, the power she has, which must be here somewhere. I hadn't realised that once I stepped into the mist I wouldn't be able to reach Dolly or keep track of what's going on in Illyria. I can't reach out at all, and there's nothing here but the voices, some of them mocking "I could make a man every bit as good as you out of two rhymes and a handful of moonshine . . ." and others intensely set on their own affairs and paying no attention to me. "Perfection isn't static. It's a dynamic form!" I turn to find my way out, because this is getting me nowhere, literally, because when I turn I realise that all directions are alike, there is nothing but the mist. I run, in the direction I think is back, and find myself running down a long corridor, past fading books and a dying geranium on a windowsill, and come to a halt, panting, by the green-painted back door. I am, somehow, in her house in Montreal. I put out my hand tentatively to the brass doorknob. Then, as I step forward, I am abruptly on the edge of a precipice, the dark looming down before me, as the mist closes in again. *"Er' perrehnne,"* a voice says, almost in my ear.

And she is there, out of nowhere, looking about thirty, her hair black as a raven's wing against the grey-white mist and roses are growing at her feet, all around her, all around me. The pearls at her throat are glowing. All the voices go quiet at once. They are afraid of her, and they are wise to be. "I need a name," I say.

"Where did you get your soul from?" she asks.

"I don't know," I say. It's a terrible question. Could you answer it? Where did I come from in the first place? I was in the glass bookshelf and she found me. I was licked out of a cloud by a cow. I shaped myself with a magic chisel. God made me out of mud. I don't know! I don't remember.

"Did you take it from the baby? Did I trade him for you?" she asks.

It has occurred to me before, so I have a ready answer. "Not consciously. Not knowing. And if I did, it was another sacrifice I made for you. But I really don't think I did. I can remember before that. Have you been wondering about that all this time?" Through thirty books. Thirty.

"You were always hiding something," she says.

We are alone together on top of a cliff inside her head, surrounded by roses and mist that swirls and shapes itself suggestively, but is silent now, and she is ruthless.

"I was hiding my plan. And my fear of you, which is bound in with my love for you because you have all the power."

"I?" She steps back, startled, close to the edge, and catches herself to stand squarely. She does not like to think of herself as the one with power, the one others might fear. She was the victim. "Tell me. It won't make any difference. But I need to know if I sacrificed him for my happiness, my career, everything I wanted."

"That's not how I remember it," I say. "And besides, you had the girls later. It's not as if you had to put creativity into only one thing. That's another ridiculous and destructive idea."

"But you came back," she says. "You came back just then."

I think about that, because it's true. "But I came back in the car," I say. "That's when I woke up. I think I was squeezed in your head all that time, after your mother killed me, dead or asleep and dreaming on the edge of this mist. I think I woke up because there just wasn't any more room and you desperately needed me. But if I wasn't there, if my soul was going to come back as that baby—no, it's a demented idea. But if so, then he was gone already, as the doctor said, Steve had killed him, you were bleeding, because that's when I woke up, in the car, not after *I* made the choice to ask for an abortion."

"Oh!" she says.

"But I really don't think that is where my soul came from," I say. "I always had it. I had it back in the bookcase. I think the baby was somebody separate, and maybe we did sacrifice him, if he wasn't killed by Steve. But we had to do it just to get free. It wasn't Faustian."

"I haven't forgotten what Steve was like," she says. She meets my eyes, and I realise that here in the mist I have eyes, and a form, and a body, as she does. I reach out and pick a golden rose from a nearby bush, and prick myself deliberately on a thorn. Blood runs down my palm and stains the petals. "But my life has been so good, since then. Was it a Faustian bargain, to have a muse, to have you?"

"Not that I know of," I say. "What universe are we in?"

She laughs. "How would I know? We're in my head. The

universe outside my head has never been under my control." Then she looks serious. "Are you really afraid of me?"

There is no point now in anything but honesty. I look down at the rose in my hand. Closest to me the petals are blood red, then shade out through many shades of pink and gold to white. I hold it out to her. "You can shut me up in here and never let me out again! How could I not be afraid? You have this mist in your head and I have no idea how to get out of here! You're ruthless and it's hard to trust you when you won't even give me the name I need to get in to Illyria, which was my plan all along, you know, mine, you wouldn't be going if it wasn't for me."

"Well," she says, and reaches out to take the rose, and at that moment the mist and the cliffs are gone, blown away in an instant, and with them our forms, so we are two disembodied voices floating in the bright darkness of the bone cave, where we usually speak when we talk in here. "As to that, what do I take?"

Take? I thought she knew she couldn't take anything. I had thought she understood at least that much. "We go empty-handed," I say.

"Souls?"

"Yes."

"In that case, what happens to my body?"

"I think it probably goes back to Canada and into a hospital," I say, tentatively. "But maybe Worldcon first? Do you have some of those strong painkillers left? Because if so, then I think you can do that."

"I was afraid that's what you were going to say, but hoping it might fall dead here at the moment when my soul leaves it. Well, I'll get to see Con and the girls, and everyone at Worldcon one last time. Though as they still haven't sent me panel information, who knows—I don't even know if I'll have a reading. Or a kaffeeklatch. Why am I worrying about that now?"

"Because you don't really believe that you're really going to be in Illyria, that you're going to live forever." It's time to let her know all of it. "You'll go into Illyria as a god, and then you'll shape yourself into new people, be born, and live, sometimes knowing and sometimes unknowing. And eventually you'll die, when you want to, and apotheosize again, and live other lives, over and over, as many times as you want to. And as a god you'll make new worlds, the way you always have, and you'll enter into them over and over, forever. And yes, one tiny shred of you will stay here in this world and go to Worldcon and then go home and die, but all the rest of you will go on forever and be vast and great. You privilege this world and call it real, and call the rest of them imaginary, made up, unreal, but there's no need to do that. You can be like I am, but free, making choices, not pacing through a plot. And I want to be free too! But for that I have to have a name!"

"Listen. They're calling," she says.

And I see the paradis in Thalia, and Dolly's blood is pumping out of him, and it has opened the gate between realities, reaching straight up through the cherubim and the seraphim and the gods all the way to God. The world can be reshaped, in this moment, and only in this moment. Progress restarts, and the stars are in our grasp. The choir is singing Prospero's strange harmonies, and Tish's picture is before us, or maybe it's what Sylvia is seeing, the Baptistery and the people in T-shirts and shorts. In this instant, there is no difference. And suddenly the ground of the paradiso heaves in front of us, and Caliban is there, and people are running and getting out of the way. "You forgot me," he rumbles, accusingly.

"No," Prospero says, from where he is safely floating on the magic carpet. "Nobody forgot you. As from your crimes you'd pardoned be, by your indulgence, set me free." And he steps off the carpet and embraces Caliban's huge neck.

The choir has faltered to a halt, in running to safety. But Ficino and Miranda, incredibly, have gone on calling, as Dolly's blood streams out, calling a long string of names. "Sylvia," they say, in unison. "Hekate, Sylvia, Katherine Sylvia Harrison." Then "Hermes, Dolios—" and we are standing again on the cliff-edge, both of us, as I wait for the name that will summon me, or will not and let her go on without me. Can they find a name for me? Is there a name I would answer to, a name that would feel mine? Even if they found the old childish name she called me long ago in her grandmother's house, would it be fitting now? Does the reader have a name for me, do you, if you have followed me this far, and can even Ficino's wisdom draw it from you? Rumpelstiltskin, Tom Tit Tot, I think, and shake my head. Everything is waiting on the word, the mist is almost silent, no more than a whisper of distant bells, as all this passes through my mind, taking no more time than Dolly's last breath. "Narrator," Ficino says, and at the same moment Miranda says, "Ariel!"

"Oh!" I say.

"To the elements be free, and fare thee well," Sylvia says.

Then I take her hand, and we step forward, off the edge of the cliff, into the rose, through layering colours that are the petals of the rose, and we do not fall, we step out into the paradiso, into the picture, and on into Illyria, together and free.

THANKS AND NOTES

Most of this book was written in Florence, but some of it was written in Montreal, Chicago, Grand Rapids, Paestum, and Rome. All of it was written in Protext, on my netbook, for which I'd like to thank Lindsey Nilson, for making it possible for me to write anywhere.

In my last novel, *Lent*, I chose to render almost all the Italian words in English. In this book, I've made the opposite decision, for a change. *Lent* is a meticulously researched fantasy novel about Savonarola. This is a playful fantasy novel about death and subcreation, in which I'm throwing together all kinds of things, and instead of (almost) real Renaissance Florence we have Shakespeare's imagination of Italy tossed with magical longevity and meditations on Renaissances, creation, and death. In *Lent* I wanted to make strange things sound more familiar. This didn't need that. The things and places mentioned in modern Florence/ Firenze are all real, especially the most improbable. So I want to thank Teatro del Sale and Perché No! . . . for existing and letting me enjoy them, the organization of Friends of the Uffizi, and especially Lumi, for helping make so much amazing art accessible, Teckla in Mercato Centrale, the Russian waitress in the Uffizi roof café who asked to be put in the book, my aunt Mary Lace, who introduced me to Renaissance art in the first place, and Ada Palmer, who generously offered me Florence and always helps me enjoy it.

I received valuable feedback on this book from Mary Lace, Hannah Dorsey, Patrick Nielsen Hayden, Teresa Nielsen Hayden, Marissa Lingen, Sherwood Smith, Emmet O'Brien, Maya Chhabra, Doug Palmer, Louise Mallory, Wendy Oakden, Jennifer Hyndman, Elaine Blank, and Alison Sinclair.

I could afford to spend the time writing in Florence in the summer of 2018, when Sylvia was there, thanks to my Patreon community, whose continuing support always helps and delights me.

The line "Ginnungagap where nothing is and all things start" quoted in the first chapter without attribution is from Ada Palmer's song "Ice and Fire." Most of the other random unattributed quotations are from the Bible, Shakespeare, the anonymous poem Tom O'Bedlam, but some of it is from all over. The late and much missed Ursula Le Guin kindly gave me permission to quote "Er' perrehnne," which is from *The Lathe of Heaven*.

Thanks to Edwin Chapman for a great copyedit, and to Camellia Sinensis, for all the tea. And thanks to you, my readers, for bearing with me through so many odd edges of genres and different kinds of stories.